HEAVEN'S LIGHT

Also by Graham Hurley

RULES OF ENGAGEMENT
REAPER
THE DEVIL'S BREATH
THUNDER IN THE BLOOD
SABBATHMAN
THE PERFECT SOLDIER

GRAHAM HURLEY

HEAVEN'S LIGHT

MACMILLAN

First published 1997 by Macmillan

an imprint of Macmillan Publishers Ltd
25 Eccleston Place, London, SW1W 9NF
and Basingstoke

Associated companies throughout the world

ISBN 0 333 65337 8

1 3 5 7 9 8 6 4 2

A CIP catalogue record for this book is available from
the British Library

Phototypeset by Intype, London

Printed by Mackays of Chatham PLC, Chatham, Kent

For Dorothy and Reg Rowden
Heavenly Lights
With Love

'Heaven's Light Our Guide'

civic motto, City of Portsmouth

'Those who persistently try and subjₗ ate distant
provinces will have to pay for it in the end . . .'

Thomas Babington Macaulay

Fantasies like this only thrive with the help of fellow conspirators. In this respect, I'm immensely indebted to John Saulet, Howard Barrington-Clark, and Robin Townsend, lawyers all three. Mike Kendall, Paul Spooner, and Roger Ching, of Portsmouth City Council, warned me of the constitutional and economic pitfalls, while Labour councillors Sarah Fry and Alan Burnett shared their hard-won political experience. Pat Forsyth, of the Portsmouth Hospital Trust, opened the doors of the Q. A. Hospital, and Anne Braisher plugged me into the mysteries of cable TV. Peter Milne, hotelier of genius, shaped The Imperial of Raymond Zhu's dreams, and his wife, Sarah, put her extensive knowledge of epilepsy at my disposal. Michael Dobbs unlocked some of the secrets of Conservative Central Office while my wife, Lin, monitored the phone taps and kept our powder dry. To her, as ever, my love. To everyone else, including a longish list of anonymous contributors, my sincere thanks.

Prologue

April 1949

Everyone wanted to leave. Across the city, amongst the teeming slums of Yangpu and Jingan, word was spreading. The Communist army was two days' march away. Out of the mountains, and across the river, they'd settle their debts in blood.

At dusk, he returned to the room where they lived. He picked his way along the alley then through the communal kitchen they shared with all the other families. The staircase wound upwards, into the darkness, and he counted the greasy treads from the bottom. Number ten was missing. Still small for his age he paused, his left foot reaching for the step beyond. His brother was waiting for him upstairs. He was still crouched on the bed, still guarding his father's body. The old man was beginning to stiffen now, his flesh cold to the touch, his slashed throat gaping blackly.

Next morning, at first light, they made their way down to the Yangtse, running through the warren of tiny streets, past the smelly bars and shuttered brothels, past the shops still bursting with silks, jades and embroideries, past the bent old men hauling carts piled high with a lifetime's possessions.

On the waterfront, under the looming granite fronts of the buildings along the Bund, they darted through the crowds pushing urgently towards the docks. Their father had talked of a fishing boat with a green funnel. The man was called Yao. They were to give him the gold bracelet. They were to tell him their names. He'd take care of them. He'd make sure they got away.

The crowd closed around them, a living thing, the people pressed tightly together, surging towards the stretch of slimy cobblestones where the tramlines ended and the fishermen laid out their daily catch. Ahead, an old woman was bent double under a bamboo yoke strung with headless chickens. The smell of the dead birds came and went, adding to the stale breath of the river. He frowned, eyeing the chickens. Every day he felt hungrier. Every day there was less and less to eat.

The crowd was at a standstill, desperate to get away. Of Mr Yao's fishing boat there was no sign but he could see tugs out in the river. They lay beyond a line of barges secured to bollards on the quayside. Tarpaulins on board had been rolled back and the holds gaped open, long black oblongs, big as a house. Getting onto the barges meant jumping off the quayside. On the falling tide the drop was ten feet at least, but there was no other way.

Beside them, a man began to shout, louder than the rest. By the look of his uniform, he came from one of the big waterfront hotels. He carried his possessions in a knotted pillowcase and the sleeve of his waiter's jacket was ripped. Somewhere he'd laid hands on a leather riding crop and in his impatience he began to use it, lashing out wildly, left and right. The old woman with the chickens, trapped by the bamboo yoke, shivered under the blows. She began to howl, and the crowd stirred, pressing forward again, responding like some clumsy animal. At the front of the crowd, men and women began to jump down to the barges, and he heard the hollow thump as their bodies disappeared into the holds. He squeezed his brother's hand, telling him not to be frightened, trying to mask his own fear. We're helpless, he thought. There are too many people. The crowd is too big, too strong.

Instinctively, carried forward by the surge of bodies, he fought for balance but he was too small and too frail to resist the pressure. His feet were off the ground now, his brother's tiny hand torn away, and he hung suspended for a moment as wave after wave of bodies toppled off the quayside. The waiter had given up with the riding crop, and he was looking down, his head bent, his face contorted, his fingers knotted tightly round the pillowcase. He reached up for the waiter, pleading for help, but the man seemed not to see him.

Then, suddenly, they found themselves on the big worn stones at the very edge of the quayside. Below, between the pilings and the barges, was a foot or two of glistening black mud. The crowd seemed to hesitate long enough for him to make out the body of a dog sprawled in the ooze. Then came the shuffle of feet again, and a push in the back. He looked round for his brother, glimpsing his tiny, frightened face, shiny with tears, and then he felt himself falling, head first, his hands reaching out, trying to shield his eyes from the onrushing darkness.

BOOK ONE

June 1994

'A town like Portsmouth should look after its own affairs, free from the toll of shires.'

Book of Fees, 1195

Chapter One

The little executive Learjet danced down the last hundred feet of the glidepath into London's Heathrow airport, a tiny black silhouette against the fierce blaze of the rising sun. It slipped over the perimeter fence, settling gently on the tarmac as the pilot throttled back the engines. Watching the aircraft flash past the queue of waiting jumbos, Ellis glanced at his watch. Last night's DTI brief had estimated touchdown at five minutes past six. Departmental timekeeping was notoriously optimistic, especially at Trade and Industry, but on this occasion someone had excelled themselves. As the Learjet slowed to turn off the runway, it was precisely 06.07.

Ellis stooped for his briefcase. He'd already talked to the overnight security supervisor at the General Aviation Terminal, and he was cleared to meet the new arrival at the aircraft steps. In the case of VCIPs, virtually any rule could be bent. Commercially Important People of this stature deserved a decent welcome.

Outside, on the tarmac, the dawn air was heavy with the bittersweet tang of aviation fuel. The aircraft was fifty metres away, nosing alongside the neat line of charter jets parked on the apron. The pilot shut down the engines and Ellis watched the aircraft's door hinge upwards and the folding steps descend. For a moment, nothing happened. Then, inside the aircraft, he saw movement. A face ducked to a window. A hand fluttered briefly in salute. Quite suddenly he was standing in the open doorway, a thin, upright figure, taller than the rare press photos had suggested. His shoulders were narrow, magnifying the size of his head, and the high, receding forehead was topped with a shock of iron-grey hair.

He was wearing creased tan slacks, his feet were bare in open sandals, and the sleeveless cotton shirt looked at least one size too big.

He manoeuvred sideways down the steps, the way an old man might, pausing at the bottom to watch a big Swissair 747 thunder past. Then he turned to greet Ellis. His handshake was light, the merest touch of flesh on flesh, and a smile ghosted across his face at the sound of his name.

'Zhu,' he repeated, offering the correct pronunciation, his lips budding in a perfect 'O', 'Raymond Zhu.'

Ellis was already peering over his shoulder, up into the plane. He didn't know how much luggage to expect, but Mr Zhu was scheduled for an early breakfast meeting at the Savoy and time was already tight.

'You have some bags, Mr Zhu? It's just a formality, of course, but Customs are ready for you now.'

He gestured over his shoulder. An official in a white shirt was standing inside the terminal building, watching.

Zhu called in Chinese to someone inside the aircraft. A younger man appeared and handed him a passport. Ellis recognized the lion and tiger of the Republic of Singapore on the cover.

They set off for the terminal building, Ellis beside his guest. Zhu walked quickly, taking tiny steps, gliding across the tarmac. When they got inside, Zhu's sandals went slap-slap on the newly polished floor. Millions of dollars in the bank, thought Ellis, and the man still wears sandals.

The Customs supervisor had disappeared. While Ellis went to find him, Zhu stood motionless by the window, watching a porter offload his bags from the aircraft and disappear round the side of the building.

At length, Ellis returned. The bags had been cleared. He extended a hand for Zhu's passport, shepherding him towards the immigration checkpoint. The woman behind the desk flipped open the passport and stamped it without a second glance. Her smile was warm. She hoped Zhu would have a lovely stay.

Outside the terminal, the DTI Rover was waiting at the kerb. The ministry driver swallowed the remains of his coffee and got out, opening the back door for Zhu. Zhu didn't move. He was watching a sleek black Daimler emerge from a nearby parking lot. At his side, Ellis was already running through a checklist of the rest of the day's appointments. After breakfast at the Savoy, Zhu was to meet a small delegation of CBI people. Sunday lunch, at the invitation of the Institute of Directors, would be in Pall Mall. A private cruise downriver was fixed for mid-afternoon, then Zhu would be flown by helicopter to cocktails with a discreet gathering of merchant bankers in a Buckinghamshire country house. With luck, the Singaporean should be back in his room at the Savoy by ten.

Ellis looked up. Zhu was standing beside the Daimler. A small squat Chinese was loading his bags into the car's boot.

'Mr Zhu?' Ellis still had the schedule in his hand. 'Is there a problem?'

Zhu was climbing into the back of the Daimler. The window purred down. He beamed up at Ellis, then gestured at the Chinese behind the wheel.

'This is Mr Hua,' he said gravely. 'He drives me everywhere.'

Sixty miles south of Heathrow, Hayden Barnaby was waist-deep in tepid water, adjusting the straps on his goggles. Comfortable at last, he submerged, his long body following the gentle slope as the pool deepened beneath him. He counted the tiles on the bottom, watching them slow then quicken as he pulled hard for the deep end. Compared to his regular morning work-outs at the municipal baths, this place was a joke, fifteen metres end to end, but the doctor had dismissed his protests and his impatience, explaining just how serious the injury to his Achilles tendon had been. Go back to serious exercise too soon and you risk permanent damage. Take things a little easier, be sensible for once, and the tear would heal completely. Your leg. Your choice. Your funeral.

Barnaby saw the wall at the deep end looming closer and he jackknifed into a perfect racing turn before surfacing again, rolling onto his back and kicking lazily at the start of another length. The little pool was part of a health club attached to the Venture Hotel.

He'd known the manager for years, and he'd managed to negotiate a generous temporary membership deal for the three months he'd need to repair the tendon. At fifteen quid a quarter, the discount was nearly 100 per cent and on top of that there'd come the promise of a little business from a couple of members of the hotel staff. A young lad in the kitchen wanting a conveyance on his first flat. The bar manageress needing advice before she took divorce proceedings. It was nothing sensational but welcome nonetheless. Acquiring new clients, even for a practice as successful as his own, had never been more difficult. For a country on the edge of an economic miracle, times were still bloody hard.

Barnaby reached backwards for the bar at the shallow end, letting himself float in the warm water. This was his first visit to the health club and, to his surprise, it had been as empty as the rest of the hotel. Next door, through the tall plate-glass windows, there was a small gymnasium. Before stripping to his swimming trunks, he'd done a brief circuit on the machines, a couple of repetitions on each, but for once he'd heeded the doctor's advice, resisting the temptation to test himself against the weights. Getting back to the squash court was his real priority. His iron-pumping days were well and truly over.

He closed his eyes a moment, willing himself to relax, trying hard not to brood about the empty hotel foyer, and the abandoned bars, and the crowds outside in the blustery sunshine, streaming towards the seafront. Today, fifty years ago, the Allied invasion fleet had been poised to set sail for Normandy. As Britain's premier naval port, the city had been in the front line. Now, exactly half a century later, Portsmouth was hosting the official celebrations. The event had attracted enormous publicity. The US President was in town, and the Queen, and the Prime Minister, and more or less everyone else in the world who seemed to matter.

Only last night, in the city's Guildhall, fourteen heads of state had sat down to a commemorative banquet, and this morning, barely half a mile away, they were convening again to attend the memorial service, taking place on Southsea Common. The service was to be transmitted live to countless nations across the globe. There were dozens of cameras, hundreds of technicians, miles of cable. There'd be marching bands, fly-pasts, a naval review. For a couple of hours, maybe longer, the eyes of the world would be on Portsmouth.

So where, in all this, was Hayden Barnaby?

He rolled over and began to swim again, a purposeful breast-stroke, the water sluicing past his body. For months he'd tried to fix himself and his wife an invitation to last night's banquet, pulling in old favours, working every connection he knew. But the more calls he made, and the more hints he dropped, the clearer the real situation became. The D-Day weekend had ballooned out of all proportion. It had acquired the status of a national event, the property of quietly spoken men in London who got together behind closed doors and determined exactly the way it would be. In theory, of course, the city was in charge of the celebrations but the real decisions, as ever, had been taken elsewhere. That, at least, was the way Barnaby saw it, and the TV pictures he'd watched had amply confirmed the real pecking order. Guests for the banquet had arrived by limousine. At the foot of the Guildhall steps, the county's Lord Lieutenant had been waiting to greet them. At the top of the steps, ideally positioned for the cameras, the Prime Minister extended another formal welcome. Whilst tucked away inside, wholly invisible, lurked Portsmouth's own Lord Mayor.

Barnaby kicked hard for the deep end, ignoring the pain in his tendon. Bill Clinton had reportedly arrived with an entourage of seven hundred. In the north of the city, White House staff had taken over virtually an entire hotel, installing their own communication links, blanketing the presidential visit with layer after layer of security. You could see the hotel from the motorway. Barnaby had driven past only the previous evening, at once excited and depressed by the forest of radio aerials sprouting from the roof. Here was his city, his birthplace, the Pompey where he'd nurtured his own dreams of power and influence suddenly awash with the real thing. The entire Royal Family. Fourteen heads of state. Including the man himself. Bill Clinton.

Barnaby slowed, brooding again. Clinton was forty-five, exactly his own age. Like Barnaby, he'd been at Oxford and, like Barnaby, he'd returned to his roots in the Deep South, a career move that

Barnaby had always admired. The man had shunned the lure of the metropolis, choosing instead to build a local power-base. By banking favours, amassing a war chest and courting the media, he'd finally put together a raft of support to float him where he really wanted to go. As a result, by the time he finally made it to Washington, it had been on his own terms. Now, as President of the USA, he was the most powerful man on earth.

Barnaby stood in the shallow end, massaging his injured calf. Yesterday, the city's daily newspaper had carried a photo of Clinton on an early-morning run, jogging cheerfully through the naval dockyard, and Barnaby remembered the image now, wondering whether the man had ever had problems with his Achilles tendon and regretting again that he'd never had the opportunity to ask.

Next door, in the gymnasium, a woman had appeared. She was working on one of the machines, and Barnaby watched her, letting his leg hang in the water, pointing his foot then rotating the ankle the way the physio at the hospital had shown him. The woman had her back to the pool. She was lying full length on a padded bench, her hands behind her head. Her feet were hooked beneath a bar and she was doing a series of stomach curls, sets of ten. She had a long, supple body, and nicely shaped legs, and the way she performed the exercises – easy, fluent – suggested someone in their physical prime.

Barnaby watched her a little longer, wanting her to turn round. She was wearing a pair of headphones and the little Sony Walkman was clipped to a heavy leather belt around her black leotard. Now and again her hand would drop to adjust the volume, and the way she did it – deft, positive, self-confident – aroused Barnaby's curiosity. Who was she? Where did she come from? What kind of life did she lead?

He lay back in the water, kicking for the deep end, feeling the muscle tighten in his bad leg. Inventing answers to questions like these was the best relaxation after a hectic week in the law courts, and he closed his eyes, letting his fantasies off the leash. She'd be a stranger in the city, someone down for the weekend, staying in the hotel. She'd be in her late twenties, maybe younger. She'd have a career, something glamorous. She'd be in fashion, or the media, or high finance. She'd have a regular boyfriend, she might even be married, but just now she was down on some kind of liaison.

Barnaby warmed to the story. She'd have a room upstairs, somewhere discreet with a huge bed and a view of the Isle of Wight, and just now she'd be killing time, waiting for her man. This guy might be part of the D-Day jamboree. He might be one of the media people, a cameraman, say, or a producer. God knows, he might even be one of Clinton's boys, a White House insider, a political heavyweight with a direct line to the President. Barnaby nodded in approval, trying to imagine the man, then – abruptly – his body came to rest in the water, his head cushioned from the tiled wall by something soft. His feet found the bottom and he stood up, pushing back the goggles. A woman was sitting on the edge of the pool. She was wearing a black Speedo one-piece, modestly cut. She had a strong, open face and her hair, drawn back, was beginning to grey at the temples. Barnaby blinked. Beyond the tall plate-glass windows, the gym was empty. The woman slipped into the pool. Her face and shoulders were pinked with recent exercise.

'Funny,' she said, 'I knew it was you.'

The smaller of the two bars was at the front of the hotel, over-looking the street. They sat at a table beside the window, Barnaby nursing a long glass of orange juice and soda. The last time he'd seen Kate Frankham in the flesh had been the winter of '92. The photos in the local paper since had done her less than justice.

'So how does it feel? Being famous?'

'Famous?' She laughed. 'Are you kidding?'

'Not at all. I'm impressed.'

'By what?'

'By what you've done. Heritage Chair in less than a year? That's some going.'

Kate ducked her head, trying to hide the grin, but when she looked at him again it was still there, as irrepressible as ever. She'd never been less than candid with him, an honesty he'd occasionally found difficult to handle.

'I've had the time,' she said simply. 'And the opposition's not up to much. Not in local politics.'

'You mean the Tories?'

'No, our lot. The comrades. Labour. We've got some good people, but not enough of them. If you put your mind to it, anyone could get there. It just needs application.'

'And time. Like you said.'

'Yes,' she nodded, 'that, too.'

She broke off, looking at him, and Barnaby found himself reaching defensively for the plastic card lying beside her purse. He tapped the date beneath the photo. Her annual membership had nearly run out.

'You come here a lot?'

'Most days, first thing normally. It's quieter then. I do as much as I can, half an hour, forty minutes, shower, then back home. The place is a rip-off but I need the discipline. Otherwise, you know,' she gestured at herself dismissively, 'it all falls apart.'

Barnaby shook his head. 'You look great,' he said frankly.

'I feel it.'

Barnaby lifted his glass in a silent toast. Kate didn't respond. An elderly couple shuffled in from the corridor, refugees from the D-Day celebrations. The man, heavy-set and overdressed, settled wearily into an armchair while his wife complained to the barmaid about the heating in the bedrooms. The thermostat was set way too low. They lived in Manitoba. They knew about central heating.

Kate finally reached for her glass. She was drinking Perrier.

'What about you?' she asked. 'Still married?'

'Yes.'

'Everything OK?'

'Everything's fine.'

'Good. I'm glad it worked out.' She paused. 'Truly.'

Barnaby glanced up, hearing the new note in her voice. He'd brought the affair to an end a year and a half ago, one chilly evening in late February. It happened to be the second anniversary of her decree absolute and she'd cooked a celebratory meal. Afterwards, they'd taken the second bottle of Chablis to bed where she'd presented him with a surprise present, a new recording of *The Marriage of Figaro*. They'd listened to it for hours, warmed by the alcohol and the plump winter duvet, and they were half-way through the last act before Kate had coaxed the truth from him. He couldn't leave his wife and family. He couldn't cope without them.

Now she was asking him about Jessie. Jessie was nineteen, blonde, quiet, immensely stubborn.

'She's fine,' Barnaby said lightly. 'Same old Jess.'

'University?'

'Didn't want to. Had the chance but turned it down, silly girl. Went to art college instead.'

'Somewhere nice?'

'Here. Pompey.'

'You sound disappointed.'

'Not at all.'

'But doesn't it help, having her at home?'

'She isn't at home.'

'She doesn't live with you?'

'No, hasn't for a while. She's got a flat – some basement place, as far as we know.'

'You've never been there?'

Barnaby shook his head, then shrugged when she asked him why. He knew where this conversation might lead and he wasn't keen to follow. A big limousine swept past outside, flanked by police motorcyclists.

'Tell me about the political stuff,' he said brightly. 'My spies tell me you're brilliant in committee. What's the secret?'

'Bluff and bullshit.' She grinned at him again, reaching for her sports bag and getting up. 'You should know that.'

Outside, in the car park, he waited beside her Audi while she searched for the keys. A man's leather jacket lay on the back seat. She saw him looking at it as she reached up to kiss his cheek.

'His name's Billy,' she said, 'in case you were wondering.' She slipped the sports bag off her shoulder, then nodded towards Southsea Common. The thump-thump of a marching band came and went on the wind. 'So why aren't you with the royals? Like everyone else I know?'

Barnaby was still looking at the jacket, remembering the lone figure in the gym. Set after set of repetitions. So fit. So supple.

'What?'

'The royals,' Kate said again. 'Why aren't you out there with them?'

'I wasn't invited.' He frowned. 'What about you?'

'Me? You're joking.'

'You had an invite?'

'Of course. Heritage Chair. Comes with the turf.'

Barnaby stared at her. 'You had an invite? And you *still* didn't go?'

'God, no. Sundays are special. Always have been.' She smiled at him. 'Don't you remember?'

She unlocked the door, not waiting for an answer, and Barnaby stepped aside, letting her get in. Excitement still smelled of shower gel and Diorella. Kate wound down the window and Barnaby did his best to return her smile.

'Take care,' he said, his eyes going back to the jacket.

Jessie Barnaby warmed her hands on a mug of hot water, willing the doorbell to ring. Haagen had left his keys, just like the last time. They lay on the floor beside the mattress. They must have fallen from his pocket when he'd pulled on his jeans, struggling towards the door, desperate to make the eleven o'clock meet. They'd both overslept, same old scene, Haagen getting in a muddle with the alarm settings on the electric clock. Haagen-time, she'd taken to calling it. Two parts vodka to one part smack.

She got up and began to circle the empty living room. The basement flat was sparsely furnished and even in midsummer the damp was almost tangible, a permanent presence, the lodger that had never left. It made everything smell. It made everything sticky. Whatever she did – aerosols, joss sticks, an hour or two's madness with the electric fire – the damp was always there, sour, malevolent, occasionally foul. She sipped the water, pulling Haagen's heavy army greatcoat around her, trying to ease the cramps in her shoulders and back. From time to time, barefoot on the greasy lino, she began to shudder, and then she had to pause, tensing herself, shutting her eyes, squeezing hard until the spasm went away.

It had been like this before, often before, but never this bad and never this long. She'd woken up early, four in the morning, dawn, and she'd wanted to tell Haagen then, but he'd been out of it, his thin body curled round hers, his breath featherlight on the back of her neck, and she'd propped herself on one elbow, smoking a couple of roll-ups until sleep had finally returned with the whine of the milk float in the street outside. She was there to take care of Haagen. He needed to rest. He was truly all she had.

The television in the corner flickered briefly and for a moment she thought it was going to give up again but then the signal strengthened and Southsea Common slipped back into focus and in close-up came the rows and rows of faces with whom she'd shared the last hour or so. The Queen. The Queen Mum. Prince Philip. Charles. Anne. The television was a cheap portable, a trophy from one of Haagen's less successful break-ins and the grainy black-and-white pictures somehow added to her icy sense of detachment. These people were real, she knew they were. They were close, too, just up the road. But caged inside this tiny set, emptied of all colour, they'd become somehow remote, visitors from outer space.

She sipped at the water and wondered about risking a slice of toast. Haagen had rigged up a little two-ring electric stove, bypassing the meter, and she knelt beside it, careful not to touch the bare wires. She thought there were a couple of slices of bread in the kitchen next door but when she went through to check she found the mice had got there first.

Beside the stove was the glass jar Haagen had brought her back the last time he'd been to Amsterdam. It was brown and fluted, and on one side it carried a gaudy stencil of a canal scene. Lately, Jessie had taken to using it as a candle holder. The flame from the candle threw a strange golden light through the glass, and if she got on her knees and looked hard at the stencil she could almost persuade herself that the barges on the canal were moving. She lit the candle now, warming her hands over the open throat of the jar. It was the only present Haagen had ever given her, and she protected it with a fierce reverence.

She carried the jar back to the living room and slipped under the blanket, staring across the room at the television. A big grey ship was ghosting past the war memorial while the commentator talked about a unique moment of history. Then the picture began to flicker again and Jessie thought of Haagen, how he was getting on, whether he'd remember which pub to go to. They were open all day today. It was part of the celebrations. She started to shiver again, and then the trembling became uncontrollable and her hands rose to her face and her nose began to run and she was up on her feet, walking back and forth, the greatcoat pulled around her.

Moments later, a shadow fell across the basement window and she heard Haagen's footsteps pause as he kicked at the abandoned cans and chip bags that littered the steps down from the street. He was still at it when she opened the door for him, standing back as he and the dog pushed past the stolen bicycles in the unlit hall, making their way to the kitchen. She heard the splash of water as Haagen turned on the tap. Then she was behind him in the semi-darkness, ready with the syringe, watching him unfolding the wrap, marvelling at the care he took, the way he held the paper between his fingers, funnelling the powder into the bowl of the waiting spoon, topping it up with water, not a fleck lost, not a drop spilled.

He turned on one of the rings on the electric stove, warming the spoon, watching the powder dissolve. Then he sucked the liquid into the barrel of the syringe, easing back the plunger. She was still behind him, transfixed by the blur of his hands as he began to shake the syringe, ignoring the bulldog's wet snout pushing at the back of her knee. Haagen went across to the window, holding up the syringe to the light; he shook it some more, and a third time, before he came back to her with that same little smile on his face.

She had the greatcoat half off by now, one arm already extended. He made her flex it a couple of times, then he put the syringe to one side and slipped the leather belt from his jeans, winding it around her arm, inches above the elbow. He tightened the belt to the usual notch, then retrieved the syringe. His fingers probed the soft flesh on the inside of her forearm, tracing the line of the raised vein until he found the spot he wanted, massaging it softly with his thumb before inserting the needle. The needle didn't hurt. It hadn't hurt for months. She watched the little trickle of blood find its way across her pale flesh as he entered the vein, and then she closed her eyes and nodded the way he liked her to, and he eased down on the plunger, emptying the syringe and loosening the belt, watching her all the time.

She stiffened with expectation, and then gasped, falling away from him, groaning as the smack hit her brain and the pain dissolved. The wave that had taken her began to curl, sucking her upwards, making her giddy, and she reached out for support, beginning to panic, aware that something was going horrifically wrong.

At her feet, the dog began to growl. It was the last sound she remembered.

Hayden Barnaby walked the half-mile back from the hotel. His route took him west, towards the corner of the island they called Old Portsmouth. He'd always loved the area – the narrow cobbled streets around the cathedral, the timber-fronted pubs, the smell of diesel and fish heads from the Camber Dock – and one day he'd promised himself he'd buy a house here. Everyone had told him he was daft – the noise, the tourists, the drunks at weekends – but he'd ignored them, bidding for a property in the street that led down to the seaward fortifications.

The house itself was odd. Like the rest of the city, Old Portsmouth had suffered heavily during the Blitz and the post-war years had seen a rash of rebuilding. Much of it was undistinguished, brick façades, flat roofs, but the architect for 20 Farthing Lane had tried a little harder, and constructed a modern three-storey house that blended surprisingly well with its Georgian neighbours. Inside, the property was like nothing else Barnaby had ever seen before: open-plan, lots of light and space, polished wooden floors, subtly lit alcoves and a wrought-iron staircase that wound upwards, giving access to the rooms above.

At the top of the house, the master bedroom looked east, over the ruins of the Garrison church, and beyond the long line of seventeenth-century fortifications lay the deep-water shipping lane that dog-legged out to the Solent and the English Channel. French windows opened onto a rooftop terrace and the day Barnaby had first viewed the property, he'd stood in the fitful sunshine with the wind in his face, watching one of the big cross-Channel ferries nosing out through the line of buoys. The rain had come and gone, washing the air clean, and the ferry had seemed close enough to touch, the water boiling at its stern, rags of smoke torn sideways by the wind. That single image had proved indelible, and every morning, when he woke up and stood at the bedroom window, he still marvelled at the limitless variations in the view. The flat, gunmetal greys that preceded an incoming weather front. The fat-bellied storm clouds that arrived hours later. The boisterous greens and blues that signalled the end of the rain. He loved it, depended on it. In so many ways it had become a consolation.

Barnaby saw his wife from the street. She was sitting in a deckchair on the roof terrace. She had a glass in one hand and a pair of binoculars in the other. He waved up at her but she was looking east, towards Southsea Common. Barnaby let himself into the house. His study was on the first floor, the desk by the window, books and files everywhere. He left his sports bag behind the door, climbing the stairs again. The big velvet curtains in the master bedroom were stirring in the wind. He stepped out into the sunshine, putting a hand on his wife's shoulder, feeling her stiffen momentarily beneath his touch. She was wearing the towelling robe he'd given her for Christmas. The bottle of Tio Pepe on the table beside her was nearly empty.

He bent down and kissed her lightly on the cheek. She lowered the binoculars and looked up at him, shielding her eyes against the sun.

'You missed *Illustrious*,' she said absently. 'I thought you'd be back.'

Barnaby shook his head. He could smell the alcohol on her

breath. He went to the railings: half a mile away he could see the reviewing stand they'd built on the Common for the memorial service. Beyond it lay a small tented city for the thousands of returned veterans. The service, he thought, must be nearly over. He turned back, easing the ache in his leg. Liz was looking up at him. Lately, she'd put on a lot of weight and it showed in her face, blunting her features. Hard to believe she'd once been a model.

She was offering him the bottle. He shook his head, said he'd prefer tea. She sighed, getting up. She was a tall woman, keenly aware of the impact she always made on men. Lately, she'd taken to wearing dresses with deeply scooped necklines, emphasizing the heaviness of her bust. I'm still in the game, she seemed to be saying. I still count.

Barnaby waved her back into the deckchair, asking whether she wanted anything to eat. He was thinking of fixing himself a sandwich. He'd bring a plateful up. She looked at him a moment, a vagueness in her eyes, before sitting down again.

'Jessie,' she said.

'What about her?'

'She's supposed to be coming to lunch.'

'*Lunch?*'

'Yes. I dropped a little note into the college a couple of days ago. She phoned back. I thought I'd told you. I'm sure I did.'

Barnaby shook his head. He remembered no such conversation. Jessie had become another of the no-go areas between them, a minefield you entered at your peril.

'Haagen coming too?'

'I don't know.'

'Did you ask him?'

'No.'

Barnaby smiled, turning away. Haagen, he was certain, was one of the reasons they saw so little of Jessie. From the day she'd set eyes on him, she'd had room for nothing else in her life. It was sweetly ironic, therefore, that Barnaby himself should have made the introductions. Not that he regretted their relationship. Far from it.

'What time?' he said, stepping back into the bedroom.

23

Liz looked at her watch. 'It's twenty past twelve.'

'I meant lunch.'

'Oh, I said four. I thought we'd eat late. That OK with you?'

Barnaby glanced back over his shoulder. Liz was reaching for the Tio Pepe again, not waiting for an answer.

Downstairs, Barnaby circled the kitchen. Most of the equipment was brand new, recently installed to Liz's specification. She'd only found out about Kate after the affair was over, a spiteful confidence from a friend, and part of the peace settlement had been a tacit understanding that their marriage should be buttressed henceforth against the outside world. That had meant money, the least of Barnaby's problems, and with the kitchen had come a bigger monthly allowance and a brand new car, visible evidence for anyone who cared to look that their relationship was out of intensive care and well into convalescence. It hadn't worked, of course, and they both knew it, but sheer exhaustion had locked them into settling for what they had. They still talked. They were still friends. They still, occasionally, made love. Even these small intimacies put them well ahead of other couples they knew, and both of them, deep down, had no appetite for starting all over again. There were worse things in life, Barnaby told himself, than a successful legal practice, and a £200,000 view of eternity.

Barnaby filled the kettle. He was still hunting for the tea-bags when he heard the front-door bell. He went to the window and peered out. Jessie never arrived early. Never. The bell rang again. A man in his forties stepped back from the door, looking up. He was wearing jeans and a sweatshirt and a pair of scuffed Reeboks. He had a holdall in one hand and a bottle of wine in the other. The blaze of blond curls was even wilder than Barnaby remembered, but there was no mistaking the big square face and the puckered grin. Charlie Epple.

Barnaby opened the door, following Charlie's pointing finger. The man never bothered with formalities. He hadn't been down for nearly a year but it didn't seem to matter.

'Lancaster,' he was saying. 'Look.'

Barnaby shielded his eyes in time to see the silhouette of the big four-engined bomber roar past. Behind it, in formation, flew

24

a Spitfire and a Hurricane. At the end of the street, the promenade on top of the sea wall was black with people. Barnaby found himself explaining about the memorial service. Behind the Lanc would come a fly-past. Tornados. Yank planes. Everything you could think of.

Charlie was still watching the Spitfire as it banked over Southsea Castle and climbed away. Finally he turned round, shaking his head, holding two fingers to his temple, cocking his thumb like a pistol. It was a gesture Barnaby remembered from years back. It meant that the sight of the aircraft had blown Charlie's mind. He stepped past Barnaby, presented him with the bottle and tucked the holdall neatly beneath the line of hanging coats. Then he was outside again, looking skywards.

'Pint?' he said. 'Somewhere with a view?'

They drank all afternoon, moving from pub to pub, never leaving Old Portsmouth. By four o'clock, they were down by the harbour mouth, joining the crowds watching the Queen reviewing the fleet. The warships were drawn up in long grey lines a mile or so offshore, straddling the stretch of water known as Spithead, and Barnaby could see the dark blue hull of the royal yacht steaming slowly past the bulk of a big American aircraft carrier.

The crowds were already six deep on the harbour front and Barnaby followed Charlie as he pushed through towards a low wall that gave access to the boatyard belonging to the sailing club. Charlie had a pint glass in one hand and a Union Jack on a stick in the other. He'd bought a flag for Barnaby, too, but Barnaby had already given his to a passing child. At the front of the crowd, Charlie handed his glass to Barnaby, then scrambled onto the wall. Another climb took them onto the flat slab roof of a sail store. The sun was in the west now, late afternoon, and they settled down against the warm brickwork at the back of the roof. The view was perfect: the ebb tide flooding out through the harbour mouth, the sunshine splintering on the dancing waves as a succession of tourist boats churned to and fro.

Barnaby reached for his glass, swallowing another mouthful of beer. It could have been his fifth pint. Or sixth. He didn't care. The afternoon had tugged him back to his youth and he'd put aside the pain in his leg and the disappointments of the weekend. Enough, for now, to be sitting in the sunshine, with the best seat in the house, listening to Charlie Epple.

He'd known the man since adolescence and he'd always been a kind of hero. They'd been classmates at the grammar school, Charlie already the rebel, already tipped for stardom. Average in more or less everything else, he had a rare talent for a certain kind of writing. Not short stories or anything literary, not the kind of turgid essays that took you up the foothills of the A-level course, but condensed little pieces, occasionally poetry, sometimes song lyrics, but more and more often the kind of casually brilliant scribblings the advertising industry called copywriting.

It was a gift that Charlie had always shrugged off. His real interests were music and women. But at Barnaby's insistence, he'd entered a national copywriting contest organized by one of the big London agencies and, to no one's surprise but his own, he'd won. With a cheque for £500 had come the offer of a job, and so Charlie had boxed his precious collection of rhythm and blues LPs, and loaded his brother's Bedford van and departed for the big city. Within six years he'd become one of the hottest properties in Adland. Poached by a succession of agencies, he'd made – and spent – a small fortune, and with the money had come the applause of his peers. His ads for Bacardi rum and Oxfam had won the industry's top awards, and by the eighties, when the Tory government decided to auction the nation's silver, Charlie had been the natural choice to shape the campaigns. He helped sell British Telecom. He was in at the rebirth of British Gas. And as Smith Square warmed to his handiwork, he got richer and richer.

Throughout this period, Barnaby had kept up with his career. Frequently in London himself on business, he'd find time to meet Charlie for a drink or a meal, amazed and delighted at the latest twist in the story. Often, these encounters included Charlie's friends, mates from the industry, and from them Barnaby was able to piece together exactly what it was that made Charlie so irreplaceable.

The advertising business ran on adrenaline. The big prizes went to the agencies who could think on their feet, make sense of impossible briefs, meet silly deadlines. This guaranteed an ongoing state of chaos, something for which Charlie had considerable affection. In consequence, he never panicked, never lost his cool, but simply came up with another half-dozen brilliant ideas. In his own phrase, they were the bullets he sent into the oncoming hordes. When the account execs were going crazy on the fourth floor, it was Charlie's nasal drawl that brought them to a halt. Barnaby had heard these men talking about him and, as far as they were concerned, Charlie Epple had two priceless assets: low blood pressure and a talent for the killer copyline. Together, they'd given him a huge helping of the one thing he couldn't handle: success.

He was talking about wife number three. She was Spanish. She was exactly half his age. And she was driving him mad.

Barnaby was watching the royal yacht steaming away down the Solent. He glanced at Charlie. None of his marriages had ever worked. This one was evidently no different.

'Why?' he asked.

'She's a kid. And she's stupid. She just wants to talk all the time. And fuck.'

'So what's the problem?'

'You ever tried it?'

'No.'

'It gets incredibly boring. Really dull. If she sits on my face again, I'll sue. Invasion of privacy. I'm serious.'

'What's the matter with her?'

'Nothing. It's greed. Pure and simple. Just helps herself. Can't stop. If it was food, she'd explode.' He paused. 'Nice thought.'

Barnaby tried to suppress a grin and failed. Charlie had never had a problem pulling new girlfriends. That bit was easy. They loved his directness, his lack of inhibition, the way he cornered them at parties or functions and talked them cheerfully into bed. It was afterwards, often weeks afterwards, when they had to swop the body oils and the laughter for real life, that it got a little trickier.

Charlie was studying his empty glass. His latest wife was called

Conchita. They had a big house in Wimbledon. He thought he might leave her the key and run away.

'Where to?'

'Anywhere. Here.' He nodded up-harbour, towards the tangle of masts in the naval dockyard. 'It's real. It's got atmosphere. It's sane. I'm serious.'

'And is that why you're down?'

'No.'

He glanced sideways at Barnaby and then explained about the new client the agency had just picked up. It seemed that Portsmouth City Council had decided to invest in a little serious self-promotion. Nineteen ninety-four was the eight-hundredth anniversary of the city's first charter. The celebrations had coincided with the D-Day jamboree, and next month, Pompey was playing host to a stage of the Tour de France. The cyclists would start and finish on Southsea Common. The world's cameras would descend on the city once again. It seemed, said Charlie, a sensible time to cash in.

Barnaby tried to follow the logic but three hours' drinking made the obvious difficult to grasp.

'You mean the city council?' he said. 'Here?'

'Yeah.'

'Our lot?'

'Yeah.'

'They want to hire you? To sell . . .' Barnaby waved his glass at the crowds below ' . . . all this?'

'That's right.'

Barnaby thought about the proposition. After another mouthful of beer it didn't sound so fanciful. You could sell anything nowadays. Even Pompey.

'And you'll do it?'

'No question.' Charlie nodded, watching a big yacht wallowing in through the harbour mouth. On the foredeck lay two girls in bikinis. One got up, stretched, then reached for the rail and began to wave at the crowds. Charlie waved back, grinning.

'Eleven o'clock,' he murmured. 'Meet the client. Discuss the brief.'

'Eleven o'clock when?'

'Tomorrow.' He blew the girl an extravagant kiss. 'Did I mention about staying the night?'

They were back home by five. Barnaby had trouble opening the front door, and when he turned to say something to Charlie he realized that his car wasn't there. He peered down the street, wondering what might have happened. Maybe Liz had gone to pick Jessie up. Maybe she'd phoned for a lift. But why should she do that when Jess had been so determined to keep them away from that flat of hers?

'Mercedes coupé,' Barnaby said vaguely, 'silver grey.'

'What is?'

'The car.'

Barnaby looked a moment longer, nonplussed, then opened the door. Inside, the table was set for three. He could smell roast beef but when he crossed the room to the kitchen he found the oven turned off. He reached for one of the saucepans on top of the hob and removed the lid. Florets of cauliflower swam in luke-warm water. He turned round. Charlie was at the table. Under a bottle of Burgundy, he'd found a note. He handed it to Barnaby without a word. Barnaby read it. Liz had been called to the hospital. Jessie was in the Emergency Unit. Barnaby looked up. Charlie was already on the phone. He was Jessie's godfather. The bond between them had always been close. He caught Barnaby's eye across the room.

'Cab,' he said tonelessly.

Portsmouth's Accident and Emergency Unit is in the Queen Alexandra Hospital on the slopes of Portsdown Hill to the north of the city. Charlie followed Barnaby into the reception area. The woman behind the desk made a note of Barnaby's name and lifted a phone. After a while, a young doctor appeared, took Barnaby by the arm and walked him towards a pair of double doors.

'Where's my wife?' Barnaby kept saying. 'Where's Liz?'

'She's through here.'

The doctor opened one of the doors, letting Barnaby pass. Right and left were lines of curtained cubicles. At the end, on a chair, sat Liz. Barnaby quickened his step. He wanted to know what had happened. He wanted Liz to tell him. She got up slowly. She looked pale and drawn, and her mascara had run, big black smudges under her eyes. The doctor stood to one side, talking to the sister in charge, who was consulting a chart and shaking her head.

'What's happening?' Barnaby said. 'What's going on?'

He felt Liz's hand on his arm and he caught it, grateful. His wife tugged him gently towards the row of empty seats.

'She's on a drip,' she said. 'She's got a tube in her arm.'

'But why? What's wrong?'

'They're saying she overdosed.'

'On what?'

'They won't tell me. But it's serious, I know it is.'

'How serious?'

'Very serious.'

'What did she take? Pills?'

'I . . .' Liz looked down, shaking her head. Her hands were trembling. Barnaby looked at her a moment, then put his arms round her. She began to sob. After a while she stopped, and wiped her nose on her sleeve. Barnaby fetched some tissues from a box on a nearby trolley. She balled them in her hand, sniffing.

Barnaby bent down to her, his mouth brushing her ear.

'Where is she?'

'Over there.' Liz pointed, indicating a cubicle at the end of the row. Barnaby got to his feet and walked unsteadily towards it. He found the edge of the curtain and peered in. He knew he was drunk but he didn't care. Sober, this scene would have been even worse.

Jessie lay on a trolley beneath a blanket. Her feet were bare, the soles cross-hatched with dirt. Machines flanked the head of the trolley and a drip hung from a stand beside Jessie's arm. It was disconnected and the bag of solution on the stand was still three-quarters full.

Barnaby stepped across to the trolley and looked down at his daughter. Her eyes were closed and she appeared to be asleep. Like this, she still had the face of a child: the blonde urchin haircut, the snub nose, Liz's perfect mouth framing the crooked tooth at the front. For years, now, Liz had wanted her to get it fixed but Jessie had always said no, a demonstration of that same quiet defiance that had finally taken her from them.

Barnaby stroked her face briefly, whispering her name. Her skin was cold and clammy to the touch. He heard footsteps outside, felt the swirl of the curtain behind him. Liz, he thought, turning round.

It was the sister again, a short, thin woman in her fifties. She looked exhausted. Barnaby straightened by the bed, determined not to apologize. His daughter. His right to be standing there beside her.

'I need to know what's the matter,' he said thickly. 'What's been going on.'

The sister was carrying a plastic bucket. She put it beside the locker at the head of the trolley. 'Your daughter was brought in this afternoon,' she said pointedly, 'about three hours ago.'

'Where from?'

'I've no idea.'

'And was she . . .' he gestured down at Jessie, ' . . . like this?'

'Yes.'

'Have you any idea why?'

The sister reached for the blanket. It was flecked with vomit. She peeled it back. Jessie was wearing a grubby white T-shirt. On the front, it said, 'Kill the Criminal Justice Bill.' The sister indicated the inside of Jessie's forearm. 'There,' she said.

Barnaby followed her pointing finger. There was a smear of dried blood around the tiny puncture wound, and bruising under the skin. He stared at it, knowing exactly what it was. He felt the blood flooding into his face. Jessie? Shooting up? The sister's finger was moving along Jessie's arm, following the thin blue line of the vein.

'And there,' she was saying, 'and there.' She glanced up. 'Is your daughter a diabetic, by any chance?'

31

'No, not to my knowledge.'

'I beg your pardon?'

'No,' he said gruffly. 'Definitely not.'

The sister nodded, replacing the blanket. Jessie stirred, one hand reaching for her face. She emitted a tiny sigh. The sister was turning to go. Barnaby stopped her. 'So what was it? What was she using?'

'I'm afraid I can't tell you.'

'Why not?'

'Because we don't know, Mr Barnaby. And if we ever do, it won't be me who tells you.'

'But what would you expect to find? May I ask you that?'

The sister blinked and Barnaby knew at once that he'd over-stepped the mark. This was neither the time nor the place for lawyerly cross-examination. He turned back to Jessie. There were scarlet blotches down the side of her neck, disappearing beneath the soiled T-shirt. Barnaby gazed at them a moment, aware of the sister beside him.

'Love bites,' she confirmed. 'Who knows? Maybe that's a positive sign?'

By the time he waved Zhu off, Ellis was exhausted. He watched the little Jet Ranger climbing away from the Battersea heliport, and then walked back to the terminal building.

Mr Hua, the chauffeur, was still waiting outside in the Daimler. Ellis stood by the driver's window, looking in. Mr Hua had a big atlas of road maps open on his lap and he was tracing a route south from London with a felt-tip pen. He did it with immense concentration, a heavy green line inching down through Surrey and Hampshire, all the way to the coast. Ellis waited until he'd finished then tapped on the window. He needed to confirm the directions out to Buckinghamshire. According to the message he'd received at lunchtime, Zhu would be ready for collection at eight thirty prompt.

Mr Hua flicked back through the atlas. Ellis showed him the way to High Wycombe. Sunday night, he said, the traffic out of

London should be light, though returning to the Savoy might be trickier. Mr Hua made a note of the directions, then reached for the ignition key. Seconds later, the Daimler was easing away from the kerbside.

Ellis stifled a yawn, watching the car disappear in the direction of Wandsworth Bridge. The route Mr Hua had been so carefully planning on his atlas would take him to Portsmouth but Ellis, try as he might, couldn't think why.

Chapter Two

Billy Goodman was still trying to tune the radio when he saw the parking space. He checked in the rear-view mirror then braked sharply. The pub car park, as usual, was full. Fifteen feet of car space, so close to the Finches, was a godsend. He eased the Audi into the gap between the two cars and turned off the engine. Only then did he notice the Cavalier waiting to back in.

He looked at it a moment, then shrugged. Parking in this city was a game. Unless you got in first, you didn't get in at all. Even guys who drove Cavaliers knew that. He reached for the radio again, looking for Virgin AM. He'd spent most of the afternoon trying to sort out a clean signal on the medium wave and he thought he'd cured the interference with a new suppressor but now he wasn't so sure. He found the station and started the engine again, cursing as the hum returned. Kate wanted the car back by ten. No excuses.

He glanced at his watch, wondering whether he ought to skip the pub. Another hour in the workshop might see the problem sorted. He glanced up, hearing a car door slam. The Cavalier was still parked in the middle of the road. A bulky youth about half his age was striding towards him. He was wearing jeans and a sports shirt and his hair was freshly gelled. His girlfriend was still sitting in the car, her body half turned in the passenger seat, watching.

The youth stopped beside Billy's window. He wrenched open the door. 'You fucking blind or something?'

Billy eyed him without enthusiasm. The boy had used far too much aftershave. 'You got a problem, son?'

'No, mate, but you do.'

'Yeah?'

'Yeah.' The youth nodded at the Cavalier. 'I was backing in. It was my space. Until you fucking nicked it.'

'Nicked it?' Billy looked injured. '*Nicked* it?'

The youth stared down at him. Anger did nothing for his composure. He glanced over his shoulder at his girlfriend. She was making a loose movement with her wrist. He nodded, turning back to Billy. 'She's fucking right,' he said. 'Wanker.'

Billy was fiddling with the radio again. When he got the station dead centre, he pulled the door shut, ignoring the string of oaths through the open window. A taxi had arrived, the cabbie leaning on the horn, and the noise brought a couple of drinkers out of the pub. They read the situation at once, settling by the kerbside with their pints of lager, awaiting developments.

The youth beside Billy's car took a step back then swung at the door panel with his boot. The Audi shuddered as he did it again, harder this time, and Billy carefully stowed his screwdriver under the dashboard before getting out. The youth looked uncertain for a second or two, then threw a long, untidy right hook. Billy ducked it, closing with the youth, seizing him by the collar and driving his forehead into his face. He heard the youth's nose break and, as his hands went up to shield his face, Billy drove his knee into his unprotected groin. The bellow of pain became a whimper as the air whistled out of him, and he collapsed onto the road, his body curled into a tight, protective ball.

His girlfriend was out of the Cavalier now, and the sound of her screams brought more drinkers flooding from the pub. She gestured hopelessly at her fallen boyfriend, begging someone to do something, but most eyes were on Billy. He was standing over the prostrate youth, gazing down. At length, he tried to stir a little movement with his foot but the youth was still fighting for breath. A moment or two later, he groaned and began to vomit. Billy bent quickly, hauled him across the road by his armpits and left him curled in the gutter, still throwing up. The girl was hysterical, flailing at Billy with her fists. She'd call the police. She had his number. He was a bastard. He was sick. She'd make him pay. Billy ignored the threats, suggesting she move the Cavalier. She was causing an obstruction. People were trying to get past. The girl stared at him, then began to wail again, and in the end Billy left her to it, getting back in the Audi and starting the engine. Driving away, he paused beside her in the road. The youth was up on one elbow, looking dazed. His nose was pulped and blood was dripping off his chin. Billy smiled at him, then indicated the parking space he'd just abandoned outside the pub.

'All yours,' he said, reaching again for the radio.

Kate Frankham sat in bed, trying to ignore the lure of the Sunday papers. They lay in an untidy pile beside her supper tray, a constant reminder of the world to which she knew she belonged. Eighteen months in local politics had taught her a great deal, and the most important lesson, by far, had been the realization that nothing was probably beyond her.

She moistened the tip of her finger and began to flick through the thick raft of paperwork on which tomorrow's meeting would float. The committee met on the first Monday of every month. In the council circulars, and on the public boards in the Civic Centre, it was known as the Cultural and Heritage Services Committee, and the first time she'd attended it, the experience had scared her witless. She'd been a stranger to this world of proposers and seconders, of minutes and addenda. She'd known nothing about procedures and protocols. Even the simple business of taking a vote had been a mystery. But Kate had never been slow to learn and it had dawned on her very quickly that the language of committees, like any other language, was simply the insiders' way of protecting their own interests. Nothing, in the end, was alarming or impenetrable. Indeed, most of the time, committee work was a statement of the blindingly obvious.

She smiled to herself, leafing through a long report on the future of the city's museums. She'd been Chairperson of the Heritage Committee for just six months. She'd been voted into the position because she belonged to the ruling group – a coalition of Labour and the Lib-Dems – and because it was generally accepted that she'd do the job well. She was young. She was bright. She was committed. And, most important of all, she'd already made her mark by winning a number of battles over local issues, some of them dauntingly complex. That, she now saw, had given her enormous clout. She'd been out there at the grass-roots. She'd done her research. She'd taken on the experts and trounced them with their own statistics. Before she'd cast a single vote, she'd acquired the aura of the veteran.

She leaned back against the pillow, stretching her arms wide, arching her back. Tomorrow, as usual, each party would hold pre-meetings before the committee formally convened. Behind closed doors, her own Labour group would thrash out a line, and the Tories would separately rehearse their objections, and half an hour later, around the committee table, they'd all go through the motions again. Any member of the public who took the trouble to attend might – first time round – be impressed by the workings of democracy, but anyone with any knowledge knew that the whole thing was a stitch-up. The real business of committee work was about scoring as many political points as you could. The decisions that mattered had already been taken.

Kate tossed the museums report onto the growing pile by the bed, then she reached for the remote control and turned on the television. The local ITV company was running the edited highlights of the day's events on the Common and she watched for a moment or two, regretting that her dad hadn't survived to be there. Unlike Kate, he'd loved occasions like these: the bands, the uniforms, the ceremony. She supposed that it must have had something to do with his war service, that unconditional loyalty to King and Country. She didn't share those feelings herself – indeed she viewed the monarchy as just another excuse to keep power out of the hands of the people – but she'd never once presumed to question her father's allegiance. It had suited him. It had made him happy. Enough said.

She leaned back against the pillows, trying to picture him. Above the bookshelf across the room hung the single framed photo that had survived the clear-out after his death. It showed him as a young able seaman on a quayside in Liverpool. In the background, on the flat grey water, rode the small corvette on which he'd spent the first two years of his war service. The boat, HMS *Kingston*, had finally hit a mine in the Western Approaches and Arthur Frankham had been one of a bare handful of survivors. He'd rarely talked about the incident but Kate was convinced that the loss of his shipmates like that had shaped the rest of his life and, looking at the big toothy grin in the photograph it seemed obvious why he'd later become such a committed trade union official. In the end, as he'd so often told her, it's down to your pals: looking after them, treasuring them, making sure they always got the best.

Kate's eyes went back to the television. The service was over. The limousines were being readied for the fourteen heads of state and the commentator was saying something portentous about the importance of treasuring images like these. Kate thought suddenly of Hayden Barnaby, wondering whether he, too, was watching. Like her dad, he'd always been a sucker for state occasions. They seemed to appeal to something primitive in him though not, she suspected, in the same way as they had to her father. Barnaby's interest had always been transparent. He loved power. He loved show. He loved an audience. That's maybe why he'd become a lawyer, she thought, smiling at this morning's memory of him standing in the pool, discomforted by the success of her little ambush. He'd put on a bit of weight and it showed in the way he'd tried to suck in his stomach as they swopped gossip in the shallow end. There'd been something different about his face, too, an air of slight wistfulness, as if life had robbed him of something indescribably important.

After the second pint, Billy Goodman knew he'd had enough. Putting the nut on the kid in the Cavalier hadn't been quite as inch-perfect as he'd have liked, and the Castlemaine was doing nothing for his headache. Out in the car park, he took several deep breaths before climbing back into the Audi. With luck, Kate would have something in the bathroom cupboard to sort him out. She suffered from migraines herself and was always dropping pain-killers.

Billy drove west, through a maze of narrow side-streets. He'd no idea whether the youth's girlfriend had been serious about calling the police but he had no appetite for getting stopped. Back on the main road, he slowed for a gaggle of D-Day veterans spilling out of a pizza restaurant, then took a right turn into the street where Kate lived. Her house was at the far end, one of a terrace of Georgian properties that had recently been tarted up. A modest conservation grant had paid for railings and a paint job, and Billy lingered in the Audi, looking up at the single lit window at the top of the house. Half past ten, he thought, and already in bed.

He let himself in through the front door, stooping to pick up the cat. The kitchen was on the first floor, and he paused to swallow half a carton of mango juice from the fridge. There was a bowl of hummus in there, too, and he broke off a dried corner of pitta bread, dipped it into the bowl and ladled the stuff into his mouth. It tasted of olive oil and lemon juice and he was going back for more when he heard footsteps descending from the bedroom above.

He turned round in the narrow kitchen. Kate was standing in the open doorway. She was wearing a long black singlet and not much else. She had a pencil in one hand and a sheaf of papers in the other.

'Go ahead,' she said drily. 'Help yourself.'

Billy wiped his mouth with the back of his hand. He'd heard this tone of voice a lot lately. It meant he'd taken liberties, trespassed. It meant he should have asked. He grinned at her. 'Hungry.' He gestured at the half-empty bowl. 'Starving.'

'Then why didn't you come earlier? Sit down for a civilized meal?'

'I couldn't.'

'Why not?'

Billy closed the fridge door with his foot. As he stepped towards her, she saw the bloodstains on his shirt. She peered at them for a moment, uncertain, then asked him what had happened. Billy described the incident outside the pub.

'So you hit him?'

'Yeah.' Billy gestured at his shirt. 'And he bled on me.'

39

'How badly?'

Billy thought about the question, remembering the youth sprawled in the road.

'It wasn't as bad as it looked,' he said defensively. 'Not as bad as she thought.'

'Who? Who thought?'

'The girlfriend.'

'There were other people there? Witnesses?'

'Yeah,' Billy nodded, 'blokes from the pub, too. You know what it's like with a fight. Everyone thinks it'll go on for ever. Thank Christ it didn't. Thank Christ I got lucky.'

'Lucky?'

Kate let the word hang between them. Like most women she had a deep mistrust of violence, believing that men were never happier than when they were belting the shit out of each other. Billy shook his head, trying to downplay the incident. The other guy had come on far too strong. He'd attacked her car. He'd been completely out of order.

'The car doesn't matter,' Kate said at once. 'Bugger the car.'

'You won't say that tomorrow. Not when you see the dents.'

'Sod the dents. It's you I worry about. Thirty-eight and still picking fights. When do you start talking your way out of these things? Why so aggressive all the time? Look at you, it's like having a kid around. Jesus, Billy, you might have really hurt him. Didn't that occur to you? Or am I being naïve?'

Kate stared at him, waiting for an answer, then turned on her heel. Billy heard her footsteps on the stairs, then the slam of the bedroom door. He looked at the fridge, wondering whether to finish the hummus. Lately, things hadn't been great with Kate. She'd become irritable, impatient, almost disenchanted, and in his heart he knew that the relationship had cooled. He still had his uses, the practical stuff she found hard to cope with by herself, but he suspected that the R&B gigs and nights of endless Guinness were probably over. Like everyone else in the Labour Party, she'd had her fling with the working class. And like the rest of them, she'd decided it was time to move on.

He bent to fondle the cat again, wondering whether he could

be bothered with the inevitable scene. When they'd first met, a week before Christmas, she'd found it hard to get enough of him. She'd dragged him back to this house of hers, poured Irish whiskey down his throat and kept him up all hours with her plans and ambitions and endless analyses of just where the party had gone wrong. His own years with the Socialist Workers Party had given him a real taste for this kind of tussle, and for a while – weeks certainly – he'd tugged her steadily leftwards until her own position had seemed indistinguishable from his. They'd agreed on the sanctity of Clause Four. They'd shared a contempt for rentier capitalism. She'd even agreed with him that sometimes – just sometimes – direct action was the only answer. How else to rid the country of the poll tax? How else to lobby for the teachers? Or the miners? Or any of the other class warriors battling this insane government?

The new year had come and gone and they'd still been friends, allies, fellow travellers on the road back to socialism. By now, the relationship had developed a physical side, her initiative, not his, and more and more often he'd find himself staying the night, waking up in the small hours to find her looming over him. From the start, she'd had a frankness about sex and about her own appetites that had first surprised and then alarmed him. Whatever he did, however often, it was never enough. She wanted to be stretched. She wanted to be tested. She wanted him, in her own phrase, to fuck her until her lights went out. This he tried to do, but with the growing certainty that his own role was entirely symbolic. He wore a leather jacket. He lived on his wits. He occasionally kept heavy company. He was, in every conceivable respect, the antithesis of the other politicos she was obliged to mix with. Thus, perhaps, his appeal.

Billy tempted the cat with a saucer of milk and toyed with beating a retreat and going home. He shared a small terrace house about a mile away with two students and an out-of-work chef. Sunday nights, they generally watched football videos. He glanced up at the clock on the wall, asking himself whether he was really up for another hour of Eric Cantona, then he abandoned the idea and began to climb the stairs. The bedroom was at the top of the house. Kate was propped against the pillows, reading the Sunday papers. The lead story speculated on the latest Tory initiative on Europe. *IS IT TIME TO LEAVE?* went the headline.

She glanced up at him, dispassionate, one eyebrow raised. 'Where's the car?'

'Outside.'

'Key?'

Billy fumbled in his pocket and tossed it onto the counterpane. He could hear the cat outside, scratching at the carpet.

'I tried to fix the radio,' he said at last, 'but it's still not sorted.'

'Don't worry.'

'No?'

She glanced up, shaking her head. There was a long silence. At length Billy took off his jacket and began to unbutton his jeans. Kate was back in the paper. By the time she looked up again he was naked beside the bed. She studied him briefly then abandoned the paper and reached out for him. Often it started like this, sometimes his call, sometimes hers. Either way, the transition was always abrupt, a shoe-horn that took them from one life into another.

Afterwards, he tried to join her in bed but she pushed him away. When he tried again, she rolled over onto her side, nodding at the pile of clothes on the carpet. 'Take the cat with you,' she said sleepily. 'He needs to go out.'

Hayden Barnaby awoke at dawn, reaching automatically for the glass of water beside the bed. According to the digital clock, it was 04.16. He blinked in the half-darkness, feeling the tightness of the bands around his head. He and Charlie had finally got to bed past midnight, the roast beef still in the oven, three bottles of Burgundy up-ended in the bin.

He slipped out of bed and padded across to the window. Liz was asleep, a long untidy comma of blonde hair splayed across the pillow. When he looked back at her face there was something in its helplessness that reminded him of Jessie at the hospital.

He stood at the window for a full minute, watching her, before shuddering and reaching for his jeans.

Outside, it was still cool, the wind off the sea. Away to the east, a ledge of cloud masked the first blush of sunrise. He used the bleep in the key-ring to unlock the Mercedes and then slipped behind the wheel. The basement flat where Jessie lived was barely a mile away, one of a series of streets that ran down into the heart of Southsea, the city's resort area. Barnaby slipped the car into gear and eased towards the main road. His route took him past the hotel where he'd exercised the previous day and he paused at the roundabout, looking across at the extension that housed the swimming pool. The heat from the pool had pebbled the smoked glass with condensation, and he tried to imagine Kate Frankham, in just a couple of hours' time, cruising back and forth, cooling down after her forty minutes on the machines.

Meeting her again had troubled him more than he cared to admit, partly because she'd taken him by surprise, the kind of social ambush he hated, and partly because she'd become so obviously independent. Leaving her had been the hardest decision he'd ever had to make and he'd believed her when she'd told him they were throwing away a relationship that neither would ever be able to duplicate. Yet here she was, barely a year and a half later, plainly in control of a life she adored. He'd seen it in her eyes, in the way she'd sat back and so openly appraised him. And he'd caught it again in the look she'd given him as she'd driven away. You don't know what you're missing, she'd been telling him. You poor, sad man.

The Mercedes purred away from the roundabout. The Common stretched away to the right, a big green buffer between the genteel terraces of Southsea and the rash of cafés and amusements along the seafront. Barnaby slowed for the bend by the Queen's Hotel, catching sight of the reviewing stand erected for yesterday's memorial service. The structure was somehow smaller than he'd expected, an untidy tangle of scaffolding, planked and timbered for rising tiers of seats. From the road, against the cold dawn light, it looked bare and empty and on an impulse he pulled in and parked, switched off the engine and let the window purr down. The air in his face tasted of low tide, a rich mixture of salt and seaweed, and Barnaby sat back, letting it sluice through him, clearing his head.

After a minute or two, he got out and crossed the road to the Common. The grass was still waterlogged after Saturday's rain and he listened to his own footsteps as he squelched around the reviewing stand. He clambered onto the scaffolding and zipped up his thin cotton jacket against the swirling wind. The chairs that had been here yesterday had gone and someone had been round with a broom, but when he reached the third tier and turned to face the sea, it was easy to people the muddy, tyre-rutted spaces, to imagine the marine bandsmen with their helmets and their glittering instruments, to hear the long keening salute from the lone bugler.

Barnaby plunged his hands deep into the pockets of his jeans, thinking of Clinton again. The big man had sat here, barely feet away. He'd listened to the Archbishop intone the service. He'd watched the seated rows of veterans, stiff-backed, attentive, bemedalled. And minutes later, when HMS *Illustrious* slipped out of the harbour mouth to take up her position for the fleet review, he'd probably reached across and touched Hillary lightly on the arm, drawing her attention to the big grey aircraft carrier ghosting slowly past the war memorial. As a piece of theatre, the service had translated wonderfully to television, and Barnaby had watched it again last night, drunk and remorseful, after returning from the hospital.

Now, he raised a weary arm to the imaginary crowds below, wondering again what it might be like to be Bill Clinton, then began to retrace his footsteps to the road. Jessie's flat lay a couple of blocks inland from the Common, and he walked the hundred yards or so to the street where she lived. The houses here were Victorian, tall forbidding mansions built for the families of naval officers but long since given over to multi-occupation. Most of the flats were let to students or families on benefit and the area had developed a shabby, unloved look: permanently curtained windows, dripping water pipes, loud music, and little nests of bulging bin bags spilling their contents onto the street.

Barnaby counted the front doors until he found number 26. At the hospital, they'd given him a small polythene bag containing Jessie's possessions. With the pound coin and the packet of Rizlas was a key. Barnaby pushed through the gate, avoiding the flattened scabs of dog turd. Steps led down to an alleyway beside the house. The walls were green with damp and he could feel broken glass underfoot. Half-way along the alley were steps down to a door. Barnaby paused at the bottom and inserted the key in the lock. It turned at once, he stepped inside, leaving the door open, feeling along the wall for a light switch. The smell was overpowering, a mixture of old fat, rising damp, and a rich oriental perfume Barnaby recognized from the days when Jess had taken to burning incense in her bedroom. His hand closed over a wall switch and he found himself surrounded by bicycles in a narrow hall. To the left, a half-open door. He pushed at it with his foot, muffling a cough then announcing his presence.

'Haagen?' He hesitated, waiting for an answer. When nothing happened, he stepped inside the room. Light from the street spilled in through the half-window at the front. The room was sparsely furnished, bare floorboards, a table, a council deckchair lifted from the beach, a television, a pile of wooden crates full of books, and a double mattress on the floor. Blankets were thrown back across the top as though someone had just got up, and there was a pile of clothes beside a candle in a saucer.

Barnaby bent to the clothes and untangled a rust-coloured halter top that Liz had given Jessie for Christmas. He lifted it to his face. It smelled of sweat and roll-ups, a sourness that reminded him at once of the prison visits he made to interview clients. He balled it in his hand, meaning to take it home, and bent to inspect the books in one of the crates. A lot were from libraries, thick biographies on various Nazi luminaries, ministers like Speer and Goering; when he looked at the return dates it was obvious that they'd been stolen. He prowled around the room again. Behind the door, on a tea chest, was a sound system. The needle was dancing on the VU meter on the cassette deck, and when he turned up the volume control he found himself listening to something sombre, heavily classical, scored for full orchestra. He lowered the volume again and noticed the flag for the first time. The Union Jack was huge, covering the entire wall, hanging limply from a line of drawing pins pressed into the picture rail. Barnaby touched it. It felt as damp as everything else.

'What is it, man? Help you at all?'

Barnaby spun round. A small figure stood in the open doorway. Under the army greatcoat, he was wearing a pair of boxer shorts. His feet were bare and his hair was brutally cropped against the bony outlines of his skull. In one hand he carried a mug of something hot. In the other was a kitchen knife.

'Haagen,' Barnaby said mildly. 'No need for that.'

Haagen stepped closer, peering at Barnaby. His face was as thin as the rest of him and though he recognized Barnaby's voice, he plainly wanted to make sure. Without his glasses, Haagen was semi-blind.

'Want these?' Barnaby had spotted them on top of the audio stack. He offered them to Haagen, who put them on. They robbed him of a little of his menace.

'Brahms,' he muttered, nodding at the cassette deck, 'Requiem.' He stood by the door for a moment or two then sucked at the liquid in the mug. Then he looked up, studying Barnaby over the rim. The steam began to mist his glasses, and he took them off, rubbing the lenses on the greatcoat. 'You want some toast or anything?'

Barnaby thought about it. He hadn't eaten for nearly a day. Toast might help the headache. He followed Haagen through to the kitchen. Another candle stood on a plate beside an ancient electric stove; its guttering flame cast a thin yellow light over the crumbling plaster walls. Haagen speared a slice of bread with a fork and held it over one of the rings.

'I thought you'd be at the hospital,' Barnaby said, after a while, 'last night.'

'I was.'

'When?'

'Before you came. And afterwards.'

'Why didn't you stay? Say hello?'

Haagen glanced over his shoulder, a smile edged with the same

46

faint derision Barnaby remembered from the first time he and Haagen had met. The social worker had done the introductions and Haagen had simply sat there in the court interview room, waiting patiently to have his say. When it came to the details on the charge sheet, he'd admitted everything with an indifference verging on contempt. He'd done the burger bar because they kept lots of ready money. The stuff about animal rights, Barnaby's suggested line of defence, was bullshit.

'This OK?'

Haagen was holding out a blackened slice of toast, thickly coated with Marmite. Barnaby bit into it, realizing how hungry he was.

'So when did you get back?' he enquired through a mouthful of crumbs. 'From the hospital.'

'Midnight. They threw me out. Sussed I wasn't a doctor.'

'Why would they think you were?'

'I'd copped a white coat. Found it in an office. It's just like anywhere. Wear a uniform, people leave you alone.'

Barnaby nodded, licking Marmite off his fingers. Haagen was the brightest nineteen-year-old he'd ever met, an East German refugee who'd fled to the West with his eldest sister and somehow ended up in Portsmouth. He'd attended schools in the city since the age of five but classroom learning had never appealed to him and at fourteen, expelled from a series of comprehensives for disruptive behaviour, he'd dropped out of formal education altogether. Thereafter, according to the social worker's case notes, he'd embarked on a fitful career of burglary and petty theft, using the proceeds to fund years of voracious reading. He'd devoured Ernst Junger. He'd gone through most of Nietzsche. He'd read everything he could find on the history of the Third Reich. And with the knowledge he'd acquired went a scalding candour that landed him in almost permanent trouble. Not once had Barnaby known Haagen stoop to telling a lie, one of the many reasons he'd fought so hard to keep him out of custody.

'So how was she?' Barnaby asked at last.

'Pretty rough. You must have seen her yourself.'

Barnaby nodded, sluicing his fingers under the cold-water tap.

Before he'd left the hospital, Jessie had been awake, sprawled on her side on the trolley, retching into a bucket. Liz had been beside her, holding her forehead, telling her that everything would be OK. Jessie had wanted them to ignore her, leave her alone, but Barnaby could sense just how badly she'd been frightened. Whatever she'd been using had nearly killed her. And she knew it.

'The sister showed me the marks in her arm,' Barnaby said quietly. 'How long has this been going on?'

'Months.'

'*Months?*'

'Yeah. I thought she could handle it. She couldn't.'

'And you?'

'I looked after her.'

'But can you handle it? Whatever it is?'

Haagen didn't answer. He'd found two more slices of bread and examined them in the light of the candle before toasting them. For the first time, Barnaby saw the tattoos on the backs of his fingers, the four fat blue letters, J – E – S – S, and the sight of his daughter's name brought the blood flooding into his face. He'd had faith in Haagen. He'd trusted him. He'd even given him a job in his own office, fulfilling his promise to the court. Now this.

'Do me a favour, Haagen,' he said thickly. 'Just tell me what we're talking about.'

Haagen was poking the toast with a knife. 'Heroin,' he said briefly. 'Smack.'

'You're telling me Jess has been on heroin? All this time?'

'Yeah. It's good for her, too. It suits.'

'You're out of your mind.'

'Not at all. She can't handle anything else. Uppers. Downers. E. Whiz. She just gets in a muddle, gets sloppy. Even alcohol breaks her up.'

'Handle? What do you mean, handle?'

'Can't take it. Can't cope.'

'Why should she have to? Who says she needs all this stuff?'

'She does. I do.'

'Why?'

'Because the rest of it is so much shit.'

48

'Rest of what?'

'This . . .' Haagen gestured round with the knife ' . . . this shit-hole we have to live in. The strokes we have to pull to get by. Not just us. Everyone.'

'She doesn't have to live here. That was her decision.'

'Sure.' Haagen pushed his glasses up his nose. 'And you know why?'

'No.' Barnaby shook his head. 'But I'm sure you'll tell me.'

'You want to know?'

'Yes.'

'OK,' Haagen said. 'Because she couldn't stand it at home with you and that nice wife of yours. The little lies. The big lies. It made her sick, physically sick. Her words, not mine.'

Barnaby nodded, letting his anger subside, knowing he should have expected a scene like this. Talking to Haagen was something you did at some peril. Softening the truth was beyond him.

'So you put her onto heroin?' he said wearily. 'Is that what you're saying?'

'Yeah,' Haagen agreed. 'We tried it and it was good for us. It worked.'

'How?'

'It gave her peace. And a bit of quiet.'

'And last night?'

'Last night was different. That wasn't smack, not the stuff we're used to, anyway.' He shrugged. 'Maybe it was purer than usual. That can be a problem. Fuck knows.'

'Where did you get it?'

'Where did I score?'

'Yes.'

'Last night?'

'Yes.'

Haagen turned away. Barnaby asked the question again. Jessie had nearly died. Someone had nearly killed her. He wanted to know who. Haagen shook his head. 'That's down to me,' he said. 'And Oz.'

'Oz?'

Haagen beckoned Barnaby over to the window. The window

was tiny, set high in the wall. Through the grime, Barnaby could see the squat bulk of a dog. When Haagen tapped on the window, the dog turned round, the cold glass clouding with its breath.

'Bull terrier.' Haagen grinned. 'Never lets go.'

Two hours later, past seven o'clock, a black Daimler took the last exit off the southbound motorway and nosed through the quiet suburban streets that covered the eastern slopes of Portsdown Hill. In the back of the car sat two men. One was Raymond Zhu. The other was a small, broad, bearded Englishman called Mike Tully. Until the journey south from London, Zhu and Tully had never met.

The Daimler drove west. At the top of the hill, opposite a pub, a car park offered spectacular views over the city. At Tully's direction, the young Chinese behind the wheel pulled the Daimler off the road and came to a halt on the edge of the tangle of couch grass and bramble that fell away to the distant housing estate below. From a hamper in the boot, the driver produced a Thermos of tea, pouring the thin green liquid into exquisite bone china cups.

Zhu and Tully were out of the car, studying the view. Below them, softened by the early morning haze, a fat tongue of land reached out from the foot of the hill, miles long, miles wide, a blur of rooftops, tower blocks, warehouses and the odd gasometer, parcelled by ribbons of motorway. Traffic raced to and fro, in and out of the city, while closer, on the lower slopes of the hill, a woman was tossing handfuls of bread to the wheeling gulls.

Zhu shaded his eyes against the glare of the sun. In the far distance, on the horizon, lay the dark blue swell of the Isle of Wight. The strip of water in between, said Tully, was called the Solent. It insulated the city to the south while east and west Portsmouth was flanked by deep natural harbours enfolded at their seaward ends by spits of sand and shingle. Tully turned from the view, pointing out a structure along the crest of the hill. It was massive, brick-built, one of the chain of nineteenth-century forts protecting the city to the north. There were three in all, and coupled with the intricate defence lines around the harbour mouth, they made Portsmouth impregnable to attack from either land or sea. It was, said Tully, a unique situation. Nowhere else had the military planners taken so much trouble to keep an English city out of foreign hands.

Zhu smiled, beckoning the young driver across and handing Tully one of the cups of steaming tea. This morning he was wearing a baggy high-necked jacket and a pair of blue serge trousers, and one hand kept going to his scalp, flattening the shock of unruly grey hair. Tully was explaining a little of the city's history. How the first settlements had grown up around the harbour mouth. How the King had ordered the construction of a primitive dock-yard. How the city's fortunes had always been tied to endless cycles of peace and war. This close to France, and the trading routes along the English Channel, Portsmouth had been a natural base for the King's fleet, and in time of conflict men had flooded into the little town, eager for work. They'd brought their families with them, putting down roots in the sprawl of slum dwellings outside the garrison walls. Commissioners from the Admiralty, befrocked and bewigged, had rattled down the turnpike from London and it had been on their decisions that the city's fortunes had always hung. If the nation was under threat, Pompey prospered. In time of peace, London turned its back. Zhu sipped his tea, catching a new note in Tully's voice. He liked this man. He liked his bulk, the quietness in his eyes, the measured way he talked, and he liked as well the respect that he showed, not just for Zhu, his new employer, but for this city of his.

Zhu gestured at the view. 'You've lived here a long time?'

'All my life, sir. Except for the service.'

'Service?'

'The Royal Marines.' He indicated the forest of cranes in the naval dockyard. 'We used to be based here but it's all gone now. Not that you stayed put at all. We were everywhere. Middle East. The Gulf. Hong Kong. You name it.'

'Good life?'

'The best.'

'But you came back?'

'Had to. My dad was ill and my wife's folks weren't too clever, either,' he said. 'It's not a bad place, Pompey. I've seen plenty worse.'

Zhu didn't respond. Tully was a partner in Quex Corporate, an investigation agency in the city. The agency specialized in commercial work, and Tully exactly met Zhu's careful stipulations. He'd wanted someone local, someone discreet, someone who'd know exactly how to access certain information. So far he'd limited the brief to business enquiries but the service he'd received from Tully had already impressed him. Responses to specific questions had seldom taken longer than a day, and as the pile of telexed reports thickened, Zhu had become more and more curious about the kind of man he'd find behind the painstaking analyses and the colourless prose. The Englishmen he dealt with in Singapore were a different breed – arrogant, young, shallow – and meeting Tully in the flesh had been a relief. There were some things in this man that money couldn't buy. And he sensed that loyalty was one of them.

Hua, the driver, had reappeared with the Thermos. Zhu told him to refill Tully's cup.

'Tell me about the hotel again,' he said. 'Can we see it from here?' Tully peered into the distance, shaking his head. 'It's down in Southsea,' he said. 'Big place on the seafront. They'll have seen my letter by now. I don't anticipate a problem, Mr Zhu. The evidence is pretty watertight.'

'And the lawyer? The one you recommended?'

'You're booked in this afternoon. Five o'clock.'

'But is he good? This Mr Barnaby?'

Tully glanced across at him, weighing the question carefully. 'Sure,' he said finally. 'He's the best.'

Chapter Three

Charlie Epple slipped into the waiting chair at the long glass table, still holding the flowers he'd bought half an hour ago from a florist behind the station. After the meeting he'd be taking a cab to the hospital. The flowers, he thought, might just cheer Jessie up.

Faces around the table studied the flowers. The meeting had been called for eleven. It was already ten past.

'Welcome . . .' A figure at the head of the table stood up, extending a hand. Introductions followed, names and titles, smiles and handshakes. The city's Strategy Unit occupied a corner of the third floor in the Civic Centre, a smoked-glass seventies building straddling two sides of the Guildhall Square, and numbered half a dozen key officers. With one exception, they were all around the table.

A secretary came in with a tray of coffee and relieved Charlie of the flowers. She admired them at arm's length and reminded him to collect them before he left. Charlie watched her retreat to the big open-plan office outside. An hour's walk along the seafront had dispelled the worst of the hangover but he'd remembered, far too late, that he'd left his file in Barnaby's spare bedroom.

'Love the concept,' he murmured to no one in particular. 'Bloody exciting.'

The man at the head of the table was on his feet again. His name was Alan Carthew and he and Charlie had already established the beginnings of a rapport on the telephone. Carthew had been routed to Charlie's agency via a business associate in the city. Charlie's agency – Braddick, Percy – had handled a key account for a big computer company, and the results had evidently been sensational. Thus the invitation for Charlie to attend an exploratory meeting to discuss ways of working a little of the agency's London magic on the city itself.

Carthew, as far as Charlie could determine, was a new recruit to the city's administration, a small, intense man with a floral waistcoat and a distinctly pugnacious manner. He'd arrived from another local authority in the north with a brief to build bridges to the private sector. What the city needed was investment, a massive infusion of money and jobs, and it was Carthew's job somehow to make that happen. On the phone he'd been candid about the difficulties he faced and his question to Charlie had been brutally direct: given the black arts of marketing and promotion, how would he go about selling Portsmouth? Charlie, whose feelings for the city were fogged by memories of cheerful excess, had sensibly refused to supply a straight answer. Pompey was a product, like everything else. Step one would be a list of the things that made it special.

Carthew was warming to his theme and Charlie found himself wondering just how many times the people round the table had heard this pitch. In his experience, sessions like these quickly became exercises in corporate reassurance, gift-wrapping the product in a thin tissue of superlatives.

'We've a story to tell here,' Carthew was saying, 'and, believe me, it's pretty damn wonderful. Take communications. London in seventy minutes. Two major airports, same journey time. Rail links in every direction. Brand new motorway up to the Midlands. And that's before we've even mentioned the ferryport.'

Charlie smiled. Trying to visualize Portsmouth as the centre of anything was a contradiction in terms. The city of his birth had always been the end of the line, the last name on the destination board at Waterloo, a blur of rabbit hutches and lean-tos and sagging lines of washing as the train clattered through mile after mile of Victorian back-to-backs. In this sense, Pompey had always seemed an orphan on the south coast, friendless, ugly, a wedge of east London torn from its mother city and left to fend for itself.

Charlie toyed fondly with the image, wondering if it had any place in Alan Carthew's hi-tech fantasy. He was talking about the skills base now, the local army of highly qualified labour that evidently gladdened the hearts of incoming personnel directors. These men, Carthew growled, were often ex-Navy. They were computer literate. They'd had hands-on experience of the latest command and control systems. And, best of all, they understood a thing or two about the meaning of the word discipline. Portsmouth had already established a bridgehead into the defence sector. What other city could offer so perfect an employee profile?

Carthew was clearly expecting a comment, and Charlie glanced up at him, masking another smile.

'My dad ran a newsagent's in Fratton,' he said. 'All this is pretty new to me.'

'But you get the point? The drift? History has made this place what it is. Economically, it's given us immense advantages. Talk about the peace dividend and you're talking about the people round this table. It's our job to cash that dividend in, to turn it into jobs, opportunities, pathways into the next millennium. That's the mission statement, Mr Epple. That's the message we'd want you to spread.'

Charlie made a note on the pad at his elbow. Then he looked up again. 'What about the heritage stuff? All those ships in the dockyard? *Victory? Mary Rose? Warrior?* Shouldn't all that figure as well?'

'Of course.' Carthew tugged at his waistcoat. 'Absolutely. You know the numbers we're getting through the city now? Tourists? Four million. Four *million*. And that was last year. This year it'll be way up.' He gestured out of the window at the flags bedecking the colonnaded Victorian façade across the Guildhall Square. 'Take D-Day, what's been going on over the weekend. This is world-class stuff. We're talking millions of viewers, countless column inches. After yesterday there won't be anyone in the UK who won't be able to put their finger on Portsmouth. We're on the map, well and truly. And that's without the Tour de France. You follow cycling at all? Know about all this?'

He pointed out a line of posters on the wall behind him, dramatic shots of the *peleton* at full throttle, and Charlie nodded. He and Barnaby had been discussing the Tour de France only yesterday, chuckling at how unlikely the whole thing seemed. An entire stage of the world's premier cycling event. Starting and ending on the bloody Common.

'Brilliant,' he conceded. 'Fucking ace.'

Carthew blinked at Charlie's comment, then recovered himself. 'You'll be there?'

'No question.'

Carthew beamed. One of the big team sponsors had extended an invitation for his kids to meet one or two of their stars. Maybe Charlie's would like to come too. Charlie looked regretful, apologizing for his lack of children, then grinned at Carthew, trying to soften the ripple of laughter around the table. He'd no desire to make an enemy of this little man but he was still having a problem bridging the gap between the Pompey of his childhood and the glitzy, dynamic fairy-tale he might soon have to sell.

'Advertising works on exclusivity,' he said carefully. 'So tell me again . . . What's so special about this place?'

'France,' Carthew said promptly. 'The continent. Europe. That's the dimension that really matters. Three hundred and forty-two million punters on our doorstep. Biggest free-trade area in the world. Believe me, we look south from this city not north. It's Le Havre, Caen, Bilbao. Not bloody Guildford. You know how successful we've been with the ferryport? Three million throughput a year. Second busiest in the UK. Major earner for the city. And still growth to come.' He nodded. 'Flagship Portsmouth. Gateway city. City for the millennium. Yessir . . .'

Charlie was scribbling another note to himself. Maybe Carthew had a point. Maybe the continental dimension was the key. He glanced up. Carthew was back on the peace dividend, using a flip-chart on an easel, pointing out areas of the city soon to be released from Ministry of Defence ownership. There were hundreds of acres involved. For commerce and manufacturing it was a unique opportunity.

He reached for a pile of brochures on a low table beside his chair, tossing a couple across to Charlie. One was a pitch for a redevelopment on reclaimed land at North Harbour. The other, thicker and glossier, promoted the attractions of a marina complex.

Charlie flicked through the pages of carefully framed photos. Expensive yachts nuzzled wooden pontoons. Handsome couples sipped aperitifs at open-air restaurants. Businessmen conferred on mobile phones against a background of eternal summer.

Charlie gestured loosely at the brochure. 'Where's this?'

'Port Solent.' Carthew's finger found a corner of the harbour on the flip-chart. 'It's very eighties, of course, but it shows you what can be done. Decent design. High build quality. Bit of imagination. Bit of style. Take a look at Port Solent and you'll see the shape of things to come. Believe me, there's nothing that investment and a bit of effort can't achieve. Absolutely nothing.'

Charlie peered at the map. Port Solent lay at the north of the harbour, at the foot of Portsdown Hill. Across the motorway was one of the roughest council estates in western Europe, a snarl on the face of a very different Pompey. Charlie thought of pushing the contrast, seeing what creative sparks might fly, then decided against it. Elements of this challenge were beginning to interest him.

'You're selling the past,' he said, 'and you're selling the future. You're selling quality of life and quality of expectation. I get a feeling of growth, of opportunity. Am I right so far?'

'Absolutely.' Carthew was beaming again. 'Absolutely.'

'But that puts you in the same frame as every other UK city. So I go back to my question. What makes Pompey Pompey?'

Carthew frowned, reaching for his coffee, giving the question some thought. Across the table, silhouetted against the window, someone stirred. He was an older man, taller than Carthew, his long body folded comfortably into the chrome-framed chair. He was wearing a well-cut suit, and when he turned his head to gesture at the Guildhall Square outside, the sunlight gleamed on his thick pebble glasses.

'Pompey gets shafted,' he said quietly, 'again and again.'

At last, Charlie heard the authentic voice of the city he counted his own. Paranoia went with the turf. Always had. Always would.

'How?' he said, leaning forward.

The man across the table offered Charlie a wry shrug. He had an air of infinite weariness, touched by a conspiratorial good humour. 'I'm a lawyer,' he said, offering the word as a kind of explanation, 'and lawyers know far too much about the small print.'

Charlie stole a glance at Carthew. Carthew was back in his chair, his lips pursed, his fingers drumming impatiently on the file that lay before him. Any minute now, Charlie thought, he'll be up on his feet again. More flip-charts. More statistics. More wish-fulfilment.

He returned to the man across the table. According to the notes he'd made earlier, his name was Dekker. 'Tell me,' Charlie murmured, 'about the small print.'

It was half past eleven before Barnaby, free of client meetings, got back to the hospital. He parked the Mercedes opposite the Accident and Emergency Unit. Inside it looked different. There were new faces behind the reception desk and the rows of seats in the waiting area were largely occupied by young mothers doing their best to quieten bored kids.

Barnaby went to the desk and gave his name to a middle-aged woman trying to juggle two telephones. He watched her scribbling his name on the back of a newly opened envelope. Finally, both phone conversations came to an end.

'Can I help you?'

Barnaby explained about Jess. His daughter had been brought in yesterday afternoon. He imagined she must have been trans-ferred to one of the hospital's wards. He wanted to see her. He needed the name of the ward. The woman was already flicking through the register and Barnaby followed her finger as it raced up and down the page, astonished at the sheer number of people who'd passed through the unit since he'd left.

The woman looked up. 'Jessie Barnaby?'

'That's right.'

'She went this morning.'

'*Went?*'

'Yes.' The woman pointed at the right-hand column and Barnaby glimpsed a name and a scribbled signature. 'Seven forty-five. She discharged herself.'

'She can do that?'

'Of course.'

'She just walked out?'

'I imagine so.'

One of the kids in the seats behind Barnaby was howling, and the woman behind the desk offered the mother a wan smile. Barnaby bent forward, getting a better look at the register. He might have been at the post office, he thought, trying to trace a missing parcel.

'I need to talk to a doctor,' he said urgently, 'someone who knows what's going on.'

The woman's hand reached for the phone again. She pressed a series of numbers and told Barnaby to take a seat. Someone would be along soon.

'But when?'

'Soon.'

'Yes, but I haven't got all day.' Barnaby tapped his watch.

The woman was talking on the phone now, looking at Barnaby and shaking her head. A small haphazard queue had formed at the counter, headed by a man in his fifties. His shirt was torn and crusted with blood and vomit. He was swaying on his feet and when the woman asked his name he spent several seconds trying to remember it. Barnaby shuddered, thinking of Jessie's flat again, the stinking basement, the shabby street outside. That's where derelicts like this lived. These were the kind of people she'd chosen as neighbours.

At length, a young doctor appeared. He had a muttered exchange with the woman behind the desk before walking across towards Barnaby, extending a hand and apologizing at once for being new. He'd been on the unit barely a week. One or two things were still a bit unfamiliar.

'It's my daughter,' Barnaby was saying, 'Jessie. It seems she's gone.'

'That's right. She went this morning.'

'Just like that?'

'So I understand.'

Barnaby gazed at him. Another blank. Another tract of no man's land where people disappeared without trace.

The doctor was fumbling irritably with his stethoscope. The hollows of his face were shadowed with exhaustion. 'You shouldn't worry too much, Mr Barnaby. I've read your daughter's notes. We gave her Narcane. It all seems pretty straightforward.'

'What's Narcane?'

'It's an antidote. We use it for morphine overdoses. It's pretty effective.' He paused. 'She'll be in no medical danger, if that's what you're thinking.'

'No *danger*? But we're talking about heroin. Heroin's a Class A drug. It's illegal. I'm a lawyer. I know about these things. Doesn't anyone talk to the police? Doesn't anyone. . .' he could no longer resist the thought '. . . take responsibility?'

A bleeper in the pocket of the doctor's white coat began to trill. He muttered an apology, stepping across to the reception desk and lifting a phone. Seconds later, he was back beside Barnaby, gently shepherding him towards the door.

'Responsibility's an interesting concept,' he said. 'Good luck with your daughter.'

Kate Frankham was holding the Audi on the clutch, waiting for the traffic lights, when her mobile rang. She reached down for it, pumping the accelerator as the queue of cars began to move. Barely a year had gone by since she'd qualified as a stress counsellor but she'd quickly acquired an ever-lengthening list of clients. Her next consultation was in the diary for noon. She was already fifteen minutes late.

'Hallo?' She wedged the mobile against her ear. The woman at the other end was evidently having trouble getting through. Kate checked the mirror, pulling the Audi into the fast lane and overtaking a big lorry. Abruptly, reception improved.

'My name's Donna,' the woman was saying, 'I'm a reporter. I work for the *Sentinel*. Can you hear me?'

Kate frowned. The *Sentinel* was Portsmouth's daily. It offered excellent political coverage and she knew lots of journalists on the paper. None of them were called Donna. She tried to put the smile back in her voice, pushing the Audi past sixty.

'If it's about the museums story,' she said, 'we're discussing it in committee. Starts at four o'clock. You're welcome to drop by or we could talk afterwards. Up to you.'

'It's not about the museums story. It's about Billy Goodman.'

Kate began to slow for a roundabout. 'Who?'

'Billy Goodman. Do you know him?'

Kate spotted a gap between the oncoming cars on the roundabout. The driver of the second car hooted furiously, standing on his brakes.

'Billy Goodman's a friend of mine,' Kate said carefully, 'if that's what you're asking.'

'How well do you know him?'

'I just told you, he's a friend.' She paused. 'Why?'

'I've been asked to find out, that's all.'

'Who asked you?'

'The news editor.' Donna was sounding flustered. 'Actually, it's about last night.'

'Last night?'

Kate was watching her rear-view mirror. The driver had given up with the horn, settling instead for anchoring his car on Kate's tailgate. Kate tried to ignore him, listening to the *Sentinel* reporter recounting the details of last night's incident. A young student had been assaulted in the street. Detectives were questioning a Mr Billy Goodman. A formal charge of some kind seemed more than likely.

'What's that got to do with me?' Kate asked.

'We understand he was driving your car.'

'Who told you that?'

There was a brief silence on the line. The driver of the car behind swept past in a blur of obscene gestures. Then Donna was back again, avoiding Kate's question, asking again about the relationship she shared with Billy Goodman. Kate felt the temperature inside the Audi beginning to rise. Someone must have taken the registration, she thought. And one of the paper's tame CID contacts must have done the rest.

'Mr Goodman had my car last night,' she conceded. 'He was sorting out the radio.'

'You're saying he's a mechanic?'

'Yes, he mends things.'

'But he's a friend as well?'

Kate didn't reply. Donna mentioned a string of previous convictions, mainly for violence.

Kate cursed under her breath. 'I beg your pardon?'

'GBH and ABH. I've got the dates here. Do you want me to read them out?'

Kate told her not to bother, asking again what possible business it was of hers, but Donna persisted just the same, reciting Billy Goodman's criminal record, a series of confrontations with sundry right-wing splinter groups. There was nothing serious, nothing to warrant more than a minor jail sentence and, listening to the voice on the mobile, Kate felt strangely proud of the man. It was never going to be the relationship she'd dreamed about but no one would ever accuse Billy of not taking his socialism seriously.

'It's all political,' she heard herself saying. 'Some of us talk. Others fight.'

'Are you defending him? Only the lad last night is still in hospital.'

'Is he?'

'Yes, I was up there this morning. Believe me, his face is a mess. You wouldn't condone that, would you?'

'Not at all. I'm just saying it's the way some people are. Why me, though? Why tell me all this?'

'Because we think it's important, Mrs Frankham.'

'Why?'

'Because you're supposed to be his partner.'

'*Partner?* Who told you that?'

'He did, Mrs Frankham.'

'Billy? Billy Goodman?'

'Yes. We asked him the question and that's what he said. He said you were partners. Have been for a while. That's why he had the car.' Kate swallowed hard. Last night, after all, hadn't been such a great idea. Maybe she should have let Billy stay. Maybe she should have made room for him. 'The news editor wants a comment from you,' Donna was saying. 'We're running the story regardless but he thinks you ought to have your say.'

'How kind.' Kate swerved to avoid a cyclist. 'And when might I expect to see this story?'

'I'm not sure. Probably tomorrow.' She broke off to answer another phone while Kate tried to work out how serious the damage might be. The *Sentinel* had recently gone tabloid and carried headlines to match. LABOUR COUNCILLOR'S LIVE-IN THUG, she thought, VICTIM POINTS THE FINGER. She shuddered at the implications. Donna's voice was on the line again, insistent, unrelenting. 'So what's your reaction, Mrs Frankham?'

Kate checked in the mirror for the cyclist. He was a hundred yards behind now, wheeling his bike along the pavement. 'No comment,' she said at last. 'But I suggest you get your facts right. It's Ms Frankham, not Mrs.'

Hayden Barnaby was back outside his office in time to meet his secretary leaving for lunch. The premises occupied the prime position in an elegant Regency terrace overlooking the main university campus. The secretary stood on the pavement, gesturing up at a tall sash window on the first floor.

'You've got a visitor.' She smiled. 'Made himself at home.'

Barnaby climbed the stairs to his office. Charlie Epple was sitting behind the big antique desk, talking into a mobile phone. A bottle of champagne stood beside the reading lamp, and from somewhere he'd found two glasses. He offered Barnaby a broad grin and waved him into the waiting chair. Barnaby hesitated a moment, then sank into the neatly buttoned leather. He couldn't remember when he'd last felt so weary, so physically drained. Jessie's basement flat had been empty. Of either Jessie or Haagen, there'd been no sign.

Charlie ended the phone conversation with a playful obscenity and pocketed the mobile. Then he stood up, reaching for the Moët.

'Brilliant,' he said. 'Fucking wipe-out.'

'What is?'

'This morning's little coup. You should meet these guys. Absolutely begging for it.'

'Begging for what?'

Barnaby stared up at him. The last time he'd seen Charlie had been several hours ago at home, the briefest glimpse through the half-open bathroom door. He'd been standing over the wash-basin, lathering his face, musing aloud about the monarchy. The royal yacht, he'd decided, was wasted on the Queen. Any other nation would have turned it into a disco years ago.

Barnaby watched Charlie untwisting the wire around the champagne cork, and then remembered the meeting his friend had come down for. Charlie had been pitching for a little business, and the Moët suggested things had gone well.

Charlie handed him a glass, then raised his own. 'To local democracy,' he said, 'and all you wonderful ratepayers.'

He swallowed most of the champagne and reached for a refill before settling behind the desk again. The guys from the council had been far sharper than he'd ever expected, and one had even risked sharing the odd home truth. Living in London, even Charlie got to believing that real life stopped at the M25. Now, thanks to his new friends, he knew different.

'I'm not with you,' Barnaby said. 'What friends?'

Charlie was leaning forward now, the Armani linen jacket even more rumpled than usual. He explained about the lawyer, Dekker, and his quiet description of just how bad a deal cities like Portsmouth could expect at the hands of the mandarins in Whitehall.

'There's real frustration,' he said, 'real drama. Faxes at dawn. All that stuff. Our guys are getting shafted, week in week out. The bastards in London are at it all the time. We're under the boot. Fourth Reich. I kid you not.'

'We?'

'Yeah, you and me and everyone else in this bloody place. You heard the one about the ferryport?'

Barnaby felt dazed by Charlie's fervour. He'd always played it this way, picking up new allies, plunging into new relationships. Men or women, it didn't matter. Just as long as Charlie had never been inside their heads before. Life, as he never tired of repeating, was one long fucking movie. And it was always the next sequence that really mattered.

He was talking about the ferryport now, pushing the bottle across towards Barnaby. The berths and the warehousing and everything else was owned by the city. They'd built it, expanded it, taken the commercial risk. The thing had exploded, a huge success, more and more ferries carting more and more cars to France. Year on year, the revenues had doubled, then doubled again. This last year, after paying for everything, the city had stashed nearly five million quid in the bank.

'That's profit,' he repeated, 'real dosh. Yours and mine. Five *million*.'

Barnaby was still bemused. 'So what's the problem?'

'*Problem?*' Charlie threw back his head, echoing the word, enjoying his new role, the instant expert. The problem, he said, was simple. The city had made heaps of money from their original docks investment, and now they wanted to push out the boat a little further. Obvious thing to do. Money makes money. So bung in a bit more.

'And?'

'And, fuck me, the answer's no. No can do. Not permitted. Not allowed. *Verboten.*'

'Who says?'

'London says. The ministry says. The civil servants. Fuck knows. Makes no difference. The point is this. My new mates up the road work their arses off getting their ferryport together. The thing works like a dream. Everyone's happy. But when it comes to expanding they can't lift a fucking finger. Why not? Because this bloody government won't let them.' He thumped his fist on the desk. 'Direct quote. Hot off the presses. To raise money, you need government permission. And the tossers just say no.'

'Why?'

'Christ knows. Because it looks bad on paper. Because it adds to their borrowing requirement. Because a bunch of non-Tories have got it together and proved public investment works. Either way, it doesn't matter. These guys down here are local authority.

That makes them the enemy. They're not allowed to make a profit, not allowed to make things happen for you and me. And here's another quote. Write it down. Those bums in London don't care a fuck about us. Never have, never will. If they could privatize everything, they'd do it tomorrow.' Charlie grinned. 'Remember, amigo, these guys are local government officers, Mr and Mrs Prim, not some bunch of left-wing loonies. So how does that sound, eh?' He lifted the champagne glass. 'I'm definitely moving down. Definitely.'

Barnaby nodded, sipping the champagne. After twenty years, sharing the city with Charlie would be a novel experience.

'So what will you be selling?' he asked. 'Frustration? Anger? Home rule?'

Raising his glass, Charlie narrowed his eyes. 'If only,' he said.

Kate Frankham parked the Audi across the road from the long sweep of Regency terrace, asking herself again whether this was such a great idea. A discreet phone call to a contact on the *Sentinel* had confirmed the editor's intention to run the Billy Goodman story. It was, in his phrase, entirely legitimate. So given the near-certainty that the wretched piece would appear, shouldn't she just accept the inevitable? Grit her teeth and brave it out? She got out of the car and gazed at the dents in the Audi's door, irresolute. Then she pulled her jacket around her and stepped off the kerb. You got nowhere in life by simply letting things happen. What mattered, what made a difference, was getting in there and sorting it out.

The receptionist's desk on the ground floor was still empty. Kate consulted her watch. A bellow of laughter floated down to her from somewhere overhead. Last time she'd been here, a year and a half ago, Barnaby's office had been the first door on the right at the top of the stairs. Given most men's reluctance to change things round, he was probably still there.

Kate made for the stairs, happy to take the chance that she'd find him in. On the first-floor landing, she paused for a second or two, looking at the careful line of eighteenth-century prints that hung on the walls between the offices. She'd had a hand in selecting them, bowing, in the end, to Barnaby's insistence on something local. The selection she'd come up with had included a couple of real-life studies in social deprivation, half-starved kids begging in the streets, harassed-looking women caged by poverty, and she saw now that those had been replaced by something altogether less offensive: panoramic views of the nineteenth-century dockyard, a quaint engraving of bathing machines on Southsea beach.

Kate smiled to herself, hearing the sound of Barnaby's voice. He was sharing a joke with somebody. There was more laughter.

She knocked lightly on the office door and stepped inside. Barnaby was sitting with his back to her. Behind the desk was someone she'd never seen before. He was in his mid-forties. He had wild hair and a beautiful jacket. Something in his grin spoke of a sense of infinite mischief.

'I'm sorry,' she said at once, 'I'm intruding.'

Barnaby eased round in his chair. He had a glass of champagne in his hand and for the second time in two days she watched that same look ghost across his face. He hadn't expected to see her. He was, in some curiously vulnerable way, disadvantaged.

He got to his feet, doing the introductions. Charlie Epple, a mate from London. Kate Frankham, a friend. She smiled at the word. How exact it was, a relationship emptied of anything remotely dangerous. Kate lingered by the door, aware of Charlie watching her.

'I'm sorry,' she said again, 'barging in like this.'

Barnaby was charging his glass with the remains of the champagne, and offered it to her. 'No problem,' he said. 'Have some fizz.'

Kate accepted the glass, wondering how to explain her sudden appearance. She remembered Charlie's name now. Barnaby had talked about him often, telling her that Charlie was the closest he'd ever come to meeting real genius. He worked in London. He wrote adverts, spun dreams, earned pots of money.

Kate raised her glass. 'Cheers,' she said. 'Here's to D-Day.'

Charlie responded at once. His glass was empty. 'Fuck D-Day. Here's to the revolution.' He was grinning again.

There was a long, awkward silence. Then Charlie got up, stretching his arms wide. He was tall, taller than Barnaby, and the sunlight through the big sash window caught in his hair, gilding it. He shot Barnaby a meaningful look and said he had to move on. He'd catch up later. There was sure to be word from Jess. He crossed the room, heading for the door, and Kate listened to the clatter of his footsteps on the stairs and the crash of the door as he stepped out onto the street.

'Interesting-looking man,' she said absently, settling into the chair in front of the desk.

Barnaby was standing by the window, watching Charlie thread a path through the afternoon traffic. Kate could hear his whistle through the open window, a tune emptied of everything except a kind of manic jauntiness. Barnaby turned back, making no effort to sit down, and Kate thought again how pale he looked. Not just vulnerable but exhausted. She glanced around her. The shelves of leather-bound legal books. The rows of carefully indexed Law Reports. The piles of annotated typescript, hole-punched and threaded with green fasteners.

'How's it going?' she said. 'I should have asked yesterday.'

Barnaby looked round as if he'd never seen the room before. 'It's going fine,' he said. 'It's a struggle, of course, but that applies to pretty much everyone. Nothing's easy any more, as I'm sure you know.'

Kate ducked her head, hiding her face. When she looked up, Barnaby was staring out of the window again. 'It's none of my business,' she said, 'but I couldn't help wondering.'

'Wondering what?'

'Jessie.' She ran her finger round the top of the champagne glass. 'Nothing the matter, is there?'

For a moment Barnaby didn't answer. When he finally turned round, pulling the chair towards him and sitting down, there were tears in his eyes. He put his head in his hands, then reached out blindly when he heard the scrape of her chair as she got up and stepped round the desk.

'She's a junkie,' he whispered. 'She's sick.' He wiped his nose with the back of his hand, turning away his head. Kate bent over him and put a hand on his shoulder, telling him how sorry she was. She'd no idea. He should have told her. Yesterday. At the health club.

'I didn't know,' he said, his face contorting again. 'Can you believe that? Months and months of it and I didn't bloody know. What kind of father does that make me? Eh?'

He didn't wait for an answer, accepted the proffered tissue, blew his nose and shook his head angrily as if something had come loose inside. Kate retrieved the champagne from the table beside her chair and held it out. Barnaby looked at the glass. 'That's no answer,' he said, 'but thank you anyway.'

'It'll make you feel better. I promise.'

'You think so?'

He gazed up at her, that same imploring look she saw on some of the clients she counselled. Tell me it won't hurt any more. Tell me the pain will stop.

'It's going to be OK,' she said quietly. 'Truly.'

'You mean that?'

'Scout's honour.' She bent to him, kissing him lightly on the forehead. He reached for her hand again, holding it tightly. Then he took a deep breath, cleared his throat and made a show of pulling himself together. She'd obviously come for a purpose. He was sorry about being so emotional.

'Don't be.' She held his hand a moment longer, then stepped back towards the chair, Barnaby watching her as she sat down. He looked, she thought, utterly bereft. 'I've got a problem too,' she said brightly. 'But I feel embarrassed even mentioning it.'

'Go on.'

'It's about . . .' she frowned ' . . . Billy.'

'Billy?'

'Billy Goodman. My so-called partner. Actually, not my partner at all. More . . .'

'A friend?'

'Yes, sort of.'

Barnaby remembered the leather jacket in the back seat of the Audi. The image was like a spongeful of cold water, forcing him to concentrate. This man of hers. Billy. He listened to her telling him about the incident outside the pub. Billy had been involved in some kind of fight. The other man, a young student, had been badly hurt. The police were involved. And now the local press.

'So what?' Barnaby asked, when she paused for breath. 'Where's the problem?'

'They're going to run an article. I've no idea why and I've no idea what they're going to say but it won't be helpful. I know it won't.'

'But what can they say?'

When she was nervous, Kate had a habit of playing with a lock of hair and she was doing it now, winding it around her little finger and then letting it uncurl.

'Billy has been living with me on and off,' she muttered, 'and he has a criminal record.'

'What for?'

'Violence.' She paused. 'He gets carried away at rallies and demos. He's not the sort to refuse a challenge.'

'And you think the *Sentinel* are interested in all that?'

'I think the *Sentinel* are interested in selling papers. Labour councillor tucked up with convicted heavy is a good story. In this city, especially.'

Barnaby gazed at the empty champagne bottle. Kate, as ever, was right. Like most local papers, the *Sentinel* had an appetite for civic outrage. The fact that a prominent local councillor was shacked up with a thug would make compelling reading. And that, in turn, made the story hard to resist.

'OK,' he said slowly. 'So what do we do about it?'

'We?'

Barnaby glanced up. Kate was looking at him, the beginnings of a smile softening the anxiety in her face. He nodded. 'We,' he confirmed. 'How do we get to the *Sentinel*? How do we phrase it?' He returned her smile. 'Just what do I say to Harry Wilcox?'

The *Sentinel* was published and printed from a low-rise modern complex in the east of the city. Harry Wilcox, the editor, occupied a glassed-in office at the head of the newsroom. Insulated from the constant trilling of phones, he could nevertheless keep an eye on the shrinking army of increasingly young reporters who generated most of the newspaper's copy.

Barnaby followed one of the newsroom secretaries into the office. Wilcox, shirtsleeved, was on the phone. He signalled a greeting with his spare hand and waved Barnaby into a chair beneath an enormous rubber plant. There was a flask of coffee bubbling on the nearby cabinet and Barnaby helped himself while Wilcox finished his conversation. He'd known Wilcox for the best part of three years, first at various Rotary gatherings, latterly on alternate Monday evenings when they joined forces with two other couples and drove out to a regular pub quiz in a pretty village near Petersfield. Recently, they'd enjoyed a series of unbroken victories and the team had become minor celebrities on the local circuit.

Wilcox put the phone down with a sigh. He was a big man, tall, bulky, physically intimidating, but his career had never kept pace with his ambitions and he made no secret of his belief that Portsmouth was a smaller pond than he felt he deserved. Drunk, five pints down, he could fantasize savagely on the opportunities he'd missed in Fleet Street, and Barnaby knew that he resented the success and the trappings that had fallen to many of his contemporaries. Like most newspapermen in their late forties, he still dreamed of the big story, the ultimate exclusive, and in Wilcox's case it had become a minor obsession, the springboard that would finally take him away from the south coast and into the big time.

Barnaby passed him a cup of coffee. Wilcox stirred the thin brown liquid without enthusiasm.

'Liz OK?'

'Fine.'

'Get that bloody wallpaper she was after?'

'Yes, as far as I know.'

Barnaby pulled a face. The last time they'd met for the pub quiz, Liz had spent most of the evening bewailing the lack of choice in the city's department stores. She was after something fancy for the spare room. It was very expensive and immensely tasteful and no one in Portsmouth had ever heard of it.

Wilcox emptied the coffee cup and dropped it in the bin beside his chair. Then he seized a copy of the paper's noon edition and began to leaf through it, shaking his head as he did so. The *Sentinel* was the cross he had to bear, he seemed to be saying. Life would be so much simpler if he was excused the chore of trying to knock it into shape.

'Listen to this,' he said, his finger resting on one of the inside pages. 'Whole bloody column on some woman's budgie. A city of 180,000 and we're driven to carrying stuff like that.'

Barnaby forced a smile, a gesture of mute sympathy, recognizing Wilcox's mock-despair for what it really was. The D-Day weekend had been the city's biggest story for a decade and Harry had masterminded special edition after special edition, splashing the paper's pages with huge colour photos of the celebrations. By common consent, the *Sentinel* had risen to the challenge with immense flair and it was plainly Barnaby's role to find a way of saying so.

'You must be knackered,' he murmured. 'Bloody hard work.'

'It was.'

'Successful, though. Looked a treat.'

'You think so?'

'Definitely.'

Wilcox permitted himself a smile, staring out at his charges in the newsroom.

'So what brings you here?' he asked, turning back.

Barnaby swirled the remains of his coffee around his cup. Anticipating this conversation had made him realize just how little he knew Harry Wilcox. They'd never risked anything as complicated as a real friendship and in his heart Barnaby recognized that bluff pub banter every other Monday night was no substitute. They were middle-aged. They were moderately successful. They pulled good salaries. And that was about it.

'It's tricky,' Barnaby heard himself saying. 'The last thing I want to do is put you in an awkward position.'

'Oh?' Wilcox was visibly interested. 'What's it about, then?'

Barnaby told him what little he knew about Billy Goodman. The man had some kind of record. He'd once lived with a local councillor, Kate Frankham.

'Lives,' Wilcox grunted. 'Present tense.'

'Oh?'

'Yeah.' Wilcox nodded. 'They're shacked up in her house. She's got a nice little pad in King Street. That's another angle, by the way. The terrace got a conservation grant and technically that falls to some committee she's on. So,' he grinned, 'guess who didn't declare an interest? And guess who ended up doing the work?'

'Goodman?'

'In one. Spot on.' He tapped the paper. 'Hellraiser boyfriend Billy Goodman.'

Wilcox sat back, pleased with himself, and it occurred to Barnaby that it might be wiser to end the conversation. Kate had mentioned nothing about the conservation grant. More to the point, before she'd left the office she'd told him that the relationship with Goodman was over.

'You know Kate?' Wilcox was smiling.

'Yes, she's a friend.'

'Known her long?'

'Couple of years. Long enough.'

Wilcox said nothing, letting the silence between them speak for itself.

Barnaby cleared his throat. 'Don't get this wrong, Harry . . .'

'Don't get what wrong?'

'Me and Kate Frankham. We're friends, buddies. I owe her a favour or two. And I also happen to think she does a bloody good job.' He paused. 'It would be a shame, that's all.'

'A shame what?'

'Messing it all up for her.'

'Messing all what up? I'm not with you, mate. We're newspapermen. We're looking at a story. If the story stands up, we'll run it.' Wilcox jabbed at the paper in front of him. 'Unless you're saying there's some good reason not to.'

Barnaby shook his head at once, acknowledging the weakness of his case. Maybe he should have dwelt on the D-Day weekend a bit longer and given Wilcox the chance to boast about the banquet he'd doubtless attended. What Clinton had said to him. What Hillary had worn. Whether or not she had good legs.

'There's no reason not to,' he agreed. 'None at all.'

73

'Then what's the problem?'

Barnaby looked him in the eye, unblinking. He could hear someone laughing in the newsroom outside. 'I don't want to see her hurt,' he said at last. 'Believe me, it's that simple.'

Wilcox shook his head. 'Nothing's that simple. Are we talking local politics here? Only you never struck me as—'

'No,' Barnaby said. 'It's nothing to do with local politics. I don't care a shit about local politics.'

'Then it must be personal.' Wilcox stuck his thumbs inside his braces.'

'Yes.'

'Very personal?'

'That's not a fair question.'

'Fair question?' Barnaby heard the braces twang. 'You come in here and ask me to spike a story? And you're talking fair question?'

'Touché.' Barnaby conceded the point, shamefaced. '*Mea culpa.*'

There was another long silence. The laughter had come to an end. Finally, Wilcox reached again for the paper, folded it up and positioned it on the desk so that Barnaby couldn't miss the front page. An elderly veteran was saluting on a beach in Normandy. His bent figure cast a long shadow across the wet sand. Over the picture, the headline read *A DAY TO REMEMBER*.

'You're right about knackered,' Wilcox mused. 'It's been a bastard. Non-stop.'

'But fascinating, I expect.'

'Yeah,' he concurred. 'Pretty bloody special.' He fingered the paper before looking up. 'Didn't make it to the Guildhall, then?'

'No.'

'Shame. History in the making. Unbelievable evening.'

The phone began to ring. Wilcox stared at it then got up, extending a hand. 'Important call,' he said, jerking his head at the phone. 'David Montgomery. Monty's son. We're doing a big profile piece.' He stepped round the desk, and patted Barnaby's shoulder. 'No promises, mate, but I'll see what I can do.'

*

Charlie Epple was still packing his bag when he heard Liz at the front door. He went to the head of the spiral staircase, watching her come in. She'd been to Waitrose and she was carrying a heavy box of shopping. Charlie clattered down the stairs, relieved her of her load, and closed the door with his foot. He could see at once that she had been crying. Like Charlie, she'd been to the hospital. And, like Charlie, she'd found Jessie gone.

Liz went at once to the kettle, filled it and plugged it in, walling herself away behind the simplest domestic routines. Charlie pulled a stool towards him, perched on it and inspected the contents of the cardboard box. Someone ate a lot of tinned tomatoes.

Liz turned round and bent to the fridge for a carton of milk. 'She loves pizza,' she muttered, 'or used to.'

Charlie nodded. Jessie had always been a favourite of his, a child so gentle, so ready to listen, so eager to please that she seemed to belong to another planet. Maybe that's why she'd taken to hard drugs, he thought.

'She'll be back,' he said aloud. 'I know she will.'

'You think so? You really think it's as simple as that?'

'Yep.'

Liz gazed at him, wanting to believe it. 'It's as if she's died,' she said quietly. 'It's as if she's dead and gone. She's not the same any more. She's different. She's someone else. Jessie would never have done that. Not her. Not Jess.'

'Are you blaming her?'

'I'm blaming nobody. Except that bloody Haagen. Him and his wretched dog.' Liz reached into the cardboard box for a packet of biscuits and tore angrily at the wrapping. She emptied them onto a plate and Charlie took one, trying to piece together in his mind the exact order of events. Haagen had been a client of Barnaby's, a local kid up on a theft charge. Barnaby, for some reason, had thought the world of him and had promised the magistrate he'd give him a job as one of the conditions of a deferred sentence. The kid had evidently performed well in the office and Barnaby had brought him home for the odd meal. Jessie, a year older, had fallen for him at first sight. Much to Liz's disbelief.

Liz was filling the caddy with tea-bags. According to her, Haagen had been trouble from the start.

'Why?'

'I don't know. It was just something about him. You could sense it the moment he walked in. He was . . . *dangerous*. Do you know what I mean?'

Charlie eyed her across the breakfast bar, helping himself to another custard cream.

'You mean different?'

'No . . .' She trailed off, thinking. 'Yes, different, of course, but something else as well, something more than that. He was looking at you all the time. He made you feel, I don't know, awkward. It wasn't anything he ever said. He wasn't abusive or rude or anything like that. It was just . . . as if . . . I don't know . . . he didn't *like* us. Nothing especially personal, just on principle. He'd made up his mind before he'd even met us. We were there to be disliked, hated even.'

The tea-caddy was full at last and she tried to force the lid down, angry again. Charlie was watching her.

'And Hayden?' he said. 'Did he feel the same way?'

'I don't know.'

'Didn't you ask him? Talk about it at all?'

'No, never.' She looked up suddenly as if she'd betrayed a confidence and flushed.

'This Haagen?' Charlie said slowly. 'Where does he figure now?' Liz scalded the tea-pot with hot water.

'God knows. They share a flat together, some ghastly basement. I'm sure that's where it all started, the heroin, whatever it is.' She looked up, the kettle still in her hand. 'She should have gone away. That's what's so silly. She should have gone away to college somewhere and got on with her life. Staying here, she's just a sitting duck. You should see them together. She'll do anything for him, absolutely anything. It's pitiful. I hate it. God, how I hate it.'

Charlie thought about trying to change the subject but knew there was no point. Jessie and her junkie boyfriend had become a running sore, a boil on the face of Liz's marriage, and her fingers would return to it again and again.

'What are you going to do,' Charlie enquired, 'when she comes back?'

'If she comes back. If.' Liz sighed. 'I don't know. That's the frustration. I went to the police this morning, asked them.'

'The *police*? What did they say?'

'They asked me if I was making a complaint.' She snorted, a short, mirthless bark of laughter. 'Actually, that's unfair. The man on the desk said that. I met someone else afterwards, someone from the drugs squad. He was nice. We just talked about it. He gave me his number. Told me to ring any time.'

'I bet.'

Liz looked up, catching the innuendo, and Charlie winked at her, Mr Nice Guy, no offence meant.

'It's good to see you,' she said suddenly. 'You do wonders for Hayden.'

'Really?'

'Yes, you make him laugh. He doesn't do much of that these days.'

'And you?'

'Me?' She glanced across at him and then slipped the tea-cosy over the steaming pot. 'I honestly don't know.'

There was a long silence and Charlie thought about getting back to London. The fast trains left at four minutes past the hour. The taxi he'd ordered would be here any minute. 'Hayden can be a head case sometimes,' he said lightly, 'but that just makes him normal.'

'You think so?'

'I know it. He worships you. He'd be lost without you. No kidding.'

'Really? You think that's true?'

'Yeah, and if it isn't then he's even more of a head case than I thought.'

Charlie slipped off the stool. His bag was at the top of the spiral staircase, ready for the off. He reached past Liz for the jacket he'd left on the back of a chair. She had a second cup in her hand. She was looking surprised.

'You're going?'

''Fraid so.'

'No time for tea?'

Charlie bent to kiss her, shaking his head. Liz tilted her face, catching his hand, giving it a little squeeze, telling him he was welcome back any time. Hayden would love to see him. She knew he would.

Charlie heard the beep of the taxi's horn in the street outside. 'Fuck Hayden,' he murmured, heading for the stairs.

Chapter Four

Barnaby stood at the window of his office, inspecting the long black Daimler double-parked in the street outside. Already the traffic was backed up towards the one-way system while the driver of the Daimler – a short, stocky Chinese – helped an older man out of the back. He, too, looked Chinese and Barnaby checked the name of the afternoon's appointment list as the two men below squeezed between the row of parked cars and made for the office door. Raymond Zhu rang no bells. Barnaby knew perhaps half a dozen Chinese in the city, men who ran restaurants and takeaways and the odd speciality food store, but none was called Zhu.

He slipped behind the desk, reaching for a fresh pad, wondering vaguely whether Mr Zhu might be bringing any work with him. Most of his business with the city's immigrant population was commercial. The domestic stuff – wills, probate, conveyancing – they tended to keep close to their chests, using family networks, but the Chinese were born entrepreneurs and whatever legal help they needed was almost entirely connected to their passion for establishing new enterprises. Barnaby would never make his fortune arranging commercial mortgages or applying to the magistrates for a liquor licence, but he had a healthy respect for these people. They worked bloody hard for their money and one or two of the city's Chinese restaurants offered food as good as Barnaby had ever tasted.

Hearing a soft knock on the door, Barnaby got to his feet. The door was an inch or two ajar but when he called, 'Come in,' nothing happened. He crossed the room. The older of the two Chinese he'd seen in the street was standing outside in the corridor.

His tunic jacket was buttoned to the neck and a pair of baggy trousers hung limply on his thin frame. He had a high forehead and a receding chin and his face carried an expression of mild detachment. Unlike the other Chinese Barnaby knew, he looked slightly bookish, a man born not to commerce but to something infinitely more academic.

'Mr Zhu?'

The Chinese accepted Barnaby's handshake. He spoke English with great care and a certain gravity, which made him sound slightly old-fashioned. He was pleased to meet with Mr Barnaby. He'd heard some excellent reports. Unused to such a formal compliment, Barnaby found himself offering Zhu a tiny inclination of the head, almost a bow, which rather surprised him. In a matter of seconds, Zhu had set the social tone. At this rate, they'd spend the rest of the afternoon swopping courtesies.

He stepped back into the office, inviting Zhu to take a seat. Zhu declined his offer of tea or coffee and Barnaby reached for the intercom. He told his secretary they wouldn't need refreshments, studying Zhu while the Chinese examined the plaster rose on the ceiling. There were liver spots high on both temples but the rest of his face betrayed nothing about his age. No wrinkles, no laugh lines, nothing obvious to indicate the passage of time.

Zhu began to talk about a hotel. It was called the Imperial. Barnaby nodded. 'It's on the seafront,' he said at once, 'big old place.'

'Are you familiar with it at all?'

Barnaby hesitated before replying. The Imperial had fallen on hard times. Inside and out the building was a wreck.

'Are you thinking of staying there, Mr Zhu? Only I could possibly recommend something a little more suitable.'

Zhu produced a silver cigarette case and, for the first time, Barnaby detected the beginnings of a smile. Zhu opened the case and offered it across the desk. Barnaby shook his head, looking for the matches he kept in the drawer.

'Tell me about this hotel, Mr Barnaby. Tell me what you know.'

'It's very big, as I said, and it's very old. It's got a wonderful position looking ... south-west, I think. It's Victorian. Lots and lots of rooms, and a great deal of history. It used to be extremely grand. Now?' He spread his hands, a sign of regret. 'I'm afraid it isn't what it was.'

'But once?'

'Once it was the best. The very best.' It crossed Barnaby's mind that he might have a photograph of the place, one of the archive shots that the city records office had started to issue as postcards. His secretary had begun a collection in the belief that one day they might come in useful. Barnaby sorted quickly through the box file in which they were kept. There were lots of shots of the naval dockyard, and the cathedral, and the Edwardian heyday of Southsea's fashionable shopping arcades, but he couldn't lay hands on the photograph he remembered. It had shown the Imperial at the turn of the century. It looked like an enormous birthday cake, a confection in elaborate white icing, and the foreground had featured women promenading in extravagant hats.

At the bottom of the box was a view of the Common. Barnaby took it out and crossed the room again, examining it in the light from the window. A path known as Ladies' Mile ran the length of the Common, flanked by trees, and at the far end stood the Imperial.

Barnaby showed the photograph to Zhu, pointing out the tiny line of horse-drawn cabs waiting in front of the hotel. The Chinese touched the photograph. The fingers of his right hand were yellowed with nicotine.

'Big,' he said slowly. 'A very important place.'

'It was.' Barnaby sat down again, pushing an ashtray across the desk. 'That was ninety years ago. I think it had a little bomb damage during the war. Afterwards, they tried to keep it going but times were difficult. I remember . . .' He was suddenly aware that he was straying from the point, but Zhu signalled for him to carry on, a tiny motion with his right hand, and Barnaby smiled, watching the curl of blue smoke drifting towards him.

Some of his earliest memories revolved around visits to the Imperial. His father had regularly entertained clients there for afternoon tea and his mother would sometimes meet him afterwards for early-evening drinks in a cluttered little cocktail bar beside the dining room. On these occasions, Barnaby would go too, largely because there was no one else to look after him. He remembered a fat porter called Mr Jones, who did tricks with an inkwell and a handkerchief, and he remembered, too, the smell of the place, a mixture of furniture polish and stale alcohol. He'd liked it in the hotel. It smacked of grown-ups and money, two items for which he'd developed an early enthusiasm.

Zhu followed his descriptions with grave interest. 'You had no brothers or sisters?'

'No, I was an only child.'

'And your father?'

'He was a barrister.' Barnaby gestured round. 'Barristers are like solicitors. But richer.'

Zhu sucked at the cigarette, ignoring the joke, and Barnaby was aware of the eyes watching him through the curtain of smoke. The conversation was fast developing into an interview, himself on the receiving end. He thought of the hotel again, the gaunt shell that housed so many memories.

'It was bought by one of the big chains,' he said. 'I'm not quite sure what happened after that.'

'And now?'

'It's very run down. The kind of people that made the place pay don't go to that sort of hotel any more. It used to be different, of course. Families came down to the coast for a couple of weeks in the summer. If they had money, they'd stay somewhere like the Imperial. And there was the navy too. Lots of officers and their families. Lots of comings and goings. The Imperial was where you'd be seen, where you'd meet for a drink or a meal. Now?' He sat back, trying to think when he'd last driven past. The place had become a blemish, an eyesore, something you wouldn't spare a second glance.

'But it's still a hotel? It still has guests?'

'I honestly don't know. Probably not. These big places have often been converted into . . .' he tried to find the right phrase, 'boarding houses for unemployed people, people without homes, people with no money.'

'So who pays the owner?'

'The state does. We do. All these people get benefit. Some of the money goes straight to whoever runs the place. It's very profitable but it's not a hotel any more, not the way I described it.' Barnaby was sure now that he'd got it right. A week or two back, he'd been duty solicitor down at the magistrates' court. A couple of the men he'd had to represent had given their domicile as the Imperial Hotel and he remembered them sharing a sour joke when he'd questioned the address. Imperial fucking dosshouse, one had told him. Stained mattresses, cracked wash basins, and a little barred window on the ground floor where you handed in your Giro cheque.

Zhu stirred in the chair, uncrossing his legs, and Barnaby leaned forward across the desk, curious to know the reason for all these questions about the Imperial.

'I want to buy it,' Zhu said simply.

'The Imperial?'

'Yes.'

'Do you mind me asking why?'

'Not at all. I intend to turn it back into a real hotel, the kind of hotel you remember from your childhood.'

'You do?' Barnaby tried to mask his astonishment.

'Yes.'

'And you're aware . . .' he hesitated, not wanting to give offence '. . . what that would involve? The amount of work? The capital outlay?'

Zhu gazed at him with an expression of mild reproof. Then his hand went to the breast pocket of his tunic and he produced a card. It read 'Mr Raymond Zhu'. Underneath, similarly embossed, was a Singapore address with phone, telex and fax numbers.

'I run a number of companies,' Zhu was saying. 'Most will be of no concern. That address will find me.'

Barnaby put the card carefully to one side. Zhu didn't look like a businessman, far from it, but personal appearance – as his father had once told him – was often the worst possible guide. He glanced up, remembering the Daimler outside in the street. That, on reflection, should have been an early clue.

'Have you . . . ah . . . begun negotiations?'

'Negotiations are complete.'

'You've agreed a price?'

'Yes.'

'May I ask how much you intend to pay?'

'Certainly.' He paused. 'Mr Seggins has agreed to accept a hundred and ten thousand pounds, plus a small percentage of my first year's trading figure. That's profit, of course.' He smiled. 'Net.'

Barnaby scribbled down the name and then the figure. £110,000 was a steal. In the eighties, at the height of the boom, hotels had been valued at £60,000 a room. The Imperial must have a hundred rooms at least, probably more. Barnaby's pen went back to the owner's name.

'You've met Mr Seggins?'

'This morning.'

'He holds title to the hotel?'

'Yes.'

'And he's happy with this figure?'

'He's accepted it.'

Barnaby caught the nuance, the hint of amusement that warmed Zhu's voice a degree or two, and he looked up, adjusting his preconceptions yet again. This man was tough as well as clever, and Barnaby began to wonder exactly how much he really knew about the hotel. Nobody would bid for the Imperial without having done a great deal of background research.

Barnaby tore the top sheet off his pad and put it to one side. Then he picked up his pen and began to take Zhu through the usual checklist. If nothing else, it might define his own relationship to this strange deal.

'You'll need a full survey,' he began. 'I can organize that if you wish. Then there's a schedule of works and a proper inventory, assuming one doesn't exist. Someone will have to talk to Mr Seggins's solicitor. You need to check his claim to title, any out-standing mortgages, any—'

'There are none.'

'No mortgages?'

'No.'

Barnaby made a note. Stuffing the Imperial full of DSS folk was even better business than he'd been led to expect.

'The local authority people?' he enquired, looking up. 'Have you talked to them at all?'

'No.'

'I'm afraid you must. There's a search to be done, just to make sure there are no orders out on the place. Does it have a bar?'

'No.'

'Then you'll need a licence when the time comes. That's an application to the magistrates' court. Will the Imperial be in your name, Mr Zhu?' He looked up. Zhu was gazing peaceably out of the window.

'Mr Zhu?' he prompted.

'Yes?'

'Will it be your name on the—?'

Zhu was getting up. He shuffled towards the window, peering down at the street. In profile, he barely had a chin at all.

'I understand you normally charge one per cent,' he said.

'That's right. There's room for negotiation, of course, but it's normally around one per cent. Plus or minus. In this case. . . .' Barnaby looked down at his pad, recognizing how little room he had for manoeuvre. Big properties like the Imperial could easily turn into a nightmare. If things got tricky, one per cent of £110,000 would barely cover the photocopying.

He looked up. Zhu was waving to somebody. 'Mr Hua,' he said absently, 'has returned.'

Barnaby checked the street below. The black Daimler was parked opposite, legally this time. 'May I assume you want us to represent you . . . ?' he asked.

Zhu nodded. 'Yes. You will be my solicitor.'

'For the purchase?'

'Yes. Afterwards there will be much to do. Building. Improvements. A very great number of things. Unlike the current negotiations, I anticipate significant costs. Also, significant problems. One per cent of a lot of money, Mr Barnaby, is a lot of money.' He lifted his arm again and then turned back into the

85

room. 'I suggest we agree a thousand pounds for the purchase of the hotel, Mr Barnaby. Does that sound acceptable?'

Barnaby fought the urge to say yes. If Zhu was serious about restoring the Imperial, then Zhu was big time. And big time people respected caution.

'There's no substantial change of use,' he mused aloud. 'What about vacant possession? Does Mr Seggins anticipate any problems getting his lodgers out?'

'None.'

'Are you sure?'

'Yes.'

Barnaby was impressed again by Zhu's lack of self-doubt, by how clear-cut he made everything sound. The deal on offer couldn't have been more explicit. As long as Barnaby kept his nose clean on the conveyancing, then the rest of the job, the real money, would be his for the asking. Tidying up a dump like the Imperial, doing it properly, wouldn't cost less than a couple of million. Conceivably, it could go well beyond that, providing ample scope for a fat management fee.

Barnaby tapped his pad. 'Will you need us to arrange a mortgage? For the purchase price?'

'No.'

'How do you intend to pay?'

'By banker's draft. I'll need the details of your client account. I intend to deposit the money at once.'

'All of it?'

'Yes.'

'Is there some kind of deadline? Is it urgent?'

'Of course.' Zhu inclined his head. 'Your city has a great future, Mr Barnaby. I intend to be part of it.'

Zhu studied him for a moment or two and Barnaby got to his feet, extending a hand, promising to speed the purchase over the inevitable hurdles. Depositing the entire sale price was extremely unusual, a gesture – Barnaby hoped – of intent.

Out in the corridor, Barnaby enquired, as a courtesy, whether there was anything else he could do. Zhu was scanning the row of framed nineteenth-century engravings hanging on the wall. The one at the end, Barnaby's favourite, showed a huge tract of the naval dockyard. Zhu was looking at it now.

'I need more,' he said. 'This is just the beginning.'

'More hotels?'

'More everything.'

'Business opportunities?'

'Of course.'

'And you want me to look?'

Zhu was peering ever more closely at the print. 'Yes, Mr Barnaby,' he said. 'I'm sure that would be advantageous.'

Liz Barnaby sat in her car, watching the drinkers milling around the garden of the pub. The Whippet was the kind of place she normally read about in the pages of the *Sentinel*. It cropped up time and time again, mostly in the special reports they carried on Mondays, gruesome descriptions of weekend vandalism, drug busts and assaults on local householders brave or silly enough to complain about the noise and the broken glass. The Whippet, by reputation, was one of the hardest pubs in the city. You went there at your peril.

Jessie was sitting at a table near the back of the garden. She was drinking something fizzy from a pint glass, taking tiny sips, no real enthusiasm. She was wearing a black T-shirt under a pair of denim dungarees and the way she kept scratching herself made Liz wonder about lice. The third time she'd called round to the basement flat, she'd summoned the courage to try the door. It had been unlocked and the flat empty, but the smell alone had been enough to make her stomach churn. From the chaos of the front room she'd collected what she could, disentangling Jessie's clothes from Haagen's, and she'd found an empty Lo-Cost bag for the books, cassette tapes and other knick-knacks that she knew belonged to her daughter.

In the kitchen, beside the gas stove, she'd found a syringe. Holding it up to the light through the back window, she'd seen the smear of fresh blood inside the barrel. When she'd returned to the electric stove and tested the rings with the back of her hand, one had still been warm. They've been back here, she'd thought. They'd made themselves a cup of something or other, and they'd used the syringe to inject more of that filthy stuff.

Afterwards, knocking at the door of the flat upstairs, Liz had managed to rouse a skinny youth who'd blinked at her in the evening sunlight and told her that Jessie and Haagen had gone out. Try the Oxford, he'd muttered, or the Whippet. The Oxford, a gloomy dive near the pier, had been virtually empty. Jessie's name had meant nothing to the woman behind the bar but at the mention of Haagen she'd bristled visibly. The boy was nothing but trouble. He'd been banned for weeks. If he ever appeared again, she'd kick his arse.

Now, watching Jessie across the road, Liz understood why. Haagen lay sprawled beside her on the grass. He'd been collecting a small pile of what looked like beer mats and from time to time he'd flick one across the garden towards the four-piece band performing in the corner nearest to the road. Each time he did it, he got up on his knees, watching the flight of the little mat, digging Jessie in the ribs when one scored a direct hit. It was an infantile game, the kind of thing you'd expect to find in a kindergarten, and Liz marvelled at the dutiful way her daughter provided the applause. Whatever the syringe contained, thought Liz, had certainly warped her sense of humour.

The band were getting louder now, the volume of the big black amplifiers turned up, and Liz wondered for the umpteenth time exactly what she should do. Simply walking across and dragging Jessie away wasn't an option. Had she been braver she might have risked it, but her real fear was of social embarrassment, of being out of place, of having everyone else stop what they were doing and look at her. That, she couldn't bear. It would be ghastly, a humiliation, infinitely worse than physical injury. All her life, she'd wanted to be looked at, admired, talked about, but not like this, not by these people. She knew in any case that the plan wouldn't work. She'd get to Jessie. She'd try to talk to her, reason with her, but one or other of them would lose their temper and then there'd be a row. She closed her eyes, imagining the audience they'd command, the cat-calls, the whistles, the howls of derision. No way, she thought. Absolutely no bloody way.

She leaned back in the seat, pushing hard with her feet against the pedals, trying to ease the tension coiled inside her. What she really needed was a man, a husband, someone close, supportive, someone who loved them both enough to care. She thought of Hayden, and of what Charlie Epple had said about him, and she asked herself yet again whether or not she could risk believing it. Did she really matter to him that much? Would he really be lost without her? She knew that the answer was immaterial. What mattered in a marriage was action. If Hayden loved her that much, why wasn't he here now? Applying that stupendous lawyer's brain to the tricky issue of his daughter's heroin addiction?

Heroin. Liz shuddered. Even the sound of the word frightened her. She read about it in the glossy style magazines she bought. She'd seen the evidence they dragged up on television. She was word-perfect on the damage it did you, the way it took a grip on your life, enslaving you, turning you into a monster. The sergeant from the drugs squad had been right. It was the devil's drug. It paved the way to hell.

Abruptly, she heard the sound of breaking glass. The heavy thump of music stopped and a girl began to scream. Liz opened her eyes, struggling upright in the seat. Across the road, some kind of fight had developed, men lashing out wildly, bottles flying, a blur of fists and boots. There was more screaming, louder this time, and the mill of drinkers fell back as the pub bouncers plunged in, seizing a small wiry youth. Liz barely had time to recognize Haagen's snarl before he folded over a heavy blow, raising his face again to spit at his attacker. One man had his head in an armlock, lifting his chin, and the other paused for a second, measuring his distance before slamming his fist into the side of Haagen's mouth. He did it again, then again, until the lower half of Haagen's face was a mask of blood. The grip around his throat relaxed and he fell to the ground, curled in a ball, trying to protect himself from the savage kicking that followed.

Liz was out of the car now, running across the road. Jessie was trying to get to Haagen, struggling through the circle of watching drinkers. Her mouth was half open and her eyes were wide. Her head kept bobbing up and down in the crowd like someone on the point of drowning.

'Jess!' Liz was calling her name, quietly at first, then louder and louder still, 'Jess! *Jessie!*'

Jessie had nearly made it through the scrum around Haagen. The bouncers had finished with him and laughed as they turned to each other, flexing their fingers, rubbing their knuckles, comparing notes. Miles away, in the distance, Liz could hear the wail of a police siren and the band responded with a hesitant chord or two, then a riff from the lead guitarist, and finally the start of a full-blown number.

Jessie was bent over Haagen's fallen body. Liz knelt beside her, putting an arm around her, feeling her shiver beneath her touch. Jessie looked up at the ring of watching faces, tears pouring down her face.

'You've killed him,' she said. 'He's dead.'

A youth in a green singlet dropped down beside her. His fingers found the big vein in Haagen's neck. He was alive. He was breathing. These guys knew when to stop. They weren't that daft. Jessie looked at him, not understanding. She seemed to be in shock. She shook her head.

'Dead,' she repeated. 'He's dead.'

The police car rounded the corner in a squeal of burning rubber and Liz heard the slam of the door and the clatter of running footsteps. One of the policemen was still pulling on his hat. The crowd fell back, giving them space. The music had stopped again.

'What happened?'

Jessie was on her feet, swaying. Her hands were covered in blood. She stared at the nearer of the two policemen then turned away. Liz put her arm around her again, guiding her gently towards the waiting car. Jessie went without complaint, needful obedience, the way a child might. Beside the car, Liz unlocked the passenger door and helped her in, half expecting the police to intervene. Pushing the door shut, she locked it. Seconds later she was behind the wheel, stirring the engine into life, checking her mirror as she accelerated away. Only at the end of the street did Jessie turn in her seat and look back.

'They killed him,' she whispered again. 'He's fucking dead.'

Hayden Barnaby sat in the Mercedes, enjoying the early-evening sunshine, looking at the Imperial Hotel. For the first time in months, he felt whole again, an abrupt return to the boundless self-confidence that had become, in so many respects, a memory. After a sequence of appalling hands, life appeared to have dealt him a winner.

In the glove box, he found a small packet of cheroots. He slipped one out and lit it, savouring the rich, bitter-sweet taste of the tobacco, narrowing his eyes as he studied the tall, five-storeyed pile across the road. To his surprise, it looked in better condition than he'd expected. The stucco was stained beneath holes in the guttering, and some of the larger pieces of ornamental plasterwork had seen better days, but the overall impression was still one of elegance and a wildly overstated grandeur. Tall, handsome windows in the dayrooms on the ground floor. An imposing entrance, the ornate canopy supported by fluted pillars, the structure big enough to house a revolving door. The door was chained and padlocked now but the wood panels and the brasswork were still intact and in the right hands, Barnaby thought, it could surely be restored to working order.

He gazed across at the door, remembering the noise it made if you pushed hard enough, the sigh of the runners on the polished floor, the chill on the backs of your legs as the sweep of the tall glass panes sucked in air behind you. On his seventh birthday, his father had arranged a modest family celebration at the hotel and after the jelly and ice cream he'd been allowed to play in the foyer. The porter, Mr Jones, had kept an eye open for other guests while Barnaby had treated himself to a twirl or two, pushing and pushing on the cold glass, eager to see just how fast the thing would go. After the third or fourth circuit, he'd begun to feel sick and it had been his mother, as ever, who'd come to the rescue. She'd appeared from the cocktail bar, talking to Mr Jones, and when he'd woven his way towards her across the foyer she'd opened her arms and scooped him up and called him her little hamster. At the time, he hadn't got the joke at all but now, trying to imagine the scene, he understood exactly how prescient she'd been. Faster and faster. The little boy in the cage.

Barnaby tapped ash through the Mercedes' open window and then got out. A broad drive swept up to the front of the hotel and he skirted the potholes before stopping and peering up. There were bedrooms from the first floor upwards and he counted the windows, multiplying by the three floors above, concluding that thirty-two rooms had a sea view. There was more accommodation at the sides and the back, of course, and he reckoned he'd been right and that the hotel had at least a hundred bedrooms.

He looked over his shoulder, down the long tree-lined expanse of Ladies' Mile, and began to share a little of Zhu's enthusiasm for the Imperial's potential. From the upper floors, the view would be sensational: the big green spaces of the Common, the zig-zag of the seafront around the battlements of Southsea Castle, and beyond the wide blue expanse of the Solent, the chalk uplands of the Isle of Wight. Add to this a decent refurbishment – tasteful décor, first-class cuisine, state-of-the-art bedrooms – and the package would be irresistible. A truly world-class hotel at last. And the entire city aware of just who had helped make it happen.

Barnaby slipped a hand into his pocket and began to saunter towards an open door. Close to, the window frames on the ground floor were falling apart. He stretched across the empty flower-beds and dug at the faded paint with a fingernail, feeling the sponginess of the wood beneath. These will have to come out, he thought. All of them. He looked up again, doing the sums for the second time. Thirty-two windows. Hundreds of pounds apiece. He smiled, stepping in from the windy sunshine, wiping his feet on the soiled scrap of matting inside.

He was standing in a narrow corridor. To his right, a flight of stairs. To his left, a row of doors. He tried one. It was locked. He looked at his hand in the half darkness, then lifted it to his nose. The door handle felt sticky to the touch and his fingers smelled suddenly of stale fat. He stood at the foot of the stairs, looking up. The carpet had long gone, and the light, unvarnished wood stretched upwards to a landing on the first floor. A child stood on the landing, barefoot, dressed only in a shabby pair of jeans. He was holding a skateboard in both hands and he turned away, kneeling on the board, pushing himself along the corridor with his hands.

Nearby, a door opened and Barnaby turned to find himself looking at an enormous man in a silver shell suit. His head looked tiny on the cavernous body and Barnaby watched while he bellowed obscenities up the stairs. The noise of the skateboard came to an abrupt halt and Barnaby heard the patter of footsteps as the child ran away.

The man in the shell suit rounded on Barnaby. His feet, surprisingly small, were shod in carpet slippers.

'Fucking kids.' He shook his head. 'What's your game, then?'

Barnaby was looking into the room behind him. A new-looking computer stood on a battered desk. Beside it, a half-empty bottle of Seven-Up.

'Just curious,' Barnaby said mildly. 'That's all.'

'*Curious?* In here?' The man stepped closer. 'Nobody's just curious. You've come for a reason. Everybody does. This isn't a fucking arcade, open to fucking anyone.'

'No,' Barnaby said. 'Obviously not.'

'So who are you, then?' Barnaby could see him eyeing the suit, the polished Guccis, the quietly flamboyant tie. 'DSS? Fucking benefits mob again?'

'Again?' Barnaby stepped back a little, giving himself a better angle on the room through the half-open door. Above the desk, beside a *Sunday Sport* calendar, was a wooden board with rows and rows of keys on little hooks. On the other side of the desk, on the floor, stood a small black safe. He could hear movement in the room now, a strange scuffling noise followed by a series of whimpers, and he raised an enquiring eyebrow.

'Dog,' the man in the shell suit said gruffly. 'Big fucker. So what's all this to you, then?'

'I told you, I'm curious. I used to come here as a kid.'

'Yeah?'

'When it was . . . you know . . . a proper hotel.'

'I bet. Fuck knows, it must have been handsome in them days.' His face was very close now. He had a neatly trimmed beard and a single gold earring. He waved at the room behind him. 'I've got pictures in there you wouldn't believe. The olden times. Stuff we found when we moved in.'

'You live here?'

'I fucking own it.'

'Mr Seggins?'

'Yeah.' He was frowning now. 'You *are* DSS.'

'Not at all. I'm a lawyer,' Barnaby said. 'I suspect we may be doing business. Does a Dr Zhu ring any bells?'

Seggins's frown deepened. Then his hand went to his face and rubbed the pouchy skin beneath one eye, a gesture of infinite weariness.

'Fuck me,' he muttered, stepping back into the office. 'The little bastard must have meant it.'

Jessie lay in the narrow bed, staring at the ceiling. The bowl of oxtail soup was cooling on her mother's lap but she shook her head again at the spoon.

'Jess, you'll make yourself ill, not eating.'

'I can't eat.'

'You have to eat, darling. Just a mouthful or two. I'm not nagging, I promise.'

Jessie looked across at her, trying to muster a smile. They'd been back home for an hour now and the pains, if anything, were worse. Her belly churned, her bones ached, her head throbbed, and through the thin nightdress, already drenched with sweat, she could feel every wrinkle on the mattress underneath. She lay back, exhausted, regretting the strength she'd shown earlier. Haagen had scored enough for both of them. Had she said yes, had she been sensible, she could have avoided all this. No pain, no torment, just another fat dose of oblivion.

Liz was trying again with the soup, tasting it herself the way she'd done when Jessie was a kid, and Jessie watched her from what seemed to be an immense distance, deeply sympathetic. Her mum didn't deserve any of this. She didn't deserve a shit-filled, skagged-out daughter. She didn't deserve the grief and hassle of not knowing what to do. Jessie tried to smile again, reaching for her mother's hand, an expression of solidarity, and she felt the soft, ringed fingers tightening around hers. Their eyes met for a second, long enough for Jessie to begin to compose a list in her mind. Names of pubs. Names of dealers. Clues to places where, God willing, she might just score the tiny twist of brown powder that would bring all the hurting to an end. Maybe Liz cared enough to run her down to Albert Road. Maybe she could lend her the fifteen quid she needed. Maybe she'd wait across the street in the car, ready with the spoon and the lighter and something to tie around her arm. Then she'd see what it was really all about. Then she'd understand.

She got up on one elbow, a sudden clumsy movement, upsetting the bowl of soup on her mother's lap. While Liz ran to the bathroom to hunt for a J-cloth, she got out of bed and threw off the nightdress. Shaking the creases out of her dungarees, she began to climb in, reaching over her shoulder for one of the straps, fumbling blindly with the fastener. She was still wrestling with the other strap when her mother returned. She was standing in the open doorway. She had a flannel in her hand.

'What are you doing?'

'I've got to go out. You can come too.'

'Where are you going?'

'Out, I just told you.'

'But why?'

'Because I have to. Because . . .'

Jessie looked at her mother, pleading, knowing already that it was going to be tough. Abandoning the strap, she searched half-heartedly for her Doc Martens then shook her head, cursing, tormented again by the pain of it all. From Old Portsmouth to Albert Road was twenty minutes on foot. She'd find the money somehow. Borrow it, maybe. Or do a deal with one of those understanding American sailors. They were everywhere. Haagen had been chatting them up all weekend. The black ones were the nicest. They practically invented the stuff. Her mother was still blocking the doorway. 'You're not going out,' Jessie heard her say. 'You're staying here.'

'I have to go out.'

'No.'

'Please, please,' she tried again, screaming to get the word out in one piece. 'PLEASE.'

Liz stepped into the room and Jessie watched the blow coming in slow motion, the palm of her mother's hand opening as it swung towards her, the meaty smack of flesh on flesh. Her fingers found her cheek. Her cheek felt hot to the touch. She began to rub it wonderingly. Then her mother's grip, stronger than she ever remembered, was lifting her bodily backwards, pushing her onto the bed, tearing at the dungarees. She closed her eyes, resigned, helpless, half aware of the rough tug of denim on her bare skin. She could hear her mother grunting with the physical effort and then, quite suddenly, the dungarees were off and she was naked on the damp sheet, her knees drawn up, her back turned. She began to shiver again, her nose inches from the Doors poster she'd Blu-tacked to the wall all those months ago, and she wondered vaguely what had happened to Haagen, whether he was dead or not, whether she really cared. Of course she cared. Of course she did. Haagen would have stopped the pain by now. Because Haagen knew.

She rolled over onto her back, letting her mother tuck the blankets around her, grimly submitting to the busy hands. Outside, at the window, it was still daylight and a phrase drifted back to her, newly minted from her childhood.

'Is Daddy back yet?' she muttered. 'Is Daddy home?'

Hayden Barnaby walked the last fifty yards to Kate Frankham's house. The terrace was deeply shadowed in the last of the sunshine but the wind had dropped now and the air was warm. He ran up the steps to the front door, turning to watch a couple of kids playing football while he waited for an answer to his knock. At length he heard footsteps along the hall and he spun round in time to see the grin on Kate's face as she opened the door.

She reached up, utterly natural, kissing him on the lips.

'You,' she said. 'Nice surprise.'

She stood to one side and Barnaby stepped into the narrow hall, letting the smell of the place envelop him. Sunshine and flowers, he thought, and the scent of something herby from the kitchen upstairs. He looked round. Everything had changed. Different paint scheme. Different pictures on the wall. He paused by a framed poster of Barcelona. It showed a heavily ornamented building climbing into a vivid blue sky. He ran his fingers over the extravagant rococo detail.

'Gaudí,' he murmured. 'Bloody wonderful.'

Kate dug him in the ribs, propelling him up the stairs, and he grinned back at her. She said she'd been brushing up her Spanish at night school. The classes were the high spot of her week.

'In here?'

Barnaby was at the door next to the kitchen. Kate had always done most of her living in the big room at the back of the house. It was full of the favourite pieces she'd rescued from her marriage: a big old leather armchair, a couple of pine bookcases, a beautiful Indian rug and an ancient upright piano. The room looked south, over a tiny walled garden, and in the evenings there was a grandstand view of the setting sun.

Now she reached past him, opening the door, apologizing for the state of the place. She'd been out counselling clients. She hadn't expected anyone round. Living alone turned you into a slut.

Barnaby was standing by the bow window. The sunset was perfect. Kate knelt quickly at his feet, tidying the litter of papers on the rug. A skinny black cat yawned and arched its back as Barnaby reached towards it.

'Hey, remember me?'

The cat studied him from a distance. Kate was on her feet again.

'I owe you a big thank you,' she said. 'I don't know how you cracked it but I'm really very grateful. I mean it.'

Barnaby dismissed her thanks with a smile. The meeting with Wilcox already belonged to another life.

'Everything OK?' he enquired.

'Better than OK. I've got mates on that bloody paper, believe it or not. One of them phoned tonight. She tells me the story's off the computer. Dead in the water. Sunk without trace.'

'Is that the end of it?'

'She says yes. She's made some enquiries and it's definitely been spiked.'

'What about . . .' Barnaby was still looking at the cat ' . . . our young friend? In hospital?'

'I sent him some flowers. She gave me his name.'

'Flowers?' Barnaby laughed. 'What on earth did you say?'

'Nothing. I sent them from an admirer.'

'How old-fashioned.'

'How cowardly, you mean. Still,' she frowned, 'it wasn't me who put him there.'

'No, it wasn't.'

Barnaby let the sentence hang in the air between them. He'd come to clear up one or two things. By far the most important was Billy Goodman. 'It's none of my business . . .' he began.

Kate shook her head. She was barefoot and wearing tracksuit bottoms and a loose singlet. She tilted her face up to Barnaby's. 'You're wrong,' she said. 'It is your business. I've made it your business by being pushy enough to beg a favour. I'm only sorry you had to waste your time like that.'

'It wasn't time wasted. Talking to Harry is never time wasted.'

'Truly?'

'Truly.'

Kate nodded, stepping back into the pool of yellow sunlight beside the window. 'So what did you say? As a matter of interest?'

'I said you were a friend of mine. I said I didn't want to see you hurt.'

'You said that?' She sounded surprised.

'Yes.'

'And what did he say?'

'He said that you and this Billy were shacked up together, living here, more or less full time.'

'That's not true. Actually, it was never true, not that it's any of his business.'

Barnaby smiled, looking down at her. She was naked under the singlet, and he could smell the lemony gel she used in the shower.

'So tell me about Billy.'

'Nothing to tell. He's gone.'

'It's over?'

'Yes, very much over. His doing as well as mine. I can be a cow sometimes. As I'm sure you remember.'

Barnaby knew it was true. 'Harry said something else as well. He said you'd applied for some kind of conservation grant.'

'He's right. We all did. The whole terrace. Is that illegal? Wanting to make the place look nice?'

'No, but he also said the grant had to go through your committee.'

'And I didn't declare an interest?'

'Yes.'

'That's bullshit.' She turned away, staring out of the window, visibly angered. 'Why don't these bloody people ever check their facts? Why do they always believe the first bit of gossip they hear?'

'You're saying it's not true?'

'Too right it's not true. Of course the grants go through committee. Everyone knows that. But this particular application was tabled last spring.'

'Before you were chair?'

'Before I was even a bloody councillor.' She pulled at a lock of hair. 'Can I sue? Mr Lawyer?'

'Only if they print.'

'Would it be worth it?'

'Definitely.'

'And will you represent me? Get a result?'

'No question.'

'Usual fee?' She glanced round at him, the grin back on her face. 'Or are we talking money?'

She gazed at him a moment then put a playful finger to his

lips, buttoning his mouth. Seconds later she was in the kitchen, throwing open the hatch between the two rooms.

'You want to be careful,' she said. 'I'm a single woman. Single women can be dangerous.'

'I know. I remember.'

'Yeah, and so do I. You brought me lots of grief, Mr Lawyer, but you're still a nice man and I owe you anyway.'

'What does that mean?'

Kate didn't answer. Barnaby heard the fridge door open and close and then she was back again, showing him a bottle of white wine. 'It's Chablis,' she said. 'I was going to drop it in tomorrow but since you're here . . .'

Barnaby stayed until nearly eleven. The first bottle led to another and over the second they shared a big bowl of pasta with a tomato and courgette sauce, sitting on the floor in the little bay window, balancing the plates on their laps.

Barnaby did most of the talking, his jacket off and his head back against the wood-panelled wall. He told her about Raymond Zhu, his last client of the afternoon, the big fat windfall that had dropped so unexpectedly into his lap. He sensed, he said, that the man had serious money and serious ambitions. The deal he'd struck for the Imperial was beyond belief. If he applied the same talent to other acquisitions, the prospects were virtually limitless.

'Prospects for what?' Kate asked.

'Success. Money.'

'And you want to be part of that?'

'Of course.'

'Why?'

Barnaby smiled. One of Kate's many gifts was the ability to phrase the perfect question and to know exactly when to ask it. It was doubtless the talent that had taken her to stress counselling, and given her the basis for a surprisingly good living.

'Why?' he repeated. 'Why do I want to be successful?'

'No. Why do you want to be rich?'

'Because money's a measure of success. Like it or not, that's the way it is. Not pound notes, necessarily, but everything that goes with it. Money talks. Money means respect. If you're not rich, no one takes a blind bit of notice.'

'That's nonsense.'

'No, it's not.' Barnaby was engaged now. 'I know what you're going to say. You're going to tell me that commitment matters, and passion, and equality and all that stuff and, of course, you're right. They do all matter. But that's not the end of the story. I'm with you. You know I am. I speak your language. I stand up in the bloody magistrates' court and I plead for all these misfits, these poor bloody inadequates that can't even tie their own shoelaces. I know these people. They're my bread and butter. Liz and I wouldn't eat without them. But wringing my hands and getting them a conditional discharge isn't enough. They just go back to it. Shoplifting. Credit cards. DSS stuff. Whatever. And they *still* can't tie their bloody shoelaces.'

'And money?'

'Money can solve that. In fact, money's the only bloody way it can be solved.'

'By you getting rich?'

'By me getting other people to take some notice of what I happen to believe.'

'Which is?'

'The need to spread it about a bit.'

'Spread what?'

'Money, of course. We used to call it taxation. Remember taxation? The rich paying their dues? The poor just a little less helpless?' Barnaby looked up.

'That was a political speech,' Kate said quietly. 'I didn't know you made political speeches.'

'Maybe you didn't listen hard enough.'

'On the contrary.' She got up, retrieving the cat from the open hatchway. 'I listened all the time. That's probably what turned you on. But you were a clown, a kid, a child. And that's what made you so attractive, believe it or not.'

Barnaby watched her stroking the cat, amazed at how effort-lessly she'd stepped from politics to something infinitely more personal. He'd come here to tell her she wouldn't be front-page news. Now she was analysing an affair that had crucified them both.

'You're saying you mothered me?'

'Not at all. I'm saying I loved your enthusiasm. Your . . . naïvety, I suppose. There was nothing you wouldn't do, no mountain you wouldn't climb. Kids are like that. Until they learn.'

'And you think I've learned?'

'I think you've changed.'

'Isn't that the same thing?'

'Possibly.'

Barnaby reached for the wine bottle. There was enough left for half a glass each.

'A vote for the Chablis party,' he said lightly. 'Never take a man seriously when he's been drinking.'

'Bullshit. Drink lowers your guard.'

Kate raised her glass, smiling. Miles away, Barnaby could hear the howl of a police siren. He closed his eyes, knowing he should change the subject, telling himself he hadn't come here to revive an old affair. The past was the past. Put to the test, he'd backed off, and nothing he could ever say or do would ever change that.

'My mate Charlie,' he began, 'also had a very good day.'

Kate sat back, cross-legged, thoughtful, listening to Barnaby describe Charlie's encounter with the city's Strategy Unit. The guys that ran the place were evidently fed up with rule from Westminster and Whitehall. They'd had enough of ministerial diktats and years of trench warfare. So much so that, according to Charlie, some seemed on the edge of open rebellion.

Barnaby paused, eyeing Kate. 'You'd know,' he said. 'True or false?'

'True. Except that we run the city. The guys Charlie met are council officers. We decide. They deliver.'

'But the real decisions are made elsewhere. That's Charlie's point. The guys that matter are up in London. What they say goes. No?'

Kate looked briefly pained. Admitting her own political impotence wasn't something that came easily. At length, with some reluctance, she nodded.

'He's right,' she said. 'In the end we control maybe fifteen per cent.'

'Of what?'

'The city's budget.'

'So what's that got to do with local democracy?'

'Nothing.' She paused. 'But, then, no one's really bothered. You know the average turnout for local elections in this bloody country?'

'No.'

'Thirty per cent.' She made a vague, despairing gesture with the empty wine glass. 'You spend weeks, months, knocking on doors, holding meetings, drawing up petitions, trying to get people motivated, but when it comes down to it just three punters out of ten take the trouble to vote.'

'You're saying we get what we deserve?'

'No, I'm saying it's a vicious circle. Your friend Charlie's right about Whitehall and Westminster. It's a huge scandal, the way they've taken charge. But they justify it by saying people like me are unrepresentative. That we have no mandate. That we're speaking for no one. In their eyes, of course, that's wonderful. It gives them the right to walk all over us and that's exactly what they want to do. We're there to be crushed because we're dangerous. And we're dangerous because we might know a thing or two about what's really going on. God forbid, we might even care enough to want to change things. But we can't, of course, because they won't let us.' She was playing with the cat's ear. 'In the end, local government's more trouble than it's worth. They'll just disinvent it. And no one'll spot the difference until it's too late.'

There was a long silence. Barnaby watched the animal nuzzle the crook of Kate's arm. 'A political speech.' He mimed applause. 'Bravo.'

'Don't be cheap.'

'I'm not. I'm impressed.'

'Are you?' She looked him in the eye. 'Impressed enough to want to do something about it? Or impressed because you're back here like this?' She gestured at the space between them.

Barnaby put down his glass and reached for her hand. She'd taken to wearing a ring on her forefinger, a big chunky thing that was slightly loose.

'You want to know the truth?' he said.

'Yes, please.'

'If I knew a way,' he nodded, 'I'd change it all tomorrow.'

Liz was still watching television when Barnaby got home. She looked up as he closed the front door then turned her attention back to the set. Barnaby carefully circled the room, bending over the sofa and kissing his wife on the cheek.

'Sorry it's so late,' he said. 'Got held up.'

'What have you been eating?'

'Pasta. Lots of garlic. Italian place.'

Liz nodded, still watching the screen. Rows of old men in berets were marching across a stretch of gleaming sand. Tiny figures on a reviewing stand offered limp salutes beneath a line of snapping tricolours.

'Normandy,' Liz said, after a while. 'Extraordinary how this stuff can still move you.'

Barnaby watched the pictures for a moment or two, picking out the faces on the reviewing stand. Mitterrand was there, and so was Major, and he thought at once of Kate, cross-legged in the bay window, telling him what a fraud it all was. Flags. Medals. Marching bands. Anything to keep the people in step. Anything to prevent them thinking for themselves.

Liz was still talking about Normandy. If only their respective fathers had still been alive, all this would have meant so much.

'My dad hated the war,' Barnaby said. 'He spent most of it being seasick.'

Liz glanced up. In the pale blue light from the television her face was empty of expression. Barnaby repeated the joke, thinking she couldn't have heard it, expecting – at the very least – a smile. Instead, she reached for the remote control, muting the sound on the television.

'Where have you been?' she said. 'I've been trying to phone you.'

Barnaby muttered something about the batteries in his mobile. In fact, he'd left it in the car. 'I've been having dinner,' he said. 'With a Chinese man.'

He began to explain about Zhu but she turned away. It dawned on Barnaby that something must have happened. 'What is it?' he asked. 'What's been going on?'

Liz didn't answer. When Barnaby stepped round the sofa she got up and walked out to the kitchen. Barnaby followed, hearing the angry rattle of cups and saucers from the sink. He stood by the breakfast bar, eyeing the silent television, waiting patiently for some clue to this mood of hers. The Queen was sharing a joke with a man in black. Kids were waving flags. A veteran in a wheelchair was trying hard not to weep.

Eventually Liz left the sink, knotting the drying-up cloth in her hands. Barnaby stared at her. Suddenly it was all too obvious what had gone wrong.

'Jessie?' he queried tonelessly.

Liz nodded. 'She was upstairs,' she took a deep breath, trying to control herself, 'but she said she couldn't wait any longer.'

BOOK TWO

March 1995

Few inhabitants in Portsmouth complain of such things as are the consequence of a garrison town, such as being examined at the gates, such as being obliged to keep garrison hours, and not be let out, or let in, after nine o'clock at night. Such things no people will count a burden where they get their bread by the very situation of the place.

Daniel Defoe, 1724

Chapter Five

Louise Carlton had fought a number of battles during a difficult year but the sweetest victory of all had delivered her one of the best views in London. From the sixth floor at MI5's new head-quarters she sometimes felt she could almost touch the Thames. It was there day and night, a constant presence beyond the metal-braced bomb-proof curtains: the muted throb of the barges pushing upstream, the impatient parp-parp of the tourist boats jostling for precedence under Lambeth Bridge, the shriek of the gulls wheeling over the litter-strewn mudflats at the foot of the Albert Embankment. She stood at the window, nursing her second slice of chocolate gateau, aware yet again of how right she'd been to fight for this office. The job, by its very nature, was already hopelessly claustrophobic. Working in one of the cubby-holes in the back of the building would have entombed her for ever.

She finished the cake and looked at her watch. Ellis was late. He'd said he'd be over by three at the latest. Maybe the MI6 people across the river had kept him longer than he'd anticipated. Or maybe he'd had to check in at the DTI. Serving trade ministers in this government had suddenly become a twenty-four-hour-a-day occupation.

Louise returned to her desk and reached for the file, polishing her glasses and then reading quickly through the second of the reports that Ellis had prepared for her. It was still difficult to justify a full surveillance operation on Raymond Zhu but it was becoming uncomfortably plain that the latest outbreak of inter-agency turf warfare would soon force her hand. The wretched man's name was beginning to crop up in too many of the intelligence digests that daily crossed her desk. So far she'd seen nothing outrageous, nothing to warrant a grade-one classification, but that, she knew, was hardly the point. For whatever reasons, Raymond Zhu was attracting a great deal of attention. And that alone was justification enough for her to gather in the various bits of the jigsaw and attempt to put them together. An office on the sixth floor with a commanding view of the Thames demanded no less.

To her quiet satisfaction, Ellis had become a bit of a fan. She'd only met him on a couple of occasions but she was extremely deft at penetrating the usual layers of bureaucratic body-armour, and she'd sensed an immediate rapport beneath the South London accent and the gruff one-liners. As a woman blessed with few illusions about her age and appearance, she knew that his warmth was probably synthetic, a gambit to secure an ally in some private tussle of his own, but in a sense that was a reassurance. The most productive relationships were rarely based on anything as unreliable as sex appeal.

She glanced over the report again to check if there was anything she'd missed. Zhu had been in and out of the country a number of times since June last year. He was based in Singapore, had business contacts in Zurich and Frankfurt, but now seemed to be making the UK his European base. He travelled from country to country in a private jet, and it was Ellis himself who had noted the registration at Heathrow and commissioned discreet enquiries. The aircraft, it transpired, was Swiss-registered and on long-term charter to Celestial Holdings, Zhu's Singapore-based trading company, and amongst other extras Zhu had stipulated a full supplement of airways maps for mainland China. Evidently he went there a great deal, though Ellis had been vague on precise destinations.

China. Louise gazed at the window-pane as the first fat drops of rain dimpled the view. Asia's sleeping giant was currently the buzzword around a handful of the key Whitehall ministries – the Foreign Office, DTI, Ministry of Defence – and everyone agreed that rich pickings awaited the UK businessmen who could turn courtship into a solid commercial marriage. 1.2 billion consumers represented the biggest market on earth and the major European players were falling over each other trying to get there first. Winning in China had suddenly become the race that mattered and, in Whitehall terms, that made the contest irresistible.

But where did Zhu belong in all this? Louise returned to the file. Ellis had been assigned to prepare the ground for Zhu's first visit. Zhu had contacted the DTI for assistance in placing an order for 50,000 sets of counter-insurgency equipment. He was representing a client whose shopping list was extensive. It included batons, body-armour, small arms, ammunition, specialist training and a comprehensive tactical communications set-up. The latter had been the juiciest plum on Zhu's tree and when the tenders came in from the handful of firms contacted by the DTI, the lowest had been priced at £47 million. That sort of money wasn't exceptional but the specification on which Zhu was insisting was extremely high, and the DTI analysts scented the possibility of more orders in the wind. As to the end-user, opinions were still mixed. Certainly not Singapore. More probably one of the bigger regional countries – Malaysia, say, or Indonesia. Maybe even the big one. China.

This conclusion, Ellis had explained in a dry aside, accounted for Zhu's instant elevation to CIP status. Commercially Important People held the keys to doors that the UK couldn't afford to ignore. No one was getting silly over forty-seven million quid's worth of batons and hand-held radios but what really mattered, what really revved up Ellis's superiors at the DTI, was the prospect of what might happen after that. The UK had already grabbed a big chunk of world defence sales. Given a step or two towards democracy, there wasn't anything we wouldn't flog our Far Eastern brothers.

Louise smiled. She liked Ellis's turn of phrase. Not just the pithiness and the cynicism but the fact that he trusted her enough to lower his guard like this, discarding the flannel that usually wrapped inter-agency reports. In another footnote, he'd briefly described his attempts to host Zhu around the standard CIP circuit. Visits to factories in the Midlands and the North had been a waste of time. Ditto the offer of an after-hours tour of the Tower of

London and the chance to share dinner with minor royalty. None of these bonbons had made the slightest impression on the man. All he'd politely requested was the chance to conduct normal commercial negotiations face to face with the firms responsible for the tenders. Beyond that, in Ellis's phrase, he'd slipped the leash and disappeared.

There was a knock at the door. Louise got up and opened it. Ellis's raincoat was dripping on the carpet. She hung it on the hat-stand beside the photocopier before sitting down again behind the desk. At once, Ellis saw the open file, his own signature scrawled over the bottom of the report's final page.

'Six seem to think he's clean,' he said at once.

Louise permitted herself a smile. MI6's brief confined the agency to gathering intelligence overseas but the end of the Cold War had forced them to revise their operational remit. Nowadays they spent more time chasing commercial intelligence than military or state secrets.

'Clean?' she enquired. 'What exactly would that mean?'

Ellis was eyeing her empty plate. For a man in his early thirties, he was already carrying a good deal of bulk. 'It means they buy him as a businessman. They've been nosing around in Singapore and it all seems to check out.'

'Oh?'

'Yes. It seems he went into construction in the early seventies after we buggered off and left them to it. Celestial was his holding company from the start. He got his hands on some of those housing projects and he never looked back.'

Louise pulled a pad from a drawer and began to scribble notes. She'd been to Singapore a couple of years back, after a quiet invitation from the people in the Ministry of Home Affairs respons-ible for the island's internal security. One of the non-stop drizzle of introductory statistics that had stuck in her memory was the sheer pace of the building programme: one apartment completed every fifteen minutes.

She looked up, her pen poised.

'And after construction? He spread his wings?'

'Yes, related industries first. Heavy plant, air-conditioning systems, big chain of wholesale carpet and furniture outlets. Stuff that would end up in the projects. That took him to the end of the seventies. The eighties, he got bolder. Ship repair. Then container leasing. And hotels, of course.'

Louise nodded, making a separate note in the file. To date, Zhu's only confirmed UK acquisition had been a run-down hotel on the south coast. She turned a page, looking for the name.

'The Imperial,' Ellis said helpfully.

Louise glanced up. She'd noticed how intuitive Ellis could be, how he liked to gamble on private hunches. More often than not, she concluded thoughtfully, the gamble paid off.

'Bournemouth, wasn't it?' she said.

'Southsea.'

'Where's that?'

'It's part of Portsmouth. The posh bit, by the seaside.'

'So where might that fit in our friend's little portfolio?'

'God knows. I asked the blokes at Six but they'd got no further than logging the bank transfer. Zhu seems to have got the place for a song. They're saying a hundred and ten thousand.'

'What about the hotels in Singapore?'

'They're all conversions. Apparently that's quite unusual out there but Six tell me he's made himself a tidy little niche. Big emphasis on Chinese food and décor. Specially reserved suites for visiting businessmen.'

'What kind of businessmen?'

'All sorts.' For the first time, Ellis consulted a small notebook. 'Japanese. Taiwanese. Hong Kong.'

'Mainly Asians?'

'Yes, that seems to be his line. The odd Westerner, but not too many.' Ellis was peering at the note book. '*Guanxi*,' he said at last.

'*Guanxi*?'

'It means family ties. One of the guys who briefed me at Six speaks Cantonese. He says this *guanxi*'s the key to it all. The Chinese are locked into clan networks. Zhu would be typical.'

'They know where he's come from?'

'Seems so.'

'And?'

'They're saying Fukien. That's one of the southern mainland provinces. Lots of merchants and traders.'

'But isn't that what he's put in his passport?'

'Yes.'

'Have they looked any further?'

'I doubt it.'

Louise leaned back in her chair, amused. Back in June last year, immigration officials at Heathrow had discreetly photocopied Zhu's Republic of Singapore passport and Ellis had faxed her the results. Against 'Birthplace', Zhu had entered the city of Amoy, capital of Fukien province.

Louise reached for the phone at last and enquired about the tea trolley. It seemed that several portions of gateau were unsold. She passed on the news, drawing a broad smile from Ellis. Then she consulted the file again.

'This equipment deal,' she said. 'Have you licensed it yet?'

'No, the FCO are hiding behind Six. They want to know where the stuff's going.'

'So what's Zhu's line? About the end-user?'

'He's saying Singapore. Like they all do.'

'Singapore?' Louise laughed, consulting Zhu's shopping list. 'Fifty thousand batons? Half a million CS canisters? I thought the place was well behaved. Crime free.'

'Singapore's a fiction. You know it and I know it. But that's not the point. Someone has to sell the stuff. Why not us?'

'Why not, indeed?'

Louise extracted a slim brown envelope from the file and emptied the photographs inside onto the desk. They were tele-photo shots of Zhu, acquired before Christmas. He'd spent several days in central London, visiting estate agents, and the photos showed him crossing a series of busy pavements. In his long shape-less overcoat and his peaked leather cap, Zhu looked unworldly and out of place, as if he'd just parachuted in from another planet. Louise had never seen a businessman quite like him. She slid one of the photos across the desk. The estate agency in the background was Knight, Frank and Rutley.

'He's been looking for somewhere to live.' She smiled. 'Properties around one and a half million.'

Ellis briefly studied the photo. 'Anything take his fancy?'

'Yes,' Louise struggled to her feet, hearing the clatter of the tea trolley in the corridor outside, 'though I understand he's just left for Singapore again.' She paused by the door. 'Did he ever mention the name Hayden Barnaby?'

It was nearly midnight, local time, when the little private jet swooped down into Singapore's Changi International Airport. The sudden rumble of wheels woke Barnaby and he pulled himself upright, tightening the seat-belt, trying to make sense of the runway lights racing past the window. Across the narrow aisle, Zhu sat in one of the rearward-facing seats, eyes closed, hands carefully composed in his lap. The last time they'd talked was hours ago, somewhere over the Bay of Bengal.

The aircraft taxied to a corner of the apron and nestled amongst a line of parked jumbos. The pilot opened the door, and by the time Barnaby stepped down into the sticky midnight heat a uniformed official was already bowing respectfully to Zhu. Inside the enormous terminal building, it was cooler, acres of gleaming floor broken by the bent shadows of hurrying passengers. Barnaby stopped to adjust the strap on his shoulder-bag, overwhelmed by the almost clinical sense of order. Airports were generally chaotic, even at midnight, but this one felt like a tomb.

The trip east had been at Zhu's suggestion. Delighted by the winter's progress on the Imperial, he'd invited Barnaby to spend a day or two looking round the city he called home. Singapore, he said, had come a long way in no time at all, and the lessons of progress might repay a little exploration. Barnaby had scribbled the phrase on the pad he kept on his desk and, after Zhu had hung up, he'd spent several minutes wondering what the other man had meant. Supervising the rebuild on the Imperial had occupied more time than he'd ever imagined possible, but his working relationship with Zhu had been a fairy-tale – every query promptly answered, no decision ducked, even the biggest invoices paid scrupulously

115

within ten working days – and by early spring he'd been able to welcome his new client back to the hotel in time to see the scaffolding come down after completion of the exterior works. For once, Zhu had allowed himself a broad smile, standing on the Common, gazing up at the newly painted stucco, and afterwards, over sandwiches in the newly restored dining room, he'd congratulated Barnaby on the fine job he'd done. He'd been told, he'd said, to expect the best. And he hadn't been disappointed.

Now, in the front of the speeding limousine, Zhu half turned, gesturing through the windscreen at the distant blaze of high-rise buildings that was the heart of downtown Singapore. After the war, he said, the place had been a mosquito-infested swamp, dotted with pig farms and tin huts. Now, just forty years later, it had become the world's fourth biggest foreign exchange centre, third busiest oil-refining centre, second largest port. Not bad, he added pointedly, for a speck of land scarcely bigger than the Isle of Wight.

Barnaby smiled at that. Zhu rarely betrayed emotion but the last couple of months, in his more recent trips to Portsmouth, Barnaby had begun to detect in him an almost fatherly pride in the city. It didn't begin to measure up to what he so obviously felt for Singapore, but on two afternoons he'd politely asked for a guided tour and both had turned into an unexpected pleasure. The man's curiosity was boundless. In Old Portsmouth, he'd wanted to understand exactly how the first settlement had expanded, insisting on walking up and down the fortified walls until the plan was clear in his head, and later, when Barnaby had sat next to Mr Hua in the Daimler, directing him around the city's rougher areas, Zhu's interest had been no less acute.

The heart of Portsmouth was ringed by high-rise council blocks, brutal neo-Stalinist relics from the sixties, and Barnaby had done his best to explain how these bleak urban landscapes had become breeding grounds for poverty and petty crime. Zhu had listened to Barnaby's careful analysis and later, at the foot of a particularly ravaged tower block, he'd told Mr Hua to stop the car while he went for a walk. Barnaby had got out too, offering to accompany him, but Zhu had insisted on going alone, shuffling away through the litter of abandoned shopping trolleys and drifts of broken glass, ignoring the cold stares of nearby youths. He'd returned ten minutes or so later, looking strangely troubled. Back in the office, when he'd enquired about the state of the city's schools, Barnaby had been glad to oblige with a brisk dissertation on the workings of the education system. People with money, he'd explained, could buy their kids a proper schooling with well-paid teachers and decent facilities while the other seven million took their chances with what was left. The result, predictably, was an early division into the haves and have-nots, with the lucky few making sure they repeated the trick with their own kids, thus widening the chasm even further. Zhu had listened to Barnaby with total incomprehension. For once, quite genuinely, he'd failed to understand.

The limousine was approaching downtown Singapore, the night sky hung with flashing Chinese characters, the air thick with the smell of garlic and frying pork. They paused at an intersection and Barnaby gazed out of the window, craning his neck, trying to count the floors on a soaring pagoda-shaped hotel. He'd got to sixteen, less than half-way up, when the traffic signals changed, and the limo surged forward again. Even at one in the morning, there were people everywhere, milling around the roadside stalls, and the place reminded him a little of New York. He voiced the comparison aloud but Zhu dismissed it with a shake of his head. Other cities, he said, were dangerous. Everyone knew it. New York had become a jungle, and even in London a sensible man stayed behind closed doors after midnight.

A mile and a half later, the limo pulled into the forecourt of a big hotel. Zhu muttered something to Mr Hua and motioned for Barnaby to get out. A uniformed concierge was already waiting on the pavement and greeted Barnaby by name, reaching for his bag. Barnaby followed Zhu and the other man into the hotel. The atrium took his breath away. Glass elevators glided from floor to floor and, looking up, Barnaby could see tier after tier of balconies, each one stepped inward.

He joined Zhu in the waiting elevator. On the fourth floor, at the reception desk, an exquisite Singaporean girl had his room pass and security key ready. There were no forms to fill in, no passport to deposit, simply a succession of deferential smiles and murmured words of welcome. The concierge was back beside the elevator, holding open the door for Barnaby. Zhu was still at the reception desk, leafing through a copy of the *Straits Times*.

Barnaby touched his arm. 'Are you booking in as well?'

Zhu shook his head. He would be staying elsewhere. He'd only thought to provide a room for Barnaby. After a wash or a shower perhaps he'd like to join Zhu for a meal. The hotel had an excellent restaurant called the Cherry Garden. After all, UK time, it was only six in the evening.

Barnaby rode the elevator with the concierge. His suite was on the nineteenth floor. An elegant sitting room was decorated in soft peach colours, and the walls were hung with beautifully framed paintings of old Singapore. Barnaby paused by the bathroom door, peeling his jacket and loosening his tie. Beside him was a print of a British man-of-war. Officers stood in groups on the quarterdeck, peering upwards, while the rigging swarmed with matelots. In the foreground, a native stood in a long canoe, his raised arm pointing to the distant hump of a tropical island.

Barnaby studied the print a moment or two longer, dazed by the way the sheer opulence of the place had softened his own landfall. He was no stranger to good hotels but nothing in his experience had readied him for this and the impact was all the greater because it was so closely associated with Zhu, a man for whom the trappings of material wealth seemed to have absolutely no importance.

Barnaby remembered the meal they'd shared aboard the chartered executive jet. In the tiny on-board galley, Barnaby had found caviar and hot blinis, and a delicious julienne of lightly smoked goose breast. There was more than enough for two but Zhu had made do with a couple of bread rolls, thinly spread with what looked like fish paste. The rolls had lasted him most of the leg from Zurich to Abu Dhabi, and he'd washed them down with half a bottle of Evian water, carefully storing the rest in the holder attached to his seat arm.

Barnaby stepped into the bathroom. The floor was paved in Italian marble and a television screen was inset into the tiled wall at the foot of the huge bath. The shower was separate and there were enough toiletries on the shelves around the sink to open a small pharmacy. Barnaby started to undress, reaching for the terry-cloth bathrobe on the gold-plated hook behind the heavy teak door. As he did so, a phone began to warble. An extension stood on a plinth beside the shower. It was an old man's voice.

'I've invited a guest to join us for dinner,' Zhu was saying. 'I hope you don't mind.'

The Cherry Garden restaurant was at the back of the hotel. A wood-roofed pavilion with walls of antique Chinese brick enclosed a landscaped courtyard, and tiny alcoves in the brickwork housed carefully chosen works of art. Making his way towards Zhu's table, Barnaby felt he'd stepped, yet again, into another world. He settled beside Zhu's guest, who asked him how he felt after the journey.

He tried to make a joke of it. 'I'm still dizzy,' he said, making a corkscrew motion with his hand, 'but it'll pass.'

The woman's name was Flora Li. She was young, no more than twenty-five, and wore an elegantly tailored two-piece trouser suit in soft blue leather. She had dark waist-length hair and the loveliest hands Barnaby had ever seen. She said she worked for the Ministry of Home Affairs. She'd evidently known Zhu for some time.

Food arrived at the table. Barnaby couldn't remember ordering but the usual protocols didn't seem to matter. For the time being, he decided, the real world had made way for a series of delicious experiences, each episode dissolving seamlessly into the next. Quite what he'd done to deserve such treatment he neither knew nor cared, and he bent over his bowl of minced-pigeon broth, picking out the tiny glistening scallops, following Flora's account of her week in the government service. As far as Barnaby could judge, she helped front the PR set-up, organizing briefing sessions for visiting businessmen. Investment was pouring into Singapore and the last year or so she'd been working flat out.

She talked quickly, in a light American accent, using her hands a great deal, and Zhu followed the torrent of gossip with his usual grave attention. When, for the second time, she used the word 'kiasu', he stopped her in mid-sentence.

'Kiasu means winning,' he explained to Barnaby. 'Very important.'

'Winning?'

Zhu nodded, gesturing round. 'All this,' he said. 'The things we've done to this island of ours. The things we mean to do.' He nodded again. 'Kiasu.'

Barnaby was looking at Flora. She'd abandoned her soup for what looked like mounds of fresh crab heaped in a basket of sliced yams.

She smiled at the expression on his face. 'From Hong Kong this morning,' she said, offering him a shred of crabmeat pincered between the ends of her chopsticks. 'Delicious.'

Barnaby accepted the crab, still thinking about kiasu. The way Zhu had used the word made it sound like a philosophy, almost a guiding light.

'Exactly.' Flora jabbed the air with her chopsticks. 'People laugh sometimes about Singapore. The way we're so tidy, so well organized. The way we care so much about what we do. But that's the point. We want to be the best. We want to win.' She dabbed the corner of her mouth with a fingertip and then sucked it dry, eyeing a bowl of deep-fried bean curd.

Barnaby helped himself to slices of beef fillet bubbling in a black bean sauce. If kiasu helped produce food of this subtlety, he'd happily sign up for life. He grinned at Flora, trying to imagine how the pursuit of excellence would play back home. 'You know England at all?'

'London, very well.'

'Portsmouth?'

'Yes. But only from Mr Zhu.'

'He's told you about us?'

'A little. I know he likes it there. He told me that.'

Barnaby looked at Zhu, who had got no further than a steaming mound of rice in a woven bamboo basket. He was peering across at Flora in a faintly abstract way, picking delicately at the rice. 'Nice city,' he said. 'Nice place.'

There was a silence and Barnaby sensed at once that it was his cue to tell Flora about Portsmouth. Etiquette, at the very least, demanded it. He wondered where to start. 'It's an island,' he said. 'Like Singapore.'

Flora nodded, as vigorous as ever. 'Big?'

'No, five miles by three. Like this.' He sketched the city's outline on the tablecloth. 'Pretty small. And very crowded.'

'Many people?'

'Two hundred thousand. Give or take.'

'But beautiful?'

Barnaby thought about the question. Just occasionally, on windy days, the views across the Solent could be sensational but, if he was honest, those rare moments were a trick of the light, a sudden fusion of towering cloudscapes and the boiling green sea beneath, nothing at all to do with Pompey.

'It's ugly,' he said. 'Not like this.'

Zhu and Flora exchanged glances. 'This is a hotel,' Zhu said. 'With money you can do anything.'

'Of course. But I meant the rest of it, the island.'

'Singapore?' Zhu shrugged. 'Singapore is mostly flat, just like Portsmouth. And wherever you go you see people.'

'Just like Portsmouth.'

'Yes. We live in a very busy place, Mr Barnaby. Maybe an ugly place, too. But we make it work.'

'*Kiasu?*'

'Exactly.'

Flora pushed her bowl of crab to one side and began to tell Barnaby what Singaporeans could expect from life in this bustling little republic. Work hard, pay your taxes, and you'd quickly earn yourself a nice place to live, good health care, clean streets, wonderful public transport, a safe environment, excellent educational prospects, and the satisfaction of knowing that you belonged to one of the world's fastest growing economies. Singapore had the good fortune to be straddling one of the great international trading routes, she said. Not to take advantage of that would, in her opinion, be extremely foolish.

Barnaby listened to the endless list of accomplishments, a paean

121

to civic virtue, wondering just how much of it she had to repeat every day. In her job it must have become a mantra, semi-religious, an hourly evocation that kept the uglier aspects of the human condition at bay. What about poverty? Crime? Injustice? Was there nothing that *kiasu* couldn't erase?

'Nothing,' she confirmed. 'We find a problem, we solve it.'

Barnaby had heard the travellers' tales of Singapore. How spitting on the street or dropping litter or chewing gum attracted huge fines. How drug trafficking or murder could send a man to the gallows. As a result, according to one or two businessmen he knew, the place was both safe and eternally spotless, a rather spooky experience after surviving the menacing slum that parts of London had become.

'I envy you,' he admitted. 'I envy your faith and your energy. Maybe we gave up trying to change people. Maybe that's where we went wrong.'

'You don't believe in progress?' Flora made it sound almost sinful, the breach of a Commandment. 'You don't think things can get better?'

'I hope things can get better. In my country, I certainly hope things can get better. But there's a world of difference between hoping and doing.'

'You mean you're lazy? In the UK?'

'No, not lazy personally. We're not idle. But we're lazy in other ways, yes.'

'What other ways?'

Barnaby was trying to gauge the direction this strange conversation had taken. There was something over-developed in her interest in Portsmouth, something that suggested an altogether less casual agenda. Did she want to settle there? Buy a nice little house in Old Portsmouth and make her peace with the traffic, the weather and the weekend drunks? Or was it something else entirely, something he'd yet to fathom?

'We're lazy,' he said carefully, 'because we've given up caring about one or two things that really matter.'

'Like?'

'Like the way we're governed. Like the fact that we ought to have some input. Like taking control of our own lives.'

'That doesn't happen?'

'No. Not locally. Not where it matters. In the UK everything comes from London. The laws that Westminster makes are the laws we have to obey. What Whitehall civil servants tell us to do, we do. Some people say that makes us puppets.'

'And you agree with them?'

'Yes, I do. But the scariest thing of all is that no one seems to care. That's laziness. And it's immensely dangerous.'

'Why?'

'Because it's turning us into a nation of vegetables. We watch television. We try to earn a crust. And that's more or less it. The kids understand that. Which is why we get so much trouble. Not that you can really blame them.'

Barnaby reached across, spooning a fresh helping of beef fillet into his bowl, slightly embarrassed by his passion and his eloquence. Most of the phrases were vintage Kate – he could hear her arguing the case for local government – but the stuff about the consequences was his own. Life in the UK had started to alarm him. People no longer talked to each other. Individuals no longer thought they could make a difference. In Singapore, perhaps because it was so small, that didn't seem to have happened. Flora was right. A couple of million people had got it together. And made the thing fly.

'Delicious.'

He lifted the bowl to his lips, savouring the smell of the black bean sauce. Zhu and Flora were talking in Chinese again, their heads together. Then Flora tapped her watch and reached beneath the table, producing a pen from her bag. She scribbled something on a piece of paper and passed it to Barnaby.

'I have to go,' she said. 'If you like, we can meet again tomorrow.'

'Of course,' he said. 'Here?'

'No, Dr Zhu will arrange for you to come out to Changi. I'll meet you there. Ask for this department at the gate.'

Barnaby looked at the piece of paper. Changi was a name he knew. 'Are we talking about the airport?' he said.

Flora was on her feet now. She was wearing a yellow halter beneath the leather jacket and her midriff was bare. 'No.' Her hand was on Zhu's shoulder. 'The prison.'

Jessie Barnaby was standing by the tea-urn in the dining room when she felt the touch of Lola's hand on her arm. She half turned, her mouth full of chocolate biscuit. Lola had been using the pay-phone in the hall and Jessie could tell at once that something terrible had happened. She followed Lola as she picked her way between the long tables, glancing at the big clock above the special-announcements board by the door. In seven minutes, they were both due back for another module one therapy session. Turning up late was guaranteed to throw them at the mercy of the group.

Jessie mounted the stairs, trying to keep up with her friend. The room they shared at Merrist House was at the end of the top corridor. Lola kicked open the door, shaking her head, close to tears. By the time Jessie joined her, she was lying full length on the bed, a pillow over her face, sobbing.

Jessie knelt beside her, the threadbare carpet rough on her knees. She stroked Lola's hand, telling her everything would be all right. She could feel the whole bed shaking.

'What's the matter, Lolly?'

Lola didn't answer. Jessie fetched a toothmug and filled it with water from the wash-basin. At length, the sobbing began to slow and Jessie helped the girl to struggle upright, holding the mug to her lips. She took a single sip, then turned away her head, staring at the uneven row of colour snaps Blu-tacked to the wall. The sight of the shy five-year-old smile in the photos made her cry again.

'Is it Candelle, Lolly? Is that what's the matter?'

Lola nodded, wiping her nose with a corner of the sheet. Something about her mother. Something about the Social.

'What have they done?'

Lola had a small dimpled face, framed by natural brown curls. Unlike more or less everyone else in the building, her complexion was flawless. When she was happy, Jessie had never met anyone so beautiful.

'She was pissed,' Lola was saying now, 'out of her fucking head.'

'Who was?'

'Mum. She could hardly talk. I knew there was something wrong. I knew it. That letter . . .'

Jessie slipped onto the bed, cradling Lola's head in her lap. Lola had shown her the letter in the kitchen after breakfast. It had come from Candelle's father, a small-time thief, junkie and heroin dealer in Guildford. It was brief and spiteful and it had warned Lola that her mother had gone off the rails. Someone had to sort Candelle out before the poor kid died of neglect.

'So what's she done? Where's she gone? What's happened?'

'The Social have taken her.'

'Where?'

'Into care. Anywhere. I don't fucking know.'

Jessie bent to Lola, kissing her forehead, rocking her gently, trying to ease a little of the pain.

'Maybe your mum's got it wrong,' she suggested.

'Never.' Lola shook her head violently. 'The only time she tells the truth is when she's pissed. You know that. You've seen it. Turning up here like that. The state of her . . .'

Jessie remembered the thin, wispy-haired woman who'd appeared in the drive last Sunday afternoon, barely able to stand up. She'd come to see her daughter, she'd told the lads on the five-a-side pitch. She'd come to tell her what a bastard Candelle's father was.

'Then maybe it's for the best. Care's not so bad.'

'How would you know?'

Jessie ignored the dig. Downstairs, she could hear the thump of a door opening and then the scrape of chairs as the module one group gathered in the room below. After nearly seven weeks in rehabilitation, Jessie was no closer to coming to terms with the therapy sessions: the cursing, the screaming, the ugliness, the raw aggression.

She tore off sheets of tissue paper from a toilet roll on the window-sill. Outside, a grey dusk was settling on the trees across the valley. Lola took the offered tissues and began to blow her nose.

'We have to go downstairs,' Jessie told her. 'You know how funny they get.'

'Fuck how funny they get. They can get as funny as they like.'

'I know, I know, but it's best we get down there.' Jessie pulled Lola to her feet and put her arms round her. 'I'll talk to my dad later. I've still got a phone call left this week. He'll know what to do. He does Social cases all the time. He'll sort something out.'

'You think so?' Lola was looking up at her. At twenty-four, she still had the eyes of a child.

Jessie hugged her again and moistened a finger, wiping away the smudged mascara. 'I don't know why you use that stuff,' she said, coaxing Lola towards the door. 'You're lovely. You don't need it.'

Lola sniffed, tilting her face to the mirror over the sink. 'That's what my mum always said.' She raised a weary smile. 'Silly cow.'

Liz Barnaby sat in her husband's study, waiting for the phone to ring. It had been raining now for the best part of an hour, the wind driving hard off the sea. Mike Tully had promised to contact her at five. He was twenty minutes late.

A car splashed slowly past outside and Liz got to her feet, peering down through the window. Mike's little maisonette was only five minutes away. Maybe he'd left work early. Maybe he'd decided to call round in person. The car drove on, rounding the corner at the end of the street, but Liz lingered at the window, her attention taken by the latest of the hand-drawn cards Jessie had been sending from Merrist House.

It had been addressed to Hayden. He'd got it only yesterday, minutes before he'd left for the airport. On the front, Jessie had sketched the face of the girl she shared a room with. All her cards were like this, little scenes from her new life, and it warmed Liz to know that the gift which had taken her to art college was still there. She had a real talent for freehand work, for capturing the essence of an individual or a landscape in a handful of pencil lines, and downstairs on the shelves around the kitchen sink Liz had circled herself with the half-dozen cards they'd received to date. It was still too early in the rehab programme to drive up there and pay a visit but this little collection of pencil studies, seemingly so simple, had bridged the gap between them. They were the real evidence that Jessie was getting better and, looking at them, it was enormously comforting to know that there were parts of her that even heroin hadn't been able to touch.

Liz picked up the card, examining it under Hayden's Anglepoise. The girl's name was Lola and she came from Guildford. According to Jessie she'd had to weather more than her fair share of life's storms. She had a little girl of five, called Candelle. Peering at the card Liz tried to work out how old Lola must be. Jessie had made her look like a child – big eyes, fetching dimples – but she guessed that her daughter's instinct would have been to soften and smooth the face, in exactly the same way that she'd sought to protect more or less everyone else who'd drifted into her life. Including Haagen.

The phone began to ring. Liz lifted it, hearing Mike Tully at the other end. He was running late. He was very sorry. Maybe they could meet in the Pembroke at the end of the street? In half an hour? Liz began to suggest that he come round and have a chat at home but Tully was already listening to a caller on another line, whispering an apology to her before putting the phone down. The place had gone mad. He was rushed off his feet. Better make it forty-five minutes.

Liz arrived at the pub to find it empty. She knew the landlord well from her days in the cathedral choir and they chatted for a minute or two before his wife called him away to the cellar. He'd left a copy of the *Sentinel* on the bar and she began to leaf through it, killing time. Coping with Jessie had occupied most of the last eight months and only now was she beginning to grasp that there might be a life beyond the endless rounds of assessments and consultations. Finding a way back from Jessie's heroin addiction, even at one remove, was a full-time job.

The door opened and Liz turned on her bar stool. She'd known Mike Tully for years, mainly through Hayden, and she suddenly realized that they'd never met alone. He was a small, broad, quietly spoken man with a neatly clipped beard and a bachelor's dress sense. Straight from the office, he was still wearing a suit although out of hours he favoured old cords and slightly scruffy polo-necked sweaters, a relic, she assumed, from his service days in the Royal Marines.

He offered her a stiff handshake, then submitted awkwardly to a peck on the cheek, ordering an orange juice for which Liz insisted on paying. For a minute or two they talked about Hayden. The Imperial Hotel, his pet project, was only ten days away from its formal opening. The guest list had topped two hundred and Liz understood that his first job when he got back from Singapore was to set something up on the media front. Harry Wilcox had evidently promised a modest spread in the *Sentinel* and Hayden had a couple of contacts in the local ITV station. With luck, said Liz, he might get something on the evening news. Tully followed Liz's account without comment. Small talk had never been one of his talents.

Finally, when Liz ran out of news, he steered her to a corner table beneath the fish tank and asked her what had prompted the afternoon's telephone call.

Liz, slightly uncomfortable at his directness, began to colour. 'I don't want any of this to get back to Hayden. Do you mind?'

'Not at all,' Tully grunted. 'So what's it all about?'

'Jessie. I thought you might have guessed.'

Tully stared impassively into his orange juice while Liz told him why she'd phoned. Jessie was in a rehab centre, trying to recover from her drug addiction. The treatment, by all accounts, was pretty rugged but the real blessing was the fact that it kept her physically away from the city. As long as she stuck with the course, she wouldn't be back in Portsmouth until early autumn, giving Liz a chance to sort something out.

Tully stirred.

'Like what?'

'Like Haagen, her boyfriend.'

Liz bent closer to him. Haagen was a waster, she said, a youth who'd turned Jessie's head. Liz had mistrusted him on sight and everything she'd feared had come true. He was a drug addict. He was a thief. He was completely destructive, and amongst the things he'd wrecked was Jessie's young life. For some reason, God knows why, Jessie had fallen in love with him and in a matter of months he'd turned her into a junkie.

Tully ran his finger along the edge of the table. 'Is Jessie still keen on him?'

'I've no idea. We don't talk about him any more. She refuses to. Her choice, not mine.'

'But do they still see each other?'

'Not at the moment. The place she's in is called Merrist House. Visitors aren't allowed, not for the first couple of months.'

For the first time, Tully looked Liz in the eye. He knew Merrist House and Liz was right. It was tough. Bloody tough.

'Tough enough to cure her?'

'Tough enough to make her think.'

'Well . . .' Liz frowned. 'I suppose that's a start.'

Tully sipped his juice while Liz filled in with the rest of Jessie's story. Back last year, in June, she'd been taken to hospital with an overdose. Over the next six months or so, she'd half lived at home while Liz had tried to find help. She'd arranged a full assessment from the city's Drugs Advisory Service, and they'd come up with a care plan, the basis of which was counselling and Jessie had submitted grimly to a series of weekly sessions but none had done much good. She'd put on a bit of weight and she'd seemed a little happier in herself, but Liz knew she was still seeing Haagen. She'd disappear for days on end without any explanation. Often he'd try to phone her at home, pretending to be someone else. Only Merrist House had finally parted them.

'So I reckon I've got about six months,' she said briskly, 'to do something about it.'

Tully regarded her over the remains of his orange juice. He had very pale skin and there was a deep tiredness in his eyes. 'So where do I fit in?' he said at last.

'I want advice. I need to know what to do, how to go about it.'

'Have you told the police? The drugs squad?'

'Yes. I spoke to someone last year. Nice man, very helpful. CID, drugs squad, whatever he was.'

'And?'

'He took all the details, wrote everything down, but Haagen's still around, I know he is, and even if they get him, arrest him, he'll only end up in court, and what good will that do?'

For the first time, Tully smiled. 'Why do you say that, as a matter of interest?'

'Because some clever lawyer will get him off. Either that or he'll get the soft option. Community service or working in someone like Hayden's bloody office. Just like last time.'

'He'd been in court before?'

'Yes, a couple of years back. He'd been stealing or breaking into cars or something. God knows what. Hayden thought he was some kind of genius. Thought he deserved a second chance.'

Tully was nodding now. 'I remember,' he said. 'Hayden gave him jobs around the office. Part of the conditional discharge.'

'That's right.'

'And he went right out and did it again.'

'Exactly. So what does that make Hayden? Apart from gullible?' She looked at Tully, expecting an answer, but he said nothing. Liz could feel herself getting angry, remembering the rows they'd had. 'Don't get me wrong, Mike,' she said. 'I didn't mind Hayden giving the boy a helping hand, even the odd meal. I just think he should have drawn the line at his own daughter. You've no idea. I watched that boy devour her, body and soul. It was terrifying, quite awful. But what can you do?'

Tully sighed. 'So you want him away? Is that what this is about?'

'I want him a million miles away. I want him so far away he'll never bother Jessie again.' Liz hesitated. 'That's why I wondered about getting him out of the country.'

'You mean deportation?'

'Yes. His second name's Schreck. It's a German name. He'll have a German passport – at least, I assume he does.'

For a while Tully sat in silence. Eventually, he took Liz's empty glass to the bar and returned with another Campari and soda.

'You've got two problems with deportation,' he said, settling behind the table again. 'One is the lad himself. I seem to remember Hayden saying he'd been brought up here. He was adopted or something. That means he'll have citizenship. Almost definitely.'

'And the other problem?'

'Even trickier. Under European law, he has the right to live here anyway. As far as I know.'

'Even if he's . . .' Liz made an angry gesture with her glass, ' . . . a junkie?'

'Yes.'

'That's absurd.'

'Of course it is, but there you go.' He gazed into the middle distance again. 'The alternative is to put together some kind of evidence. Take out a private prosecution. Drag him along to court yourself. You know where he lives?'

'He's still in the basement place he shared with Jess. Elphinstone Road. I checked this morning.'

'And we know what he looks like?'

'I've got a couple of photos. I found them in Jessie's room.' Liz opened her bag and took out a white envelope. She emptied the photos onto the table. Tully picked one up. Haagen was sitting cross-legged on a beach, grinning at the camera.

'We normally charge twenty-six pounds an hour,' Tully said. 'That buys you everything except disbursements. There's VAT on top, of course.' He paused. 'In your case, let's say fifteen pounds an hour.'

Liz blinked. For some reason she hadn't expected Tully to be quite so businesslike.

'And what does fifteen pounds an hour buy me?'

'Surveillance. Leg work. If we're to pull in the goodies, we need to poke around a bit.'

'Goodies?'

'Evidence. And it has to be admissible. In court. Which brings you back to square one.' Tully looked briefly apologetic. 'You haven't got much faith in the police because you haven't got much faith in the courts. Getting him into the dock a different way solves nothing. A court's still a court. Whichever route you take.'

Liz did her best to absorb the logic, testing each link in the chain, forced to concede that Tully was right. Natural justice demanded that Haagen be put away. Any mother, any parent, would surely agree with that. But the courts, for God knows what reasons, seemed to have other ideas. She sipped at her Campari, watching the landlord putting up a poster for the cathedral's latest organ recital, reflecting bitterly on just how powerless she'd become. Jessie was 19. Like any other adult, she could choose whoever she liked to wreck her life.

At length, deflated, she turned back to Tully. If anything, he was looking even gloomier.

'But as a friend, Mike, what would you do?'

'In this situation?'

'Yes. Say you had a daughter, say you had Jessie, say there was a Haagen, what would you do?'

Tully sat back, his eyes on the ceiling. Then he ran a tired hand over his face, smothering a yawn. 'If it was me,' he said, 'I'd go and see a friend.'

'That's exactly what I'm doing.'

'A different kind of friend. And when I saw him, I'd give him an envelope.' He glanced sideways. 'You follow me?'

Liz returned the look, totally blank. 'No,' she said. 'What's in the envelope?'

Tully was silent again. He seemed to be conducting some kind of inner debate. At length, he frowned.

'Ten thousand pounds,' he said quietly, 'which is about the going rate.'

Kate Frankham heard the phone from the street. She ran up the stairs to the front door, fumbling for her key, remembering the promise she'd made to the secretary of the local Labour Party. The woman was a stickler for punctuality. She'd said she'd phone at eight and Kate had promised faithfully she'd be in.

The cordless telephone was on the small occasional table in the hall. She picked it up, trying to picture her diary for the next couple of weeks. The meeting to elect the next parliamentary candidate was rumoured to have been fixed for early March. Deliberately, she'd rescheduled her counselling sessions to leave every evening free.

'Kate Frankham,' she said breathlessly. 'Can I help you?' She heard a far-away series of clicks, then a man's voice, clear as a bell. He was asking her how she'd been coping. He said he missed her more than he could say. She frowned.

'Hayden?'

'Me.'

'In Singapore? Already?'

'Yes. Got in tonight. It's four in the bloody morning. Unbelievable place. You'd love it.'

He began to tell her about the suite they'd given him, the way the sitting room was furnished, the map they'd forgotten to supply with the bed.

'Map?' she said blankly, at last unbuttoning her raincoat.

'It's huge, enormous, I'll need a bloody map to get out.'

She could hear him laughing at the other end. He sounded slightly drunk. She tried to think of something to say, something that might short-circuit his account of the meal he'd just eaten and clear the line for the incoming call.

'Must cost a fortune, phoning me like this,' she said, when he paused for breath. 'You know how hotels load the bill.'

'It's free, my love. Zhu's picking up the tab for everything.'

Kate stiffened at the mention of Zhu's name. She'd met him a couple of weeks back when he'd come down to check on progress at the Imperial, and Hayden had insisted that she join them both for dinner. Normally, she had no difficulty getting on with people, indeed it was one of the talents that convinced her she'd make a good MP, but Zhu had remained stubbornly beyond her reach. After an hour and a half's conversation, she hadn't been an inch closer to knowing the man, and that had bothered her.

She bent to the phone. Barnaby was still talking about the meal. He wanted to know where, in Portsmouth, he could buy fresh pigeon.

'Is he there with you?' she interrupted.

'Who?'

'Zhu.'

'No, he's off somewhere else. He must have a place of his own here.'

'And has he told you what he's up to? Flying you out?'

'Not really. He's got some kind of programme for me, things he wants me to see. Then there's the hotel side, of course. I think he must own some. Not this one. He doesn't seem to know the people behind the desk.'

Barnaby began to describe the hotel again, a child's excitement with a new toy, and in the background Kate heard the tone that announced another call waiting. Someone was trying to get through and, thanks to Barnaby, they couldn't. He was telling her about the giveaways in the suite. Might she find house room for a pair of pearl-backed hairbrushes and a leather-bound '96 diary? Kate muttered something about a visitor knocking at the door. She had to go. Maybe he could phone back later.

'Later?' she heard him laughing again. 'I told you, my love, it's four in the morning.'

She looked at the phone a moment. Nothing was more important than the selection meeting. The sooner she got to know the date, the easier it would be to concentrate her mind on those vital ten minutes when she had to stand up in front of all those people and convince them she'd make a bloody good MP. Barnaby was talking about a prison now, and she closed her eyes, slipping the phone back onto the base station, cutting him off. It began to ring at once and she lifted it to her ear again.

Another male voice, rougher this time, but no less familiar. 'It's Billy. Just to wish you good luck.'

'Oh?' Kate sank onto the stairs, pulling her coat around her.

'Yeah. The meeting's been postponed. It's on the twenty-seventh now. Monday night.'

'How do you know?'

'They just told me.'

'Who did?'

'Sally, the secretary.' He paused. 'Haven't you heard?'

'Heard what?'

'I'm standing too.' He laughed. 'Just in case anyone's still interested in socialism.'

Chapter Six

Charlie Epple's final session with the estate agent was even briefer than the first. They met on the pavement in Old Portsmouth beside the block of newly completed maisonettes. Charlie had his eye on number three, the one with the red door. The estate agent had the key and Charlie followed him from room to room, interested chiefly in the outlook. The last time he'd been round he'd had too much to drink, and he couldn't remember how far up you had to go to get a clear view of the sea.

The maisonettes were built on three floors. Across the road stood a length of thick, stone-blocked fortifications known locally as Hot Walls. Beyond lay the harbour mouth and the deep-water shipping lane, a regular succession of ferries and warships so close you could almost reach out and touch them. There was an apron of beach on the seaward side of the walls and, since childhood, Charlie had been crazy about the place, sunbathing on the tarry pebbles, hurling himself into the sea from the top of the nearby Square Tower. Being able to live here, with this fabulous view as a neighbour, would be truly wild.

The estate agent pushed open the door to the living room. From the little bow window the view was curtained by Hot Walls. Even on tiptoe, almost touching the ceiling, Charlie could see only a thin grey strip of the Solent, with the humpy silhouette of the Isle of Wight beyond. He mounted the stairs again. On the top floor there were bedrooms and from here the view was perfect. Charlie grinned, getting to the window in time to watch a cross-Channel ferry nosing out of the harbour mouth. It was huge, slab-sided, as big as a block of flats. For the time it took to rumble past, it shadowed the street outside.

Charlie stood in the empty bedroom, transfixed. '*How* much was it?'

He heard a rustle of papers behind him as the estate agent looked for the purchase price. 'A hundred and thirty-nine thousand, sir,' he said.

Another ferry had appeared from behind the squat grey mass of the Square Tower. It was French this time, one of the elegant Brittany Ferry boats inbound from the Normandy coast.

'Hundred and ten,' Charlie said.

'I'm not sure the price is subject to negotiation, sir.'

'Better check, eh?'

'Of course, sir.'

The agent retreated down the stairs. Charlie heard him talking on his mobile. He knew the developers were desperate to find buyers and his only worry was that £110,000 was too generous. Maybe he should have offered £100,000. Or less. The estate agent was coming back. £110,000 would, after all, be acceptable.

'Great.' Charlie produced a cheque book. 'Who do I pay?'

Mike Tully took lunch on the seafront, sitting in his Cavalier, tackling the corned-beef sandwiches he'd made first thing. Every now and then he checked up and down the road, trying to guess which way Owens would come. Straight from the suite of Special Branch offices at central police station he'd take the fun-fair route. Called out on some other job, he could appear from anywhere.

Tully finished the last sandwich and brushed the crumbs from his lap before dipping into his briefcase. He still had the photos Liz had shown him the previous evening and he was almost certain now that the boy Haagen was one of the names Owens had mentioned on the phone. The call had come last week, entirely unsolicited. Owens had talked vaguely about a National Front 'event' and wondered whether Tully had picked anything up. The intelligence had come down from Special Branch sources in

London, together with a list of names, though there was nothing specific in terms of dates or targets.

Tully hadn't been able to help but after last night he'd called Owens back, suggesting a meet. Owens had been less than enthusiastic. For one thing, his missis was ill and he was supposed to take the dog to the vet. For another, he was swamped by paperwork. The Home Office had ordered yet another manpower review. If he buggered up their bloody self-assessment form, he'd probably be out of a job.

Tully propped the photos on the dashboard, thinking of Liz. Recently he'd seen less than usual of Barnaby, partly because the man was so busy and partly because Zhu was as keen as ever on keeping them professionally apart. Tully was still doing work for the Singaporean, feeding him a series of reports on potential bid opportunities in the city, but in all conscience he knew he was getting out of his depth. After more than a decade in the game, his expertise was pretty wide – anything from insurance fraud to the protection of commercially sensitive data – but Zhu's appetite for intelligence and analysis seemed limitless. His success with the Imperial Hotel, delivered on a plate by Barnaby, had fuelled a non-stop stream of telexes from Singapore and the sheer scale of his ambition had begun to make Tully just a little nervous. What on earth made him think he could buy an entire industrial estate? What would be the point?

A jogger struggled past, then another, heads down against the bitter wind. They were both women, both middle-aged, and Tully thought again of Liz, wondering what she'd made of their conversation in the pub. It was the first occasion he'd spent with her alone, and he hadn't felt at ease. Living by yourself, you lost the knack of being comfortable with people, and the sheer depth of her anger had made him even warier than usual. Folk in that state were unpredictable, which made his parting aside about the ten grand all the more dodgy. A line like that, quoting the going rate for a contract killing, was the sort of half-joke you probably limited to men. They would be impressed but do fuck-all about it. Women, on the other hand, were a lot more ballsy. Mothers, especially.

He picked up the smaller of the two photos. He was still

examining it when the windscreen was briefly shadowed by Owens's thin frame.

Tully leaned across and unlocked the passenger door. Owens must have parked his car and walked. He was wrapped up against the wind, his neck swathed in folds of scarf. He got in and shut the door. He unbuttoned the thick coat and handed a blue file to Tully without a word. He had a pale, thin face, with lank strands of greying hair combed sideways across his skull. In another life, Tully thought, he would have made a perfect undertaker.

'What's this?'

'I thought you wanted the SP,' he was eyeing the photos on the dashboard, 'so I sorted something out.'

Tully opened the file. The photograph clipped to the standard ID form looked more recent than the prints he'd got from Liz. It had been carefully scissored from a newspaper and it showed a head-and-shoulders shot of Haagen that might almost have been posed in a studio. His face was half turned to the camera. Clever lighting emphasized the hollows of his cheeks and the smile was knowing, rather than manic. His hair was closely cropped and a small silver swastika hung from his left earlobe. Clearly visible, beneath his left eye, was a two-inch scar, running diagonally towards the corner of his mouth.

Tully compared the photo to the shots on the dashboard. The scar was new. 'What happened? How come the scar?'

Owens was blowing into his cupped hands, trying to restore a little warmth. He looked like a man on the edge of flu. He squinted at the photo. 'Got beaten up,' he said briefly. 'Pub brawl last summer.'

'Here?'

'The Whippet.'

'Political?'

Owens shook his head. 'Too many snakebites,' he said. 'He likes to fuck about when he's had a few.'

Tully leafed quickly through the file, absorbing the contents as he went. Haagen had come to the attention of the Special Branch via a publication called the *National Front News*. Since October he'd been writing a regular column. There were photocopies of the column and Tully slipped one out. It seemed to boil down to a ferocious attack on Albert Speer, Hitler's architect. Speer, wrote Haagen, had been a brilliant organizer, sorting out the bottlenecks in German industrial production. He'd sensibly put the Jews to work in slave-labour camps and achieved a series of minor miracles with the V2 programme. More or less single-handedly, he'd kept Hitler's war going. But all that good work had been wrecked by the noises he'd made before his own death in 1981. He'd condemned the slaughter of the Jews. Worse still, he'd labelled the Führer 'a monster'. 'Who knows?' Haagen had snarled in his closing line. 'Maybe Speer was a closet Yid himself?'

Tully read the column again, fascinated. It was a strange combination of scholarship and rant. In places it read like a degree treatise; in others it was the purest garbage. Tully slipped the photocopy back inside the file.

'So why the interest?' Owens queried, blowing his nose.

Tully told him briefly about Liz. A friend of his had a daughter. The girl was up to her neck in hard drugs and the mother was blaming Haagen. Owens looked across at Tully and sniffed. His coat was covered in long brown hairs and he smelt powerfully of golden retriever. Tully wound down the window, letting in a blast of cold air.

'What else have you got on him?'

'Not much. Lives down here. Signs on at the DSS every other Thursday. Claims not to be working.'

'What about the newspaper stuff?'

'Says it's unpaid, according to the benefits people. Apparently he's working on a book, too. Something about the League of St George.'

'League of what?'

'St George. It's a branch of the NF. Way out to the right. Cops all the real loonies.'

'Including our friend here?'

'I doubt it. He's too bright for that.'

Tully rolled up the window. Owens looked chilled to the bone. 'I've been talking to the Met again,' he went on. 'Five have got a wire on one of the NF lines and our lads at the Yard have been getting a look at the transcripts. Bloke I talk to's a pal of mine and he thinks they're on to something.'

'Like what?'

'Some kind of event. Down here.'

'When?'

'Soon.' Owens fumbled for tissues. 'Only there's a financial problem.'

'Money?'

'Exactly. They're planning something big and they don't want to fuck it up by under-spending. I gather we're talking transport, mainly. Plus collaterals.' He indicated the photo on the dashboard. 'That was our friend's word for it.'

'Does he figure on the transcripts?'

'Yes.'

'So what does he mean by collaterals?'

'Fuck knows.'

'What do you think he means?'

Owens looked at him and Tully sensed that at last they were getting to the heart of it. Special Branch attracted a certain breed. They were far from stupid and they never made a move without devoting a great deal of thought to the consequences. So why had Owens phoned him last week? Why the sudden interest in the National Front?

'This event, whatever it is,' Tully said carefully, 'why tell me about it?'

Owens looked briefly pained. Then he reached for the file. 'Most of these guys are animals,' he said. 'They come down for the piss-up and the aggro. All they ask for is a target. The softer the better.'

'And?'

'I think your mate Haagen's found them a target.'

'Who?'

There was a long silence. For the second time Owens checked his watch. Then he slipped the file inside his coat, nodding at the newly painted bulk of the Imperial Hotel, clearly visible across the Common.

'There's a bloke called Seggins,' he said. 'I gather you've had dealings.'

Tully stared at him. Arthur Seggins, the previous owner of the Imperial, was a small-time entrepreneur who'd been making a fortune from bogus DSS claims. The last time Tully had seen him was on completion of Zhu's purchase when he'd returned the evidence that could so easily have put Seggins in court.

'You're telling me Seggins is a target?'

'Not at all.' Owens's hand at last found the door handle. 'I'm telling you Seggins has signed on with the NF boys.'

There was no sign of Zhu when the limo returned to the hotel to collect Hayden Barnaby. It was mid-morning but already the temperature was heading for thirty degrees and Barnaby felt the heat engulf him as he stepped out of the air-conditioned cool of the towering hotel atrium. He slipped quickly into the back of the limo, sinking into the soft leather as the car surged away. The rendezvous at the prison with Flora Li had been fixed for eleven o'clock and he sat back, stretching his long legs, wondering exactly where the meeting might lead. He and Zhu were to spend the afternoon discussing plans for the Imperial's Southsea opening. Zhu had already signalled his desire for a lavish eight-course banquet and was preparing to fly in a special team of chefs and front-of-house waiters to ensure that every last detail was authentic. Whatever Flora had in mind couldn't take longer than an hour.

They drove along the coast, back towards the airport. The other side of the expressway was thick with inbound city traffic while, overhead, neatly uniformed workers tended the rich green loops of ivy trailing over the concrete flyovers. Both sides of the expressway were lined with soaring apartment blocks, each carefully sited around little clumps of co-ordinated trees. Winding past at a steady fifty miles an hour, this intricate urban landscape felt like a page ripped from an architect's sketchbook, every detail and perspective carefully planned. After the colour and bustle of the downtown shopping area, this was another Singapore, no less impressive, and Barnaby found himself musing on the lives these people must lead, caged by constant exhortation.

There'd been something slightly frightening in the sheer intensity of Flora's self-belief. She belonged to a society that worked. It was her job, her responsibility, to make it even better and all that stood in her way was the tiresome weakness of the human condition. Barnaby fingered the beautifully stitched leather, remembering the sight of her leaving the restaurant. She walked like a model, erect, purposeful and, like everyone else he met in Singapore, left behind her the scent of something immensely expensive.

Changi prison lay to the north of the airport. The driver used a pass to negotiate his way through two sets of security checks and at the third gate Barnaby handed in the scrap of paper Flora had given him. The guard studied it briefly, eyed Barnaby, then muttered to the driver. In a corner of the big courtyard ahead were parking spaces for visitors. They were to wait there.

Minutes later, Flora emerged from a long low building set apart from the main prison compound. This morning she was wearing a dark knee-length skirt, severely cut, with a tailored jacket to match. Her hair hung down her back in a French braid, secured at the top by a twist of scarlet ribbon. Barnaby watched her walk towards the car. In Manhattan, he thought, she'd have been a bond dealer or an advertising executive, someone with a big desk, a hectic sex life and wonderful prospects. Here, she preached the gospel of hard work, family values and incessant self-improvement.

She bent to the car, offering Barnaby a tight smile through the tinted glass. He opened the door, feeling the first prickles of heat even as his feet touched the tarmac. Flora was hoping he'd slept well. She had much to show him.

Barnaby followed her into the welcome chill of the building she'd just left. At the end of a corridor, she led him into a small office. From the wall across the desk, an enormous pair of eyes stared at newcomers. Across the top of the poster, above a line of Chinese characters, the message read *ALERT! TOGETHER WE CAN STOP CRIME!*. Barnaby stepped closer, trying to decipher a much smaller line of type at the bottom. 'Crime Watch', it went. 'Special Issue for the Festive Season.'

Barnaby smiled, aware that Flora was waiting for his reaction. She had a small leather zip-up briefcase tucked beneath one arm. In her other hand, she held a thick sheaf of papers. She gave them to him.

'This is Mr Zhu's idea,' she said at once. 'He thinks you should see the bad side, too.'

'Bad side?'

'This is a prison. We're not perfect, Mr Barnaby.'

She shepherded him towards the door. Changi, she said, was one of two prisons on Singapore Island. The regime was tough and widely publicized. That, in itself, served as a deterrent to crime but there were also big fines and, for serious offences, the certainty of the death penalty.

They were walking down another corridor. Right and left, through squares of wired glass inset in steel doors, Barnaby could see rows of iron-framed beds. The dormitories appeared to be empty.

'You hang lots of people?'

'Last year,' she glanced over her shoulder, 'seventy-six.'

'And does it work?'

'They die, sure.'

'I know, but . . .'

They were at the end of a long hall. To the right, through another door, Barnaby could hear movement, an occasional voice, the shuffle of footsteps. Flora was looking at her watch and frowning. For once, she seemed hesitant.

Barnaby glanced down at the briefing papers. According to the Minister of Trade and Industry, Singapore manufactured more than half the world's supply of computer disk-drives. He looked up again. Flora had half opened the door. Inside, Barnaby could see what looked like a gymnasium. There were climbing bars on the walls and thick ropes hanging from iron rings in the ceiling.

He heard a sharp hissing noise, then a fleshy smack and a deep-pitched grunt, semi-human. Puzzled, he stepped round the door. On the far side of the gym stood perhaps a dozen men. They were all naked. One was spreadeagled over an upright wooden frame, similar to an artist's easel. His hands and his ankles were strapped, and Barnaby could see what looked like a handkerchief twisted between his teeth. Several metres behind him, at the end of a length of coconut matting, stood a short, squat man in a sky blue Adidas tracksuit. He was carrying a long thin cane and, as Barnaby watched, he flexed it in his hands then swept it left and right, producing the hissing noise again. Finally, he turned round. With a curious skipping motion, he came sideways down the coconut matting, slashing at the man's back, putting all his strength into the blow. The man jerked with the impact, shaking his head, and Barnaby saw his eyes widen and then shut tight as the footsteps came dancing down the mat again and the cane descended for a third time. Each blow raised a long, scarlet welt across the pale skin and Barnaby realized that the grunting noise came not from the man lashed to the easel but from the daunting figure in the tracksuit.

The flogging went on, five lashes, six, and some of the other men had turned away, not wanting to watch. At last the man in the tracksuit tossed the cane to one side, mopped his face with his bare hand then gestured towards two attendants, clad in spotless white tunics. They ran to the easel, released the straps and helped the wounded youth towards a long trestle table, keeping him at arm's length to avoid soiling their clothes. There was a bowl of something yellow on the table and they began to sponge away the blood on his back, telling a couple of the other men to hold him up as they did so. Barnaby watched them at their work, sickened by how slick and familiar this operation had obviously become. The next luckless target was already being tied to the easel, his legs spread wide, the muscles of his back visibly tensing.

Barnaby felt the touch of Flora's hand on his arm. She was wondering about coffee? Did he take milk? Sugar? Barnaby shook his head. He was looking at the man in the tracksuit. Occasionally, when he caught someone's eye, he'd smile.

'What have these guys done?' he asked. 'Why the punishment?'

Flora looked confused, then began to apologize. 'I'm sorry,' she said. 'I thought Mr Zhu had told you.'

'Told me what?'

'This is our drugs rehabilitation unit.' She gestured at the man spreadeagled at the end of the coconut matting. 'There's a note on the success rate in your briefing. Mr Zhu thought you might be interested.'

Jessie was sitting in her usual position next to the door when the group turned on Lola. The session had started at two o'clock, half an hour earlier than normal, and so far Jessie had managed to deflect the odd asides that, on a different day, might have developed into something ugly.

There were nine in the group including the staff member they called the moderator. The moderator's name was Alan, a thin, cadaverous ex-junkie from Camberwell who'd survived a year-long rehab course in a similar set-up near Oxford and then become a founder member of the Merrist House community. Jessie had leaned hard on him during the five weeks of her assessment module but now knew that she could expect little help if the groups got rough.

A languid black twenty-six-year-old called Chester was currently under attack. The three-hour session was designed to develop emotional honesty and openness and two of the younger residents felt that Chester had no interest in either. So far, he'd got no further than mumbling something about not wanting any of this shit. In group terms this was the verbal equivalent of turning his back and Jessie winced, knowing that this kind of reaction was bound to unleash the real pit bulls in the room.

One was called Brent, a small, thick-set, aggressive youth from Reading. His face and upper body were cratered with acne and he'd demonstrated his indifference by adding a number of heavy-duty tattoos. Jessie and Lola knew about the tattoos because recently Brent had developed a habit of appearing semi-naked on the corridor outside their room up on the first floor. On the street, Brent's problem had been alcohol, not hard drugs, and Lola had twice had to fend off his attentions, warning Jessie he was close to psychopathic. Brent had been referred to Merrist House as a condition of discharge after an ABH conviction. Out of his head on vodka, he'd crushed a glass in a student's face.

Now, cleverly, he was carrying the attack to Lola. In what passed for group dynamics, Jessie had come to recognize this as one of the subtler tactics. If Chester wouldn't be goaded by frontal attack, enlist him in someone else's war until he opens up enough to present a worthwhile target of his own.

The group sat in a wide circle. Brent was bent forward on his chair, directly opposite Lola. 'You've been on the phone again,' he said. 'Fucking squawking. Squawk. Squawk. Look at me. Squawk. Squawk.' Lola turned her head away. Brent might have been a bad smell. 'Well?' he yelled at her. 'Haven't you?'

Lola nodded. Normally her voice was low. Often, in their room, Jessie had to strain to catch what she was saying. Now she looked Brent in the eye.

'What if I fucking have? What's it to you?'

'It's everything to fucking me. Everything.'

'Why?'

'Because you're telling me something. You're telling me what a tragic little cunt you are. Crying your fucking eyes out all the time. Me, me, me. That's what you're saying. Me, me, me, and that squitty little daughter of yours. Candelle? What kind of fucking name's that?'

Jessie could see the colour draining from Lola's face. Brent was so pleased with the reaction he seemed to have abandoned Chester altogether.

'Well, cunt?' he screamed. 'Are you telling me I'm fucking wrong or what?'

Lola was looking towards Alan. Her hands were shaking. She wanted help.

'You're out of order, Brent,' Jessie heard herself saying. 'You don't have the first fucking idea.'

Brent turned on Jessie. The veins were cording on the sides of his neck and his face was scarlet. 'Was I asking you? Little Miss Tight Arse?'

'No, but I'm telling you just the same. One day you might have a daughter, God help her, and then maybe you'll understand.'

'Understand, understand.' Brent mimicked Jessie's accent. Before Merrist House, Jessie had never given a thought to the way she spoke but the last six weeks she'd been crucified for her manners and her pronunciation. Getting through an entire sentence without an obscenity, she'd quickly discovered, was the very worst form of verbal insult.

Brent had stopped to draw breath. Chester appeared to have gone to sleep. Lola, her head down again, was fighting to control herself.

Another youth stepped in. His street nickname was Manik and Jessie knew him from her days with Haagen, trying to score in Pompey pubs.

'Look at you,' Manik sneered, gesturing derisively at Lola, 'the fucking state of you. Brent's right. All you fucking want is sympathy. Me, me, me.'

Brent took up the chant. Lola had been flashing pictures of her daughter since the day she'd arrived at the place. She was so fucking thick, she thought they'd protect her.

'Too fucking right.' Manik nodded vigorously. 'Fucking dishonest, that. Don't touch me. Don't be nasty to me. I'm a mother, look, proof, my little Candelle.' He leaned towards Lola and blew hard, the way a child might blow on a birthday cake. 'Oooops!' he said. 'Sorry! Just blown the little cunt away!'

Brent barked with laughter. One or two others in the group sniggered. Lola was sitting bolt upright, her knees pressed together, her hands bunched into tiny fists. Jessie wanted to reach out, touch her, comfort her, but group rules prohibited physical contact.

Very slowly, Lola got to her feet. She was wearing jeans and a sweatshirt. She unzipped the jeans and pulled them down. Underneath, she had a pair of black bikini briefs. She pulled these down too, her eyes never leaving Brent's face.

'OK?' she said quietly. 'Is that what you want?'

Brent was staring at her. Embarrassment and anger inflamed his acne. The rest of the group were looking at him. Some were grinning. Lola had come out fighting at last. Everyone knew what Brent had been after since the day he'd met Lola. He'd made it very public because that's the way he was. He wanted to shag her and shag her and shag her and one day, he'd assure anyone who cared to listen, he would.

Now he sat back and Jessie sensed at once how dangerous the situation had become. People like Brent reckoned they could handle anything. Except humiliation.

Lola was zipping up her jeans. Then she sat down. No one moved. No one said anything. Jessie swallowed hard. She could taste the shepherd's pie from lunchtime.

At length, Brent sighed. 'You wouldn't know a dick from a fucking hole in the road,' he said, 'so I'd be wasting my time.'

'Oh, yeah?' Lola was smiling now. 'So why all the aggro? Why all the attention? And how come I got to have a daughter?'

'Fuck knows. Probably got it off a catalogue. Mail order. How should I fucking know?'

'Because you've been trying hard enough, that's why.' Lola glanced at Jessie for confirmation and Jessie nodded. 'Up and down the corridor, cock hanging out under your towel, really subtle that, real turn-on. What do you do for an encore? Stick it through the keyhole?'

'You should know, dear.'

'What does that mean?'

'You should know. You told me.'

'Told you what?'

There was another silence. Brent was studying the wreckage of his fingernails, playing a new role, the principled guy who wouldn't dream of betraying a confidence. The eyes of the group were on him again. He seemed to have won back a little of the initiative.

Alan, the moderator, stirred in his chair. So far he, too, might have been asleep.

'This is about openness and honesty,' he reminded Lola. 'It's a direct challenge. You should answer.'

Brent was looking aggrieved now, the man betrayed. 'You telling me you never fucking said it? Or you telling me it's not true?'

Lola shook her head violently. Colour had flooded into her face. 'I don't know what you're talking about.'

Brent had her hooked now and he knew it. He let her struggle on the line a little longer. Everyone was watching her. Everyone wanted an answer.

'Well?'

'Fuck off.'

'That's not what you said.'

'It is. It's what I meant.'

'No, it's not. What you said was . . .' He made a show of reining himself in again, deeply regretful. 'I can't grass you up, love. Ain't fair. Can't do it.'

Lola was looking helplessly at Jessie. On her other side, Alan cleared his throat.

'Are we talking house rules here? Or what?'

Brent shrugged, holding up his hands, palms out. 'Can't say, guv. Straight up.'

'Lola?'

'Fuck off.'

'Lola?'

'He's winding you up. Can't you see? It's a game.'

'But what does he mean? What did you tell him?' Alan asked. 'This is group time, you know that. Nothing's held against you. Anything goes.' He frowned. 'We have a dysfunction here. It's not working the way it should. Honesty, Lola, and openness. Take it easy. Trust us.'

Lola was mute, turning down his invitation with a tiny shake of her head. Brent was watching her every move.

Chester uncrossed his legs. 'Speak your mind, man,' he said, with a yawn. 'You're the only one's gonna tell us.'

'No, Lola'll tell us, won't you . . . Lolly?' Brent grinned.

Jessie watched Lola trying to fight her temper. Finally, she snapped. 'I'm telling you fuck all,' she screamed. 'I'm telling you you're a fucking liar. I'm telling you you're scum. Worse than scum. No wonder you never used. No wonder you couldn't handle it. Junk's too fucking good for you.'

Brent drew in his breath sharply, wagging his head in mock reproof. Lola had lost her rag. Time, now, for the last twist of the knife. He looked across at Jessie, the leer back on his face.

'Takes two to break this rule.' He tapped the side of his nose. 'So what's she like in bed, Tight Arse? Good shag or a waste of fucking time?'

Late afternoon, Kate inched through the Portsmouth traffic, determined to have it out with Billy. She'd phoned him twice since he'd told her about the candidate selection meeting but both times he'd been out. On the second occasion she'd managed a brief conversation with one of the students with whom he shared the house. To the best of his knowledge, Billy was working with the lads up at the arts centre.

Kate parked the Audi and let herself in through the big double doors, wondering how Billy had come to be working here. He'd always had a natural rapport with kids and he'd spent several seasons running a successful football team in one of the local tyro leagues, but to her knowledge he had absolutely no teaching experience. Indeed, he'd always made a virtue of his lack of educational qualifications. Street wisdom, he'd often told her, is the only knowledge that really counts.

The area that served as a classroom was on the top floor. The corridor was in semi-darkness and Kate walked towards the square of light at the end, hearing a low murmur of voices. She stood at the door. Billy was at the head of a long table. Eight kids were crouched over the enormous sand tray that took up most of the working space. On it, in neat formations, stood dozens of model soldiers, one army ranged against another. The sand was carefully moulded into a series of features, and a winding blue line down the middle of a valley represented a river.

As Kate watched, Billy was leaning forward, rearranging a line of red-coated infantrymen. As he did so one of the kids disputed the move. Others joined in the argument. Voices were raised. Someone fetched a book from a nearby shelf. Heads bent over lines of text, fingers pointed to a map. Kate couldn't imagine what lay at the heart of the wrangle. Were they fighting a real battle? Or was the encounter pure fiction? Either way, it didn't matter. Far more important was the fact that the kids were well and truly engaged. As an example of education in the raw, of attention sought and offered, it was flawless.

Kate pushed at the heavy swing door and the conversation died as she came in. Heads turned towards her and she was conscious of the smile that ghosted across Billy's face. 'I'm interrupting,' she said. 'I'm just wondering whether you might be free for a drink later?'

There was a stir round the table. A couple of the kids exchanged glances. Billy evidently had a lot of credit already and this surprise invitation was doing him no harm.

'We can talk here if you like.' Billy was looking at his watch. 'I was through twenty minutes ago.'

'What about . . .' Kate gesticulated at the table.

Billy reached for a big cardboard box. 'It's endgame,' he said. 'Prince Jerome's over-committed on the left and it's stalemate in the middle. The irresistible force meets the immovable object. Carry on, and we'll be here all night.'

One of the taller youths looked troubled. 'That it, then?'

'Yeah, till next week.'

'What about the gear?'

'Comes back with me.' Billy made to cuff him playfully round the ear. 'You think I'm that stupid?'

The youth mimed an elaborate feint, grinning broadly. Then he pointed at a line of carefully sited cannon. 'No barrage?'

'Postponed.'

'Until when?'

'Next week. I just told you.'

Billy began to gather in his armies, stowing them carefully in the box. A couple of the youths helped him. The rest drifted across to the pool table in the corner and Kate heard the clack of balls being readied. There was a TV in the corner, bodies slumped in the circle of threadbare armchairs and someone with the remote control prowling aimlessly through the channels.

Kate picked up one of the lead soldiers. Billy had often told her about his passion for military history, and she knew how deeply he'd read on the subject, but not that his interest extended this far. The figures were intricately painted, every last detail carefully picked out. Red tunics. White cross-belts. Buff facings.

'You did these?'

'Yeah.'

'You never showed me before, never mentioned it.'

'You never asked.'

Kate sat down while Billy made coffee. He said he'd been doing special-needs sessions for several months. He came every week and, contrary to what everyone had told him to expect, the class had grown in size. At the start, he'd had just three kids. Now, as she could see, it was full house.

'That's a credit to you. You should be pleased.'

'Yeah, I am.' He was looking at the sand table. 'They come for the violence, really. Even on this scale Waterloo's better than the telly.'

He sat down beside her on the sofa. The mug of black coffee was scalding hot. She put it on the floor beside her foot.

'It's about the selection meeting,' she said. 'It was a bit of a surprise, that's all.'

'Me standing?'

'Yes, to be frank.'

'You thought you had a clear run?'

'Not at all. Frank Perry's the favourite. He's got the union vote. You know he has.'

'I meant a clear run against him.'

'Oh, I see.' Kate hesitated. 'Then yes, I did. I thought it would just be the two of us. Not that you didn't have a perfect right . . . Who nominated you? Do you mind me asking?'

'Not at all. Tipner branch.' Billy raised his mug. 'Bless their hearts.'

Kate reached down for her coffee. Portsmouth was big enough to support a pair of MPs and the city was divided into two constituencies, East and West. The Tory MP in Portsmouth West, a young ex-banker called Philip Biscoe, was currently defending a majority of 2,700, a margin that put the constituency comfortably within Labour's grasp.

'I'm amazed they haven't parachuted someone in,' Billy was saying, 'nice off-the-shelf candidate from Walworth Road.'

'We prefer to keep it local. You know we do.'

'Yeah, but that's Old Labour, old thinking. Blair's people will do anything.'

'Is that why you're standing? Bloody-mindedness?'

'Partly that.'

'Then it won't make any difference. You'll just split the vote.' Billy had his eyes on the television across the room. The kids round the pool table were now watching *Neighbours*.

'What if it makes a difference to me?' he said.

'Then that would be selfish. And pretty pointless.'

'I see.' Billy glanced at her. 'But what if there were people around, people in Tipner say, who might want a voice?'

'I'd speak for them.'

'*You*'d speak for them?' Billy laughed softly. 'What would you say? How would you know what they wanted? How they felt?' He lifted his mug, gesturing towards the shadowed faces around the TV. 'A couple of these kids come from Tipner. Broken homes. Shit schools. Dad on the piss every night, shacked up with some bird round the corner. Mother on the Social. Do you know what goes on inside their heads? Do you?'

Kate knew him well enough to recognize the anger in his voice.

'I want change,' she said simply. 'Just like you.'

'No, you don't, you want power. They're not the same thing.'

'They are. The one follows the other.'

'Not at all. Power's something else completely.'

'You really believe that?'

'Yes, I do.' He offered her a cold smile. 'You want to be in the middle of it all, up in London, where you think it matters. Of course you do. It's natural. It's where people like you belong. That's the power thing again. You're junkies. You're physically addicted. All of you.' He shrugged. 'Good luck. I hope it goes well for you. I hope you get what you want. But God help the rest of us. Back in the real world.'

Kate thought briefly about leaving, then decided against it.

Walking out would be an admission of defeat and she hadn't got this far simply to jack it in. This is politics, she reminded herself, not friendship. And in politics, as someone up at last year's party conference had remarked, only winning matters.

She picked at the loose threads around a hole in the upholstery. 'Is there anything I can say to convince you?' she asked.

'Convince me of what? Of you needing to stand? Or about this wonderful new party of ours?'

'Both, as it happens.'

'You think they're connected?' He was incredulous.

'I know they're connected. We have to get our act together. Gesture politics aren't enough. To do anything we have to get into power, and getting into power means persuading people to vote for us. The old slogans are wonderful but they frighten people stiff.'

Billy lifted his T-shirt and scratched his belly. Over the winter, he seemed to have put on a bit of weight and Kate wondered who he'd taken up with. He'd never had a problem finding a woman – in fact, he probably had more offers than he knew what to do with.

'OK,' he said at last. 'So what's your line on the Clause Four thing?'

Kate ducked her head. Of course, the question had to come. Blair had electrified the Blackpool conference with his plans to revise the party's constitution. The language, as ever, had been carefully coded but everyone in the Winter Gardens had known exactly what he'd meant. The days of public ownership were numbered. Privatization was here to stay. Exit Clause Four.

'It has to go,' she said. 'And it will.'

'With your blessing?'

'Yes.'

'You'll vote in April?'

'Of course.' Blair had called a special conference on the issue. The votes against Clause Four were already stacking up. The April decision was a foregone conclusion.

'What about water? Gas? Electricity? Where does profit belong in all that?'

'There's nothing wrong with profit. Sometimes the market does it better than we do. We have to use that. We have to be big enough to admit it. Profit's an engine. It drives things.'

'It drives greed, and it drives envy.' Billy's eyes were on the television. 'So where does that leave my kids there? My faithful grenadiers? You think they'll ever benefit? You think they'll ever own shares? Get their snouts in the trough?'

'They'll have the option. Like all of us.'

'Bollocks. The only option they'll ever have is which fucking channel to watch, which soap opera. Still,' he looked across at her, 'I suppose that's choice of a kind. Isn't that the magic word? Choice?'

'Be realistic, Billy. We're talking about the wheel here. You can't disinvent it, no matter how hard you might try.' Then, encouraged by his silence, she plunged on. 'OK, I admit it, the party's moved to the right, no question. And yes, so have I. But not very far, not as far as you think. Make a list, put ten pledges down on paper and I bet I agree with every one of them. The only difference between you and me is gender. Women are realistic. Men are the dreamers. We're both after the same thing so why be awkward? Why make it so difficult for yourself?'

'It's not difficult. It's very easy. Socialism's about sharing. These kids deserve something better than a poor man's Tory Party. And so do I.'

'You really think we're like the Tories?'

'I think we're worse.'

'Is that why you're standing?'

'Yes.'

'Then you're wrong. What's happening is inevitable. We have to adjust. We have to modernize. Otherwise we'll die. And what would be the point in that?'

Billy gazed at her without comment. Then he drained the mug and got up. The box of toy soldiers was on the other end of the sand tray. He picked it up and wedged it under his arm. When he called goodbye to the kids round the television only one bothered to answer. Making for the door, he stopped beside the sofa. Then he shook the box lightly and Kate heard the soft rattle of lead figures inside.

'Death or glory.' He smiled. '*Plus ça change.*'

Jessie sat at the corner table in the lounge bar, waiting for Lola to come back from the loo. They'd been in the pub for nearly an hour. According to the timetable in the village square, the last bus north left at ten past seven.

One of the local lads called from the bar again. The offer of a drink was still there. He and his mate had a van. He'd seen Jessie's rucksack and Lola's suitcase, overheard the girls talking. They'd have a couple of bevvies then they'd run them both up to Guildford. Be a pleasure. Jessie refused for the second time but asked herself if maybe it wouldn't be better. The bus would take hours and they'd have to change at Alton. Leaving Merrist had been the hard bit. Why make the rest such a trial?

The loo door opened and Lola came back. She was wearing a low-cut vest tucked into her jeans and the weight she'd put on during rehab had restored the figure Jessie had glimpsed in some of her photos. She sat down, ignoring a whistle from the bar.

'OK, girls?'

Jessie grinned at her. The lads at the bar weren't taking no for an answer. One was coming across, juggling two glasses of what looked like cider. He lowered them carefully to the table. Lola looked at them a moment then gave him a smile. He couldn't take his eyes off her cleavage.

'Cheers.' Lola took a glass. She'd had two pints already.

The lad from the bar slid into the seat beside her. His mate did the same on Jessie's side, trapping the two girls between them. Lola took a long pull at the cider, then returned the glass to the table. Her hand found Jessie's and she squeezed it softly. The youth with the van was talking about another pub, out in the country, much quieter. Maybe they should go there *en route* to Guildford. It had a wood fire and a dart-board.

Lola smiled dreamily. Her tongue had found the inside of

Jessie's ear and her hand was circling her face, caressing it. 'Great,' she murmured. 'Let's do it.'

The youth was staring at her. He'd started saying something about everyone being on for the ride but he'd stopped in mid-sentence. 'Girls?' he said uncertainly.

Chapter Seven

Liz Barnaby was half-way to Winchester in the Mercedes when the phone rang. She reached for the radio console and turned down the morning edition of *Woman's Hour*. The voice on the phone was all too familiar.

'Dad? It's me, Jess.'

Liz swerved to avoid a big puddle by the side of the road, wondering what a young child was doing in Merrist House. She could hear it quite clearly in the background, howling.

'Jessie?'

Jessie was talking to someone else now. A door slammed. Then she was back again. The howling had stopped.

'Mum? Is that you?'

'Yes.'

'Where's Dad?'

'He's gone to Singapore.'

'Oh . . .'

Liz touched the brakes as she approached a queue of traffic dawdling along behind a tractor. Jessie usually called from Merrist in the evening. Evidently it was difficult getting to the phone during the day.

'Got the morning off, Jess? How's it going?'

There was another silence and Liz thought the connection had gone funny. Then Jess was on the line again, telling her that things had been difficult. Her best friend, Lolly, was in trouble. She was worried sick about her little girl. In the end there'd been no other solution.

Liz was in third gear now, tucked in behind a big milk lorry.

It began to dawn on her that something had happened. Something serious.

'Where are you?' she asked. 'What's been going on?'

She heard Jessie laughing. She said there was nothing to worry about. She was up in Guildford, looking after Lolly and Candelle. She had a little money saved and Lolly had borrowed forty quid from a friend round the corner. Everything was working out fine.

'What does that mean?' Liz saw a lay-by approaching and signalled left, pulling the Mercedes out of the traffic stream.

Jessie was telling her about Candelle, Lolly's little girl. She was supposed to be in care but the social workers had brought her round for the morning. She was a real dreamboat. She had blonde ringlets and little dimples that matched Lolly's almost exactly. No wonder Lolly had been in such a state.

Liz cut in, her voice icier than she'd intended. 'Are you on leave? Have they given you a pass or something?'

'Who?'

'The people at Merrist. The drug people.'

'Oh, no.' Jessie was laughing again. 'Once you've split, that's it. There's no way back. Ever.'

Liz stared at the long ribbon of road. The queue of traffic behind the tractor was a blur in the distance.

'Shit,' she muttered. 'Shit, shit.'

'Mum?'

Liz looked at her watch, making a series of rapid calculations. 'I can't believe this,' she said aloud. 'I can't believe you're doing this. After six weeks? When it's gone so well? And you just give it all up?'

'It's no problem, Mum. I'm better, I promise.'

'You said that before.'

'I know. It's different this time.'

'You said that, too.' Liz checked the rear-view mirror and restarted the engine. 'So are you coming home or what?'

Jessie said that was impossible. It wouldn't work and it wouldn't be fair. Then she started talking about Lolly again. She needed support, she needed looking after. The pair of them would be up in Guildford for as long as it took. Liz shut her eyes, squeezing hard until red blobs swam out of the darkness. It was something she did involuntarily, in moments of great crisis.

'Do you have an address?'

'Yes.'

'May I have it?'

'Of course.'

Liz reached for a petrol receipt and scribbled the address on the back. Nine months of living with a junkie told her it was probably false.

'And what about Haagen?' she said thickly. 'Where does he come into all this?'

'Who?'

'Haagen. Your German friend.'

'Oh, him.' Jessie sounded vague, as if she'd misplaced a half-forgotten card from her filing index. 'He's tried to get in touch but I haven't had time to do anything about it.'

'Am I supposed to believe that?'

'Mum . . .' Jessie sounded reproachful, and Liz found herself on the edge of an apology. Maybe she was being too harsh. Maybe the people at Merrist really had worked a miracle.

Jessie was talking about Charlie Epple. She wanted his home telephone number.

'Why?' Liz said at once.

'He's been very sweet. He sent me some money.'

'Really?'

'Yes. I think he'd even have come down to see me except it wasn't allowed.'

Liz slipped the Mercedes into gear and began to inch forward, struck by a sudden idea. She'd seen the place in Old Portsmouth that Charlie was buying. It was far too big for a single man and there was plenty of room for Jess. Better still, it was just round the corner, no more than a couple of minutes' walk, and if Jess wouldn't live at home then it was definitely the next best thing.

'Do you want me to get in touch with Charlie?' she suggested, rather too quickly. 'Tell him you're better?'

'Please, Mum.'

'You'll ring again?'

'Of course.'

'And you'll . . .' Liz was unable to finish the sentence. She knew nothing about this new friend of Jessie's except the obvious. She, too, had been in Merrist House so she, too, had presumably been a junkie. In the background, Liz heard a door opening and a child's voice. She checked the road behind her, and pulled the Mercedes into a savage U-turn. Whatever it took, she had to get Jessie back to Portsmouth before this new-found independence landed her in yet more trouble.

'Mum?' Jessie was back on the phone. She was talking about Haagen again. She said he'd written her a couple of sweet letters. To be honest, she felt guilty not writing back. Had Liz seen him around? Had he phoned at all?

Liz eyed the speedometer. The bends were on the tight side for eighty miles an hour. 'No, darling,' she said. 'Someone told me he's gone back to Germany.'

Louise Carlton didn't bother to queue for the shuttle mini-bus over to the Home Office but took a taxi instead. The interdepartmental meeting was scheduled to start promptly at eleven and there were limits, she told herself, to the current obsession with cutting costs.

The traffic was surprisingly light and the cab dropped her outside Queen Anne's Gate with ten minutes to spare. *En route* to the conference room on the fourth floor, she shared a lift with two of the New Scotland Yard people and they spent half a minute or so exchanging small-talk about the morning's headlines. There were City rumours about a big financial scandal in Singapore. Someone from a UK bank had been taking crazy positions on the Tokyo stock market and the fall-out was substantial.

The lift door opened and Louise led the way along the corridor to the room at the end. The deputy permanent secretary was already sitting at the head of the long table, his papers carefully arranged in front of him. Although the Home Secretary, technically, had ordered the F4 division of his police department to convene the meeting, Louise knew that the real concern had come from the civil servants. The interdepartmental turf wars were getting out of hand. MI5 designs on areas of traditional policing were increasingly blatant. Something had to be resolved before the squabbling in the nursery woke the grown-ups.

Five minutes later the meeting started. Louise was part of a three-strong delegation from MI5 and she sat in silence for nearly an hour, listening to the heavyweights slugging it out. The Assistant Commissioner from the Yard was obdurate about the precise limits of police responsibility. Clean-up rates, he grimly reminded the meeting, depended essentially on secure convictions. And convictions, in turn, were the consequence of evidence. Without evidence, properly gathered and fully admissible in court, there would be no prospect of bringing a single investigation to a successful conclusion. So where did that leave the shadowy ciphers from MI5? Men and women who couldn't appear in court without the shield of a curtain and an alias?

He looked around, tabling the question, registering his own antipathy with an indifferent shrug. The law was the law. The police were the proper agency to enforce it. The gentlemen from Thames House, while a useful source of background intelligence, surely had wars of their own to fight.

The Assistant Commissioner's sidekick stirred. Mickey Allder was a tiny florid man with a reputation for a short fuse. One of his hands-on responsibilities was the Met's substantial Special Branch, six hundred strong. He would, he said acidly, value a little practical guidance. His men were operating in the dark. They'd always acted as the front office for MI5, assuming co-operation at every level, but on more and more operations they were bumping into bodies from Thames House who had neither right nor reason to be there. Lately, it had got beyond a joke. People had given up talking to each other. Was this really the way to run the forces of law and order in a so-called modern democracy?

The deputy permanent secretary looked pained. 'Examples?' he murmured.

Allder had been expecting that and he turned, at once, on Louise. He knew very well that she headed F7, the task force responsible for monitoring fringe political groups. Indeed, she and his Special Branch co-ordinator often pooled intelligence but this partnership depended on a degree of trust on both sides. So what role was she playing in the current National Front operation? He leaned forward, shadowing his blotter, spelling out the detail. Five had got a blanket intercept order on a number of NF phone lines. On the face of it they'd been scrupulous about sharing the intelligence yield. They'd read the ministerial edicts about collaboration in the interests of efficiency and justice and they were insisting that they had no other agenda. Yet day by day he was seeing reports from around the country that indicated something very different on the ground.

Louise abandoned her doodles and looked up. She liked declarations of war. They gave life a certain edge.

'Meaning?' She smiled at him.

'Meaning you're putting bodies into play. Quite needlessly.'

'Duplicating effort?'

'Getting in our way.'

'How? Where?'

The little policeman leaned back in his chair, arms crossed. On the south coast he'd come across a prime example. Young German lad. A name that cropped up time and again in the telephone transcripts.

'Haagen Schreck?' Louise had seen it coming.

'Yes. You're denying an interest?'

'On the contrary.'

'You know we're already watching him?'

'Yes, as a matter of fact.'

'Then why are you bothering?'

Louise offered Allder a motherly smile. She was about to describe the security considerations that made Haagen Schreck a legitimate MI5 target when the deputy permanent secretary intervened. 'This is operational,' he said pointedly, glancing at his watch. 'Let's keep to the big picture.' He looked down the table at Louise. 'I suggest you two get together this afternoon. Might that be fruitful?'

Louise was still watching Allder. Denied a full-blown row, he was scribbling furiously on the pad at his elbow. At length, he looked up.

'Delighted,' he snapped.

Liz Barnaby was back in Portsmouth before midday. She drove through the centre of the city, following the swirl of traffic around the new one-way system. In Southsea she parked on the double yellow line outside Haagen's basement flat. She picked up her bag and locked the car. She could hear music coming from Haagen's flat and knew he had to be in.

He answered her second knock. The scar on his face that she'd glimpsed a couple of days earlier looked infinitely worse close up, a livid welt of tissue that sliced down across his cheek.

'It's you.' He stepped back. 'Come in.'

Nonplussed by his matter-of-factness, Liz did as she was told, bracing herself for the stench. The last time she'd been here, rescuing Jessie's pathetic bundle of belongings, the place had been a tip. Now, to her astonishment, there was a pleasant smell of fresh flowers. She followed Haagen into the big room at the front. A proper table stood in the bay window, covered with a heavy chenille drape. Beside a chessboard and a pile of books was a glass bowl full of fruit. She looked round. In front of the hissing gas fire were two leather-bound armchairs, a little scuffed but otherwise well preserved, and between them stood a low wooden table, piled high with yet more books. The flowers were on the mantelpiece, a bunch of fresh-looking freesias in a fluted china vase. The only reminder of the old Haagen was Oz, his beloved bull terrier, sprawled in front of the fire, asleep.

Haagen was waving her into one of the armchairs. Did she want tea? Coffee? Liz loosened the silk scarf at her neck. For a hideous moment she wondered whether Jessie might already be back here, out in the kitchen maybe, but then she remembered the call on the car phone, and the child yelling in the background, and dismissed the thought. Not even Jessie could be that devious.

Haagen was looking at her, amused. 'Nothing?'

'I'm sorry?'

'To drink?'

Liz shook her head, desperate now to regain the initiative. She'd come with one intention only and she wasn't leaving without the answer she needed. 'I want to make you an offer,' she said brusquely. 'Give you a present, if you like. Only there are strings.'

Haagen sank into one of the armchairs, gesturing at the other, but Liz ignored the invitation. To sit down would be to accept his hospitality. The last thing she needed was any form of indebtedness.

'I have a cheque for a thousand pounds.' She touched her bag. 'It's yours on one condition.'

'What's that?'

'You leave the country.'

At first, Liz thought Haagen was going to laugh. Instead, he leaned back, the armchair swallowing his slight frame.

'Why should I do that?' he asked at last.

'Because I want you out of my daughter's life.'

Haagen took off his glasses and began to polish them. For the first time, Liz saw the fan of typescript at his feet, pages and pages of it.

'What makes you think there's anything between us?'

'You're telling me there isn't?'

'No, I'm asking you why you think that way. She's not around any more. She's getting herself straightened out. Good decision. Very wise move.'

Liz was taken aback. This was a new Haagen, not at all the cocky young thug she'd met last year.

'You've been writing her letters,' Liz said carefully.

'She told you that?'

'Yes.' Liz nodded. 'It's true, isn't it?'

Haagen didn't reply but got up and left the room. Next door, from the kitchen, Liz heard the clatter of cups. When he returned, he was carrying a small wooden tray. Against her better judgement, Liz at last sat down and accepted a cup of tea.

'Well?' she said.

Haagen was tidying the typescript into a pile. The dog had woken up and was nosing wetly around Liz's ankles.

'A thousand's not enough,' he said. 'And I need to know about the rest of it.'

'Rest of it?'

'These strings of yours.' He pointed at her bag beside the armchair. 'What exactly am I supposed to do?'

Liz took a deep breath. She'd worked out most of it on the drive back. The rest she'd make up as she went along.

'I'd lodge the money at a travel agency. They'd give you a ticket home and the balance in currency. I'd want you to promise me you'd stay away for at least a year.'

'You want me to sign something?'

'There's no point. I'll accept your word.' She stared at him. 'And I'll expect you to keep it.'

Haagen patted the dog and adjusted the flame on the gas fire. He was wearing a green collarless shirt and a pair of nicely cut jeans. With his round gold-rimmed glasses, and his look of intense concentration, he might have passed for the kind of student Liz had always wanted Jessie to meet.

'Where's home supposed to be?' Haagen was asking. 'As a matter of interest.'

'Germany, I imagine. That's what Jessie always told me.'

'You think I've got relatives there? Somewhere to stay? Somewhere to call my own?'

'I've no idea.'

'You think it's that easy? Just up and go?'

'Probably not.' Liz reached down for her bag, suddenly wanting to get this scene over. 'Two thousand. I'm afraid that's my limit.'

Haagen sat back in the chair again, his legs crossed beneath him. His smile was emptied of everything except curiosity. He gestured round: the wall-mounted spotlights, the framed poster advertising pre-war Baden-Baden, the neat rows of paperbacks on home-made shelves.

'This is as good as it's ever got,' he said. 'Why should I leave it? Why should I just bail out?'

'I can think of reasons.'

'Like?'

'Like it's not your country, not your home. And it must be difficult getting by sometimes . . .' She moved uneasily in the chair. 'I take it you don't have a job?'

'I'm busy. I work.' He waved at the typescript on the floor. 'But you're right. It doesn't pay.'

'Then take it with you. Whatever it is.'

Haagen said nothing, and for a moment Liz had the feeling she was making progress. 'You need to be gone within a week,' she said. 'That's the other condition. I'll lodge the cheque with Thomas Cook. They'll have instructions to return it to me if you don't cash it in for a ticket and currency. You know how to find Thomas Cook?'

Haagen looked up at her. His eyes were the lightest blue.

'Five thousand,' he said quietly. 'And we'll shake on it.'

'*Five?*'

'Yes.' He got to his feet, a hint of the old contempt back in his face. 'This country is falling apart. It has nothing left for me, nothing. Five thousand's cheap. You should call it an investment.'

Hayden Barnaby dialled Kate's mobile from the private aviation terminal at Zurich airport. Through the double-glazed windows, he could see the swept taxiways, black ribbons against the startling white of the morning's snowfall. Zhu was still aboard the little executive jet out on the apron. The pilot had already filed a flight plan for the final leg to London. As soon as refuelling was complete, they'd be off.

At last Kate answered the phone. She sounded irritable, as if she wasn't pleased to hear from him, but when Barnaby asked her why she dismissed it. Time of the month, she said briskly. Plus one or two other little niggles.

Barnaby glanced at his watch. They'd be touching down at Heathrow around five. He could be back in Central London by early evening. He'd booked a hotel. He'd meet her there.

'Where?'

'The Orchid. Same as last time.'

'I'm tied up,' she said at once. 'Until late.'

'In town?'

'Yes.'

'How late?' Barnaby's impatience showed in his voice. He'd hardly slept at all on the hopscotch flight back from Singapore, bemused by the number of airports *en route* where Zhu needed to touch down to attend brief meetings.

Kate was talking about some party contacts from Blair's private office. She knew a couple of staffers there, people she'd run into at conference. They were getting together for a drink and a meal. It could be important for her.

'Obviously.'

'I mean it. The parliamentary selection meeting's in a couple of days. Every contact counts. Believe me.'

Barnaby was watching the fuel bowser beside the tiny jet. The driver was disconnecting the hose and wiping the drips of fuel from the crescent of fuselage beneath the filler pipe. In a couple of minutes they'd be ready to leave.

'Maybe you should go straight home,' Kate was saying. 'Perhaps that would be best.'

'Home?'

'Portsmouth. I could see you tomorrow. There might be time for lunch.'

Barnaby frowned, trying to clear the fog of indecision in his brain. A night at the Orchid had been part of their plans since he'd learned of the trip to Singapore. They'd have the evening in town. The'd have a meal, the chance to catch up with each other, the chance to talk. Going home was inconceivable.

'I'll see you at the hotel,' he said briefly. 'Whenever you can make it.'

Owens was trying to manhandle the dog out of the back of his estate car when he heard the knocking at the upstairs window. He stood upright in the icy drive, the golden retriever sagging in his arms, seeing the shadowy outline of his wife behind the net curtains. She had one hand raised to her ear, their private semaphore for an urgent phone call. Owens stepped back, breathless, trying to close the tailgate with his foot. The sudden adjustment as he nearly lost his balance made the dog stir. Still sleepy after the anaesthetic, it raised its head and looked round, bemused.

Owens struggled indoors. He could hear his wife coming downstairs. She was wearing his plaid dressing gown, tightly belted, and he was glad to see a bit of colour back in her face. She passed him the cordless phone. 'The office,' she said, bending to inspect the dog.

Owens lifted the phone. For once in his life he'd formally booked a day off, and he'd made a point of asking his oppo to be sensible about calls. Only real emergencies, he'd said. And only if there's no other bugger around.

'DS Owens,' he grunted.

He heard an unfamiliar voice at the other end. He thought he caught the word 'Commander' but he wasn't sure. Finally it dawned on him that he was talking to someone from the Met.

'Who are you on about?'

'Schreck. Haagen Schreck. Your guv'nor said he was down to you.'

'He is. Sort of. Why?'

'Long story. Your guv'nor's got the details. Give him a ring, will you?'

The line went dead and Owens looked at the phone. His wife and the dog were locked in a sloppy embrace across the kitchen table. In the absence of kids, the dog had always been the target for some heavy rapport.

Owens took the phone next door. The lounge was dominated by trophies from his fishing expeditions. As well as photographs and the odd cup, there was a big scrapbook full of press cuttings. Owens sank into the armchair beneath the 15-pound mounted pike, not bothering to undo the buttons on his raincoat. He'd been through leave days like this before. He knew the pattern only too well.

The superintendent answered his call on the second ring. Bairstow wasn't a man to soften a conversation with anything remotely domestic. As far as he was concerned, Owens could have been in an office downstairs.

'The Met were on,' he said.

'I know. Bloke just phoned.'

'About that German kid? Our Nazi friend?'

'Yeah.'

'OK. Got a pencil handy?'

Owens found a biro on the mantelpiece. In the absence of paper, he used the palm of his hand. Schreck had been under surveillance for a couple of days. The guys involved had been from London, not local. They'd staked out his flat and this afternoon they'd followed him to the nearby shopping precinct. There, he'd collected £2,800 in foreign currency, plus a rail ticket.

Owens frowned. His hand wasn't that big and he was fast running out of space.

'Where to?' he said.

'Amsterdam, via Brussels. Eurostar for the first bit.' Owens could hear the shuffle of papers on the superintendent's desk. 'The currency is part guilders, part US dollars. I've got the breakdown here. It's mostly dollars.'

'So where is he now?'

'Back in his flat. According to the travel agency, the Eurostar ticket's booked for tomorrow. Ten thirty-five out of Waterloo.'

'And what do the Met boys say?'

'Which Met boys?'

'The guys who've been doing the leg work? The ones you mentioned just now.'

'Ah, now there's a thing.' The superintendent's voice hardened. 'Turns out they weren't Met boys at all. They were MI5. The Yard's been trying to sort it out all afternoon. Latest I hear, we're taking precedence. Not only that but the Met wants us to handle it this end. Must be desperate, trusting us. I'm looking at the currency now.'

'What currency?'

'Yours, son. He'll take the train to Waterloo. Bound to. You're with him on the Eurostar as well. Same carriage.' He erupted, a bark of derisive laughter. 'First bloody class.'

*

When Barnaby awoke in the hotel room, Kate was standing at the foot of the big double bed. 'The door was open,' she said. 'I just gave it a push.'

Barnaby got up on one elbow, rubbing his face. His jacket hung over the back of a nearby chair and his shoes were on the floor somewhere but he was still fully dressed.

'Must have dropped off.' He swung his legs off the bed. 'How are you?'

'Fine. How about you?'

'Knackered. Come here.'

Kate didn't move. Her trench-coat was unbuttoned, and underneath he could see the black skirt and low-cut scarlet top she favoured for special occasions.

'What's the time?' Barnaby asked.

'Gone nine.'

'Good evening? Meet your chums OK?'

Kate studied him a moment, then stepped back towards the door and shut it. Crossing the room, she pulled the curtains over the dormer windows before running her fingertips over the back of the armchair in the corner, feeling the heavy brocade.

'Nice,' she said.

Barnaby was still watching her. The boots looked brand new, black leather, knee-length. He began to wonder who she'd dressed up for.

'Where did you go?'

'Belgravia. Little French place.'

'Good?'

'Excellent. Very tasteful. Very understated. Kind of restaurant that makes you feel . . . I don't know . . . metropolitan, I suppose.'

'And what was the food like?'

'I'm not sure. It looked lovely.'

'Didn't you eat?'

'No, there was no point.' She raised a thin smile. 'He didn't turn up.'

'Why not?'

'God knows. You tell me.'

She turned away, slipped off the coat and hung it carefully in the wardrobe. Only then did she join him, sitting on the edge of the bed, her back towards him, her hands clenched tightly in her lap. Barnaby kissed the nape of her neck. He could feel how cold she was, and how remote.

'Bastard.' She bit her lip. 'Bastard, bastard.'

'Who was he?'

'Doesn't matter, just a friend. Not even that. An associate, a colleague, someone I met at conference. He's highly placed, no question, a real flier and I thought . . . you know . . .' She gestured helplessly at the boots. 'Pathetic, isn't it?'

Barnaby lay back against the pillows, disturbed now, his suspicion confirmed that the ensemble hadn't been for his benefit.

'When did you fix it up? This meal?'

'Days ago. I should have expected it, I know I should, the lives these people lead. Why should I get special treatment?'

'So what happened? Where did he get to?'

'God knows. Some television station or other? New York? Washington? Brussels? Who cares?'

'Did he phone?'

'No.'

'Did you?'

'Yes, in the end I did. There's only so much you can do with a bread roll.' She sniffed, more anger than grief, her back still turned to Barnaby. 'I got through to some girl in his office. She thought he'd gone to a briefing. It's probably the standard line. When I gave her my name she'd obviously never heard of it. Bitch.'

Barnaby eyed her. When she bent over to loosen the boots, he stood up and reached for his jacket. Kate glanced round. Her face was white and pinched and her lipstick was smudged at the corner of her mouth. She looked, for once, extraordinarily vulnerable.

She got to her feet, uncertain, watching him lacing up his shoes. He walked across to the dressing table and checked his tie in the mirror, then he joined her by the bed. He could smell the perfume he'd left under her pillow on Christmas Eve. To his knowledge it was the first time she'd worn it.

'Hungry?' he murmured.

She looked up at him. Then she grinned the old grin. 'Starving.'

They ate at a Moroccan restaurant round the corner in Knights-bridge, Kate's choice. They had a tagine of chicken and prunes with a steaming mountain of couscous and were half-way through the second bottle of red wine by the time Barnaby finished enthusing about Singapore.

His visit, he admitted, had been conducted at breakneck speed and all he could offer was a series of snapshots, but first impressions were important and it was hard to do justice to the impact the place had made on him. OK, their democracy was a thin excuse for one-party rule, and the government came up with comic-book ideas like Courtesy Month and the National Ideals and Identity Programme, but this was a small price to pay for a society that so manifestly worked. A pulse beat through Singapore. You could feel it on the streets and in the shopping malls. These people had a pride in the lives they led, the society they'd built, the ends to which they put their working hours. He'd visited hospitals, schools and public housing projects that put Britain's equivalents to shame. On the streets he'd seen no graffiti, no litter, no beggars. Every-where he'd been, he'd met nothing but courtesy and a determination to make things better. To someone from the UK, with its tired culture and weary sense of personal defeat, this brimming optimism had felt, at first, like a piss-take. Could these people possibly mean it? Had they really built this gleaming city? They undoubtedly had – and, to his astonishment, by the week's end he'd buried his cynicism and concluded that this little glimpse of the future was absolutely for real.

Kate looked at him over the tiny vase of wild mint. She was tackling the last of the chicken leg with her hands, shredding the meat from the bone.

'I get the feeling you liked it,' she said drily.

'I loved it.'

'No reservations? None at all?'

Barnaby thought of his visit to the prison. Corporal punishment, in the flesh, was abhorrent. No question. But a bare ten minutes' conversation with the rehab unit's director had prompted him to look at the issue anew. There was a tariff for caning. Any inmate who physically attacked another got three strokes. Someone drug-testing positive could expect six. It was brutal justice but all the surveys suggested that, once again, it worked. The only benchmark that mattered in Singapore was success, and given the enormous challenge of trying to wrestle someone away from drug addiction, who could say that caning should be banned?

Barnaby wiped his mouth with his napkin and recharged his glass. His visit to Changi had touched another nerve, altogether more personal.

'Jessie's apparently bailed out of the rehab place,' he said. 'I tried to phone her last night.'

'Does that worry you?'

'Of course it does.' He grimaced. 'Liz says she's in Guildford with some friend or other.'

'You've talked to Liz, then?'

'Yes.' He smiled. 'She's my wife.'

'And she knows you're here, in London?'

'No, she thinks I'm still in Zurich. With Zhu.'

Kate reached for her glass. The second bottle of wine was nearly empty.

'Maybe we should go public,' she said softly. 'Would you drink to that?'

Barnaby returned her smile. Exhaustion was catching up with him again. The last thing he needed was another lap or two around this particular track. 'I'd drink to anything,' he said lightly. 'As long as it was just you and me.'

'But it isn't, is it? It's you and me and Liz and poor Jessie and your home and that wonderful view you keep telling me about and . . .' She frowned, six fingers raised. 'Shall I go on?'

'I'd prefer you didn't.'

'I bet you would.' She leaned forward, the candlelight spilling shadows over her cleavage. 'I've missed you, Hayden, and this is just another way of saying it. I'm a quarrelsome old bat. Take no notice.'

'I won't.'

'No?'

She was waiting for an answer, and he captured her fingers, giving them a little squeeze, a private signal that it might be time for bed. Kate withdrew her hand. The dessert menu was beside the wine and she opened it. Barnaby watched her eyes go filmy as she tried to concentrate.

'Tell me about Zhu,' she said absently. 'Get to know him, did you? Pals now?'

'Not really, he's not that kind of guy. We spent time together, of course, but the whole thing was tightly organized. Lots to see, lots to find out. No.' He shook his head. 'I wouldn't call him a friend.'

'What then? A patron? A benefactor? The tooth fairy?'

'No, he's a client, that's all.'

'Pretty mega client.'

'Of course, but a client nevertheless.' Barnaby began to fold his napkin. 'He's been talking about more buys in Portsmouth. I don't think capital's a problem and he seems fond of the place. The Imperial's been a doddle, a real delight. If there are any more in the pipeline like that . . .' He left the sentence unfinished. Kate's foot had found his leg under the table. He could feel the soft leather of her boot running up and down the inside of his calf.

'You really think there'll be more?'

'God knows. We all have our fantasies and Zhu just might be mine.'

'I think he is.'

'Why?'

'You should have heard your voice on the phone from Singapore. You were like a kid in a toy shop. It's been a while since I heard you like that.'

'Yeah,' Barnaby conceded, wryly. 'It's been a while since anyone made that kind of fuss of me.'

He held up both hands at once, stemming the flood of mock sympathy. Sober or drunk, Kate knew him inside out and what made it worse was the knowledge that he loved it that way. It spoke of the deepest intimacy, a delicious violation that occasionally overwhelmed him. Kate could be rough, abrasive, demanding, illogical, and selfish, but none of that had ever altered the fact that he loved her in ways he'd never thought remotely possible.

'Tell me about your meeting,' he said.

'Meeting?'

'The constituency thing. Your big chance.'

'Ah . . .' She leaned back in the chair, nursing her glass of wine, rehearsing the line she'd take before the constituency membership. The nomination was there for the taking, she said. Frank Perry, her main rival, had been at it far too long for his own good and she knew there was a real appetite amongst the membership for change. Everyone in the local party would have a vote and a simple majority would see her adopted as constituency parliamentary candidate. Given the rightward shift in Labour's leadership, and the residue of doubts about what had been left behind, she'd decided to pitch it dead centre. The market should deliver but the people should profit. Health and education should be top priorities, but taxation shouldn't strangle enterprise. People should have obligations as well as rights. Looking out for your neighbour was as important as looking out for yourself.

'Sounds like Singapore,' Barnaby said softly, listening to her ticking off the phrases one by one, aware of her eagerness and her hunger, wondering how much of this pretty speech she'd been rehearsing for her earlier date.

She was talking about Europe now. She was pro the Social Chapter but against a big Brussels bureaucracy. One of the things she'd wanted to check with her New Labour friend was the leadership's line on QMV.

'QMV?'

'Qualified Majority Voting.'

'Ah.' Barnaby had reached for the dessert menu. The waiter was hovering again. Barnaby looked up, wondering aloud about the warm figs in Madeira, but Kate was already fumbling under the table for her bag. She produced a credit card from her wallet and gave it to the waiter. When Barnaby protested, she got up, shaking the creases out of her coat.

'I thought you were still hungry?'

'I am. I thought we might go to bed.' She grinned down at

him, waiting for the Visa slip. 'I don't want to sound political,' she said, 'but here's a promise.'

'What's that?'

Kate bent to his ear. Her breath was warm on his cheek. 'When it comes to me getting screwed,' she squeezed his hand, 'you can do it any way you like.'

Owens had nearly finished sucking his second Strepsil of the morning when he saw the taxi turning into the top of Elphinstone Road. He watched it squeal to a halt outside Haagen's basement flat, the driver leaning on the horn.

'We're on,' he muttered throatily.

The duty CID driver beside him was deep in a copy of the *Daily Mail*. She looked up to see Haagen appear on the pavement. He was wearing jeans and a thick green anorak, and he was carrying a black holdall. Seconds later, the taxi was on the move and the CID girl followed at a discreet distance. When they got to the harbour station, Owens checked his watch. The fast Waterloo train left in seven minutes' time. So far he'd got it exactly right.

He reached behind him, hauling out his own bag. His wife had washed it twice since the last competition but she still hadn't got rid of the fishy smell. Haagen was out of the taxi now, twenty yards ahead, paying the driver. Any minute now he'd look up.

'Sorry about the cold.' Owens was genuinely apologetic. 'But you'd better kiss me.'

An hour and a half later, he was tracking Haagen across the concourse at Waterloo. The new international station was on a lower level and Owens let him get to the foot of the escalator before riding down. In the departure lounge, Haagen treated himself to a cappuccino and what looked like a Danish pastry. When the Brussels departure was ready for boarding, Owens took a chance and stationed himself at the head of the queue. His Eurostar seat allocation put him four rows in front of Haagen and he knew that the best cover of all lay in being first on the train. If Haagen saw him already seated, he'd hardly suspect surveillance.

First class on the brand-new train was quietly comfortable and

Owens settled himself beside the window. He'd bought a copy of *Angling Times* in the departure lounge and he was half-way through an article on ground bait when the train plunged into the Channel Tunnel. Twenty minutes later they were out again, picking up speed for the dash to Lille, and he sat back, watching the flat expanse of Picardy unrolling beyond the occasional blur of a track-side building. The CID girl who'd driven him to the station had given him a mobile phone that would hook into the European digital network, and when the train stopped for signals in the suburbs of Tournai, he tried it out. Back in Portsmouth Bairstow had appointed himself Owen's primary contact, and Owens got through to him without difficulty. As usual, they'd agreed the simplest of codes and Owens signed off after less than a minute's conversation. 'Tell Derek I think it'll probably be OK,' he said. 'I'll get back to you again when there's more news.'

In Brussels, Haagen and Owens changed trains. Like Haagen, Owens's ticket took him through to Amsterdam but this time he rode in a different carriage. The train was Dutch, a long yellow thing, and it wound slowly up through Belgium and into Holland, stopping at station after station. Each stop found Owens in his seat beside the pneumatic door, his bag at his feet, his eyes never leaving the platform. Haagen was riding in a carriage at the end of the train. If he chose to get off, he'd have to pass Owens. And if that happened, Owens would be out too.

By four o'clock the train was easing into Amsterdam's central station. In the busy forecourt, amongst the crush of bicycles, Haagen paused beside the taxi rank, consulting his watch. Owens was still inside the station entrance, half hidden by an advertising display, and when Haagen abandoned the taxi rank for a nearby tram stop, he stepped out, pushing his way through the crowds of commuters hurrying into the station. Across the cobbled forecourt, he could see Haagen at the back of a long queue. There were trams everywhere. One stopped, hiding Haagen from view, Owens began to sprint. To lose him now would look foolish indeed. A vision of Bairstow swam into his mind. Running errands for the Met was far from uncommon but there was something about this operation that had got under the superintendent's skin. Owens had caught it in his voice when he'd used the mobile phone. He was paranoid by nature but he'd sounded even more suspicious than usual. Phoning in again to report a blank would really make his day.

The tram was beginning to move. The kerbside queue was down to three women. Of Haagen there was no sign. Owens headed for the nearest taxi, cursing. Then he stopped. He'd kept track of the passengers as they'd filed onto the tram. He was certain that Haagen hadn't been amongst them.

On the other side of a canal a big main road ran left to right, thick with traffic. At right angles to the main road, spearing into the heart of the city, was a wide boulevard. The traffic lights at red, Owens joined the flood of pedestrians crossing. On the other side, he knew he had to make a decision.

He stopped again, trying to visualize the map he'd committed to memory on the train. Left, right or straight on, three options, a 33 per cent chance of not fucking up. He was about to settle on the second option, the boulevard into the city, when he spotted the cluster of phone kiosks. Haagen was in the nearest one, his back turned, his hand chopping up and down on the thin metal shelf as he made a series of emphatic points. Owens backed away slowly, the adrenaline washing through his system. Haagen had a notebook out. He was scribbling something down, the phone wedged between his shoulder and his ear. Any minute now the conversation would be over.

Owens felt a nudge in the small of his back and turned to find himself beside a florist's stall. The woman was holding out a bunch of early daffodils. Owens took them without a word, fumbling for a twenty-guilder note. By the time the woman had tallied the change, he was thirty metres away, hurrying along beside the canal, trying to make the corner before Haagen disappeared again.

It was nearly dark by the time Ellis found the entrance to the drive. On the phone to the ministry, Zhu had been surprisingly vague in his directions, telling Ellis that the house was half-way between

Wentworth and Bagshot. Only on his third pass had Ellis found the sign indicating Bentwaters.

He followed the drive between thick hedges of dripping laurel. At the end, beyond a turning circle of newly laid black tarmac, stood a substantial, brick-built house flanked on both sides by double garages. Ellis parked behind a white delivery van and got out. Beside the front door was a big iron bell-pull. He yanked on it twice but heard nothing. He was about to try again when the door opened. Zhu was dressed exactly the way he'd first seen him at Heathrow, the baggy cotton shirt hanging on his thin frame. Ellis shook the outstretched hand and stepped inside. The hall was enormous, panelled in oak. At the foot of the stairs that led to the first-floor gallery were a number of heavy-duty cardboard boxes. Some were open and inside, cradled in white polystyrene, Ellis could see computer terminals and keyboards.

Zhu led the way into a lounge. At the far end of the room, a Labrador lay in front of a roaring log fire. Through big french windows, in the gathering dusk, Ellis glimpsed a stone-flagged terrace and beyond it, still crusted with snow, an expanse of lawn.

At Zhu's invitation, Ellis sank into one of the plump armchairs beside the fire. A tray of tea had already appeared and Zhu was bent over the pot, peering down at the thin yellow liquid. As ever, he had no interest in small-talk.

'Thank you for coming,' he said. 'I have a proposition.'

Ellis put his attaché case on his knees and opened it. The case was on loan from MI5 and Louise Carlton hadn't let him leave Thames House without proving to the F branch technicians that he could operate it. The microphone was built into the bottom of the case and Ellis moved his chair a little, ensuring that the case was angled directly at Zhu.

Zhu was pouring the tea. 'You'll know we've placed an order for the equipment.'

'Of course.' Most of the counter-insurgency stuff in the original deal that the DTI had helped facilitate was coming from a company in Derby. Their quote had been substantially less keen than the rest but, quality-wise, their products were in a different league. Zhu's judgement in this respect had attracted much comment within the ministry. Businessmen with an interest in excellence, rather than the bottom line, were an increasingly rare breed.

'And you'll know our client intends to place supplementary orders?'

'So I hear.'

'Good.' Zhu's hand hovered enquiringly over the sugar bowl. Ellis shook his head, curious to know where this conversation might lead. Discreet enquiries in Singapore had capitalized Zhu's various stockholdings at a fraction over $857 million. By anyone's standards, that made him a very rich man indeed. Hence, perhaps, his acquisition of a property like Bentwaters. If you were looking for a UK base, somewhere with a bit of privacy but a global reach, you could do worse than a £1.4 million mansion in the Surrey woods, stuffed full of computers.

Ellis accepted the tea, balancing the saucer on his attaché case. The hope in Whitehall was that Zhu would cap this first order with something truly substantial. Armoured vehicles, perhaps, or something in the guided missiles line.

'Does your client have a time-frame for whatever he needs next?' Ellis asked.

'Yes. Very soon now I hope to have the documentation.'

'And do you want us to arrange another meeting? At Victoria Street?'

'That may well be necessary. Unless, of course, we meet here.' Zhu beamed, already very much at home.

Ellis said something polite about the panelwork in the hall. He asked about the age of the property and Zhu said he didn't know. Maybe the nineteen thirties. Maybe earlier. He was standing by the fire now, gazing down at the dog.

'I've been in Portsmouth,' he said at last. 'You know Portsmouth?' Ellis shook his head. Zhu's file had recorded a number of recent visits to the south coast and full details of his purchase of a local hotel. Quite where this fitted into his portfolio was a mystery, although he had hotel interests back in Singapore.

'Nice place, Portsmouth,' Ellis remarked.

'Very pleasant. Good people.' The dog began to stir and Zhu

tickled its ear with a slippered foot. 'Good prospects too. I like it there.'

He glanced up, a slightly contemplative smile on his face. Outside, in the hall, Ellis could hear a whispered conversation about cable ducting.

'They have a dockyard,' Zhu was musing, 'down in Portsmouth.'

Ellis reached for his tea. 'That's right. Home of the Royal Navy. Always has been.'

'So I understand.' Zhu's attention had returned to the dog. 'How would I go about buying it?'

Owens waited until he'd crossed the road before he made the call. From the corner, beside the canal bridge, he could still see the entrance to the café and the men in profile drinking at the bar. Most were watching football on the television at the end. The couple beside Haagen were locked in a gentle embrace.

Owens checked his watch, wondering why Bairstow wouldn't answer his phone. After half past seven he'd said he'd be at home, and it was already way past eight. At long last the call was answered.

'Me,' Owens said, turning his body towards the canal, dispensing with the code. 'He's in a bar in Amsterdam. It's a pick-up, I swear it.'

'Pick up what?'

'Fuck knows. It's in his holdall. And it cost him a fair bit. He paid in US dollars. At least two grand's worth.'

'What did it look like?'

'It's in packets.'

'Big? Small?'

Owens frowned, picturing the way he stored his fishing bait. 'Tobacco tins,' he said. 'Eight-ounce.'

'Resin?'

'Could be.'

'Something heavier?'

'Maybe.' Owens glanced over his shoulder. Haagen was buying another drink. For someone holding, he was either brainless or the goodies had already left with someone else. Either way, Owens needed orders.

He bent over the phone again. 'What do you want me to do?'

He heard a grunt at the other end. Lights from the street were dancing on the black waters of the canal. Bairstow was back on the phone. He wanted to know more about Haagen. Where had he been? Who had he met? Owens felt his patience beginning to wear thin. Put the big guys behind a desk, he thought, and they rapidly lose touch.

'He's been nowhere,' he said. 'He's made a phone call, he's walked from the station to the bar, and now he's sitting on a couple of thousand dollars' worth of something naughty.' He stepped back to let a bicycle sweep past. 'Shall I talk to the locals? Get him pulled in?'

At the other end there was a minor explosion. It sounded like a sneeze and Owens was suddenly back in the world of soggy tissues and hourly doses of throat linctus. Then Bairstow was coherent again. On no account was Owens to think in terms of arrest. Haagen was to run and run. In the end Owens would lose him but that wouldn't be an issue. The more they had on the boy the better it would be.

Owens was getting lost. 'Better for who?' he said. 'Who are we talking about?'

There was a brief, mirthless bark of laughter. Then Bairstow was back on the line. 'Don't ask me, son,' he snorted, 'I'm only a fucking policeman.'

Chapter Eight

Two days later Louise Carlton drove out to the Heathrow Marriott hotel for breakfast. It was still early, barely seven, but the eastbound M4 was already at a virtual standstill, three lines of headlights crawling slowly through the thin drizzle. She left her Saab in the hotel car park and asked reception to check whether David Jephson had yet arrived. The F branch director was booked on the first BA flight out of Brussels. According to the directorate schedule faxed to her home last night, he should have landed twenty minutes ago.

The young American behind the reception desk had no news of Jephson. Louise thanked him and followed the stream of executives into the hotel restaurant. Breakfast was served from a buffet and she lingered beside the chafing dishes of scrambled eggs and newly grilled sausages, wondering how long she could hold out. The drive over from her house in Kew had been simplicity itself but getting up at five thirty had sharpened her appetite and, savouring the smell of bacon and fresh coffee, she realized just how hungry she'd become.

She was weighing the possibility of two separate breakfasts when she felt the lightest pressure on her elbow. As ever, Jephson was immaculate: the dark suit perfectly cut, the black brogues newly polished, the crisp white shirt carrying the subtlest blue stripe. Louise submitted to a kiss on the cheek and then shepherded him towards the queue for cereals, marvelling at the man's stamina. At noon, he was due to address a closed-door gathering of chief constables at the ACPO conference in Leeds. Just getting there by road would take at least three hours. Yet here he was, eyeing the kippers as if time was the least of his problems.

They carried their trays to a corner by the emergency exit. The nearest occupied table was comfortably out of earshot. Jephson slipped his mobile phone out of his pocket and turned it off before storing it in his briefcase. He was currently commuting to Brussels on a near-weekly basis, attending regular meetings of one of the Europol working groups. This was an arrangement that should, fingers crossed, give MI5 the key intelligence liaison role between UK law-enforcement agencies and sister organizations on the continent. In the brave new world of transnational policing, this was a very big prize indeed and, as a direct consequence, the bureaucratic in-fighting was ferocious. The Metropolitan Police were convinced that the responsibility was properly theirs, and Jephson's elegant reports from Brussels, circulated around Whitehall, had become a legend at Thames House. They were, in the parlance, Five's very own smart bomb, scoring direct hit after direct hit on the uniformed bodies over at New Scotland Yard. Whether or not MI5 would prevail was anyone's guess, but Jephson had turned the exercise into a textbook campaign, winning the agency the kind of friends who might, in time, turn the tide of battle.

Now, loading his fried bread with grilled tomato, Jephson wanted to know about Haagen Schreck. The last of Louise's encrypted reports had reached him eighteen hours ago in Brussels. The youth had left Amsterdam aboard a KLM flight for Heathrow. Intelligence from Hampshire Special Branch suggested he was carrying a quantity of unspecified narcotics and a call to the Customs and Excise controller at Terminal Four had cleared his path through the green channel. A team of watchers from A branch had picked him up on the arrivals concourse and followed him into Central London. He'd visited two addresses in Shepherd's Bush, both belonging to known drug dealers. Emerging from the second address, a three-storey terrace house off Goldhawk Road, he'd no longer been carrying his holdall.

Jephson reached for his coffee. 'Where did it get to?'

'We're assuming he left it there.'

'Anyone tempted to find out?'

'Not so far, thank God.'

Jephson concealed a grin with his napkin. New Scotland Yard

and Thames House were often looking for different yields from an operation. In an instance like this, with the net closing around an original MI5 target, it could often be difficult to dissuade the drugs squad sharp-end heavies from forcing the pace.

'What did you tell them?'

'We're saying he should run.'

'Rationale?'

'Unspecified. If they really push it, I think we should take it to the top.'

The beginnings of a frown shadowed Jephson's face. The top, in the first instance, meant the Home Secretary. Thereafter, at his discretion, referral could reach as far as Downing Street.

Jephson picked warily at a disc of black pudding. 'You're confident about this?' he murmured. 'If we have to show our hand?'

'Absolutely. Schreck anchors a new NF network. That's a matter of fact. He keeps it no secret. On the contrary, you can read it in his column every month if you can bother wading through the rest of the wretched paper.'

'*National Front News*?'

'Yes.'

'But what's new? What are we really saying?'

'That remains to be seen. My guess is a link between Schreck's lot and one of the bigger West London drug cartels.'

'You think he's got rid of the stuff from Amsterdam?'

'I think he's sold it on, yes.'

'Drugs money funding the extreme right?'

'Exactly.'

Jephson mopped up the last of his scrambled egg, visibly impressed. Keeping an eye on the nastier edges of the political fringe had always been accepted as a legitimate MI5 concern but recently Thames House had been eyeing a number of other areas of police work that might fall to some determined poaching. The biggest plum from this particular tree was so-called narcocrime, a phrase that covered everything from student cannabis busts to international money-laundering. Proving a link between drug money and the shock troops of the far right would be a very exciting development indeed, giving MI5 a bridgehead into the heartlands of traditional police work.

Jephson was coaxing a tablet of butter onto a triangle of toast.

'Do you think you can do it?'

'I think we're very close, yes.'

'And you think this Schreck's the key?'

'I think he'd make the point very nicely. We've no idea how much he might have made but on the usual tariff he'd have trebled his investment, at least.'

'Meaning?'

'Six thousand dollars, maybe more.'

Jephson was looking out of the window. Some of the more harassed executives were already on the forecourt waiting for the shuttle bus to the airport. Jephson lifted his cup, swallowing the last of the coffee.

'Some of the Met people will be up in Leeds,' he said thoughtfully. 'The boy Schreck. You used the word investment. What does it mean?'

'I don't know. Schreck went out to Shepperton yesterday, once he'd got his money.'

'Shepperton?' Jephson had spotted his driver. 'Why?'

'We're not sure. He went to an old farm. It belongs to a stage designer who used to work at the film studios. Evidently he still picks up private commissions.' Louise paused. 'He has a converted barn on the property. He uses it as a workshop. I'm putting someone in tonight.'

Jephson pushed back his chair. 'So what do I tell our friends in Leeds when they start whingeing about trespass again?'

'I'm not sure.' Louise smiled. 'National security? Isn't that the phrase?'

Jephson was on his feet now, reaching for his briefcase and overnight bag. He beamed down at her, apologizing for a hasty exit. Traffic on the motorways north was always a nightmare and the weather would make it worse. On the point of leaving, he was struck by a sudden thought. 'You mentioned an event in the last briefing I read,' he said. 'Anything specific?'

'Nothing confirmed.'

'But anything I should know about? Given the company I'm keeping.'

Louise permitted herself a moment's reflection. She'd taken home the logs on the NF phone taps. The codes they used were remarkably sophisticated but Louise was as certain as she could be that something was planned for the south coast. Probably Portsmouth. Probably tomorrow. Prudence argued for sharing this information but she had already decided that the longer-term advantage lay in holding off. Headlines about the menace of the National Front would be the neatest way of making MI5's case and the last thing she wanted was something promising nipped in the bud.

Jephson had his raincoat folded over his arm. He was still waiting for an answer. 'Well?'

Louise shook her head. 'Nothing definite,' she said. 'Nothing worth your while.'

'Are you sure?'

'Positive.' Her eyes went to the Thames House driver, waiting in the car outside.

Jephson hung on for a second or two, unconvinced, then turned on his heel and left. Minutes later, returning to her table with a second plate of food, Louise heard the trill of her mobile phone. She retrieved it from the Harrods bag beside her chair. It was one of the team she'd tasked to watch Schreck's flat in Southsea. He said he'd completed his enquiries at the travel agency where Schreck had picked up his ticket and the currency. According to the local manager at Thomas Cook, the covering cheque had been tendered by a Mrs Elizabeth Barnaby.

Louise wrote down the name then returned to the phone.

'Anything else?' she asked lightly.

'Yes.' The voice chuckled. 'She's married to a lawyer. Can you believe that?'

Hayden Barnaby awoke to the opening headlines on the morning news. Normally he was at the health club by eight but today, exhausted by the aftermath of his trip with Zhu, he'd overslept.

He rolled over, reaching for his wife, but found the bed empty. Liz was standing at the door in her new dressing gown. He'd bought two at Changi airport. Liz had the red one and it fitted her beautifully.

'You should have stayed there,' she said, holding out a cup of tea. 'Singapore. It's all over the news. Some trader or other. A Brit.'

'What's he done?'

'No one seems to know. He's gone missing.'

Barnaby struggled half upright in the bed, grateful for the tea. The newscaster was talking about a young merchant banker. He'd fled Singapore, leaving a large hole in the company's trading account. Liz was perched on the side of the bed, opening an envelope.

'What's that?'

'A letter. Charlie wants me to sort out the gas people before he moves down.'

'Has he got a date?'

'Apparently not. Typical, isn't it?'

Barnaby laughed. He was running his fingertips up and down Liz's back. He could feel the contours of her body through the thin silk. She began to shiver, reached back and caught his hand.

'Cold?'

'No.'

'Like it?'

'Yes.'

'The dressing gown?'

'That, too.'

Liz glanced over her shoulder. Aroused, her face acquired a fuller, softer look. She had another envelope on her lap. She opened it, pulling out a card. It came from Zhu, an exquisite nineteenth-century engraving of the view east over Southsea Common. Inside, Zhu had penned a personal invitation for Liz to join him for the opening of the newly restored Imperial. 'It will be a pleasure to repay you for your patience and your many kindnesses,' he'd written.

'But you're invited already.' Barnaby looked mystified. 'Why this?'

'He's being a gentleman. It's nice.' She read the card again. 'It means he knows how much you've put into it. The time it's taken. He's saying sorry.'

'Sorry for what?'

'Sorry for taking you away.' She folded the card and put it back in the envelope. 'Isn't that right?'

Barnaby didn't reply. He finished the tea and got out of bed. A thin rain was drifting in from the sea, a gauzy curtain that softened everything it touched. Barnaby could just make out the big wheel in the fun-fair, barely a quarter of a mile away. He yawned, stretching his arms wide, running through the checklists in his head.

As agreed, Zhu had flown in a catering team from Singapore for the reception. Once the celebrations were over, the hotel would open for normal business and one or two of the Singapore people would be staying on to help form a core group around Zhu's new manager. He, too, was Singaporean, a young Chinese with impeccable English and limitless self-confidence. He'd been working at one of the prestige hotels in Brighton and, with Zhu's money, had been able to attract some first-class people for the rest of the management posts. In this, as in everything else he touched, Zhu seemed to have a faultless gift for converting an idea, or a vision, into something that had all the makings of a solid commercial success. Over the past six months, Barnaby had watched this process at work. It had never ceased to amaze him. It was, he thought, so utterly different from the way in which the English might tackle something similar. Instead of caution, boldness. In place of buckpassing and indecision, a wholehearted preparedness to take the lead.

'Hayden?'

Barnaby glanced round, still preoccupied with everything he had to chase before tomorrow. The unacknowledged invitations on the guest list. A follow-up call to the local TV station. The full page ad in the *Sentinel*. Liz was lying on the bed, her back propped up on the pillows. The dressing gown lay open and she was naked underneath. She smiled at him, her hand opening the drawer on the bedside cabinet. She produced a tiny bottle of coconut oil and unscrewed the top. She dribbled a little into the palm of her hand and then began to rub it softly between her breasts. Barnaby watched her, feeling himself stir. In recent months, Liz had lost well over a stone. Not drinking quite so much had done wonders for their sex life, as Barnaby was the first to admit.

The bottle of oil was back on the bedside cabinet. Liz's fingers were between her thighs. She closed her eyes and told him to go downstairs. He'd find the fruit bowl on the breakfast bar and the yoghurt in the fridge. Aroused now, Barnaby fetched them. As well as bananas, there were mangoes and tangerines. He lifted a mango to his nose. He loved the smell. He put the bowl on the bed. Liz's hand found a banana. He peeled it slowly and coated it thickly in yoghurt, straddling her chest while she enfolded her breasts around him. She had big breasts, beautifully shaped, and he began to move, back and forth, very slowly, touching her on the lips with each upward stroke, drawing her tongue from her mouth. After a while, the yoghurt a little warmer, he reached back and her hand met his, taking the banana, guiding it inside herself, then letting him take over. She was moist already and he slid it in and out, an inch, no more, matching her rhythm to his own.

For a while they made love this way, Liz teasing him with her tongue, flicking at him, scalding little touches, and Barnaby let himself drift away, flooded with warmth. Eight brief months had shaken his world inside out. Gone were the feelings of inadequacy and creeping middle age. Gone were the worries about the legal practice and the near-conviction that his career had bogged down. Gone, too, was the numb defeat he'd seen every morning in the mirror, waking up to a dead marriage and a social life stuck firmly in bottom gear. The key to it all, of course, was Kate. She'd blessed him with a second chance, and this time neither of them was going to let the real world intrude. Kate understood him like no other woman ever had. She understood his pride, his fear of failure, his need to succeed. She'd mapped his path to her cave, and she'd guaranteed the kind of privacy he knew to be beyond violation. No one would be hurt this time. Because no one would ever know.

Barnaby looked down at Liz, a mute question in his smile, and when she closed her eyes and nodded, he slipped round, his mouth finding the banana through the warm yoghurt, eating it slowly, savouring the strange sharpness of the taste. Liz was teasing him again, her tongue like a tiny soft dagger, and then she took him deep inside her mouth, sucking and sucking, and suddenly he was back in June, back in the pool at the health club, fretting and fretting about the D-Day celebrations. That weekend seemed a million light years away, part of some other life. Fuck Clinton, he thought gleefully. Fuck the banquet and the fat cats and the crowds flocking to the Common to see their precious Queen. Could any of them match this? Could any of their lives possibly compare?

He felt Liz stiffening beneath him and he withdrew from her mouth and turned again, easing himself into her, as far as he could go. When the phone began to ring, he ignored it, feeling her pushing and pushing against him, her hands round his buttocks, her nails scoring his flesh. Finally she gasped, her whole body arching upwards while Barnaby drove on and on until he felt the world splintering around him.

After a while, prone on top of Liz, it occurred to Barnaby that the phone was still ringing. His hand crabbed across the bedside cabinet. Happiness was the spreading pool of creamy wetness between his wife's thighs.

'Hallo?'

For a moment, Barnaby heard nothing. Then, unmistakably, came the sound of Kate's voice. 'Hayden? Is that you?'

Charlie Epple was in the shower when he heard the peal of the front-door bell. He let it ring for more than a minute, working the shampoo into his scalp, letting the hot water sluice the suds down his chest. This was his last morning in the Wimbledon house. If it was the estate agent again, she could come back later. If it was the guys from the removals firm, they were too bloody early. The ringing went on and on. The shampoo rinsed away, Charlie stepped out of the shower. Most of the stuff in the bathroom was already crated, ready for the move, and he stood on the bare floorboards, watching the water pool at his feet. Then he reached for a towel and padded downstairs.

Outside, in the spring sunshine, stood Jessie. Beside her, smiling up at him, another girl, much smaller. Charlie beckoned them inside but Jessie was saying something about a cab. The driver was still waiting. The fare had been more than they'd expected. Might Charlie oblige with a loan? He peered past her, into the street. A big Vauxhall was parked beyond the hedge.

'Where have you come from?'

'Guildford.'

'*Guildford*? Fuck me. How much?'

'Forty pounds.'

Charlie tut-tutted then disappeared inside the house. He kept an emergency supply of spare cash in a jam jar on the fridge. He emptied it, giving Jessie two twenty-pound notes. Outside, from the street, he could hear the chink of coins as the cabbie gave her change. When she came back, she hugged him. 'It was forty pounds,' she said. 'Exactly.'

Charlie got dressed and gave the girls breakfast, astonished at how much they ate. Jessie's friend, Lolly, was definitely noshing for England. After the last of the Weetabix and two boiled eggs, she began to work her way through a small pile of toast. For someone so tiny, so delicate, her appetite was prodigious. 'No one been feeding you?'

'Long story.' Jessie pulled a face, telling Charlie about the re-hab centre. She and Lolly had been abused, day and night. Not just by the residents but a couple of the staff, too. Jessie had done her best to protect them both but against a couple of dozen men they'd been virtually helpless. Thankfully, the pregnancy tests had been negative.

Charlie blinked, still watching Lolly. She seemed so fragile, so flawless. She had the kind of face certain art directors would kill for. Meeting someone like Lolly was the moment you chucked the whole campaign in the bin and started again. 'You serious? You were raped?'

Jessie nodded, wide-eyed. 'Often.'

'Been to the police?'

'We can't.'

'Why not?'

Jessie began a long, rambling story about a couple of the residents. She said they were pretty heavy. One had convictions for GBH. The other belonged in the nut-house. Both had made it plain that grassing them up would be unwise.

Charlie no longer believed a word. 'So you've done a runner?'

'Had to. No choice. Mum's livid.'

'I bet.'

'Hasn't she been on to you?'

Something in Jessie's voice sounded an alarm in Charlie's head. He knew from Barnaby that she had been referred for therapy and the last couple of weeks he'd been meaning to get an address so that he could drop her a line but things had been so chaotic after the decree absolute that he hadn't got round to it. He was sure, though, that the course had been long-term. Six months. Maybe more.

'So are you better? The pair of you?' he said.

Lolly nodded, looking at the coffee pot, and Charlie took the hint, hunting for the jar of instant he'd been saving for the removal men. The last of the milk had gone on the cereals.

'Black I'm afraid, girls.'

Jessie's hands closed around the mug and Charlie wondered what had happened to her nails. Like Liz, Jess had always had beautiful hands but now the nails were bitten to the quick. She had a ring, too, a tiny cheap-looking thing with a fake ruby set in peeling gold. Jessie saw him looking at it.

'Lolly's,' she said proudly. 'She's letting me wear it.'

Nearly an hour later, when the removal men arrived, Charlie was close to getting to the bottom of it. Lolly's daughter Candelle was in care and the social workers had a problem with letting her out. Lolly's mother, meanwhile, had taken up with an unemployed truck driver who was permanently on the piss. When provoked, he often turned violent and life in Guildford had become impossible. He'd throw stuff around, smash up the place. Last night he'd up-ended the goldfish tank and poured the contents over Lolly's mum's head. After a fruitless search for the goldfish, Lolly had had enough. From now on, her mother was on her own.

Jessie was standing by the kitchen door, watching the removal men emptying the front room. 'Mum told me about your new place,' she said. 'Sounds lovely.'

'Yeah?'

'Yes,' she agreed. 'She said it had two bedrooms. Old Portsmouth, isn't it?'

'That's right. Opposite Hot Walls.'

'Yummy.' Jess turned to Lolly, explaining the geography of Old Portsmouth. In summer, Hot Walls could be wicked.

Charlie shuttled up and down the hall with more mugs of coffee. He was due at a meeting in Portsmouth at half past two. It was already ten forty but there was a fast train from Waterloo in an hour and he was assured by the removals people that they would leave the empty house secure.

Jessie was talking about Liz again. Evidently she was keen to have her daughter back home.

'Do it,' Charlie said at once. 'Sounds a terrific idea.'

'I couldn't. It wouldn't work. I know it wouldn't. A couple of days and we'd be at each other's throats. You know what she's like, banging on all the time. I couldn't cope with all that. Besides . . .' She looked at Lolly. 'There's two of us.'

Charlie shook the last of the coffee granules into a beer tumbler. The mugs had all gone.

'Two of you?' he said carefully.

'Yes, me and Lolly.'

'Ah.' He looked up, the kettle poised, at last scenting a solution to Jessie's unvoiced plea for somewhere to crash. To be honest, he wasn't keen on taking sole responsibility for Jessie but a couple of lodgers might just work. Mutual support, he told himself. Someone for Jessie to confide in.

'Actually, it's got three bedrooms.' He smiled at Lolly. 'Not two.' Jessie grinned back at him, a reminder at last of the shy adolescent he'd smuggled into one or two of Soho's wilder jazz clubs.

'Is that an offer?' she said. 'Only two bedrooms would be more than enough.'

Kate got through to Barnaby at noon. She'd been phoning all morning, desperate to explain her wake-up call, but every time she'd rung, the receptionist had told her that Mr Barnaby was tied up. That, in itself, was a bad sign. Barnaby had never before refused to take her calls. Now she could feel the chill in his voice.

'I'm sorry about this morning,' she said, for the second time, 'but it just felt important, that's all.'

'Why?'

'It's complicated. I can't really explain on the phone.'

'Where were you?'

'At the health club. I'd been waiting for you. I just . . .' She was sitting on a stool in the kitchen, staring at the unwashed dishes in the sink. She was eight hours away from the most important speech she'd ever had to make. Success or failure could literally shape the rest of her life. Yet there she was, behaving like some schoolgirl, rubbing salt in a self-inflicted wound. She looked up at the clock on the wall. 'I'm at home,' she began, 'I don't know whether—'

Barnaby cut in. 'I'm running late. Today's a nightmare.'

'I'm sure. I just . . . It would be nice, that's all. I wouldn't keep you long. It's just . . . I don't know . . .' Her voice trailed off. Whatever she said just made it worse. She'd never felt this pathetic. Ever.

Barnaby was on the phone again. His voice was softer, kinder, and she sensed that someone must have been in the room with him and had gone. That's why he'd been so matter-of-fact, so insensitive.

'Lunchtime,' he was saying, 'I've got half an hour. We could go to the pub on the corner. One fifteen? Pick me up here?'

Kate began to say yes but a click on the line told her that Barnaby had hung up, doubtless turning to yet another contract, another fat pile of business opportunities. Over the last few months, she'd watched him become the most talked-about solicitor in the city, the brief who'd stitched together an extraordinary deal on the Imperial and now travelled everywhere by private jet. She sat on the stool for a moment or two longer, trying to rid her mind of the conversation she'd pieced together in the changing room. She'd been showering after her workout. The splash of the falling water had made it hard to be certain yet the two women had definitely been talking about Liz Barnaby, she knew they had. Second honeymoon, one had said. Second coming, the other had suggested, giggling enviously.

When the courier arrived, Zhu happened to be in the Imperial's foyer. He pushed through the revolving door, pausing to admire the new décor. After exhaustive discussions with their demanding new client, the Knightsbridge design consultancy had finally settled on pale greys and a deep shade of blue, with details picked out in a rich burgundy. The mix of colours, echoed in the luxury suites at the front of the hotel, combined a cool serenity with something altogether more opulent. The latter was understated, a quiet smile rather than a bear-hug, and Zhu was delighted with the impact the hotel made on first-time visitors.

He took the package from the courier. There was a bubbling pot of coffee in the alcove beside reception and Zhu insisted he help himself before returning to his van outside. The youth broke into a smile, attacking the plate of biscuits as well, while Zhu scissored through the big, heavy-duty plastic bag. Inside, tightly folded, was a long banner. He pulled it out, signalling to the receptionist to help him. She took one end, walking away towards the restaurant as the banner unfurled. From one end to the other, it measured forty feet, and there were instructions inside the bag on how it was to be fixed to the hotel's façade.

The courier was still standing beside reception, finishing his coffee. Neither Zhu nor the receptionist could read the message inscribed on the banner. The courier was trying to hide a grin.

'What does it say?' Zhu called.

The courier shook his head. He was a thin, crop-haired youth in his early twenties. 'It's a wind-up,' he said. 'Don't let it worry you.'

'What?'

'It's a piss-take. Forget it, mate.' He drained his cup. 'Cheers for the coffee.'

'But what does it say?'

The courier eyed the receptionist. She was Singaporean, a vivacious, raven-haired girl, taller than most Chinese. Unlike Zhu, she'd sensed at once that something was wrong.

Zhu was getting impatient. 'Read it to me,' he said. 'Please.'

The courier wiped his mouth with the back of his hand. His eyes were still on the banner.

'Fuck Off Back To Chinkieland,' he dropped his voice, 'Wog Cunts.'

Charlie Epple walked the half-mile from the city's railway station to the Regency terrace where Barnaby had his offices. The train had made good time and he still had an hour in hand before the start of his meeting. In June, the city's Strategy Unit were sending a delegation to an important trade fair in New Jersey, and the afternoon's meeting would finalize the pitch the Portsmouth team would be making to attract investment. To Charlie, these opportunities were priceless. With the right words and the right pictures, as he kept telling his new colleagues, anything was possible.

He stopped outside Barnaby's office. He'd rung from Waterloo and the receptionist had assured him that Barnaby would be at his desk. He had pressing appointments all day but lunchtime he'd fenced off for paperwork.

Charlie took the stairs two at a time, wondering what Barnaby would make of Jessie's plans. He'd left the girls at home in Wimbledon with instructions to close the place up once the removal men had finished. He'd found another ninety quid for their tickets down and told them to spend the change on champagne. His first night back in Pompey deserved a modest celebration.

The door to Barnaby's office was an inch or two open. Charlie stepped inside. Sitting behind the desk was a woman he recognized.

She had a strong, open face with a wide mouth and wonderful cheekbones. Her hair was longer than he'd last seen it and she was wearing big gold earrings that bounced around as she got to her feet.

Charlie extended a hand, introducing himself. 'We met last year,' he reminded her, 'me sitting there, you this side. I can't remember your name, though.'

'Kate. Kate Frankham.'

'Ah, yes, the politician, Red Kate, gotcha.'

'Who told you that?'

'Barnaby. Terrible gossip. Tell him something interesting and he'll share it with anyone, even me. Bit troubling in a lawyer, don't you think?'

Charlie sat down in front of the desk. Kate did the same, resuming her seat and pulling her coat around her. There was a longish silence. At last, Charlie burst into laughter. 'So where is he?' he said. 'What have you done with him?'

'Nothing.' Kate consulted her watch. 'We were supposed to be having lunch. Half an hour ago.'

'And he hasn't turned up?'

'No.'

'Typical.' Charlie got to his feet, crossed the room and opened the door with a flourish. 'My pleasure,' he said. 'Never trust a married man.'

At Kate's insistence, they went to the pub on the corner. Charlie ordered a pastie and chips but Kate said she didn't want anything. They sat at a table by the window, Kate's eyes rarely leaving the door. He might still turn up, she explained, when Charlie asked why.

'You were going to meet him here?'

'No, the office, but we come here for lunch,' she offered him a faint smile, 'occasionally.'

Charlie laced his pastie with brown sauce and used a paper napkin to pick it up, curious to know why conversation was so difficult. Barnaby had mentioned Kate on a number of occasions. She was active in the Labour Party. She had a talent for getting things done. And she hated the bloody Conservatives.

'I'm in advertising,' Charlie mumbled, through a mouthful of mince and carrots. 'I used to work on some of the privatization campaigns. Fat cat bastard Tory ministers. Unbelievable people.' For the first time, Charlie thought he detected a flicker of interest in her face, though she was still watching the door.

'Really?'

'Yeah, money for old rope, whichever way you cut it. We made a packet. They made a packet. Even Joe Soap wound up with a share or two. Magic, pure magic. Bloke I worked with used to call it the Paul Daniels school of economics. It's all smoke and mirrors. You wave the wand, bribe the great unwashed with their own money, and wait for the votes to roll in. Never fails.'

Kate reached for a chip. 'They'll be wiped out,' she said briskly, 'starting in May.'

'There's an election then?'

'Yes,' she replied. 'It's only local and your lot'll say they don't count but they do, believe me they do.'

Charlie tried not to choke on the pastie. He swallowed a mouthful of Guinness.

'My lot?' he gasped. 'Are you serious?'

Kate was looking at him now, the door abandoned. 'All that money?' she said. 'All that work they pushed your way? Surely to God you're not telling me you're a socialist.'

'You're right.' Charlie nodded vigorously. 'I'm not telling you bloody anything. Except I hate the bastards.'

'What bastards?'

'Politicians.'

'Any particular brand?'

'Yeah, London politicians, the sort I run into. We used to get them round to the agency, vetting the rough cuts on the British Gas ads. Remember all that? Remember Sid? They used to stand there, these clowns, looking at the crap we dished up, wagging their heads, telling each other how clever it all was, how witty.' He lifted his Guinness again. 'Here's to politicians. Clueless bastards.'

'You're talking about the Tories. We're not all like that.'

'Wrong. I'm talking about power. Power does something to

people. Have you ever noticed that? Doesn't matter which party, that's irrelevant. It's power, full stop.'

Kate was looking thoughtful now, toying with her drink.

'I'm speaking at a selection meeting tonight,' she said. 'If I win, I get to be a parliamentary candidate. And if that happens, I might end up an MP.'

'You kidding?' Charlie was staring at her.

'Not at all. It's a logical progression.'

'And you'd *want* to be an MP?'

'I want to make a difference, yes.'

'And you think that's the way to do it?'

'I do, yes. Unless you can think of another.'

Charlie returned to his plate, and began to mop up the pool of brown sauce with his last few chips.

'MPs are lobby fodder,' he said. 'It's a cliché but it's true. And by the time they get to be ministers, they've lost it anyway.'

'Lost what?'

'Any clue about the real world. The lot I've come across could have been on another planet.' He looked up. 'You serious about this meeting? Tonight?'

'Yes, why?'

'Sounds a laugh, that's all.' He pushed away his plate. 'Can anyone come? Or is it ticket only?'

'Ticket only, I'm afraid. You have to have been a member for a year. House rules.'

'A year? That's absurd. Why a year?'

Kate looked briefly uncomfortable. Finally she explained how the rule was supposed to prevent the candidates from packing the meeting with their own supporters.

Charlie was sitting back in his chair, his hands clasped behind his head, delighted. 'See?' he said. 'See what it does? Power?'

Owens said yes to the offer of a second cup of tea. For the first time in weeks, he felt half normal. No pains in his sinuses. No thickness in his head. No little curls of foil wrap from the endless tubes of Strepsils in his pocket.

He reached across the table for the plastic bag again, double-checking the despatch numbers on the consignment note against the figures he'd passed on to TNT Express. The package had been handed in to their Brentford depot late yesterday afternoon. The sender's name was listed as Arthur Hengist, and under 'Address', the clerk had scribbled 245 Hankisson Road. Owens had phoned the address through to Special Branch at the Yard and the reply had come back within minutes: 245 Hankisson Road didn't exist. Not, at any rate, within the Greater London area.

The lawyer, Barnaby, passed Owens the tea. The little Chinese guy was still at the back of the hotel's restaurant, supervising his staff as they put up decorations. Tomorrow, in keeping with some tradition or other, he'd be celebrating the hotel's opening with fireworks and a snake dance.

Owens glanced at his watch. 'We should talk about tomorrow. We've been getting intelligence from London.' He nodded at the banner, neatly folded on a neighbouring table. 'This may be starters. Main course to come.'

'I'm not with you.'

'It's nothing specific. I can't give you names, numbers, times, nothing like that. All we've got is smoke in the wind.'

'I see.' Barnaby sat back, looking at Zhu again. 'And what are you planning to do about it?'

'The superintendent will be down within the hour.'

'Bairstow?'

'Yes.'

Barnaby frowned. He knew Bairstow well, a bluff, bad-tempered Yorkshireman with a brilliant clear-up rate and absolutely no talent for public relations. Giving him the run of the hotel during the opening banquet would be a nightmare.

'Are you serious?' he said slowly. 'You think there's a real threat?'

'We think there may be. Mr Bairstow gets possessive about his city. You've probably noticed.'

Barnaby nodded. Coachloads of visiting football supporters were routinely hauled off the motorway on the edge of the city

for body searches and a brisk lecture. Down here we like it nice
and quiet, went the official line, so behave your fucking selves.

'So what are we saying? Vehicle checks? Riot police? The
works?'

'I've no idea.'

'But will he tell me? Mr Bairstow?'

'Depends if he knows. Intelligence is saying National Front.'
His eyes returned to the banner. 'Does that ring any bells?'

Ellis was already examining the cake trolley when Louise Carlton
stepped into the Palm Court restaurant at the Ritz Hotel. A uniformed waiter led her to his table, pulling back the chair to let her
sit down. Beneath the huge chandelier, refugees from Harrods and
Harvey Nichols were locked in conversation over plates heaped
with scones and teacakes. Ellis, by contrast, was settling for two
thick slices of chocolate gateau.

Louise let the waiter take her plate, ordering a pot of Lapsang.
Then she turned to Ellis, waving away his apologies for having
started. He had to be back at Victoria Street by five at the latest.
The possibility of a bid for Portsmouth's naval dockyard had triggered a classic Whitehall stand-off, and there was some imprecision
on the line the DTI should take.

Louise smiled. She liked Ellis's use of the word 'imprecision'.
In fact she liked Ellis. Very much indeed.

'You think he's serious? Our Mr Zhu?'

'I don't know. He can raise the money, certainly.'

'How much are we talking about?'

'Two hundred and fifty million. That's ballpark, DTI figures.
Nothing's agreed.'

Louise used her fork to carve herself a fat wedge of gateau. As
ever, it was delicious, one of life's more dependable pleasures. She
looked up. In a phone call to her office before lunch, Ellis had
outlined Zhu's interest in buying the dockyard. Given MI5's
responsibility for protecting UK economic interests, there was, for
once, no interdepartmental clash. Selling off the nation's premier
naval port had profound security implications.

'What are the MoD saying?'

'The Navy Board are horrified. They think it's a joke in extremely poor taste. The Army brass will be gloating, of course. Until it's their turn.'

'What about the politicians?'

'They're taking the Treasury line, or at least the ultras are. These guys all sing from the same hymn sheet. Anything that reduces the PSBR. Anything that lowers the wage bill. You know the way it goes . . .'

Louise helped herself to another forkful of gateau. Thanks to some inspired rearguard actions, MI5 had managed so far to avoid the worst of the cultural revolution that had swept through White-hall. Unlike the other security agencies, MI6 and GCHQ, Five was outside the direct control of the powerful Joint Intelligence Committee. This ensured a degree of immunity from ministerial diktat, an invaluable dispensation that dug a moat around the daily grind of intelligence work.

Ellis was still musing about Portsmouth dockyard. Evidently, Zhu had come up with a scheme to lease some of the key facilities back to the MoD.

'The politicians would buy that?'

'It's cheaper, they're bound to. It gets them off the hook as well. They can say that nothing's really changed.'

'Except ownership.'

'Sure, but the warships still get serviced. The place looks the same. The mateys are still in jobs, some of them. Who's going to worry about the small print?'

'We might, if it came to a war.'

'Quite. But you know the way it is with politicos. They're permanently at war. And two hundred and fifty million's a tidy windfall if it happened to coincide with an election.'

'Has Zhu got a date in mind?'

'Nothing specific. I get the impression he'd buy the place tomorrow if he could.'

Louise moistened her fingertip and picked up tiny flakes of chocolate from her plate.

'Why does he want it?' she asked. 'Why bother? If the Navy can't make it pay, what's he got up his sleeve?'

The waiter arrived with a plate of warm scones for Ellis, who cut one in half, and freighted it with strawberry jam and a big dollop of cream before passing it to Louise. Louise beamed at him, still waiting for an answer.

'I don't know,' he said at last. 'The place is huge, hundreds of acres. There's a lot of fixed plant, some of it quite modern. He's got shipbuilding and repair interests in Singapore. I imagine he might fancy the same thing here. Maybe he'll put work our way. Construction? Maintenance? Oil rigs? It's an opportunity. We should grab it. That'll be the DTI line, at any rate.'

'And you? What do you think?'

'I think we should be careful.'

'Why?'

'Because . . .' Ellis frowned, gazing out at the traffic, inching down Piccadilly ' . . . there's a hole in his past. What we know, genuinely *know* about him, goes back to the sixties. Before that, if we're honest, it's a mystery. He says Fukien province but he could have come from anywhere.'

'Does that matter?'

'It might. Depending where you're sat at the time.'

Louise looked amused. 'I don't want to risk a compliment,' she said lightly, 'but you're talking like one of us.'

'I know. And you can imagine how popular that makes me at Victoria Street. My guys are in it for the money. Find them a customer and they'll sell him anything. Zhu could be Saddam Hussein's brother for all they care.'

Louise's eyes shone behind the enormous glasses. 'You realize Six should be doing the legwork?'

'Yes.'

'But you've decided to talk to me? Is that it?'

'Obviously.'

Louise signalled the waiter. When he'd written out the bill, she produced a twenty-pound note from her purse, telling him to keep the change and complimenting him on the gateau. Only when they were outside, flagging down an approaching taxi, did she take the conversation further.

'Do you know it at all?' she said. 'Singapore?'

Labour Party headquarters for the constituency of Portsmouth West comprised four ground-floor rooms in a property that had once served as a fruit and veg shop. Kate Frankham found a parking spot half a block away from the premises. A small typed notice on the door directed the membership to the nearby Baptist church hall. Meetings to select the constituency candidate traditionally attracted a biggish turnout, far too many for the converted corner shop, and Kate could hear the clatter of chairs through the open door across the road. She pulled her coat around her and checked her watch. The meeting was due to begin at eight. Ideally, she wanted a full house before she made her entrance.

She returned to her car and got in. She'd spent most of the afternoon rehearsing her speech, pacing up and down her living room, trying to shut out every other distraction. In the first place, she'd handwritten it, drawing on a check-list of what the ex-poly lecturer on the executive committee liked to call 'bullet points'. This list included items from the Walworth Road menu that she knew she couldn't afford to ignore, but as the speech began to take shape on paper, she'd done her best to fashion it into a personal statement of beliefs. Why it was right to acknowledge the free market. Why the old abuses of union power could never return. Why the party had to shed its reputation for high spending and high taxation. Why the Tory quango state was an insult to democracy. Why education and jobs should be the priorities for anyone interested in creating a half-decent society. Why the Social Chapter belonged at the very heart of Labour's first Queen's Speech.

The list went on and on, a sensible, moderate, voter-friendly mix of traditional Labour Party values and realpolitik. When it came to labels, as it always did, Kate had settled on 'ethical socialism' as the closest she could get to describing her own political credo. She'd picked up the term at conference, in conversation with a young researcher, and she was pleased with the way she'd managed to build it into her peroration. Candidates for selection had just ten minutes to make their case, and her eighteen months as a councillor had already taught her the importance of seeming to speak from the heart. People, in the end, weren't interested in the small print. What mattered – what made the real difference – was passion.

She glanced in the mirror, folded her speech and returned it to her bag. The stream of figures hurrying into the hall had slowed to a dribble and she knew she ought to join them. She got out of the car and locked it, glad she'd worn the jersey trouser suit against the bitter wind. She crossed the road, quickening her step, suddenly alarmed that she might be late, but when she got inside the hall she found the usual buzz of conversation as people stood in groups, gossiping.

Seats on the platform at the front were reserved for party officers. Kate spotted the secretary, a formidable ex-teacher whom she still found slightly intimidating, and offered her a sheepish wave, making her way through the mill of people. The secretary kissed her cheek briskly and wished her luck. Straws had already been drawn for the order of speeches and Kate was to go second after Frank Perry. The secretary squeezed her arm and turned away to join the rest of the executive committee up on the stage. Seconds later, she was calling the meeting to order.

Kate found her name on a seat at the front. Billy Goodman was already sitting beside her. He was wearing jeans and a plaid shirt beneath his leather jacket. On his lap lay a folded copy of *Militant*. Kate sat down. She'd known this moment would arrive and she'd been dreading it. Billy Goodman was her conscience, the watching face in the front row that she knew she couldn't avoid. He'd declared his own candidacy, she was convinced, to make things difficult for her, to remind her of all the times they'd tried to pull the issues apart, all the times they'd tried to disentangle the bullshit from the people's real interest. In most of these discussions she'd agreed with him, she knew she had, though more recently she'd come to accept that gaining power wasn't simply a matter of proclaiming one's beliefs. You had to gauge the public mood. You had to sniff the electoral wind and trim your sails accordingly. Otherwise, you'd be in opposition for ever.

Billy was watching Frank Perry climbing the steps to the stage. The chairman's brief opening remarks were over and for the next ten minutes the meeting would be his. There was a microphone on a stand in front of the long committee table and Perry stood behind it, looking uncomfortable. He was a tall, thin, stooped man with a smoker's cough and a wardrobe of nylon shirts. He'd spent his entire working life in the dockyard and his devotion to the party was unconditional. As a councillor, he'd laboured tirelessly for his constituents and he'd won a substantial following but he had neither the talent nor the appetite for public speaking and Kate knew he'd be a disaster on the hustings. Frank Perry was what happened when you refused to turn your back on the past. Only a party with a death wish would ever nominate him for a parliamentary seat.

As Frank began to speak, Kate followed Billy out of the hall, remembering to her relief that party rules forbade rival candidates to be present during each other's addresses. A room behind the stage had been set aside for the candidates' use and Billy made sure he left the door an inch or two open. Kate could hear Frank Perry's thin voice fighting a heavy cold.

'He's got it all sewn up.' Billy had found himself a chair in the corner. 'Did you see the fax from Walworth Road?'

Kate shook her head.

'What fax?'

'Bloke called Beatty. Blair's office. Official endorsement.'

'Kelvin Beatty?'

'Yeah, that's him.'

Kate felt the blood pulsing into her face. Kelvin Beatty was the staffer she'd been supposed to meet at the restaurant in Belgravia, the young turk she'd run into at conference. He'd spent the best part of an hour telling her why people like Frank Perry were a luxury the party could no longer afford. They had to be marginalized. They had to be pensioned off.

'Are you sure?'

'Positive. I saw it just now.'

'Who showed you?'

'Frank.'

Kate looked away. Outside, on the stage, Frank Perry was lost already, bogged down in the small print of some ward dispute. The noise regulations simply weren't being enforced. The police should be under firmer democratic control. Quangos had turned them into an arm of the Tory Party. The line drew a ripple of applause. Billy Goodman was smiling.

'I thought you knew this bloke Beatty?'

'I do.'

'Friend of yours?'

Kate didn't answer. She opened her bag, fingering the speech inside it. Beatty, she thought, could have written every line. Indeed, the prospect of his approval, his blessing, was partly what had shaped it in the first place. She closed the bag again, her confusion giving way to something far closer to anger. She'd seen it his way. She'd listened to his elegant little lectures. She'd pored through his carefully highlighted photocopies from *The Economist* and the *Guardian*. She was word-perfect on why the party machine needed overhauling, on why effective power had to be pooled in London. Politics, she'd believed, was about winning. And now this.

Frank Perry was coming to the end of his speech, a traffic jam of promises that tailed into silence. There was a brief round of applause, shyly acknowledged, and Kate heard him blowing his nose before calling for questions from the audience. The questions lasted less than ten minutes, then the secretary appeared at the door, beckoning to Kate. Meeting Frank outside in the narrow corridor, she felt the touch of his hand on her arm, and she dimly heard his whispered good luck before she was up on the stage herself, her speech forgotten, her careful précis of the Walworth Road masterplan utterly discarded.

She gazed out at the blur of faces in the hall. Politics, she began, is about people. People you know. People you care about. People whose lives you shape, and improve, and help dignify. Being an MP should be part of that process, but being an MP had – instead – become part of the problem. Why? Because the party had become too restrictive. Because discipline had become too

209

tight. Because the struggle for power had become all-consuming. Power mattered, of course it did, but power should never become an end in itself. But that's what was happening. Up in London. Away from the grass-roots. Away from the people.

Kate bent to the microphone, her anger and her contempt driving her on. Parliament had become a charade, she said. MPs with any courage, MPs with any voice of their own were ignored, or sidelined, or quietly threatened with de-selection. The only line that mattered was the party line and if you refused to toe it, you were out. She paused, only too conscious that she was arguing herself out of a job she hadn't even got, but she didn't care. She was speaking from the heart. She was telling it the way she saw it. What might happen to her candidacy was irrelevant.

A voice behind her asked if she'd finished. She nodded and left the stage without a backward glance, not bothering to stay for questions. Billy Goodman was waiting for her in the corridor. There was a smile on his face. Plainly, he'd heard every word. The secretary appeared again, calling for Billy to take the stage. He shook his head, still gazing at Kate.

'No need,' he murmured. 'My colleague said it all.'

The closest Barnaby could park the Mercedes was nearly a hundred metres down the road. He had the Dom Perignon and the glasses in his sports bag on the back seat. In his heart, he knew that Kate would win.

Ten minutes later, much earlier than he'd anticipated, figures began to emerge from the hall. Kate, another surprise, was amongst them. She was standing under the porch beside the open door, deep in conversation with a man in a leather jacket. Barnaby was too far away to see the man's face but he could sense that the two were friends. Kate was doing most of the talking, using her hands a lot the way she did when she was excited. At one point, the man put a restraining hand on her arm and when they parted shortly afterwards she kissed him on the lips before he turned on his heel and disappeared back inside the hall.

Barnaby flashed the Mercedes' headlights, attracting Kate's

attention. He'd told her he'd be outside. He'd said he'd be waiting. He watched her hurrying towards him, aware of the knot the last couple of minutes had tied in his stomach. This morning he'd been angry with her, shocked at her breach of the agreed rules. Phoning him at home was something she'd promised she'd never do. His life with Liz was his own affair, nothing to do with her. That was the pact they'd made. That was why it had worked so well. Yet here he was, half a day later, insanely jealous, wanting her back in the car, wanting every last particle of her.

Barnaby leaned across, unlocking the door. He'd never been so pleased to see her. He kissed her, smelling the cigarette smoke on her coat, and he felt her responding, burying her face in his sheepskin jacket. At length, they disengaged and Barnaby looked at her, the obvious question unvoiced. She offered him a small, tired smile and he saw how close she was to tears.

'Frank,' she said. 'By a mile.'

'*Frank*? Frank *Perry*?'

'Yes. I blew it, my love. The most important ten minutes of my life and I blew it.'

They drove to the top of Portsdown Hill. The car park overlooking the city was deserted. He pulled the Mercedes to a halt and switched off the lights. The island lay below them, mapped by street lights.

Kate's hand found his. She'd told him about the meeting, about the speech she'd made, about her refusal even to call for questions. The audience had been bemused.

'I expect they thought I was being hysterical, just another bloody woman. Maybe they're right. Maybe they're better off with Frank.' She sniffed, staring woodenly into the darkness.

There was a long silence. Barnaby squeezed her hand. A car sped past on the hilltop road behind them.

'What happened this morning?' he asked. 'Why the phone call?'

'I missed you,' she said simply.

'You were at the pool?'

'Yes.' She glanced across at him. 'I've just got used to it, I suppose. It's become a routine. I'm not supposed to like routines, am I?'

'No.'

'Well, there's another surprise. I'm human, after all.' She was silent briefly. 'There was something else, too.'

'What's that?'

'You'll think this is crazy. Maybe it is crazy.' She withdrew her hand. 'There were a couple of women in the changing room. I think they must know your wife.'

'And?'

'I was in the shower. They were talking about her.'

'What did they say?'

'They said . . . that things were pretty good, you know, for her . . .' She tailed off. ' . . . It's not the kind of thing women say, not without good reason.' She twisted a lock of hair. 'That's all really. But it upset me.'

'So you decided to phone?'

'Yes. I don't really know why. I just did. I felt . . . helpless, especially after, you know, everything in London. How good it was.'

Barnaby sensed relief flood through him. This woman loved him, she really did, and here was the proof. He kissed her softly on the lips. Then he reached into the sports bag for the champagne. The bottle was still cold to the touch and he began to untwist the wire around the cork.

Kate was looking at him, uncomprehending.

'There's a couple of glasses in the bag,' he said lightly. 'I thought we'd celebrate.'

'But I lost.'

Barnaby smiled at her in the darkness. 'You think so?' he said, the cork beginning to ease as he levered it upwards.

Louise Carlton was on her way to bed when the call came through from Shepperton. The intruder team had been lucky. The property had been empty all evening and they'd had the place to themselves. Entry to the barn had been a doddle. Louise smiled, still half-way up the stairs with the cordless phone, listening to the account of exactly what they'd found. The thing had looked amazing, a real work of art, must have cost a fortune, and there'd been a note attached with a location and a time. Someone was calling tomorrow at dawn. They'd need a truck to ship it south.

The conversation came to an end shortly afterwards and Louise returned to the lounge, searching for a notebook in a drawer before picking up the phone again, and dialling the Thames House switchboard. The duty officer put her through to Registry and the woman in charge of the night shift apologized for the delay in checking her PIN number.

Finally, Louise's clearance confirmed, the woman asked how she could help. Louise had found a biro now, and a clean page in the notebook. 'I'm interested in the Anti-Racist Alliance,' she said. 'Check if there's a Portsmouth branch.'

Billy Goodman heard the phone from the kitchen. Picking up the takeaway vindaloo, he went through to the tiny hall. The phone was on the floor beside his bicycle. Kate had mentioned she might ring. 'Yeah?'

The voice at the other end belonged to a woman, someone a good deal older than Kate. She spoke slowly, the way you might pass an important message to a child, or a foreigner, and then she put down the phone. Billy sank to the floor, his back against the wall, balancing the takeaway on his knees. He picked at the chicken, deep in thought. Then he got to his feet again and returned to the kitchen, storing the takeaway in the oven. His address book was in his bedroom. He fetched it down, trying to remember who had access to transport. His first call went to a fellow ex-Trot, now living in Petersfield. He described what had happened. The woman had given him a time and a place and one or two other details. She sounded kosher. They should get bodies organized. They should be ready.

'Wheels?' he enquired. 'Can you help out at all?'

The contact in Petersfield obliged at once. He did a morning run for disabled kids, hauling them round to a day centre. The

Sherpa minibus was standing in the road outside his flat. It was brand new. He was looking at it now.

'A van for the disabled?' Billy grinned. 'Perfect.'

Next morning, as promised, Barnaby was at the Imperial Hotel by nine o'clock. Bairstow, the police superintendent, was waiting for him inside the foyer.

'No promises,' he muttered, 'but I think we've cracked it.'

The two men walked through to the restaurant. All the decorations were in place now and a two-man news unit from the local ITV station was busy getting pictures of the extravagant display of paper lanterns, silk hangings and elaborate lacquerwork. Barnaby watched them as they wandered around with the big video camera, glad he'd managed to limit the fall-out from the banner incident the previous afternoon. Not even the *Sentinel* had picked it up.

Bairstow was talking about the arrangements he'd made. The afternoon's home match against Millwall meant that most police leave had already been cancelled but he'd secured extra manpower from neighbouring forces and with this he'd put a choke hold on all three major roads into the city. Anyone planning a serious demo would have to run the gauntlet of radio-linked patrol cars, and he'd be backing these assets with five hours' turn-time on one of the headquarters helicopters from Winchester.

'Turn-time?' Barnaby noticed a waitress approach with a tray of coffee.

'Blade time, time in the air. The chopper gives us extra reach. Bloody expensive, though.'

'What about trains?'

'BR police have been fully briefed. We've officers at Waterloo, Woking and Guildford. Stations east and west are covered, too.'

Barnaby pushed back his chair, making room as the waitress began to unload the tray. 'Sounds foolproof,' he said. 'I'm impressed.'

'Impressed?' Bairstow shot him a look. 'Bloody sauce.'

The reception at the hotel was scheduled to start at noon. Zhu had stipulated champagne for the first hour, followed by the banquet. The eight courses were carefully timetabled to end by mid-afternoon, after which bamboo screens towards the rear of the restaurant would be folded back to reveal a series of elaborate tableaux. These would all have a Singaporean theme and the celebrations would end with a traditional Chinese snake dance and a big fireworks display outside on the Common. Given the guest list, more than two hundred of the city's key players, Barnaby couldn't imagine a more high-profile launch for the hotel. It would, in every sense, confirm that Raymond Zhu had truly arrived.

By half past twelve, the reception was in full swing, the foyer and the big lounge bar packed with guests. Barnaby circulated with Zhu, introducing his new client, accepting compliment after compliment from men and women he'd always dreamed of impressing on this scale. He was on his third glass of champagne by now and the tension of the morning was beginning to ease. The Imperial was going to be a huge success – he could feel it in the buzz of conversation around him, the stolen glances at the TV crew, the look of startled admiration when yet another flawless Singaporean waitress appeared with a tray of exquisite canapés.

Barnaby smiled, joining Harry Wilcox in the big bay window. The editor of the *Sentinel*, for once upstaged, was generous with his praise. 'Wonderful,' he said, 'bloody marvellous. Bit of class at last. Just what the city needs.'

Wilcox was with his newly promoted features editor, a young journalist called Donna, and Barnaby was describing his trip to Singapore when he caught sight of three big furniture vans moving towards the hotel along the main road that skirted the Common. Wilcox had interrupted him, wanting to know more about the drug rehabilitation set-up. He'd passed a drugs brief to Donna only the other day. A Far Eastern perspective might sit well with whatever she was planning to do.

Barnaby heard himself describing the scene he'd witnessed at Changi prison. The Singapore authorities met fire with fire. And who could say that they were wrong? Wilcox took up the theme while Barnaby's eyes went back to the road. The first of the vans had stopped outside the hotel. The other two were also rolling to a halt. Three abreast, they blocked the traffic in both directions.

Barnaby knew something was wrong now and his eyes searched the room for Bairstow. The big policeman liked a drink. His height and bulk made him easy to spot but he was nowhere to be seen. Wilcox, his back to the window, nudged Barnaby. He was asking about Zhu. What kind of clout did he have in Singapore? Could he fix access to Changi? Could he help with flights out? Barnaby offered him a grim smile. The rear doors on the nearest van were swinging out, pushed open by unseen hands. Then the trailing board clattered down and as it did so the whole vehicle began to rock. He heard a low chant, almost tribal, then came the sound of stamping boots.

Wilcox at last turned round and looked out of the window. Bodies were pouring from the back of the furniture van, tattooed skinheads in tight white T-shirts, older men in denim jackets and high-laced Army boots. They milled around in the road for a moment or two before a smaller, slighter figure emerged, clad entirely in black, taking control at once. Barnaby stared at the face beneath the peaked SS cap, the livid scar, the gleam of madness behind the round, wire-rimmed glasses. Haagen. Haagen Schreck. The kid he'd rescued from a near-certain prison sentence. The kid he'd befriended and trusted and given the run of the office. The kid who'd repaid him by turning his daughter into a junkie.

Barnaby got to the phone, dialled 999. When the operator asked him which service he wanted he told her police. Several seconds later, another voice.

'Your name, sir?'

'I'm at the Imperial Hotel,' Barnaby announced bleakly. 'Tell Bairstow he's got a riot on his hands.'

He passed the phone to a startled guest and returned to the window. The TV crew were already on the pavement, taping the skinheads as they marched and counter-marched, roaring abuse.

> *'Chinkie bastards, we are here*
> *Shag your women, drink your beer,*
> *Sieg heil! Sieg heil!'*

The first missiles shattered the window beside Wilcox. Women screamed, backing away, and Wilcox began to shake splinters of glass from his jacket, amazed. Suddenly there was rice everywhere, small hard grains underfoot, and Barnaby ducked as another missile came tumbling up from the street below. Unlike the last, it didn't burst and Barnaby picked up a polythene-wrapped ball the size of his fist, packed tight with rice. He went back to the window, peering round the curtain, feeling the cold wind on his face. From one of the other vans, a giant snake-like creature was emerging. It was painted red, white and blue, a long, wriggling Union Jack, shouldered by a line of bearers. It wound across the road then turned and began to parade to and fro in front of the hotel, the line of Doc Martens at last in step with Haagen's barked orders.

From deep in the city came the howl of a police siren and the noise triggered a fresh barrage of missiles, paint-filled this time, the reds, whites and blues splattering the newly painted façade of the hotel. With the vans blocking the road, the traffic had come to a halt but across the Common, on the grass, Barnaby glimpsed a speeding minivan. It was white. He could see faces peering out and as the van bounced to a halt he could read the line of lettering along the side: 'Wheels for the Disabled. Donated by the Petersfield Lions Club'.

The men inside piled out and ran headlong into the waiting skinheads. Fighting started in earnest, men wrestling each other to the ground, vicious flurries of violence. One of the newcomers, an older man in jeans and a leather jacket, was attacking the head of the serpent, using his boots, and there was a roar from the skinheads as the long snake began to sag and then collapse. Four or five surrounded the man in the leather jacket, ordered into action by Haagen. A couple had baseball bats and one of the first blows caught the older man high on the side of his head. He staggered, blood pouring from the wound, then his hands went up in a protective gesture as the skinheads tore into him.

Barnaby watched, sickened. Wilcox was beside him. He seemed to be in shock.

'Scum,' he kept hissing. 'Bastard scum.'

The man in the leather jacket had gone down now and Barnaby

caught sight of Haagen again. He was striding up and down the snake, urging the men inside to their feet. Barnaby fought to control himself, then turned away from the window and threaded a path through the watching guests, elbowing them aside. On the reception desk was an empty champagne bottle. He seized it and shouldered his way through the revolving door.

Outside, on the hotel steps, the TV crew had beaten a retreat. Barnaby paused beside them, glancing back, fuelled by an anger he could almost taste. He glimpsed Liz's face behind a nearby window. She looked pale and frightened. She was waving to him, beseeching him to come back, but he ignored her, taking the steps two at a time, keeping his eyes on Haagen.

The line of skinheads on the pavement parted as he plunged through. The head of the serpent, with its crude John Bull leer, was still lying in the road. Beside it, under a blur of boots, lay the man in the leather jacket. Haagen was beyond them, urging them on. Barnaby shattered the bottle on the back of the first head he could reach. The youth collapsed and the rest turned to face him. He had the broken throat of the bottle by the neck, and he began to jab at the line of faces, determined to carve himself a path to the small strutting figure beyond. He felt the bottle slice into flesh and pushed harder, twisting it, then lashed out left and right as the line began to tighten into a circle around him. The nearest skinhead lunged at him with a baseball bat, and he felt a searing pain as it smashed against his wrist. The remains of the bottle flew from his grasp and he heard it skidding away across the road.

Then, quite suddenly, he was surrounded. The first blows numbed him to pain. He rode them as best he could, bellowing with anger and frustration, his arms shielding his face. Boots were coming in too, knee high, and he twisted away from them, knowing with a terrible certainty that going down would probably be fatal. Then, from nowhere, came an explosion of blinding white light that seemed to shatter the inside of his skull, and as the thin daylight drained away and the darkness enveloped him, he heard the wail of the siren again, slowly fading into silence.

BOOK THREE

December 1995

'Mutiny brewing at Spithead'
Captain Patton, 13 April 1797,
semaphore to the Admiralty

Chapter Nine

Hayden Barnaby sat in the darkened editing suite, transfixed. Charlie had told him very little about his plans for the commercial. He knew his friend had been talking to the television people in Southampton. He knew he'd hired post-production facilities, here in the university's media centre. And he knew he'd been out of circulation for the last couple of days, tucked away with a young video editor, cutting and recutting. But nothing had prepared him for this.

'Show me again.'

The editor respooled the tape. The screen went black. Then two lines of type appeared. *'If I am not for myself, who will be for me? If I am only for myself, what am I? If not now, when?'* Underneath the quote, briefly, appeared a name, Rabbi Hillel. Then came the swelling noise of a riot, voices chanting, glass smashing, and abruptly the text disappeared, submerged beneath a tidal wave of images, each one uglier than the last.

Barnaby had recognized the scene at once. These were images that still haunted his nightmares – lines of snarling skinheads, the blur of whirling baseball bats, the derisive taunt of an enormous Union Jack – but Charlie had done something to the composition of the pictures, changing their texture and slowing down the motion to give the sequence a strange, almost ageless look.

Barnaby could date the riot to the second. He'd been there in the Imperial when Haagen's thugs arrived. He'd been in the firing line when the first missiles shattered windows in the hotel. He'd joined the fighting down in the street, plunging into the thick of it, making things worse. He even appeared in some of the shots.

Yet watching the event again, through the prism of Charlie's special effects, was like watching an episode in a play. It was unreal. It was remote. Yet it somehow carried the assurance of still greater violence to come. Behind the roar of the skinheads, Charlie had laid a slow pulse of music, faint at first, then building and building until it drowned the sounds of the riot, giving the ugly, contorted faces a sense of implacable menace, a sign, perhaps, of things to come. The last image in the sequence, a close-up of a body sprawled in the road, remained on screen for at least five seconds. Then it slowly faded, mixing into a glorious shot of the harbour mouth, the medieval Round Tower silhouetted against the sunset. Finally, another message, shorter this time. POMPEY FIRST, it went, BETTER THAN THE STATE WE'RE IN.

The picture cut to black. Charlie reached forward and stopped the machine. He glanced round, his face shadowed by the bank of flickering screens behind him. 'What do you think?'

'I think it's incredible. What's Pompey First?'

Charlie and the editor exchanged glances. They'd been through this scene before, anticipating the obvious question. Charlie reached for the light switch.

'Our new party,' he said. 'The one you're going to start.'

They had lunch at a pub in Old Portsmouth. Barnaby sat at a table in the corner, letting Charlie order the drinks at the bar, more shaken than he cared to admit. Physically, he'd survived the riot in far better shape than he'd deserved: the blow to his head that had knocked him unconscious had been followed by a flurry of boots, and doctors at the hospital had at first suspected a fracture of the skull, but X-rays had revealed nothing. After an overnight stay under observation, Barnaby had been released to go home.

The next few weeks had been difficult. Painkillers had masked the worst of the headaches but nothing seemed to ease a profound conviction that the nightmare was about to recur. Everywhere he went, he expected fresh violence. Every stranger in the street was a potential assailant. In company, even with lifelong friends, the slightest movement made him flinch. After a month, the anxiety began to recede and by midsummer, busier than ever with Zhu's expanding empire, he could count on days when memories of the Imperial's launch never once crossed his mind. Lock them in a box, he told himself, and throw away the key. This he thought he'd done. Until Charlie's little treat.

Charlie was back with the drinks. For months, Barnaby had risked nothing stronger than shandy.

'Where did you get the pictures?'

'From the telly people. They wouldn't do anything officially but a mate of mine joined them last month. He's on the post-production side. He has access to the library. I got him to do me a dub of the rushes.'

'What does that mean?'

'I've got the lot. Everything they shot.'

Barnaby nodded, toying with his glass. The police had also acquired the TV footage of the riot. They'd invited him to head-quarters back in March to identify Haagen Schreck. They'd spared him the full coverage, showing him only a couple of still frames, close-up studies of the thin, scarred face beneath the peaked Sturm-bannführer's hat. Watching the shots, Barnaby had been enveloped again by the choking anger that had taken him down to the street, and he'd readily agreed to act as a prosecution witness, should the police ever lay hands on Haagen. In the immediate aftermath of the riot, he'd disappeared. Wilcox, watching from the hotel, claimed to have seen him commandeer a passing car but whatever his means of escape, the hunt had now been extended to Europe. The smart money was apparently on Amsterdam although, privately, Barnaby saw no reason why he shouldn't be back in his native Germany. Either way, though, it made little difference. Wherever Haagen went, Barnaby thought grimly, he'd be dripping the same poison.

Charlie was talking about his brainchild again, a brand new party, locally rooted, serving nothing but the interests of the city. He wanted to call it Pompey First. Hence the final message in the commercial.

Barnaby reached for the menu. Steak and kidney pudding sounded nice.

'What's the point?' he asked. 'Who'd be interested?'

'We would. The city would. Anyone who wants a say in their own lives.'

'You believe that?'

'Yeah.' Charlie offered an emphatic nod. 'I do.'

Barnaby smiled, amused by Charlie's passion. The last eight months had administered a dose of fervent citizenship, embedding him anew in the city of his childhood. The house in Wimbledon had been sold, his ex-wife had returned to Spain, and he'd finally parted company with the London advertising agency. His consultancy with the city's Strategy Unit had been judged a success and a busy year had been crowned by a potful of money from the Millennium Fund. By the turn of the century, according to Charlie and his colleagues, Pompey would be showing a new face to the world, no longer a run-down slum at the end of the line but the UK's most exciting landfall.

Barnaby was looking for the waitress.

'Pompey First?' he mused aloud.

'Exactly.'

'What difference would it make?'

'Everything. Every conceivable difference. No more kow-towing to fucking London. No more faxes telling us what we can and can't do.' He leaned forward across the table. 'They've kicked us around forever. It's time to get off our fucking knees. This place is great. You know it. I know it. It's got an amazing future. Why share it with the rest of the bloody country?'

For the first time, Barnaby felt a flicker of interest. Over the summer, sheer pressure of work had limited his attention to Zhu's constant string of acquisitions. After the success of the hotel had come the restaurants. Then the one-stop travel shops. And now, God help us, the naval dockyard. Zhu always kept initial negotiations close to his chest but the small print of each agreed deal had meant an ever-growing mountain of legal work and, on Zhu's insistence, Barnaby had kept the tightest possible grip on the swelling portfolio. Each new step had incurred fresh risks but Zhu had an uncanny eye for growth opportunities and the revenue streams were broader and deeper than Barnaby had ever dared hope. Pompey was, indeed, on the move. And Zhu was the living proof.

Charlie was fumbling beneath the table. Lately, he'd taken to carrying a big, shoulder-slung folio case, an elegant Italian design in soft black leather. He produced a sheaf of papers, clearing a space on the table. 'Roughs,' he explained, 'but you'll get the idea.' He handed Barnaby a sketch for a poster. The illustration showed the interior of the House of Commons. Politicians crowded the benches. The Speaker sat at one end. A figure stood at the despatch box, ignoring the forest of order papers waving at him across the aisle. Beneath the illustration, two more questions: 'Real Democracy? Or Just Going Through the Motions?'

The line brought a smile to Barnaby's face. Very Charlie Epple, he thought. Clever, barbed, provocative. He looked up. Charlie was ready with another offering. This time, the background was a jigsaw of press headlines, all attacking sleaze and corruption. Tory MPs on the make. Undeclared junkets to exotic locations. Multi-client consultancies. Refusals to toe the Nolan line. Stripped across the poster, in heavy black scrawl, another of Charlie's copylines: ALL GOOD THINGS COME TO AN END, it announced. VOTE POMPEY FIRST.

The waitress was at Barnaby's elbow. He ordered steak and kidney pudding, watching her face as her eyes strayed to the poster. When she grinned, he asked her why. 'I just wish it was true,' she said. 'That lot never listen to anyone.'

Charlie roared with laughter, then blew her a kiss. 'See?' he said. 'See what I mean?'

She blushed, scribbled down Charlie's order for egg and chips, then hurried away. A third poster rough had appeared at Barnaby's elbow. This time the message was simpler. The pen-and-ink sketch showed a grinning footballer saluting the terraces. The opposition goalkeeper lay sprawled in the mud. Beneath, in the same rough scrawl, Charlie had sent the city another message. POMPEY FIRST, it read. ANOTHER HOME WIN.

Barnaby smiled. Pompey's football team was in deep trouble. 'They're nearly bottom,' he protested.

'I know. That's the point. We needn't be.'

'You're serious?'

'Absolutely. We start a new party. We get our shit together. We contest the next elections. Here. Look.'

The last poster was different in tone, more sombre, more gritty. An upturned supermarket trolley lay at the foot of a council tower block. Kids hung around, crop-haired, watchful. In the background, the burned-out carcass of a car. The artwork was infinitely more detailed than the rest, an essay in urban bleakness, and underneath Charlie had penned a simple question. WHOSE PEACE DIVIDEND? it asked.

Barnaby nodded. Of all the posters, he felt that this one hit the mark. Anyone in the city who bothered to keep their eyes open would recognize the scene. It made you angry. It made you want to change things. For centuries, Pompey had been spilling blood for crown and country. But when it came to peace, who were the real winners?

Barnaby tapped the sheaf of roughs. 'They're excellent,' he said quietly. 'Who else has seen them?'

'Kate.'

'And what did she say?'

'Not much. I chose a bad time.'

'Billy?'

'Yes.'

Back in February, Billy Goodman had led the charge that turned Haagen's demo into a full-scale riot. By the time the ambulance men fought their way through to him, he'd been unconscious. Ten weeks in hospital had mended his broken bones but mentally he'd become a ghost, functioning only with the help of a cocktail of anti-convulsant drugs. Kate visited him daily. A discreet cheque from Zhu had bought him a fourth-floor seafront flat with views across the Solent but his life had contracted around him, and he seldom ventured out. Lately, according to Kate, he'd become depressed to the point of threatening suicide and she'd taken the precaution of removing the key to the balcony. Not that there weren't a million other ways of taking a life if it no longer seemed to promise very much.

Barnaby reached for the posters. Kate's current interest in politics, as he knew only too well, was restricted to venomous asides about Labour's rightward drift. A brand new party, the chance of a fresh start, might restore her political appetite and, with it, a little of the warmth that had once cocooned them.

Barnaby held each of the posters at arm's length, trying to imagine them on billboards across the city. Local elections took place in May. Normally only a third of the seats were up for grabs but next year, unusually, the entire council was to be re-elected. Charlie was watching him again, his new-found earnestness tinged with a little of the old mischief.

'Well?' he asked. 'Are we up for it?'

Jessie got back to Charlie's house earlier than usual, winding the bull terrier's chain around the railings while she dug in her jeans for the key. Normally, she walked Oz to the pier and back, three miles at least, but today Haagen's pride and joy had been more than usually boisterous.

The door opened and Oz plunged into the lounge. Lolly was lying full length on the sofa and as the dog began to tug at the trailing belt of her dressing gown, Jessie saw the corner of the blue air-mail envelope slipping out of the pocket.

Lolly was trying to fight off the dog. As she tumbled head first from the sofa, the letter fell onto the floor. Jessie picked it up. Her own name. Haagen's unmistakable scrawl.

'When did this come?'

'Just now. Second post.' Lolly's face had reddened. 'I opened it by mistake.'

'Liar.'

'I did. I thought it was for me.'

'Who do you know abroad?'

'Loads of people.'

'Like who?'

Lolly was on her feet again. The dog had lost interest. 'I thought you weren't in touch any more. I thought it was all over.'

'It is.'

'Fucking liar yourself. Bloody read it. Go on, read it.'

Jessie shut Oz in the hall, then sank into Charlie's only armchair. The letter was brief, a single flimsy sheet of paper. Haagen was still crashing with friends. The friends were OK but he was bored out of his head. He'd no objection to reading but he'd already gone through all the books in the house twice. Going out was risky but he owed his brain a bit of stimulus. Maybe he'd try the local bookshop. It didn't close until six and it was dark by then.

Lolly had picked up the envelope, discarded by the armchair. She was peering at the postmark. 'Where's Den Helder?'

'Haven't a clue.'

'Liar. Look on the other side.'

Jessie turned over the page. In a long postscript, Haagen had thanked her for her other letters. He'd been reading them again. They were, he explained in a rare flourish, like water in the desert. They kept him alive. They kept him sane. He'd have gone mad without them. Jessie read the postscript a second time, oblivious to Lolly's accusing glare, feeling the warmth flood through her.

'Well?' Lolly snarled.

Jessie looked up. 'Holland,' she said. 'Somewhere by the sea.'

'But why are you writing to him?'

'Because I wanted to.'

'But why? Tell me why.'

Jessie stared at her for a long time, recognizing the technique, the tone of voice. This was the way things went in Merrist House, those long, ugly afternoons when they all sat in a circle and screamed at each other. Aggression was the key. That's what loosened it all up for you. That's what was supposed to set you free.

Lolly was folding the envelope into ever smaller pieces. Her face had gone pale. 'You told me it was over.'

'It is over. He's abroad. He's gone.'

'But you want him back. It says so. As good as.'

'No, it doesn't. Writing to somebody isn't the same as wanting them back. He's a friend, that's all.'

'But you miss him.'

'I feel sorry for him.'

'Feel *sorry* for him?' Lolly was staring at her. 'The bloke that caused all the trouble? Nearly killed your dad? *Sorry* for him?'

Jessie felt the blood pulsing into her face. The riot outside the Imperial had been on television. There'd been no mistaking Haagen's role and the shots of the beating her father had taken had made her physically sick. Yet even these images she'd somehow managed to lock away, persuading herself that they had nothing to do with the Haagen she'd known.

'He's a head case sometimes,' she said defensively, 'but you're right, I do miss him – bits of him, anyway.'

'Cow.' Lolly stamped her foot, then collapsed in a heap on the sofa. She began to sob uncontrollably, a signal to Jessie that she wanted comfort, reassurance, sole possession, with nothing left for anyone else. Least of all, Haagen Schreck.

Jessie got to her feet and joined her on the sofa. She began to run her fingers through Lolly's hair but Lolly turned her face to the wall.

'Cow,' she said again. 'How could you?'

'How could I what?'

'Write to him like that? Behind my back? Not telling me?' In the absence of a reply, Lolly turned round, struggling up on one elbow. 'How many?' she said.

'How many what?'

'How many letters? How many have you sent?'

Jessie thought. She'd been writing for at least a couple of months, ever since Haagen had broken the silence with a phone call to a mutual friend. He'd fled to Antwerp. Then to Amsterdam. And then again to Den Helder where he now had a semi-permanent address. 'Four or five,' she said uncertainly.

'And he writes back?'

'Not until now. This is the first time he's bothered.'

Lolly reached out, her tiny hands closing around Jessie's throat. When she began to squeeze, her strength surprised Jessie and it was a moment or two before she was able to fight her off.

Lolly was sobbing again, incoherent with anger. 'I've looked,' she got out at last. 'I've been upstairs and fucking looked. I found them. Just where you hid them. Under the fucking bed.'

Jessie closed her eyes and took a deep breath. In her heart, she'd always known that keeping secrets from Lolly was a contradiction in terms. With Lolly, it was all or nothing. Always had been. Always would be.

'I wrote first because of the dog,' she said simply. 'And that's the truth.'

'Oz?'

'Yes. I thought he'd miss him and I was right.'

'But you kept writing.'

'Obviously.'

'And he wrote back.'

'Yes.'

'Why?'

Jessie turned away, one hand still rubbing her throat. The sheer violence of Lolly's anger had frightened her. Someone so small, so physically perfect, should be immune from that kind of ugliness.

'I don't know,' she admitted. 'It just happened, that's all. We were together a long time.'

'A year and a bit. And he fucked you up.'

'We fucked each other up.'

'That's not what you said before.'

'It's true, though.'

Lolly pulled a cushion towards her, hugging it. To Jessie's relief, she seemed to have calmed down. From the pocket of her dressing gown, she produced a stick of gum, stripping off the silver paper and tearing it in half. Jessie accepted the peace-offering. They'd seldom talked about Haagen but now was obviously the time.

'What was it about him?' Lolly was asking. 'Sex?'

'No.'

'What, then?'

'I don't know. He was special, that's all. Different. I'd never met anyone quite like him. It was the way he dressed. The way he thought. He knew so much. He took so many risks. He never seemed afraid.'

'And?'

'And?' Jessie shrugged. 'We just got it on. It just seemed natural. Nothing else really mattered.'

Lolly was frowning. 'Did you trust him?'

'Completely.'

'Even when he turned you on?'

'Yes. That was no big deal. You know how it happens. Everyone thinks that smack's, like, huge but it isn't at all. It's just another drug. It was there and we did it. He said we could stop whenever, and I believed him.'

'He was lying, though.'

'No.' Jessie shook her head. 'When he wanted to stop, he stopped. That's the whole point, you see. He's so amazingly strong. He wants to do something, he just does it. Regardless.' She looked up. 'If I couldn't stop, then that was my fault. Not his.'

'That's shit. You're talking shit.'

'No, it's not. I believe it. Whatever you do, whatever happens, it's down to you. No one else. Just you. In the end, we're all alone.'

'Who told you that?'

'He did.'

'And you still believe it?'

'Yes, I do.'

'So what does that make him?'

'A friend. Someone who writes me letters.'

'And me?'

'You're different.'

Lolly thought about the answer, chewing furiously. Then she looked up, the sudden grin emptying her face of anger.

'Let's go upstairs,' she said.

Louise Carlton waited until the interval before broaching the subject of Portsmouth dockyard. The visit to Covent Garden had been her idea, an invitation casually extended over the telephone, and she'd been gratified by the extent of Ellis's enthusiasm for Puccini. Of all the operas, *La Bohème* was his favourite and, better still, he had a passion for the pale young Australian soprano who was singing Mimi.

They were standing in the crush bar, Ellis guarding the remains of a bottle of Bollinger.

'If I ever settled down,' he said glumly, 'it would be with someone like her.'

Louise did her best to look maternal. Over the summer, she'd treated him to a number of evenings out, surprised by the austerity of his private life. He lived alone in a soulless maisonette in Carshalton. She'd been down there once for a meal, instantly depressed by the smeary windows, the cobwebbed lampshades and the second-hand chintz. When she'd asked tactfully about his plans for redecoration, he'd mumbled something about not being bothered. Most of his waking life was spent in the office or on the train. He returned home, quite literally, to sleep. That may have been true but even a man as dedicated and single-minded as Ellis deserved better than this, she'd thought.

Now, swallowing the last of her champagne, she mentioned Zhu. She'd heard that the dockyard negotiations were in trouble. True or false?

Ellis turned his back on the crowded bar, looking instantly relieved. Small-talk was the least of his talents. 'True,' he said at once.

'May I ask why?'

'Of course.' He offered her one of his rare smiles. 'It's because he's smarter than we are. It's as simple as that.'

He bent towards her, explaining how the sale had bogged down in a mish-mash of conflicting interests. The minister, with Treasury backing, was only too eager to get rid of the yard. A sale to Zhu would save the taxpayer around £150 million a year whilst safeguarding jobs and maintaining certain facilities for the Navy. The latter condition had been built into the negotiations at an early stage, evidently with Zhu's blessing. He'd be only too pleased, he'd said, to be able to bid for Navy work. This offer had been music to the minister's ears. With the Navy's other two dockyards at Devonport and Rosyth currently in the hands of private contractors, the price of repair and maintenance tenders could only go down. More good news for the taxpayer. Another round of applause at the party conference.

Ellis refilled Louise's glass.

'So what's the problem?' she asked.

'The asking price,' Ellis said. 'The place is unsaleable and Zhu knows that. The MoD started the bidding at three hundred million. That was back in the spring. Now we're looking at a dowry situation. Giving him money to take the bloody place off our hands.'

'Are you serious?'

Ellis inclined his head, almost gleeful. 'It's happened before, with other disposals. Dockyards get contaminated. It's the nature of the beast. PCBs. Asbestos. Heavy metals. Contaminants from ammunition, electroplating, you name it.' He sighed. 'Under current laws, the liabilities are already frightening. In twenty years' time it could be even worse. Zhu knows that. And he's not about to spend a third of a billion quid for the privilege of getting sued.'

Louise was studying the remains of her champagne. 'Any other tenders?'

'None. Aside from the environmental stuff, you've got serious problems with employment laws, and then there's all the nonsense about heritage. A lot of Pompey dockyard's listed. Grades one and two. You could buy it but afterwards you couldn't touch it. Which makes redevelopment a bit tricky.'

'So Zhu has a clear run?'

'Absolutely. And that means he can name his price – or even lift the thing for free. Not that the Treasury's losing sleep. Until we get to capital-cost accounting, they're only interested in what it takes to run the place. A hundred and fifty million a year off the PSBR sounds good to them.'

'But what would Zhu do with it?'

'No one knows. And not too many people care.'

Louise heard the bitterness in his voice. Recently she'd concluded that Ellis was a patriot of the old school, his vision of England untainted by the rush somehow to balance the government's books.

'What about the Navy? What's their line?'

'They're doing their best but they know they're stuffed. We've got one too many dockyards. Get any admiral drunk and he'll tell you Pompey's useless if it ever comes to war. Badly sited. Wrong ocean. Too far to steam before you get to the bits that matter. It's just a shame that half the Navy's based down there.'

Louise acknowledged the logic of Ellis's case. Missile-carrying submarines had made Portsmouth redundant but history had ringed the city with dozens of other service facilities. The school of marine engineering was nearby. Ditto the establishments that taught weaponry, communications and tactical operations. Thousands of serving personnel. Hundreds of millions of pounds' worth of hi-tech investment. Without warships and a dockyard in the middle of this sprawl, the web would lose its spider.

Behind the bar, a bell signalled the imminent start of act two. People emptied their glasses and began to move towards the door. Ellis hadn't stirred. 'It's classic,' he said with relish, 'absolutely classic. A little Chinese guy arrives with a bundle of fivers and the politicians think it's Christmas. A couple of months later he's leading us by the nose. You know something?'

'Tell me.'

'There's nothing in this country that isn't for sale.'

Ellis raised an eyebrow as if cheered by the thought, then stepped aside, allowing Louise to pursue the eddies of expensive perfume as the last of the drinkers returned to their seats.

Over supper, she'd make sure there was more champagne. They'd eat somewhere nice, somewhere fitting, somewhere expensive and oriental like Hai Tien Lo or Li Bai, and Ellis would tell her exactly how far he'd got with the Singapore people.

By the door, Louise paused. The memory of Mimi's voice still lingered in her mind and she wondered, for the first time, whether Ellis was ever lonely.

The principal drug prescribed for Billy Goodman was called Epanutin. It mixed badly with alcohol but most evenings, around ten, he slumped in the armchair by the window and emptied the best part of a quarter bottle of malt whisky. Invariably he'd wake hours later with a foul mouth and a blinding headache but since both were already listed amongst the drug's side effects, he'd decided the Scotch made no difference. If booze was invented for anything, it was for precisely this. An hour or two watching the world soften beyond the big picture windows was all that remained between himself and oblivion.

Kate sat at his feet, her back against the armchair, her knees drawn up. She'd spent the last ten minutes musing about Charlie Epple's latest wheeze.

'Tell me again,' Billy mumbled.

'There's not much to tell. He's thinking of starting a brand new party. He wants to call it Pompey First. That's about it.'

'What's the party for?'

'Us. The city. Portsmouth.'

'And who'd be in charge?'

'I don't know. It hasn't got that far. Charlie's from advertising. He never thinks things through. Not if he can help it.'

'So why's he bothering?'

It was a question that had been niggling Kate most of the day, ever since the phone call had summoned her to watch the video he'd put together. Her friendship with Charlie Epple had deepened over the summer, a welcome counterpoint to the gloom that had begun to envelop her. She needed a court jester in her life and he'd played the role to perfection. With Barnaby preoccupied with business, and her political career at a standstill, he'd been a welcome, if erratic, source of company. They'd had half a dozen meals together, been to the movies, shared a wild day out on the Isle of Wight. He was good fun and, underneath the manic one-liners, she'd sensed a real outrage about the direction the country was taking, but until she'd seen the video she'd never suspected that his disgust extended as far as political commitment.

Billy struggled out of the armchair and pulled the curtains. Despite months of physiotherapy on his damaged knee, he was still walking with a limp. He turned round, staring down at Kate. He'd put on a lot of weight, and it was beginning to show in the folds of grey flesh beneath his chin.

'Has he written a constitution? Got himself something to believe in? Or is it *à la carte*? Open house? Anyone's party?'

'I've told you, I don't know.' Kate extended a hand, feeling him flinch as her fingers brushed his thigh. 'I can't imagine he's got that far. He's great with the headlines but legal stuff just isn't his thing.'

'What about your lawyer friend, then? Can't he help?'

Kate turned her face away, refusing to be goaded. She'd talked to a lot of neurologists in the last eight months and all of them had told her the same thing. Brain injuries as severe as Billy's had lifelong consequences: feelings of inadequacy, low self-esteem, of being pushed aside from the mainstream of events. Prior to the riot, Billy had been philosophical about Hayden Barnaby. Afterwards he'd come to hate him.

'Well?' He wanted an answer.

'I don't know.'

'Haven't you asked him?'

'No.'

'Why not? I thought he was involved? Keen?'

'He is, or was.' She looked directly up at him. 'But what do you think? Do you think it's a good idea? Breaking away? Giving people the choice?'

'Choice? Choosing between two kinds of capitalism? Two kinds of greed? Two ways of stuffing your neighbour? What kind of choice is that?'

'Who said anything about capitalism?'

'No one. But you don't have to. It goes with the territory.' Billy was reaching for the bottle of whisky. Uncapped, it stood on the carpet beside the armchair. Kate's hand closed around it. He stared down at her, red-eyed, belligerent. 'Give me that bottle.'

'No.'

'I said give it to me.'

'No. Not until you tell me what you think.'

'I just did.'

'I mean what you really think. Charlie's come up with an idea. It might be very good. It might be hopeless. But the way things are, at least it's some kind of alternative. Don't you have a view on that? Without slagging us all off?'

Billy began to sway. He reached down for the arm of his chair, supporting himself. He looked about ninety.

'Socialism's the alternative,' he whispered thickly. 'Always was. Always will be. Not that it fucking matters to you.'

'That's unfair.'

'No, it's not. Pompey First. New Labour. Lib-Dems. You're pissing in the wind, all of you. It's words, just words. You come here telling me about the new Jerusalem and it turns out to be some adman's wet dream. Words are cheap. It's action that counts.'

'What's that supposed to mean?'

'Work it out for yourself. You've got eyes, haven't you?'

Kate got to her feet, angry now. She still had the bottle and when Billy tried to wrestle it out of her grasp she took a step backwards, nearly tripping over. Billy blundered after her, cursing. The open door behind her led to his bedroom. As she backed into the semi-darkness, she smelt bleach and urine. She reached for the light switch beside the door, wanting this scene over. She'd been wrong to talk about politics. The notion that it might help, that it might tempt him out of his misery and his isolation, had been hopelessly wide of the mark. Instead, it had done the reverse, adding insult to injury, swamping him with half-remembered griefs.

His head was turned away, his hand shielding his eyes from the overhead light. He was mumbling to himself, the same word over and over again, the needle stuck in the groove. She leaned forward, trying to understand him. The word was choice. He said it again and again, choice, choice, choice, then quicker and quicker until the sound became primitive and inhuman, a steam train at full throttle. Abruptly, he stopped, and his head began to shake, little flurries of movement, as if he was trying to rid himself of some demon.

Kate put her arms around him, only too certain of what was to follow, but he reared away from her with a tiny involuntary cry, his eyes rolling upwards into his head. Unconscious, he collapsed sideways, his skull cracking against the corner of the chest of drawers as his legs buckled beneath him. Kate knelt on the carpet, cradling his head as blood began to trickle from the gash above his ear. His eyes were wide open, the pupils dilated. She hauled him onto his back, gasping with the effort, and then bent to his mouth, trying to force air between his clenched teeth. When nothing happened, she straddled his chest, both hands flattened on his breastbone, pressing down hard, regular thrusts, both arms straight, the way the instructor at the health club had taught her. Billy's face was tinged with blue and she pressed harder, increasing the frequency, measuring the distance to the bedside telephone, wondering whether she dared leave him long enough to call for an ambulance. Then she felt his limbs begin to jerk beneath her, powerful spasms of movement, seismic aftershocks. Fitfully, his breathing returned and a froth of tiny white bubbles appeared around the corner of his mouth.

She began to relax, easing backwards, the sweat cooling on her face. Very gently, she turned his head sideways, letting the saliva trickle onto the carpet. Billy was breathing regularly, his jaw relaxed, his eyes closed, his limbs still. Once he gave a little sigh, the way a child might, regret perhaps, or disappointment.

In the bedside cabinet, Kate found some tissues and a tube of antiseptic cream. She dabbed at the wound on his temple, cleaning up the trickle of blood that was already beginning to crust. By the time full consciousness returned, she had an Elastoplast ready, the backing torn off, and she held it where he could see it while his eyes battled to focus. From the expression on his face, part curiosity, part bewilderment, she knew he had no memory of what had happened. She covered the wound with the plaster and sealed it with a kiss. Billy could smell the urine now, and Kate watched his hand explore the spreading pool of wetness around the crotch of his jeans. Then she bent to him again, kissing him on the lips.

'Little mishap,' she whispered, 'nothing serious.'

Louise Carlton sat in the back of the minicab as it sped south towards Carshalton. It was raining hard and Streatham High Road was a blur of empty, over-lit shop fronts as the tyres hissed on the wet tarmac. Ellis sat beside her, a bulky hunched figure in the shapeless blue raincoat. In a carrier bag between them, still warm, were the containers of chop suey and egg foo yung they'd been unable to eat at the restaurant. As ever, Louise had over-ordered, and as ever the attentive young waiters had parcelled up the left-overs, smiled at her jokes about doggy-bags and wished her a polite good night.

Ellis was talking about the Singapore people again. He'd been in touch with their Department of Commercial Affairs, trying to gauge the exact strength of the deal on offer. The Singaporeans had been badly burned by the Nick Leeson scandal. The young broker had been working for Barings, the City of London's oldest merchant bank, and the sheer scale of the losses he'd incurred had driven the bank into liquidation. The resulting headlines had shadowed the reputation of the Singapore financial exchanges and the local regulators were keen to place the blame where they felt it rightly belonged. Leeson himself had recently returned to Singapore, successfully extradited from a German prison, but there were other names on the investigator's list, way above Leeson in the Barings hierarchy, and some were still sitting behind desks in the City of London's Square Mile. So far, the English authorities had refused to co-operate in any investigation but Ellis's insistent enquiries about Raymond Zhu had evidently given the Singaporeans a little extra leverage. Whatever they knew about Zhu was only available in return for help on the Leeson case, preferably in the shape of access to certain named Barings executives.

The minicab had stopped at traffic lights. Louise was still thinking about the bankers.

'You mean they want us to arrest the Barings people? Fly them out in chains?'

'More or less.'

'And will it happen?'

'Of course not. Why should we hand them all our dirty washing?'

'Quite.'

Louise watched a couple necking in a bus shelter. At last, the lights went green and the car lurched forward.

'So where does that leave you?' she pondered. 'And our Singaporean friends?'

'Nowhere. They're absolutely intransigent. No deal on the Barings thing. No leads on Zhu.'

'You think they've got anything?'

'I'm sure they have. Whether or not it's useful . . .' Ellis left the sentence unfinished.

Louise glanced across at him, her eyes opaque behind the huge glasses. Back in the summer, she'd opened one or two doors for Ellis, offering him the promise of certain Thames House assets in his private hunt for background information on Zhu. The potential benefits to herself were obvious, stealing a big juicy plum from a tree that properly belonged in MI6's orchard, but the timing of her offer had been woeful, coinciding as it had with an abrupt change of gear in the negotiations over Portsmouth dockyard. With Zhu in the driving seat, and the Treasury ever more determined to get the dockyard off its books, Ellis had been officially tasked to prepare a DTI background file on Zhu: his origins, assets, liabilities, and that complex web of debts and allegiances that might, one day, prove embarrassing. Preparing the file, all too sadly, had meant the use of official channels. And official channels, of course, had led straight to MI6's South-east Asia desk. Six, though, had so far proved worse than useless, providing nothing more solid than a sheet or two of business connections and a rehash of old newspaper cuttings that Ellis had long ago committed to memory.

Louise patted him fondly on the thigh. Ellis had vented his impatience with Six in regular phone calls to Louise. He'd called them incompetent, a bunch of patronizing old tarts. From experience, Louise knew exactly what he meant but was convinced that Six were playing games. So far, they'd had nearly four months to shake Zhu down. In that time, given their reach and their connections, they couldn't have failed to rattle the odd skeleton. So why not share the intelligence? Why leave the DTI in the dark?

She could only assume that the Matrix-Churchill fiasco had inflicted deeper wounds than anyone had suspected. With morale at rock bottom, Six were in desperate need of a *coup de théâtre*, something really spectacular, and with half of Whitehall as an audience, an abrupt exposé of Raymond Zhu might do very nicely indeed. Politically, the timing would be crucial. Let the dockyard negotiations run and run. Let the public controversy build and build. Let the pens be poised over the final contract. Then send the killer fax, the one that revealed the truth about Zhu, the one that cut the ground from beneath the politicians' feet, the one that kept the Union Jack flying over the nation's favourite dockyard.

Louise's hand dropped into the carrier bag beside her, her square-trimmed nails finding the little crimped edges of the foil containers. The MI6 ploy she understood only too well. She'd done exactly the same with the boy Schreck, back in the spring. Find something newsworthy, something guaranteed to get the tabloids foaming at the mouth. Seed the situation, nurture it with care. And when the politicians were suddenly beset by headlines, make the most of your inside track.

With the National Front, it had been simplicity itself. The Southsea riot had made the front page of every paper in the country. The television pictures had been shown world-wide. And next morning, when the Home Secretary had been desperate for instant solutions, David Jephson had quietly pointed out the wisdom of confirming MI5 as the lead agency with respect to political extremism.

It was true, of course, that Thames House had always kept files on the lunatic fringe but intelligence had traditionally been separated from operations. Schreck, though, had put the police blockade to shame, driving through every checkpoint on the road south, and after the very public débâcle outside the Imperial Hotel, the battle in this particular corner of the turf war had been well and truly over. Henceforth, when it came to planning operations, Five would be guaranteed a key seat at the table.

Louise eased the lid from the container, slid her fingers inside, then licked them one by one. The oyster sauce was truly delicious. Beside her, Ellis was staring out of the window. She motioned towards the carrier bag, inviting him to help himself. Then she was struck by another thought. 'There's a chap down in Portsmouth called Tully,' she mused. 'I think you ought to meet him.'

*

Kate was still in bed when Barnaby called round next morning. He let himself into the house, stopping off in the kitchen to test the kettle. Finding it cold, he prepared a tray of tea, making room beside the sugar bowl for the brand new foolscap pad he'd picked up at the office. Minutes later, he was perched on the end of Kate's bed, the pad on his lap, explaining again why they had to get the small print right.

'We're setting ourselves up,' he said. 'We'll be a threat, a target. One chink in the armour, and we'll blow it.'

'You're talking like a lawyer.'

'That's because I am a lawyer.'

'Sure.' Kate scowled sleepily. 'And don't I know it.' Barnaby abandoned the pad long enough to kiss her. She tasted, very faintly, of Scotch.

'Tell me about this threat.' She pulled him down beside her. 'Who's going to be bothered?'

'Labour for one.'

'Why?'

'Losing you.'

'Who says I'm joining?'

Barnaby looked at her. When his hand found her breast beneath the T-shirt, she told him to behave.

'I'm serious,' she said. 'This is boys' talk, a new toy, you and Charlie having a little fantasy. Politics is too important to be left to you lot. Bloody men, you're all the same.'

'Not fair,' Barnaby remonstrated. 'Absolutely not fair.'

'You really care enough to do it? Go along with it? All those envelopes to be stuffed? All those doors to be knocked on?'

'Charlie thinks there might be alternatives.'

'Like what?'

'He wouldn't say but you know what he's like with hi-tech.'

'Too right. If you can plug it in or screw it, wonderful. Otherwise, forget it. So where does that leave boring old local elections? And that's another thing.'

'What?'

'Where does all the money come from?'

Barnaby uncapped the fountain pen he liked to use for legal

drafting. For the time being, money was the least of his problems. Zhu's acquisitions in the city had resulted in a flood of detailed contract work and the accountant who kept an eye on the practice's books was anticipating a 270 per cent increase in gross revenues.

'The money's fine,' he said lightly. 'It's the rest I worry about. We've got a clean sheet of paper. Literally.' He gestured at the pad. 'Isn't that every politician's dream?'

Kate countered the question with a shrug. The cat had sprawled across her chest, begging for attention.

'It's not as easy as that. Politics is subtler than you think. You can't just write a shopping list.'

'I don't intend to. We need a constitution, a legal shell. I thought you might have some ideas. I'm just trying to be demo-cratic. Anything wrong with that?'

'Nothing – nothing at all. I'm just wondering how seriously you're taking all this.' She fondled the cat. 'It's a nice idea. In fact it's brilliant. I can think of a dozen politicians in this city who'd die for the chance of a fresh start, and two of them are Tory MPs. But . . .' her eyes were still fixed thoughtfully on the cat ' . . . it's you really, your motives.' She looked up. 'Why get involved? Why bother? When everything's so sweet for you?'

Barnaby was vaguely aware of his pen doodling triangles across the top of the page. He'd been half anticipating this scene for weeks. The past half year had been truly hectic. With his time strictly rationed, the relationship had been forced into odd corners of his schedule, and Kate was far too competitive to put up with second best. Her jealousy of Liz had developed into a resentment of anything that stood between them and it was harder and harder to make her believe that he still wanted her, that he still cared. He looked up, seeing the unvoiced accusation in her eyes. Instead of flowers, or a bottle of wine, he'd brought her something rather special. Was that why he was here? An early Christmas present? A brand new party of her very own?

He shook his head, refusing to be distracted, inching himself onto firmer ground. When it came to rows, he was hopeless. 'We need to make ourselves into an association,' he began, 'unincorpor-ated. Answerable only to our own rules. That's step one.'

Kate was smiling now. 'We did that,' she said, 'some time ago. Before you took leave of absence.'

'I'm serious. This way we'll be under no obligation to publish accounts. Financially it's wonderful. No corporation tax. In fact, no tax of any kind. As long as no one comes away with a profit.'

'Can you do that?'

'No problem. It's the same with any association. I'm drafting constitutions all the time. Bowls clubs. Veterans' associations. Allotment societies. The concept's called mutuality. You write yourself a constitution, define what you're about and off you go. Beautiful.'

'But we're talking about a political party, not the Darby and Joan club.'

'Makes no difference. How do you think the Tories get away with concealing all those foreign donations?' He prodded the pad. 'They're just a network of associations, all over the country, with nothing very much in the middle – just a bunch of guys getting together for their mutual benefit. There's no chief executive, no profit motive. They've got party officials, and directors and so forth, and I think there's a board of management and treasurers to oversee the financial bits, but that's about it. Locally, we could set up exactly the same structure.' He grinned. 'No problem.'

Kate looked surprised. 'Is that really the way they do it? I thought they just steam-rollered on. Breaking all the rules.'

Barnaby shook his head. 'They can't. They wrote the rules in the first place. That's why it's so important to get the constitution right. They *are* the rules.'

'I see.' Kate reached at last for the mug of tea, mollified. 'So what do we say?'

'We?'

'You.' She grinned back. 'Mr Lawyer.'

Barnaby paused a moment. Scarcely a day had gone past since Charlie had broached the possibility of creating a brand new political party. In truth, between them, they had nothing but a name. But the name, in a sense, said it all. Pompey First.

'Let's do it a different way,' he said. 'Forget the legal stuff. I'll take care of that. Let's think about what we want to do with it, what it's there for in the first place.' He began to scribble on the pad. Then he looked up. 'I've kept it simple,' he said. 'Five points.'

He returned to the pad, listing the imperatives. Pompey First would focus entirely on the needs of the city. It would attack the problems of crime, unemployment and poverty. It would involve local people in their own governance. It would attract investment from national and international sources. And it would make sure that the proceeds of that investment found its way to every corner of the community.

Kate nodded, engaged now. 'What about equality? Fairness? Justice?'

Barnaby pointed at his notes. 'It's all there. It's implicit.'

'No, it's not. You need to spell it out,' she said. 'Go on, do it.'

Barnaby hesitated, then set to work. Point Six registered Pompey First's commitment to building a fair society in the city, based on the principles of justice, equality and mutual tolerance.

'Excellent,' Kate mimed applause, 'except for the last bit. Put respect, not tolerance.'

Barnaby's pen hovered. Then he glanced at her, curious. Words were his business. The change of nuance was important.

'Why respect? Why not tolerance?'

'Because respect is what matters. Tolerance is wishy-washy. Too much tolerance and the whole thing falls apart. Ask Jessie. She'd know.'

'That's uncalled-for.'

'No, it's not, it's the truth. If I didn't love you, I wouldn't say it.' She nodded briskly at the pad. 'Read it again. From the start.'

Barnaby did as he was told, swallowing his pique at her comment about Jessie, warming anew to his brief. Several phrases needed reworking and there were other areas that might repay a little exploration but overall it had a nice feel. He got to the end and capped his pen. Kate had dipped her finger in the milk jug and the cat was licking it.

'It's great,' she said. 'But you know what it reminds me of?'

'No.'

'Singapore,' she said quietly, at last making room for him in the bed.

Charlie Epple was into the last mile of his morning run before the strategy began to slip into focus. All his life he'd wanted to sell something he truly believed in. Not just consumer goodies, like foreign lagers or designer ice creams, not just financial scams, like privatization, but something with which he'd feel a real kinship. His consultancy with the council people had very nearly done it. Selling the city of his birth, having to package views and history he'd always taken for granted, had opened his eyes to what might be possible. The process, as ever, had been hampered by the inevitable compromises, and it was a pain in the arse to have to kiss goodbye to some of his wilder copylines, but the freedoms extended by the guys on the Strategy Unit had brought him within sight of the ultimate challenge: not simply selling the city but having a hand in shaping an entire way of life.

He was on the seafront now, passing the war memorial, the tall column of names that commemorated Pompey's fallen. From here to the fun-fair was a good quarter of a mile and the last few weeks he'd been pushing harder and harder, forcing himself into a sprint for the imaginary tape that signalled the end of his run.

It was a beautiful day, bright sunshine, broken skies, and a moist, blustery wind swirling around the beach-side cafés. He bit deeper into that precious reserve he kept for these last few seconds, aware of the slap-slap of his new Reeboks on the paving stones. Ahead of him, the big hovercraft from the Isle of Wight was surging up the beach from the deep water channel and he could taste the salt on his lips as the fine cloud of spray enveloped him. He fixed his eyes on the pilot up in the hovercraft's cockpit, trying to ignore the rasping in his throat, telling himself that his legs would only jelly when he stopped. Then, moments later, he was there, bent double in the pale sunshine outside the amusement arcade, sucking the air back into his lungs. At length, he stood upright again, sweat pouring off his face, trying to ignore the stares of disembarking passengers. Happiness smelled of stale fish and chips, he thought. God bless Pompey.

He began to jog through the fun-fair, keeping warm. The rides were dismantled for the winter, the big wheel stripped of its gondolas, the Waltzer padlocked, the dodgem cars crated. On the adjoining pier, a couple of kids were fishing, and on the long stretch of promenade that reached towards the harbour mouth Charlie could see one or two elderly couples, walking arm in arm, but otherwise the seafront was empty. Beside the thick-walled stone redoubt that marked the seaward end of Old Portsmouth's fortifications, Charlie stopped again, leaning back against the railings and staring out across the tumble of rooftops around the cathedral. Fifteen giddy years in the advertising business had taught him that there was nothing that couldn't be sold. By carefully crafting the message, by appealing to exactly the right measures of greed, or envy, or insecurity, a good campaign could trigger responses that translated within weeks into hard cash. It was a process that had never ceased to amaze him. Get the ad right, and the product, any product, simply got up and walked off the shelves. It had happened time and time again and the only downer was the fact that the money, by and large, went into the pockets of people he despised. Advertising, he'd always thought, was wasted on commerce. Businessmen had no soul, no real appreciation of the things that mattered. Much better, thought Charlie, to try and apply his skills in an altogether worthier cause.

He nodded to himself, feeling the sweat cooling on his face. The commercial he'd shown Barnaby had been the first step. He'd put it together because he'd seen what had happened outside the Imperial and he couldn't think of any other way of getting at the animals responsible. He hated the National Front. He loathed racism. But when he began to build the commercial, shot by shot, he realized that this ugly eruption of violence, so graphically captured, was the perfect image for a much wider brutality. The eighties had taken the gloves off. Thatcher's shock troops had carried all before them, slashing and burning, and there was fuck-all left of that rather comfortable, rather safe society he remembered from his Pompey days. Much of the onslaught had been fuelled by advertising, and few who had been better placed to watch the process than Charlie, but after the glitz and the promises of the boom years, there'd come the reckoning. Bits of Britain were a wasteland, truly ravaged, and in his gloomier moments Charlie saw no reason why the process should ever stop. Thatcher's tiger was out of the cage. And no politician had the bollocks to put it back again.

Charlie clambered down to a tiny beach beneath the walls. He stooped for a small flat pebble and sent it skipping across the water. In a society close to disintegration, the video commercial had shown him a way forward. Why? Because the logic at the end of the piece had been irresistible. Images as strong as these, with all their implications of a wider violence, led to only one conclusion. Things had to change. And if you couldn't start nationally, with the big picture, then you had to think on an altogether smaller scale. Pompey, as it happened, was perfect. Lots of people jigsawed together, nicely curtained away on the south coast. Lots of debris from the eighties: houses repossessed, schools falling apart, kids out of control, jobs non-existent. Lots of scope, in short, for a fucking good shake-out. Pompey First!

Charlie grinned in approval, wondering what Kate and Barnaby had made of it, whether or not they'd seize the baton and run. In their separate ways, he sensed that they both loved power, and the invitation to be in on the birth would give them almost parental rights. He knew that Barnaby, especially, was keen. He'd seen it in his eyes when he'd shown him the posters in the pub, and he had virtually admitted it, outside on the pavement, when he had asked about display rates for the big roadside billboards.

Charlie returned to the promenade. At the head of the steps that led down to the street, he paused, still thinking about Barnaby. Across the road was his new house. Up on the top floor, the curtains in Lolly's bedroom were still closed and he found himself wondering whether her sexual curiosity ever extended as far as men.

Chapter Ten

Once the meetings were over, Ellis was glad to get out in the fresh air again. He'd driven down to Portsmouth last night, his Datsun developing a leak when the rain got really heavy, and he'd booked into a hotel within sight of the marina development where Askew's, the London accountants, had built their new complex.

This southern outpost of the big City firm had been retained by the MoD to advise on the negotiations over the sale of the dockyard, and Ellis had spent the morning being briefed by a succession of accountants on the fiscal implications of various options Zhu was currently tabling for discussion. Ellis had no formal training in accountancy, but his years at the DTI had given him little faith in paper qualifications and he was confident that he'd grasped the essence of what the Askew's people were saying.

Zhu's business plans were ambitious and almost impossible to test against any contemporary benchmark. Whenever the accountants tried to tie down his figures – his tourist revenue projections, for instance, or his anticipated yield from maintenance and repair work – he simply shifted the goalposts. In a fast-moving world, he kept pointing out, the big prizes went to the swift and the brave. Where this left the politicians was anyone's guess. Given the imminence of an election, the last thing they could afford was protracted negotiations.

Ellis folded his raincoat over his arm and made his way across the car park. Last night's rain was still puddled beneath the dashboard on the passenger side of the Datsun and Ellis wondered if he should mop it up before meeting Tully. They'd agreed a rendezvous at a pub on the marina's boardwalk for half past twelve, and it was just possible that he might be in need of a lift afterwards. He got in and started the engine. The man worked for an investigation agency, for God's sake. He was bound to have transport of his own.

A road around the edge of the marina took Ellis to the pub where he'd agreed to meet Tully. Beyond a smart executive housing development was a forest of masts, and further down the road he could see a big crescent of apartments, encircling a yacht basin. The apartments looked newly built, each balcony carefully sited to take advantage of the view, and the feel of the place was at odds with the impression of Portsmouth he'd built up from conversations in London. According to colleagues in the DTI, Pompey was the kind of destination for which you bought a day return. Spending any serious time there was beyond the call of duty.

Tully was already in the pub when Ellis walked in. He was sitting beside a window, a small glass of orange juice barely touched. When he saw Ellis he lifted his copy of the *Daily Telegraph*, got up and extended a hand. He was a small, broad, stocky man with a full beard and deep-set eyes. The flannels and the blazer blended nicely with the view from the window.

Ellis said something complimentary about the marina, then fetched himself a pint of lager from the bar and sat down.

'It's about Zhu,' he said, 'as I expect you've gathered.'

Tully didn't react. His range of facial expression seemed limited to a wariness verging on acute suspicion. Finally, he asked Ellis for his ID. Ellis extracted a ministry pass from his wallet and handed it across. The photograph, though recent, was horrible. It had been taken when he'd only just recovered from flu and it showed.

Tully grunted and handed it back. 'Zhu was a client of mine,' he said, 'which makes it tricky.'

'Was?'

'Yeah. I've done nothing for him since the summer. Still,' he added, 'that's not the point. Business is business. There's a code here. If a man pays me money, he expects confidentiality. You wouldn't want me to break it.'

Ellis said nothing, but opened his briefcase and took out a file. Louise Carlton had warned him that Tully would be difficult. He had a service background in the Royal Marines. His posting to the Special Boat Squadron had led to a series of covert engagements, and his MoD file, which Ellis had seen, had a great deal to say about his two-year posting to Brunei. This was a man of cast-iron integrity, impeccably motivated, a textbook soldier. For the right cause, he'd do literally anything. Under fire, when others had faltered, he'd fulfilled his mission to the letter. His last commanding officer, a thoughtful Scot now heading the UK division of a major American oil company, had described him as 'solitary, old-fashioned and utterly trustworthy'.

Ellis handed over the file. Inside, with the exception of the detail of the dockyard negotiations, was a précis of everything he currently knew about Zhu. The fact that nothing in the three-page summary merited even the lowest security classification was a measure of his desperation.

He watched Tully's eyes move steadily through the text. At the end of each page, he licked a fingertip before turning over. Finally he looked up, his puzzlement edged with impatience. 'The man's in business. He's very successful. Shipping, hotels, construction, he's a good operator,' he said. 'Does that make him a problem?'

'It might.'

'Why?' Ellis didn't answer. The lager was warmer than he might have liked. He offered the menu to Tully, who declined. 'Why all the fuss?' he repeated.

Ellis reclaimed the file. The people at MI6 had confirmed Zhu's birthplace as Amoy, a city in the southern Chinese province of Fukien. According to them, he was fifty-seven years old and had fled to Hong Kong when Mao's Communists swept to power in 1949. He'd stayed there for twenty years, laying the foundations of the empire he'd chosen to build in Singapore.

Ellis looked up. 'You know he's bidding for the dockyard? Here? In Portsmouth?'

'Yes, of course.'

'Did he ever discuss it with you? Before he opened nego-tiations?'

'No, he didn't.'

'Does that surprise you?'

'Not at all. I was an employee, Mr Ellis, a foot soldier. I did the small stuff, the preliminaries, finding little bits and pieces for him to bid for. Zhu was out of my league way before the dockyard.'

Ellis asked him what he meant. Tully explained Zhu's appetite for land zoned for development. Portsmouth was a crowded little island but there was still space within the city for the odd industrial estate.

'And he wanted to buy one?'

'Several.'

'And you helped him?' Tully cocked an eyebrow and Ellis knew at once that he'd gone too far. The query had sounded like an accusation. He rephrased it. 'You were still involved? At this stage?'

'To some degree. I certainly helped where I could, but the bigger stuff was beyond me. I don't know about you, Mr Ellis, but in my business it pays to be candid. Never oversell yourself. If you're out of your depth, you drown.'

Ellis nodded. There was something reassuring about this man. His commanding officer had been right. He was old-fashioned. In a world addicted to small deceits and petty advantage, he had a blunt preoccupation with the truth. Ellis looked at his hands as they tugged at the creases on his flannel trousers. He could see no rings and he began to wonder about his private life. Was he married? Or was he as solitary as he appeared to be?

Tully was gazing at the file. 'Tell me about this dockyard thing,' he grunted. 'How far has it got?'

'Not that far. There's a bid on the table. The MoD have formed a committee, as you might imagine.'

'Who's represented?'

Ellis was surprised at the depth of Tully's interest. 'Defence Lands,' he said slowly. 'Legal advisers. Someone from the Navy Staff Secretariat. The Chief of Fleet Support. All the usual suspects.' He frowned. 'Plus some guys from Askew's up the road.'

'Askew's are involved?'

'Very much so. This is a complex negotiation. Getting the figures right matters more than anything. So it pays to have the best.'

'Pays whom?'

'Us.'

'Who's us?'

At last Ellis sensed an opening, a tiny crack in Tully's carefully maintained defences. The man, after all, cared. And cared deeply.

'The nation,' Ellis said lightly. 'Who else?'

Tully reached for his orange juice, refusing to be drawn. At length, he enquired about the schedule for the negotiations. Was there a deadline? A pressing need to get the dockyard off the Navy's hands?

'Not officially, no.'

'What does that mean?'

'It means that we're bound by ministry rules. There are hoops we have to jump through. Due diligence is one of them. You can't hurry these things.'

'Unless the politicians bend the rules.'

'Exactly.'

'So there is a deadline?'

'Of course there is. There's an election in sight. And we're talking big money.'

'How big?'

'I'm afraid I can't say.'

Tully was staring out of the window. In profile, his face tilted up, he looked like a man facing a strong wind.

'Zhu's extremely sharp,' he said quietly. 'You'll know that already. He doesn't pay big money. Not if he can help it.'

'Then perhaps he can't help it.'

The beginnings of a smile briefly creased the pale skin around Tully's eyes. 'That I doubt. Especially if he's the sole bidder.'

'Who said that?'

'He did. In the local paper. Yesterday.' He paused. 'I've watched him, been with him. I like the man, don't get me wrong, but he'll eat you alive, I guarantee it. That's the way these guys are made. I've been out there, in the service. I've seen it first hand. It's bred into them. It comes with their mother's milk. There are thousands of Zhus in Hong Kong, in Singapore. Form all the committees you like, you'll never lay a finger on people like Zhu.'

'You make him sound like a gangster.'

'Not at all. He's just very good at what he does. It's all down to excellence. If you don't win, you're nowhere, you're history. It's as simple as that.'

Not quite knowing why, Ellis had produced a pen. Part of him wanted to register the usual objections, to talk about the burdens of democracy, the handicap of having to play by a certain set of civil-service rules. Another part of him simply agreed.

'You're right,' he conceded eventually. 'But does it matter?'

'Of course it bloody matters.'

'Why?'

'Because you're dealing with a national asset. This is a working dockyard, for God's sake, not some ancient monument. We're talking about live skills, key facilities, all the stuff the Navy needs to keep going. You can't just flog it off to some foreigner. Just because he's got the money. Just because he might help you get elected again.'

'Maybe he hasn't got the money.'

'He's got loads of money.'

'Then maybe he doesn't need to spend it.'

Tully looked startled. 'What?' he growled. 'What did you say?'

'I've said nothing. I'm just suggesting the situation might be less clear cut than it seems. You're right about the other bidders. There aren't any. Zhu's got a clear run. And you're right about Zhu, too. He's bloody sharp. He won't part with a penny unless he has to.'

'So what are you telling me? Exactly?'

Ellis was toying with his pen, capping and uncapping it. The conversation had gone further than he'd intended but he sensed that this was the only way to get Tully onside. There had to be a degree of trust, an agreement on shared objectives. And that, God help us, meant a glimpse or two of the truth.

'This is in confidence,' he said carefully. 'Zhu wants to buy the dockyard, and he wants us to put up most of the money.'

'How does he figure that?'

'Because he thinks it's a liability. Not an asset at all.'

'Then he's crazy.'

'Sadly not.' Ellis gave Tully a bleak smile. 'Liability's our word, not his. The politicians are using it all the time. Things we have to shed. Items the state has to get rid of. You may have noticed.'

There was a long silence. Tully was staring out of the window again but nothing could mask his anger. He emptied his glass.

'So will he get it? The dockyard?'

'Yes, I think he will.'

'And what will he do with it, once it's his?'

Ellis reached for the remains of his lager. 'I've no idea,' he said. 'That's why I'm here.'

Lolly was still in bed when she heard the phone begin to ring. She lay on her back, staring up at the ceiling, wondering whether anyone else was in. She'd been up most of the night trying to write a letter to Jess, trying to wrestle her feelings onto paper, but none of it had made any sense. Waking up at noon, she'd started the letter afresh in her head, hitting the same bumps in the road, the same blind bends. Maybe a letter wasn't such a great idea. Face to face she'd probably manage it much better.

The phone was still ringing. She got out of bed, wrapping the eiderdown around her. Her bedroom door was already open, the standing invitation to Jessie, and she slipped onto the landing and down the stairs in time to lift the phone before the trilling stopped.

The voice at the other end belonged to a man. He asked for Jessie. Alert at once, Lolly said Jessie was out. She'd be back whenever. In the meantime, Lolly would be glad to take a message. There was a long silence.

Then the voice returned. 'OK,' he said. 'Tell her I'm thinking of coming back.'

'Who are you?'

'Doesn't matter. Just tell her that.'

'Shall I say a date?'

'No, but it'll be pretty soon, though.' There was a silence. 'Tell her something else, too.'

'What's that?'

'Tell her she was right to keep hassling. This place is shit.' The phone went dead and Lolly found herself sitting on the bottom stair, hugging her knees. Haagen, she thought, Haagen fucking Schreck. Even the name had come to obsess her, a big fat cloud that shadowed the relationship that she and Jessie had now sustained for nearly eight months. Together they'd managed to stay clean, stay healthy. Together they'd travelled further than any of the dickheads at Merrist House. By settling down and getting herself a permanent address she'd even impressed the social workers back in Guildford. With luck, they might even let her look after her daughter again.

After a while, she went upstairs. She'd found the letters in a box under Jessie's bed. With them had been a brown glass jar, crusted with candle wax. On the side of the jar, partly peeled off, was a picture of a canal. She'd no idea exactly how but she was sure that the jar had been a keepsake from Jessie's days with Haagen. It was exactly the kind of rubbish the silly cow would hang onto. Emotionally, she never let go of anything.

Lolly pushed open the door of Jessie's bedroom and slipped in. The duvet on the bed was thrown back. On the pillow was a half-completed pencil sketch of the view from the window. Lolly got down on her knees and felt under the bed for the box. The jar was still inside. She lifted it out. It was cheap and nasty, the glass rim already chipped. She held it in her hand, remembering the voice on the telephone, then she hurled it at the wall. The broken glass showered onto the bed and Lolly grinned, looking down at it, before running upstairs to her own room and slamming the door.

Minutes later, dressed, she was back in the hall, hunting for Jessie's mum's address in the phone book.

Charlie Epple was due at the cable TV headquarters for a two o'clock meeting. The studios were ten miles inland, off the old London trunk road, and, at the top of Portsdown Hill, with half an hour in hand, he pulled his sleek new Calibra onto one of the car parks that looked out over the city.

The view from the hill had always fascinated him, the tricks that height and distance played with the grid of endless streets, the big council tower blocks and the tangle of distant cranes that hung over the warships in the dockyard. Up here, where the wind always seemed to blow, you could half close your eyes and play God with the city below, demolishing the gasworks that disfigured the Hilsea industrial estate, realigning the sweep of motorway that funnelled traffic across the upper harbour, expanding the roll-on, roll-off berths in the commercial docks choked with cross-Channel ferries. It was a fun thing to do, ridiculously easy, and he sauntered back across the car park, his hands deep in his pockets, wondering whether Pompey First might bring the fantasy alive.

The last few days he'd done nothing but explore the implications of founding a brand new political party, all too aware that the difference between success and failure would lie in the small print. To his surprise, the business of fielding candidates in the city's thirteen wards was remarkably simple. A phone call to the council's electoral officer had produced a thick envelope stuffed full of nomination forms. They came in two versions: signature of one testified that the candidate either lived or worked within the electoral borough; completion of the other required eight seconders to support the candidate's nomination. Neither of these hurdles was especially daunting and, with five months to go before the local elections, it shouldn't be impossible to find the right individuals to put themselves forward. Within each ward there were three council seats. That made a total of thirty-nine candidates, local men and women committed enough to their own city to turn the political system on its head and break the stranglehold of the three major parties.

Charlie kicked a stone and watched it tumble down the hillside. He'd seen Barnaby only this morning, dropping off some stuff he'd got together with a local graphics student. Barnaby had given him coffee, shown him the draft constitution, together with the bones of the manifesto that he and Kate were knocking into shape. The latter had a beautiful simplicity: here was a message addressed to no one but the inhabitants of a specific city. Nothing had been blurred by the interests of Westminster or Whitehall. Nothing had been fudged to accommodate some national interest group. Just

Pompey, First, Last and Always. Charlie played with the phrase, trying to imagine it on billboards beside the city's major roads, and when he got back to the car, he made a note of it, scribbling the line on the back of his electricity bill.

The sight of the bill brought a smile to his face. Behind him, across the rolling countryside on the other side of the hill, a line of pylons carried electricity to the city. Already, in conversation with Barnaby, he'd explored the logic of Pompey First. What if they cleaned up at the May elections? What if they'd identified a real appetite for putting the city's interests first? What if that hunger extended as far as a bid for genuine independence?

Charlie wound down his window. Pompey's only power station had been demolished years ago. Every household in the city was dependent on the national grid. Given some form of independence, who'd guarantee that the lights stayed on? Charlie folded the bill into his pocket, blissfully happy, knowing that questions like these were the stuff of the best adventures, infinitely more challenging than campaigns for aftershave or ice lollies. Pompey First, he thought, midwife to Europe's youngest city-state.

The cable TV headquarters comprised one half of a modern, system-built office block on an industrial estate outside the suburb of Waterlooville. The tiny reception area was criss-crossed by busy young men on mobile phones, and a line of framed faces on the wall beamed down at prospective customers. Each belonged to a salesman of the month, and while Charlie waited to meet the PR manager, he listened to the swirl of conversation around him. This kind of language was all too familiar: it came straight from America, and over the last couple of years it had swamped the companies he was used to dealing with in London. These people were dedicated to the aggressive sell, everything up-front, everything in your face, and they fired their bullets with total conviction, immensely proud of the product. Hitching onto the cable was a steal. It gave you options, choice. Something for Mum. Something for Dad. Loads of stuff for the kids. Charlie grinned. If fourteen quid a month bought you lifestyle, science, sport, music and kids' cartoons, why not Pompey First as well?

The woman who ran the PR operation invited him upstairs.

Her name was Nicky. She was neat and businesslike, with bobbed blonde hair and a lovely mouth. She had a desk and a spare chair in a big open-plan office, and there was room beside her computer for a teddy bear dressed in Pompey colours. While Charlie explained the excitement of launching a brand new political party, she made notes on a pad at her elbow. When he had finished, she offered him a polite smile.

'I'm not quite with you,' she said. 'Where do we fit in all this?'

Charlie was looking at a map on the wall. At the bottom was the city of Portsmouth. Across the island, and inland to the north, colour-coded pins recorded the advance of the fibreoptic cable that carried the company's thirty-two channels. Charlie had seen maps like this before in some of the other cable franchises. In national terms, the industry had been a big disappointment but he'd heard rumours that the Pompey operation was the exception to the rule. 'How many homes are we talking here?'

'Serviceable? Seventy-four thousand.'

'And how many have signed up?'

'Eighteen thousand.'

Charlie nodded. The rumours had been spot on. Eighteen thousand homes was a penetration rate of nearly 25 per cent, way above the national average. He looked at the map again, trying to calculate how many of the customers lived within the city itself. Inland, where the monied folk tended to settle, the take-up rate would be low. The cable people hated admitting it, but signing on for Sky and the Disney package was still emphatically down-market.

'Do you look at the demographics?' Charlie asked. 'Area by area?'

Nicky smiled. She was bright. She'd seen the question coming. 'Yes,' she said. 'And you're right. Cold calling on the council estates is a doddle. Ask any of the blokes.'

Charlie thought briefly of the faces on the wall downstairs. No wonder the salesmen of the month looked so cheerful. In Paulsgrove or Portsea, you could sell anything that kept the kids off the street.

Nicky fetched coffee from a nearby machine. Her earlier bemusement seemed to have gone. She was looking at the wall map again. 'Where have you drawn the line?' she asked. 'Where does Pompey First begin and end?'

'Existing city boundaries. All thirteen wards are up for grabs in May.' He sensed an ally in this undeclared war. 'You think that's sensible?'

'I think it's perfect. More to the point, it's what the punters think too. Did you see the MORI poll in ninety-three?'

Charlie hadn't. Nicky explained that the city council had commissioned an opinion poll as part of its submission for something called unitary status. Under the current arrangements, the city was administered jointly from the Civic Centre and from County Council Headquarters, twenty-five miles away in Winchester. The division of responsibilities was confusing and inefficient, and the local officers naturally wanted to be masters in their own house. Charlie had heard a little of this before from colleagues in the Strategy Unit, and knew that the city had won its case. The MORI poll, though, was a mystery.

'What did it say?'

'It was a questionnaire. People were given various options. Did they want Pompey to amalgamate with Fareham and Gosport? With Havant? With East Hampshire? Did they want to stick with the current arrangement? Or would they prefer to go it alone?'

'And?'

'Forty-seven per cent said go it alone.'

'Meaning?'

'Draw the line at the city boundaries.' She smiled again. 'Just like Pompey First.'

Charlie reached for a pen. This was a killer figure, rock-solid evidence that Pompey First would hit a nerve city-wide. In marketing terms, 47 per cent was the jackpot.

'Do you want the rest of it?' Nicky asked.

'There's more?'

'Absolutely. You know it's the densest-populated city in the country outside London? You measure these things by the hectare. Up country, in Hampshire, we've got four people per hectare. You know the figure for Pompey?'

Charlie's pen was poised.

'Twenty?' he guessed. 'Thirty?'

'Forty-five. It's written on my heart. It's one of the reasons the board give us so much rope. Pompey's perfect for cable. Tightly packed housing. The right demographics. Strong local feel. You know the employment profile? How many people in work find jobs within the city?'

'Tell me.'

'Eighty-six per cent. That's unheard of. And it's the same for shopping, too. Ninety per cent of householders never leave the city. It's all here for them.'

Charlie's pen raced across the pad. Better and better, he thought. He looked up. 'How come you know all this stuff?'

'I used to work for the council. And it's handy for this job, too. As you might imagine.'

Charlie frowned. Nicky Bannister wasn't a name he'd come across during his sessions with the Strategy Unit.

'What did you do?'

'PR stuff, organizing mainly. I was on board for the whole of 'ninety-four. All the major celebrations.'

'D-Day? Tour de France?'

'Yes, all that.' She looked at the teddy bear. 'I was Nicky Elliott then. I remarried last year.'

Charlie sat back. Nicky Elliott was a minor legend amongst certain council officers. Almost single-handed, she'd held the ring while various heavyweights from Whitehall and Washington fought tooth and nail over the arrangements for the fiftieth anniversary of the D-Day landings. Portsmouth, for one wet June weekend, had become the focus of the world's attention, and Charlie remembered his own amazement, coming home to find the city thick with foreign heads of state.

'How was it?' he asked at once. 'Busy? Mad? Huge buzz?'

'Enormous buzz. Good fun. But interesting, too.'

She told him about the constant battles with Westminster and Whitehall, bits of turf fought over again and again, often literally.

'How do you mean?'

'Southsea Common. They were always wanting to dig it up,

lay more cables, sink more drainage. I don't think it ever occurred to them that it might belong to someone.'

'Like who?'

'Like all of us. It was odd. We lived here. It was our city. But the bigger the event became, the more fingers there were in the pie. Security was the real nightmare. You can imagine, fourteen heads of state, people like Clinton, Major, Mitterrand, and all with their own little plans – top-secret, of course. We were the poor relations, really. Us and the veterans. They were the ones that really mattered. Which is why we fought so hard to keep them in the picture.'

Charlie was transfixed. The TV images from the D-Day weekend were still pin-sharp in his mind. Clinton and the Queen at the drumhead memorial service. The royal yacht gliding out through the harbour mouth. A Spitfire and a Hurricane dancing in the wake of the big black Lancaster bomber the RAF rolled out for special occasions. He glanced down at the pad. He'd circled the word TV.

'There's stuff in your licence about providing a community service, isn't there?' he said.

'Yes. We run a text and graphics operation, a sort of electronic billboard. Channel Eight, if you're interested.'

'Nothing more elaborate?'

'Next year, yes. Come March, we'll be running a weekly special. Reporters, pictures, the lot.'

'How long?'

'An hour.'

'An hour a *week*?'

'Yes.'

Nicky looked briefly shamefaced. Money was tight. Production costs were astronomic. But it was, at least, a start. 'You should try the BBC,' she suggested. 'Or Meridian, if you're looking to run stories.'

'We will, we will. It would just be nice to have a local tie-in,' Charlie said. 'That's the essence of the thing. That's the message. Your city. Your vote.' His eyes drifted back to the map. 'Have you lived here long?'

'All my life. Born and bred.'

'So what do you think? Seriously?'

'I love it. Always have.'

'And Pompey First?'

Nicky's hand found the polystyrene cup beside the teddy bear. She sipped the coffee. 'You want the truth?' she said. 'I think it's a great idea. I think it's years overdue. And I think it's absolutely in tune with the way the city's going.'

'And do you think it'll work?'

'No.' She smiled. 'You haven't got a prayer.'

Hayden Barnaby was leaving the health club at the Venture Hotel when he spotted Harry Wilcox. The *Sentinel*'s editor was emerging from the restaurant. With him was one of the city's two MPs.

Hayden watched the ritual exchange of handshakes as the two men said their goodbyes. A taxi was waiting on the hotel's forecourt. The lunch had been excellent. Their respective secretaries would be in touch. The MP swept across the lobby and disappeared into the gloom of a foggy afternoon. When Barnaby suggested a drink, Wilcox consulted his watch.

'Twenty minutes,' he said, 'else I'm in bloody trouble.'

'You're the boss, Harry. You're never in bloody trouble.'

'Don't you believe it. Mind you . . .' he was leaning against the reception desk, watching the MP folding his long frame into the back of the taxi ' . . . there's trouble and trouble. Compared to some, we're bloody lucky. The Tories are dead in the water. And they know it.'

They went into the bar. Wilcox ordered a double brandy. Barnaby settled for a long glass of orange juice topped with soda. They carried the drinks to a corner table, Wilcox eyeing the bulky sports bag. 'Any reason for torturing yourself?' he enquired. 'Or is it still vanity?'

He patted Barnaby's shoulder, no offence meant, and Barnaby countered with the usual dig about Wilcox's fondness for big lunches. The experience of the riot outside the Imperial Hotel had warmed the relationship between the two men. Over the summer, they'd swopped notes on the phone, met for the odd drink, musing about the way the country was going. The comforts of middle age had embattled them. They'd become, to a surprising degree, comrades in arms.

Barnaby was asking about developments amongst the *Sentinel*'s owners. The paper belonged to a successful group of provincial dailies and the annual trading figures, due next week, were rumoured to be exceptionally good. So good that a modest expansion might be on the cards.

'Am I right?'

Wilcox frowned, his left hand patting his chest. 'Scout's honour. Couldn't possibly comment.'

'That's your wallet, Harry. Your heart's on the left.'

'I know.' He grinned. 'Why else do you think I stay?'

Barnaby laughed – just occasionally, when the mood took him, Wilcox could be genuinely funny. He reached down. The envelope Charlie Epple had dropped at the office was still in the pocket on the side of the sports bag. He took it out and emptied the contents onto the table, aware of Wilcox watching him. Like most journalists, he was eternally nosy.

Barnaby picked up one of the little calling cards and showed it to him. 'It's only a rough,' he said, 'but what do you think?'

Wilcox peered at the card. A thin blue line across the middle represented the horizon. A disc of crimson signalled sunrise. The word Pompey lay across the surface of the sea, flattened like a Welcome mat, while the word First occupied the sky around the rising sun. Beneath the logo, in elegant black script, was Barnaby's name. Below it, slightly smaller, 'Founder-President'.

Wilcox was looking baffled.

'Founder-President of what?'

'Pompey First.'

'What's Pompey First?'

'Our new party.'

'Really? Can anyone come?'

'Sure.' Barnaby nodded. 'You can join if you like. We'll even find you a ward to fight. How does Charles Dickens sound?'

Wilcox held the card at arm's length, narrowing his eyes, pretending he hadn't heard. The Charles Dickens ward included some of the toughest areas of the city, problem families caged in sixteen-storey tower blocks. Harry Wilcox hadn't made it to the *Sentinel*'s editorial chair to dirty his hands with real life.

Barnaby gestured at the card. 'Charlie's been working with a young guy from the art college. That's his first attempt. "Heaven's Light. Pompey First." The word made flesh.'

Wilcox had the grace to smile. 'Heaven's Light Our Guide' was the city's official motto, inscribed on the scroll beneath Portsmouth's civic crest. He put down the card and sifted through the rest. Finding no other names, he looked up. 'Who else is involved?'

'At the moment? Kate, and that's about it. It's early days, yet. It's a gleam in Charlie's eye, and mine. But that's the point, Harry. It's a great story. And you're absolutely the first to know.'

'Kate Frankham? Your pal?'

'My colleague.'

'She's leaving the Labour group?'

'Obviously.'

'Do they know yet?'

Barnaby glanced round. The bar was empty but Wilcox had the newsman's knack of pushing the conversation faster and further than Barnaby would have liked. He thought about Kate, wondering whether he was being premature.

'No,' he said finally. 'They don't know yet.'

'When will they?'

'When Kate tells them.'

'And when will that be?'

'God knows.'

Barnaby began to shuffle the cards back into the envelope, unsure that it had been wise to have shared their little secret with the likes of Harry Wilcox, a pressman. He himself was a lawyer, for God's sake. And lawyers were supposed to be cautious. He began to outline the case for a brand new voice in the city's political affairs but sensed straight away that Wilcox wasn't listening. Instead, he wanted to know about the small print. 'Where will you run candidates?'

'In every ward. We'll contest the lot.'

'And where will you find them?'

'The candidates? We're launching next week. We're planning a press conference – here as it happens. We'll have a draft manifesto and a top table of founder-members.'

'Like who?'

'Can't say yet. But the bid'll be there, out in the open, and we anticipate major coverage.' He paused, a delicate invitation for Wilcox to confirm the *Sentinel*'s interest.

Wilcox was warming his glass, his big hand cupping the balloon of brandy. Barnaby picked up the threads again. A constitution was under debate. Charlie was working on poster ideas. The time had come to return the city to the people who had its interests most at heart.

'Like who?' Wilcox asked again.

Barnaby sat back. He'd barely had time to bounce the idea off a handful of his friends but in every case he'd met with nothing but enthusiasm. Whether or not this would translate into solid support was far from certain. Recently people had wearied of the political game but the novelty of Charlie's idea, the unwavering focus on a single community, seemed to have penetrated the growing sense of cynicism and Barnaby had been heartened by some of the comments his cautious phone calls had provoked. One fellow Rotarian, a top manager in the city's hospital trust, had been positively gleeful: Ministry of Health demands for a savage management cut-back had just landed on his desk and he was sick to death of taking the knife to yet more of his employees. 'These bastards just don't understand how it is at the coalface,' he'd muttered. 'All they know is smoke and mirrors.'

Barnaby repeated the quote to Wilcox.

'You've chosen a good time,' Wilcox said slowly. 'An excellent time.' He waved towards the door, a reference, Barnaby assumed, to the guest he'd just lunched. 'Nationally, the bloody Tories are all over the place. You don't even have to get them pissed any more. It just pours out. Right wing, left wing, pro-Europe, anti-Brussels, One Nation, Ten Nations, they can't wait to lose the election and get stuck in. The party's falling apart. It'll be bloody and it'll be brief but God knows what kind of shape they'll be in afterwards. I shudder to think.'

'And Labour?'

'Even worse. The polls are looking wonderful and the loonies are under lock and key for the time being but it won't last. Give them six months in power, a couple of head-to-heads with the City, and the wheels will come off. It always happens. You can't change society without spending money, and there ain't no money to spend. Blair's lot know that. They're not stupid. But the loonies think otherwise. Did I say six months? Make that three.'

For once Barnaby was impressed. Kate had been telling him exactly the same, almost phrase for phrase. In her view, New Labour was heading for a place in the history books, perpetrators of the biggest political con-trick ever. Was individual choice really the same as equality? Wasn't talk of empowerment and stake-holding just more meaningless flannel?

Wilcox picked up the calling cards again, thinking aloud. 'We'd be the first city,' he mused, 'if you get it right.'

'You mean win?'

'No, I mean setting the thing up. It has to be serious. Good people. Strong candidates. It has to be resourced, too. Where's the money coming from?'

'Money won't be a problem.'

'That means you don't know.' Wilcox began to lay out the cards between them on the table, a hand of patience, column after column. 'Have you talked to anyone? Tapped up any of the big players? IBM? Marconi?'

'The money's fine,' Barnaby said again. 'I guarantee it.'

'You'll fund it yourself?'

'It's possible, just to begin with, until the subscriptions come in.'

'Thirty-nine candidates? Advertising? Phone bills? Transport? Publicity? Have you really thought this thing through?'

'Yes. You think we'd be sitting here if I hadn't?'

Wilcox heard the new note in his voice, a veiled warning that he was serious. 'Of course I'll send someone to your press conference,' he said. 'Be glad to. Who else are you inviting? Telly? Local radio?'

Barnaby nodded. Charlie had a hit list. He was up in Waterlooville now, talking to the cable people.

Wilcox looked dismissive. 'Cable's irrelevant,' he said briskly. 'They've got a community channel but fuck all's on it, no pictures anyway. You're wasting your time.'

Barnaby hesitated. His media knowledge was far from extensive and the last thing he wanted was an argument with Wilcox. The *Sentinel* would be the key to Pompey First's success. One way or another, it went into every household in the city and he'd yet to meet a local politician who didn't swear by its influence. When the *Sentinel* spoke, the voters listened.

Wilcox was toying with the last of his brandy. 'You might think of giving us first bite,' he frowned. 'What time's the conference?'

'We're thinking mid-morning. Charlie wants to catch the midday bulletins.'

Wilcox shook his head. 'Make it two p.m. Give them lunch or something. Nibbles. Drinks. We'll put on a special for our first edition. You're talking midday on the newsstands.'

'What about the rest? Telly? Radio?'

'They'll be pissed off but it won't matter. In fact, it'll probably help. The telly people don't believe anything until it's been in print and we only publish locally. The Beeb and the Meridian boys go region-wide. If you live in Brighton or Portsmouth, it'll sound like breaking news.'

'OK.' Barnaby found a pen in his inside pocket. 'So what do you need from us?'

'Names, principally. Who's backing you, who might stand. Leave the reactive stuff to us. The Tories will do their best to ignore you. The Lib-Dems won't say much, either, but the Labour lot will go ballistic. Especially about Kate.'

Barnaby interrupted: he wanted nothing mentioned, no conversations, until the day of the press conference. Otherwise the thing would go off at half-cock.

Wilcox agreed. 'No problem. We'll need to talk to Kate,

though. Proper interview, embargoed until launch day. I'll send someone round with a photographer. She loves all that.'

Barnaby collected the cards and slipped the envelope back into the pocket of the sports bag. Wilcox checked his watch and got up. He was out of time. He had to run.

'I'm surprised,' he said. 'I thought you might have something for me on the dockyard story. Your Chinese mate. Zhu.'

Wilcox was struggling into his coat. Barnaby picked up his bag. 'Mr Zhu keeps his cards close to his chest,' he said. 'Democratic he ain't.'

'But profitable?'

'Very.'

'Good.' Wilcox led the way towards the door. 'So why aren't you holding the press conference at the Imperial? Why this dosshouse?'

Barnaby shrugged. The Imperial would make a wonderful venue but something inside him argued for keeping his distance. Charlie was especially sensitive to nuance and the Imperial, with its subtle décor and glorious cuisine, oozed serious money. Wrong image, Charlie would say. Wrong vibe.

Barnaby caught up with Wilcox in reception.

'One thing we haven't discussed,' he said.

'Oh? What's that?'

'Our manifesto. Our credo. What we believe in.'

Wilcox turned round, beaming. Barnaby could smell the cigar smoke in the folds of his long cashmere coat. 'Fax it over,' he said, and produced a pair of leather gloves. 'You were always rather good with the bullshit.'

It was mid-afternoon when the call came through to Mike Tully's office. He was sitting at the desk in the window, writing out an interim invoice for a big industrial customer. A week's surveillance work, mob-handed, came to four figures, and some of the technical gizmos they'd specified would more than treble the bill. Tully reached for the phone, still trying to work out the VAT on £4,378.12.

'Hallo?'

'It's Liz. Liz Barnaby.'

Tully's fingers hung over the calculator. He hadn't seen Liz since before the summer, though a couple of brief conversations with Barnaby had suggested that family life was blooming.

'How's that daughter of yours?' Tully asked.

'Dreadful.'

'Oh?'

Tully sat back, the calculator abandoned. Outside, it was nearly dark, the odd shopper hurrying home through the gloom laden with early Christmas presents. Liz came to an end. Tully checked his watch. His secretary would type the invoice. The rest of the day's paperwork could wait.

'I'll come right over,' he said. 'Give me ten minutes.'

Liz opened the door to his second knock. She was wearing a pair of tracksuit bottoms and a big green pullover that Tully had last seen on Hayden Barnaby. She looked fit and well and her face had lost the puffiness that Tully remembered from their last meeting. She asked him to come in, indicating the long sofa beside the fireplace. One end was piled with holiday literature, the brochure on the top offering luxury breaks in Malaysia and Singapore.

Tully sat down. 'How's Hayden?' he began. 'Ever see him these days?'

'Hardly. It's politics, now. That's the latest.'

'Oh?'

'Yes. I think he wants to change the world. This week, anyway.'

Tully felt warmed by the fond look on her face. He had a great deal of respect for Hayden Barnaby but he couldn't be the easiest person to live with. Too active. Too impatient. Too bloody clever. He watched Liz carrying a tray from the breakfast bar. She'd had time to brew a pot of tea and lay out slices of what looked like chocolate cake. Tully had been going to ask more about Hayden's latest brainchild but Liz was already talking about Jessie. She was living in the house of a friend in Old Portsmouth, Charlie Epple. There was another lodger there, a girl called Lolly.

Tully nodded. Liz had got this far on the phone. 'She's the one who came round,' he said. 'This afternoon.'

'Yes. She's . . . you know . . . she and Jess . . . they're . . .'

'Together.'

'Exactly.'

'And you didn't know until this afternoon.'

'No, I didn't, and frankly it would never have crossed my mind. Sweet little thing, Lolly. Pretty, too.'

Tully accepted a slice of cake. Jessie's new friend had burst in earlier, Liz said. She'd been hysterical. It had taken Liz most of the afternoon to calm her down and when she'd finally coaxed some sense from her, she'd rather wished she hadn't bothered. Lolly and Jess were lovers. Had been since Merrist House. They'd spent a wonderful summer together, hatching all kinds of plans, but now everything had been wrecked.

'By Haagen?'

'Exactly.'

'Hence your call.'

'Yes.' Liz began to pour the tea. Just the mention of his name gave her face a haunted, despairing look. With Haagen evidently abroad, the nightmare was over. Or so she'd thought.

Tully refused another slice of cake. It was a little too rich for him. 'You mentioned letters,' he said.

'Yes. Haagen's been writing to her, or so Lolly says. Actually, it must be true. She had one of the letters with her. That's what the fight was about.'

'Fight?'

'Yes.' Lolly had intercepted some letter or other. From Haagen. She'd read it. She'd found some others. Then she'd taken this phone call. Liz explained that Haagen was threatening to come back. Soon.

'How soon?'

'Lolly doesn't know. But soon is soon enough.'

'Has he sorted himself a passport? A new one?'

'God knows. Is that something he'd have to do?'

'Obviously. Unless he wants to get nicked. His name's on the computer. He'd never get past Immigration.'

Liz nodded, briefly heartened by the thought of Haagen behind bars. Tully asked why Haagen would want to return to the UK.

Liz, pouring another cup of tea, made a hopeless gesture with her spare hand. 'That's what I asked Lolly. All she could come up with was loneliness. She thinks the wretched boy's fed up. She thinks he needs someone to talk to, someone to lean on, someone to share all his troubles – and, of course, that's Jess all over. A couple of bars on the violin and she's anyone's. Always has been, silly girl.'

Tully cradled the cup on his lap, eyeing the framed photos on the piano top. Fifteen years of trawling through the small print of other people's lives had poisoned his view of human nature. Most of his private clients, indeed most of the people he knew, he regarded as greedy, insecure and incapable of distinguishing between self-interest and the truth. Liz, oddly enough, had always been an exception. He admired the way she'd protected her marriage, the way she'd battled for her daughter against Haagen, the way she'd come to him for advice but never returned to bleat or complain. She was a strong woman. She had pride, self-respect. Hayden Barnaby had been lucky to find her.

Tully emptied his cup and returned it to the tray. 'So what do you want me to do?'

'I'm not sure. I thought you might have some ideas. That's why I phoned.'

Tully frowned. The issue, in essence, was simple, exactly the same question Liz had posed at the start of the year: how to keep Jessie away from Haagen Schreck. 'Is she working? Jessie?'

'Off and on. Mainly off.'

'Does she have any money? Any savings?'

'Not that I know of. All that went last year.'

'So she wouldn't be in a position to join him in Holland.'

'I'd have thought not.'

The beginnings of a strategy were shaping in Tully's mind.

'Let me ask you something else,' he said. 'This man Charlie you mentioned. It's his house where Jessie's living?'

'Yes. Charlie's Jess's godfather.'

272

'Are they close?'

'Very. Always have been.'

'And Charlie keeps an eye on her?'

'Not really. Charlie's the eternal adolescent. Keeping an eye on anyone just isn't his style. If anyone does the looking after, it's probably Jess.'

'So you wouldn't trust him to keep a secret from her?'

'God, no. Why do you ask?'

Tully stood up, searching in his pocket for the packet of cheroots he normally carried. Liz found a box of matches. He sat down again.

'You mentioned a phone call. If it really is this Haagen, he'll phone again. Bound to. We need to tap into the phone calls. If he means what he says about coming back, we need advance warning.' He fiddled with the matches. 'I can put a device on the line.'

'What line?'

'Jessie's line. The phone line at the house.'

'But that's Charlie's line.'

'Precisely.'

Liz stared at him, the penny beginning to drop. 'You want to bug Charlie's telephone calls?'

'To keep tabs on Haagen, yes.'

'What good will that do?'

'It might enable us to have him picked up at the port of entry. Harwich, say, if he takes the boat from Holland. Or maybe Heathrow, if he flies.'

'You can do that?'

'Easily.'

Liz began to warm to the idea. Tully could see it in her face. She got up and went across to the breakfast bar. Keys hung on ribbons from a line of hooks beneath a pinboard. She selected one and brought it back, winding the ribbon between her fingers. She offered it to Tully. 'It's Charlie's,' she said. 'He sent it down to me before he moved in. I had to sort out the gas people.'

'Where does he live?'

Liz gave him the address. The girls were probably home a

good deal but, as far as she knew, Charlie was out most of the time.

'How long would you need to plant this thing?' she asked.

'Five minutes. Absolute maximum.'

'And it just records by itself?'

'No. It transmits the conversation on a radio link. The range isn't enormous but I'll find somewhere safe for the recorder.'

'How close would you have to be?'

'Quarter of a mile. Give or take.'

'Then put it here. I'll sort out a place. Charlie's just round the corner.' She paused. 'Are you sure he won't find it? Spot it? Whatever you need to plant?'

Tully was examining Charlie's key. He shook his head, then slipped the key into his pocket and got up. The biggest of the photos on the piano was a formal wedding portrait. He stood beside it, buttoning his jacket. In the photo, Hayden and Liz were standing beneath a small tree. Liz looked extraordinarily young, her face in profile, beaming up at Hayden, and in the background he recognized the honeyed stonework of the cathedral. Tully lingered a moment longer, glad that one couple at least had made it through to middle age. Then he remembered Liz's offer. 'Here will be fine,' he said. 'I'll drop it in tomorrow.'

Jessie was drunk when she found the broken glass. She'd borrowed some money from Charlie and had hauled Lolly up the High Street for a pint or two of cider to celebrate a Christmas job she'd just secured at one of the city's department stores. They'd stayed in the pub for most of the evening, scoring more drinks from a party of insurance salesmen, and by the time they returned to Charlie's house, they were both paralytic.

Lolly, who'd forgotten all about the glass jar, suggested they raid Charlie's supplies of vodka. Jessie, who hated spirits, said she wanted to go to bed. She mounted the stairs in darkness, not bothering with the light, and pushed open her bedroom door. She stepped out of her clothes and collapsed on the unmade bed. At first, she felt nothing. Then she became aware of a wet stickiness beneath her arm. She rolled over, fumbling for the bedside light. The sheet beneath her arm was scarlet with fresh blood. She gazed at it wonderingly. Every time she moved on the mattress, there was a clink-clink of broken glass.

She stood up, fighting for balance, trying to make sense of the bed. There was more blood on the sheets, a blotch here, a blotch there. She narrowed her eyes, trying to find a pattern. Then the door opened and Lolly was standing outside in the corridor. Swaying, she reached for the door frame.

'You're bleeding. Shit.'

Lolly came in. On her hands and knees, she started to pick tiny shards of glass out of Jessie's legs, working slowly up, cupping the splinters in her hand. Jessie did as she was told, standing motionless beside the bed, wondering aloud about the mark on the wall. At length, her eyes returned to the bed and she spotted a fragment of canal boat. She bent to pick it up and showed it to Lolly.

'That's from my jar,' she said vaguely. 'My lovely jar.'

Lolly had found a pair of tweezers. A tiny splinter had lodged in the fold of flesh beneath Jessie's shoulder blade. Jessie was still staring at the bed, tussling with cause and effect. 'What happened?' she kept asking. 'What's been going on?'

Lolly opened the window and Jessie heard the tinkle of glass on the pavement below. Then Lolly was back, taking her by the hand, leading her towards the door. She was covered in blood. Some of the deeper cuts might need plasters. She'd sort something out in the bathroom. Outside, on the landing, Jessie pulled Lolly to a halt.

'You did it,' she said uncertainly. 'You broke my jar.'

Lolly nodded. 'Horrible thing,' she said. 'Cheap and nasty.'

Chapter Eleven

He'd been waiting in St James's Park for nearly half an hour before it dawned on Ellis that he'd chosen the wrong bench. It was lunchtime and civil servants from the Foreign Office and the Treasury were striding along the newly swept paths, some alone, some in company, one or two in tracksuits and running shoes, tucking in a circuit or two of the park before returning to their desks. Ellis got up, cursing himself for misunderstanding the directions on the phone. North side, she'd said. Up by the Cake House.

He hurried across the bridge over the lake, wondering whether she'd bother to wait. He knew she was fond of him, she'd signalled her affection in a dozen tiny ways, but he knew as well how unforgiving she could be about people who let her down. In Louise Carlton's world, there were a number of cardinal sins. And lack of punctuality was one of them.

Seconds later he caught sight of her. She was sitting on a bench in the icy sunshine, her bulk unmistakable. On her lap she had a plastic shopping bag. Pigeons pecked at the crumbs round her feet, and as Ellis watched she produced more cake from the bag, tossing it clumsily across the path and into the water. Ducks paddled towards the cake, and a pair of swans splashed heavily off the bank in anticipation of more.

Louise saw Ellis coming, shading her eyes against the low sunshine and then fluttering a gloved hand in greeting. As soon as he sat down, she reached in the bag and produced a thick slab of icing. She broke it in two, handing half to Ellis.

'I've been thinking about Zhu again,' she said. 'I thought we might review developments in a little more detail.'

She favoured him with a chilly smile, half encouragement, half enquiry, and Ellis added what he could to the account he'd already given her on the phone. He'd been down to Portsmouth. He'd taken Mike Tully to lunch. And he'd been able to confirm, to no one's surprise, that Zhu was an able businessman with a talent for spotting high-yield business opportunities. Beyond that Tully hadn't been prepared to go, though Ellis had sensed an unease about Zhu's plans for the naval dockyard.

Louise was shaking the last of the crumbs out of her bag. 'He hasn't got it yet.'

'No, but Tully thinks he will. He knows Zhu. He admires the way he works. And I don't think he's got a lot of time for the opposition.'

'Opposition?'

'Us.' Ellis nodded towards the ramparts of Whitehall across the pond. 'The civil service. God's elect.'

'He's wrong.' Louise was adamant. 'We're not the opposition. We're enablers, facilitators, agents of change. We're shrinking the state, thinking the unthinkable. We're on his side. Doesn't the poor man understand that?'

Ellis picked a crumb from Louise's lap. The relationship they'd built depended on conspiratorial moments like these, a joint recognition that whole swathes of Whitehall had become agents in their own destruction, spectators at their own funeral, presiding over a process that could lead only to the dole queue. It was one of the more powerful reasons that Ellis had begun to wonder about a transfer to MI5. There, at least for the time being, you were still invisible. And there, as well, it was possible to remain beyond the clutches of the politicians.

Louise patted his hand. She had an uncanny knack of being able to read his mind, of getting behind the gruff wariness with which he kept most of the world at bay.

'How did you get on with Tully? Personally?'

'Fine. In fact I liked him.'

'You'll see him again?'

Ellis glanced across. Most of her questions were orders in disguise. 'You think I should?'

'If you think it might be important, certainly.' She waited for an answer, and Ellis thought again of the hour and a half he'd shared with Tully. After talking in the pub, they'd walked the length of the yacht basin, as far as the heavy timber gates that gave onto the upper harbour. It was low tide, and across the gleaming mudflats Tully had pointed out the nearby bulk of Portchester Castle. The Romans had established a settlement there. The place was steeped in history. Something in Tully's face as he'd turned for the walk back to the car park had stuck in Ellis's mind. Part of it had to do with pride. Tully obviously loved the place. But part of it had to do with something more corrosive, something – Ellis thought – closer to resignation. Strolling back past the lines of moored yachts, Ellis had tried to probe a little deeper, tried to fathom what Tully's interminable silences might mask. But nothing he could say provoked even a smile, and when he'd said goodbye, Tully had barely acknowledged him.

Louise was still waiting for an answer. 'Well?'

'He's a difficult man. It could take a long time.'

'A long time to what?'

'To get close to him, to win his confidence.'

'I understand that. But would it be worth it? A wise investment?'

'Depends.' Ellis was frowning now. 'What exactly are you after?'

Louise didn't answer. A Japanese couple were having trouble with their camera. The ducks had swum away. Ellis felt the weight of Louise's body against his shoulder. When she spoke, her breath was warm on his ear.

'I want you to run him,' she said, 'strictly freelance, nothing on paper, nothing formal. I want you to befriend him, nurture him, make him trust you. It's spare-time work, evenings, weekends. I'll fund your expenses, and there's scope for a small subvention at the end. You'll report to no one but me. Only use the office phone to arrange meetings. Keep them social. We're friends, remember.' Her hand closed over his, and Ellis felt her fingers tighten inside the leather gloves. He let her kiss his cheek and gave her hand a little squeeze in return. The last thing he wanted to do was encourage her.

*

Charlie Epple's invitation to join the harbour cruise had been an afterthought, a late decision by the Strategy Unit's director, Alan Carthew. The cruise was the first in a series that was to run throughout the following year. Aboard a luxury launch, Carthew and a handful of colleagues would host a briefing for a dozen or so businessmen who'd expressed a serious interest in moving their operations to Portsmouth.

The briefing began half an hour into the cruise. Out beyond Southsea Castle, Carthew mustered the guests in the main saloon and bombarded them with the good news about the city's prospects. How tourism had blossomed. How investment was pouring in. What sense it would make to relocate to one of the UK's most dynamic locations.

Afterwards, as the launch wallowed back towards the harbour mouth, it was Charlie's turn to pitch for business. In the wake of Carthew's fervent optimism, he was deliberately low-key. He talked about the history of the place, how settled it was, generations of Pompey families barely leaving the same street. He talked of loyalty and fortitude and a number of other civic virtues, increasingly rare. Phrase by phrase, he built a picture of a workforce that no sane businessman could resist, and before he called for questions, he ended on what he admitted was a frankly personal note. There was a case, he said, for genuine city governance: the people's votes, the people's faith, the people's money vested in local leaders whom they themselves had chosen. The idea was by no means new but lately it had taken real shape. The party, he said, was called Pompey First. And big business, in particular, should take note.

An hour later, way up-harbour beyond the ferryport, Carthew trapped Charlie in the stern of the launch. 'You had no right,' he said at once. 'That was extraordinarily ill-judged.'

Charlie eyed him without comment. 'Why?' he asked. 'What's so outrageous about believing in the product?'

'It's political, that's why.'

'Really? So when does belief become political? And who cares about the difference? I want to sell the city because I believe in the city. If Pompey First makes it a better city, surely that's all to the good. I'm adding value, Alan. Look on the bright side.'

'You're being naïve.'

'Bollocks, I'm pissed off just like you are. We could do it better by ourselves, that's all I'm saying. Anything wrong with that?'

Carthew seemed lost for words. Behind him, one of the big French ferries was nosing into the terminal. Charlie nodded at it. 'Our ferryport,' he pointed out, 'our money, our investment, our expertise, five million quid in the black and now those pillocks in London say we can't spend a penny more. Does that sound logical to you?'

'No, of course not. But that's the way things are.'

'Bullshit, Alan. I know what you really think. You really think what we all think. You really think, deep down, that we could do it better ourselves. Only no one dares say so.'

'We can't say so.'

'*Can't?* What's can't? You ever hear about the eighties? Looking after yourself? Looking after number one? This is a new game, Alan. We're in it for what we can get. Bugger London.'

Charlie turned away, suddenly tired of arguing, but Carthew caught his arm.

'There are rules, Charlie. We're council officers. We're account-able. Even you – even you're accountable.'

'Oh, yeah? To whom?'

'The Secretary of State.'

'Wrong. We're accountable to the councillors. They're local, for God's sake, and they'd probably see it our way too. If only someone had the bottle to ask them.' Carthew looked round – he seemed nervous of being overheard, as if he'd suddenly found himself behind enemy lines. Charlie patted him on the shoulder. 'Join the party.' He grinned. 'Join Pompey First. Help us make it through the night.'

'You're crazy. I've told you. We're supposed to be apolitical. You're not *allowed* to do these things. I keep telling you. There are rules here. Protocols. Dos and Don'ts.'

'OK, OK.' Charlie held up his hands. 'Then dream a little. Wouldn't you *like* things to change?'

Carthew studied him, trying to weigh the seriousness of the inquiry. Eventually, he permitted himself a tiny nod.

'Yes,' he said guardedly. 'Of course I'd like things to change.'

'Then wouldn't it be nice to try? Have a little punt? Couple of quid on democracy?'

'Of course it would. But you're underestimating the difficulties.'

'You mean the enemy?'

'I mean the difficulties. Have you any idea what this government's done? The legislation they've pushed through? Fencing us in? Tying our hands? Making sure we behave ourselves?'

'No.' Charlie shook his head. 'I haven't a clue.'

'Then talk to Johnny Dekker. He knows it inside out. He says it's war. That's the word he uses.' Carthew was emphatic now. 'War. If we step an inch over the line, they hammer us. It starts with the District Auditor and it gets worse.'

'How much worse?'

'Infinitely worse.'

'Sarajevo?'

'Exactly.'

'Then we have to fight back. Like the Muslims. No?'

Carthew looked at him for a long moment, then placed a cautionary hand on Charlie's arm.

'Fine,' he said. 'You do what you have to do. But ask yourself one question. Ask yourself where all this leads.'

Charlie turned away, more convinced than ever that he was right. Only when he got to the companionway that led to the saloon did he realize that John Dekker, one of the city's lawyers, had been listening. He was standing at the rail, enveloped in a duffel coat, smoking a cigarette.

'Alan's right,' he said softly, as Charlie stepped past. 'But there are ways and means, believe me.'

Tully had been waiting in his car for nearly an hour before he saw the two girls leave with a dog. He recognized Jessie at once, the tumble of curly blonde hair, the way she loped off down the street, long, rangy strides, just like her mother. The girl beside her must be Lolly, he thought, remembering Liz's description. Small, she'd said, and dainty.

He watched until the two girls rounded the corner and disappeared, then dialled Charlie Epple's number. It rang for perhaps twenty seconds before the answerphone engaged. A man's voice asked for messages and expressions of eternal love. Tully rang off with a snort, climbed out of the car and hurried across the road. It was a cold grey afternoon, a sharp wind gusting off the sea. At Charlie's door, he used Liz's key and locked it again from the inside. He saw the phone at once, a cordless Betacom cradled on a base station, the cable from which routed along the skirting board to a standard BT junction box. Tully knelt beside it and unscrewed the cover. Inside, working with a penknife and a tiny pair of pliers, he fitted the transmitter into the circuit. The aerial was tiny, a whisker of plastic-coated wire. It was nearly invisible to the naked eye and he ran it beneath the junction box, millimetres above the carpet. Finally he replaced the cover and screwed it tight before he got up and retreated to the front door.

Back in the car, he unboxed the device that acted as both receiver and recorder. This was much bigger, the size of a modest transistor radio, and he extended the aerial before dialling Charlie's number again. The needle on the meter began to dance the moment the message triggered on the answerphone, and he replayed the recording afterwards, satisfied that the system worked.

Round the corner in Farthing Lane, Liz answered his knock. He showed her the recorder and asked her where she'd like to site it. She took him to the hiding place she'd prepared in the spare bedroom and he lodged it firmly behind the vase of flowers, trailing the aerial over the back of the table.

'Anyone ever come in here at all? Guests? Kids?'

'No, not even Hayden. Best he doesn't know.'

'Are you sure?'

'Positive. He's great pals with Charlie. And I feel bad enough as it is.'

When Tully got to the front door, he remembered the spare audio cassettes. He fetched them from the car, explaining that each ran for ninety minutes. When the first one was full, or she heard something especially interesting, she was to give him a ring. Liz took them without enthusiasm.

Tully stood by the car, feeling unaccountably guilty. He rarely trusted his sense of humour, but the circumstances seemed to warrant a joke. 'Maybe you should have spent the ten thousand on a contract.' He smiled. 'Like I suggested.'

Liz shivered, pulling her cardigan around her. 'I spent three on a present,' she said, 'and it didn't work.'

Kate Frankham normally left her Christmas shopping until the last possible moment but this year was an exception. She had the usual network of friends and relatives, the Christmas card list she kept in the back of her leatherbound address book, but she wanted, above all, to find something special for Hayden. After a difficult summer trying to sort out her feelings for him, she'd concluded that love was as good a word as any. It certainly wasn't perfect. No relationship that depended on stolen time ever could be. But stolen time added an excitement of its own and Kate had enough first-hand experience of the torpor of marriage not to begrudge Hayden a little boredom of his own. If he chose to stay with his dull wife and junkie daughter, so be it. Kate, at least, had the best of him.

She pushed through the heavy swing doors into Knight and Lee, a big Southsea department store, unbuttoning her coat as she did so. She'd set aside the afternoon for getting Hayden's present just right, and she began to drift through the displays of crystal glass, wondering exactly what sort of gift would bridge the yawning gap between Christmas Eve and the start of real life again, days and days into the New Year. She'd been this way before, the first time they'd had an affair, and she knew how empty Christmas could be without a partner. The ritual meals with her mother and her widowed aunt. The interminable hours of bad television and Spanish brandy and stale mince pies. The incessant urge to tiptoe into the hall, lift the phone and dial his number, stealing just a minute or two of his Christmas. She'd hated it, resenting every second of the nine days he'd spent with his wife and daughter, but this time round she was determined to be stronger, to fence him off from her life, to pretend for a week or so that she was back on her own again, answerable to no one but herself.

Upstairs, on the first floor, there was a section devoted to the kind of framed prints that ended up on the walls of so many Southsea homes. Impressionist classics by Monet and Degas. A couple of Lowry's industrial townscapes. Even an early piece from Egon Schiele. She stepped back, looking at the Schiele print. It was called *La Danseuse*, a wonderfully poignant study of a young dancer at rest, her knees drawn up to her chest, her body cloaked, her head resting on her shoulder. She looked pensive and physically drained, and there was something in her face that spoke to Kate of all the other Schiele prints she'd collected, the ones she'd framed for her bedroom wall, bodies intertwined, lives knotted, relationships caught at moments of overwhelming frankness. She reached for the print, meaning to buy it, then changed her mind. The only place he'd ever hang it was in her own house. She didn't want that. It would only confirm how narrow a ledge they shared.

She went downstairs again but wherever she looked she encountered the same dead end. The aftershave his wife would smell. The simple silver ring he'd never wear. The exquisite leather gloves he'd have to pass off as a present from a grateful client. In a while, she found herself back upstairs, within touching distance of the Schiele print. What she needed wasn't an object at all. What she really needed was an experience, something they could share together, an hour or two or an evening that would lodge itself deep inside him, an everlasting memory, indelibly date-stamped, no one else's property but their own. She smiled to herself, glad to have made a decision. They'd start, as ever, with a bottle of wine. There'd be music, something different, something new. Then a meal, and more wine, and afterwards, an hour or two that he'd never forget.

She made for the stairs. At the perfumerie, she bought a handful of tiny bottles of body oil – coconut, primrose, musk. Then, nearby, a box of scented candles, deliciously thin, the colour of spilled blood. In an off-licence across the precinct she found four bottles of a '91 Rioja, an outstanding vintage she'd come across only the previous week. She returned to the precinct, wondering about the music, about the meal, building the present item by item, hour by hour, the way a playwright might compose a series of scenes. Hayden loved pasta, adored seafood. She'd marry the two with home-made linguini and fat Dublin Bay prawns, and bless the union with the best olive oil she could find. Afterwards, they'd have fresh fruit, something raunchy and tropical, laced with yoghurt or *crème fraîche*. She hurried towards the supermarket, delighted that she'd staked out territory of her own, found a way of detaching him, all too briefly, from the tyranny of real life.

The supermarket was crowded. She drifted up and down the aisles, selecting items that caught her eye, adding a box of crackers and a ripe Camembert to the meal she'd prepare. Beside the display of fresh produce, she began to hunt for tropical fruit, testing the lychees and paw-paws. She was about to settle for a particularly ripe mango when she felt a hand on her arm. Frank Perry was standing guard beside a trolley. His wife and daughter were nearby, filling a plastic bag with apples. Frank looked neat, tidy and unusually cheerful. Being MP-in-waiting for Portsmouth West obviously suited him.

Kate kissed him on the cheek. Absurdly, she couldn't think of anything to say.

'Coming to the Christmas do on the nineteenth?' Frank asked brightly. 'Only I know there's a rush on the tickets.'

Kate felt her face go pink. She'd been meaning to write to the constituency secretary, offering some excuse or other, fending off the inevitable invitation. By the nineteenth, she'd be a founder-member of Pompey First, a traitor, a turncoat, the target of every Labour supporter in the city. The last place she'd want to be was the party's annual thrash.

'I can't,' she said quickly. 'I'd love to but I'm otherwise engaged.'

'Shame. Anything nice?'

'Not really.' Kate swallowed hard, reaching for a plausible excuse. 'It's Billy, Billy Goodman. He's not, you know, too well. I try and cheer him up whenever I can.'

Frank nodded gravely and his eyes went down to the contents

of Kate's basket. 'Lucky man,' he said. 'Shame the wife never stretches to stuff like that.'

Charlie Epple was back in Old Portsmouth before nightfall. The harbour cruise, by common consent, had been highly successful, Alan Carthew securing expressions of serious interest from six of the nine guests as they filed off the launch and shook his out-stretched hand. They'd been impressed, they said, and they'd certainly be in touch again once they'd had time to marshal their thoughts.

Charlie parked his Calibra in the shadow of Hot Walls and crossed the road to his house. The lights were on in Lolly's room on the first floor and he heard the girls talking as he let himself in. He called upstairs, telling Jessie he was home, and detected the bounce of bedsprings as she went to the door to yell back. Then the door closed and he hesitated a moment, hearing her footsteps dance across the ceiling before the conversation dissolved into giggles.

The phone rang minutes later. Charlie was in the kitchen making toast. He picked up the cordless in the hall, wedging it between his shoulder and his ear as he licked the butter from his fingers. The last time he'd seen John Dekker was an hour or so ago, climbing into a taxi outside the harbour station. Now he seemed to be back in his office at the Civic Centre. 'I've been talking to Carthew,' he said. 'I know a worried man when I see one.'

'What's he worried about?'

'You.'

'Why?'

'He thinks your little speech was out of order. He's asked me to have a quiet word.'

'Really?' Charlie laughed. 'So what do you think?'

'I think I'm extremely interested. But Carthew's right. You should ask yourself where all this leads. It might not be as simple as you think.'

Charlie returned to the kitchen. Dekker was talking now about

Pompey First. Just the phrase had fired his imagination. It had the merit of sounding obvious from the off. Charlie was spreading Marmite on the toast. 'What do you mean, obvious?'

'Obvious in the sense that it should have been done years ago. Obvious to me, at least.'

'Glad to hear it. So where are we going wrong?'

Dekker laughed. If Pompey First was to lead anywhere, then it would have to flag the path to some form of independence. And if that were to happen, it would find itself at war.

'With whom?'

'Our masters in London. Carthew's right – they can open up on several fronts. The District Auditor's only one, but that's bad enough, believe me.'

Charlie pulled a stool towards him with his foot, slipping another slice of bread into the toaster. I ought to make notes, he thought. I ought to be writing all this down. Dekker was briskly tallying the bullets in the Auditor's gun. If Pompey First ended up by holding the balance of power within the city council, and if the party's programme incurred any serious expense, both councillors and council officers were potentially at legal risk.

'Of what?'

'You want the list?'

'Please.'

Dekker began to go through it. Under Section 19 of the 1982 Local Government Act, the Auditor could make application to the court for a declaration that a particular item of expense was unlawful. Under Section 20, councillors or officials could be sur-charged. Under Section 25a, the Auditor could issue a prohibition order, blocking a particular financial initiative. Under Section 25d, he could further apply for judicial review.

Dekker waited for Charlie to emerge from the blizzard of legislation.

'I'm lost,' Charlie said, 'don't understand a word of it.'

'It's simple. It's a restraint. You're handcuffed, bound hand and foot. Whitehall allows you to spend just so much. Spend any more and you'll end up paying the bills yourself.'

'Or what?'

'Or face contempt of court.'

'Meaning?'

'A big fine. Or a prison sentence.'

Charlie did his best to absorb the news. He was still woolly about the connection with Pompey First. 'We're fighting a local election,' he began. 'Is that illegal?'

'Absolutely not.'

'Then what's the problem?'

'There isn't one – unless you win. If you win, then you'll face choices, like any other party. Those choices are incredibly narrow. That's all I'm saying.'

'So narrow we couldn't change things?'

'So narrow no one would ever know the difference.'

'That's appalling.'

'You're right.'

'Even worse than I thought.'

'Good. Best give it some thought, eh?'

Charlie was unsure now where Dekker stood. Was this another shot across his bows? Subtler than Carthew's but motivated by the same old reluctance to rock the boat? Or did Dekker have another agenda, a longer game that might, conceivably, work to Pompey First's advantage? He bent to the phone, still tasting the Marmite on his lips.

'Straight question,' he said. 'Where are you in all this?'

'Me?'

'Yeah, you. Say the launch goes well. Say we pick up support, field some decent candidates. Say people have the guts to vote us in. Say we win in May. What then? For you?'

There was a long silence. Dekker had a spacious office up on the third floor in the Civic Centre, and Charlie could picture him behind his desk, slowly revolving in the swivel chair, half a turn to the left, half a turn to the right, chewing the question over.

'I'm a lawyer,' he said finally, 'and I have great respect for the law.'

'So you're against us?'

'On the contrary.'

'You're *not*?' Charlie was lost again.

'No, I'm with you every step of the way.' He paused. 'This won't mean anything to you but last year the government pushed through something called the Deregulation and Contracting Out Act. It was in the papers. A lot of people were very unhappy.'

'Why?'

'Because it gave the government *carte blanche* to do exactly as it chose. Laws are made in Parliament. This particular law enables ministers to amend or repeal more or less anything. Without a proper reference back.'

'Back to what?'

'The House of Commons. In effect, ministers can ignore or change any law they like. In peace, it's unprecedented. The last bloke to try it on was Henry VIII.'

Charlie barked with laughter. He could hear the anger behind Dekker's silky tones. If we ever need an attorney-general, he thought, then Dekker's our man.

'You're pissed off,' he ventured. 'These guys make you crazy.'

'You're right. They're cowboys, bandits. We're the most over-centralized country in the free world. And you can forget democracy, too. It's an elective dictatorship, pure and simple.'

Charlie had found an old shopping list. He began to scribble the phrases on the back. Whatever Dekker had been drinking had definitely done the trick.

'Elective what?'

'Dictatorship. They talk about the sovereignty of Parliament but it's a myth. Ministers do what they like. MPs are here to make it legal. It's all about turf. It's all about power. As long as we have the set-up we have, the guys at the top will always want more.'

'So where does that leave us?'

'Us?'

'Down here.'

'Ah.' Dekker laughed. 'You mean local government? We're the enemy, my friend, we're not part of the constitution at all. We're an irritant, a nasty species of insect. If they could, they'd get rid of us completely.'

'And do what?'

'God knows. Open a chain of one-stop offices, I should think, administered by some quango or other. Why take the risk with democracy if the locals have ideas of their own?'

Charlie heard Dekker laughing again. More in sorrow than in anger. 'So what's the answer?' he asked.

There was a long silence. Charlie bit into the toast. Then Dekker was back on the phone. 'I'm not sure,' he said, 'but Pompey First might be a bloody good start.'

Hayden Barnaby sat behind the wheel of the Mercedes, anchored in the fast lane of the motorway. Fired by Charlie's vision of the sunlit political uplands which might lie beyond victory in the local elections, he'd spent half an hour on the phone to one of the local programming editors at Meridian Broadcasting, the local ITV station. The conversation had led to a lunch invitation, and the lunch had lasted most of the afternoon.

The editor was a sallow young man called Hendricks. His brief at Meridian included local politics and Barnaby's talk of Pompey First had interested him. Over spaghetti Marinara and a good Chianti he'd pushed to find out just how robust a political infant Barnaby and his colleagues might deliver.

The Mercedes crested Portsdown Hill and began the long descent to the tangle of exits beside the new marina complex. Away to the right, the city was webbed with orange street lights and Barnaby wondered whether the notion of Pompey going it alone might not be so far-fetched, after all. As Hendricks had pointed out, there were already a number of precedents, little bits of the UK that had wriggled free from Whitehall's grip and acquired a degree of real independence. Jersey was one, Guernsey another, the Isle of Man a third. If they could do it, why not Portsmouth?

When he arrived Kate was in the bath. The room was tiny, shelves overflowing with potted plants. Barnaby shut the door, sitting on the linen box, his shoes discarded, his feet on the side of the tub. Kate's toes poked through a mountain of bubbles. Every now and again, she pushed at the hot-water tap, thickening the clouds of steam.

Barnaby had been telling her about Hendricks's enthusiasm for

Pompey First. He controlled the weekly political programme. He had real influence.

'What's he going to do?'

'Depends on us. If we come up with something interesting, something original, he's talking about a full-blown studio debate, us and the other major parties. Can you imagine that? Forty-five minutes? Region-wide?'

Kate was soaping her face, her eyes tightly shut. 'So what did you tell him?'

'I told him we'd be there. I told him we'd be very keen indeed.'

'But what have we got to show him?'

Barnaby reached for the flannel in the sink. Steam had mottled his image in the mirror but nothing could disguise the breadth of his smile. He fingered a tiny scab on his chin. 'I said our investment was in people, in a genuinely local democracy. We wanted lots more councillors. We wanted them paid. We wanted mediation groups, neighbourhood by neighbourhood, citizens' juries sitting on all the big policy issues, city-wide referenda before the final decision.'

There was a surge of water in the bath behind him. He turned round and handed Kate the flannel. She was sitting upright, mopping the soap from her face.

'You've been reading all those articles I gave you.'

'You're right.'

'So what did he say?'

'He said he agreed. He said the Brits were political infants. That's the phrase he used. He talked about Europe a lot. He knows their systems inside out, the way they organize themselves, the way power's stayed with the regions.'

'Where in Europe?'

'France, Germany, Italy, Spain, you name it. These places are light years ahead of us. You want something to happen in Barcelona and, bang, it's there. None of this fannying up and down to London. None of those queues at the minister's door. These people have real authority, real discretion, and they use it.'

Kate was still peering up at him. She looked, if anything, a little nervous. She liked this shiny new car Hayden had found. But she wasn't sure, yet, about the top speed.

'I thought we were talking about Pompey First,' she said uncertainly. 'Isn't Barcelona just a little bit bigger?'

Barnaby shook his head. 'Same principle,' he said briefly. 'Size is no bar.'

'But Spain's different, my love. So are Germany and France. To be like them we'd need to change everything. Either that or opt out entirely.'

'I agree.'

'What do you mean you agree? You agree to change? Or you agree to opting out entirely?'

'Either. Makes no difference.'

'Nonsense. Just listen to yourself. It makes every difference. If you think we can change the entire country, I'm afraid you're out of your head. The only other option . . .' she pursued a small plastic duck with the flannel '. . . is going it alone.' She looked up again. 'Is that what you're saying? We blow up the bridges and float away?'

Barnaby told her about the Channel Islands and the Isle of Man. Apart from defence and foreign affairs, they had total autonomy. They could raise their own taxes and spend them exactly as they chose.

Kate shook her head.

'Jersey's stuffed full of millionaires,' she said. 'So's the Isle of Man.'

'Doesn't matter. The precedent's there. And, in any case, it's the money that follows the set-up, not the other way round. Get the set-up right, keep the taxes low, and the money floods in. After that, you can do anything. Look at Liechtenstein and Monaco. Buckets of money. Both of them.'

'And you really think that would happen here?' Kate's toe found the chain at the end of the bath. 'In Pompey?'

Barnaby stretched out his hand for a towel. 'I know it would. It's happening already.'

'Oh?' Kate stood up, the water cascading down her body. 'Really?'

'Yes. His name's Zhu.' Barnaby grinned, taking off his jacket. 'In case you'd forgotten.'

The tall thin figure in the shadows made Jessie jump. She was hauling the dog along the apron of pebble beach across from Charlie's house. Normally she avoided walking alone after dark but Oz was all the security anyone could ever need. Scenting the stranger, he began to strain at the leash, growling.

'It's me, Manik. Tell that fucker to behave himself.'

Relieved, Jessie bent to the dog and fondled him behind the ears. Manik was one of the few friends she'd shared with Haagen. Like her, he'd ended up in Merrist House and, like her, he'd done a runner.

'You get the call from Haagen?'

'No.'

'He's coming home.'

'When?'

'The next week or two. He's got new documents, new passport, the lot. Asked me to pass the word.'

'When?'

'Tonight. He phoned a couple of hours ago.' He jerked his thumb at the row of houses across the road. 'I was going to call by but you saved me the trouble.'

Jessie caught the slur in his voice and knew he'd been shooting up. There was an uncomfortable silence. Then Manik laughed. 'I can fucking sell you some,' he said, 'if you're that desperate.'

'I'm not.'

'Good girl.' He reached for the support of the wall. 'Be good to have H back, eh?'

Hayden Barnaby was still on the mobile to Charlie Epple when he signalled left and swung the Mercedes into Farthing Lane. He'd rung Charlie to pass on Hendricks's thoughts about the various constitutional doors that a Pompey First victory at the polls might unlock, but the moment he'd mentioned the Channel Islands, speculating about a modest degree of independence, Charlie had countered with news of his own. He'd been talking to John Dekker again, the lawyer advising the Strategy Unit. This was the guy with the book of rules, the guy who really understood the small print and, according to Charlie, he was barely a step away from open rebellion. He'd never heard such anger, such contempt. If a lawyer was this committed, surely the punters would take the hint. If only they knew. If only Pompey First had the bottle to push the cause as far and as fast as it could possibly go.

Barnaby eased the Mercedes into a parking bay opposite his house. He could still smell the lemony shower gel with which Kate had soaped him down.

'What cause?' he enquired idly.

'UDI. Unilateral Declaration of Independence. Going it alone. We have to do it. We have to.'

Listening to Charlie, Barnaby wondered whether they were both certifiable or whether there might be a way. As far as Charlie was concerned, of course, there were no doubts. Independence, genuine independence, was a great fat apple just waiting to fall from Whitehall's tree. All it needed, he kept saying, was a single issue, a single headline. Something to make the punters understand. Something to march them off to the barricades.

Charlie broke off, laughing. 'So where were you?' he said.

'When?'

'When I phoned earlier to tell you all this?'

Barnaby hesitated a moment, gazing out at the shell of the Garrison Church. Charlie had guessed about him and Kate. He knew he had. 'Debating policy,' he said lightly. 'With our Labour friend.'

'Yeah? Getting one or two things straight?'

'Mmmm . . . maybe.'

Barnaby brought the conversation to an end and slipped the mobile into his pocket. Locking the car door, he glanced over his shoulder. Liz was up in the spare room, gazing down at him, but when he waved she turned away.

BOOK FOUR

April/May 1996

'You are warned that the pier and adjacent hotel are liable to be cleared away at a day's notice in the event of war . . .'

Guidebook issued for the annual
BMA conference at Southsea, May 1899

Chapter Twelve

From the hospitality suite, high above Meridian's biggest studio, Hayden Barnaby had a perfect view of the set of *The South Decides*. The recording had been in progress now for nearly twenty minutes, pictures fed to the big transmission monitor at the other end of the room, but Barnaby couldn't resist the view from the window. From here, through the thick soundproof glass, he could look down on the semi-circle of black leather chairs in the pool of brilliant light. Beyond the rostrum, in the half-darkness, the big studio cameras prowled back and forth, eavesdropping on the conversation, responding to the director's every command. Barnaby tried to visualize the technical wizardry that took these pictures and fed them on to hundreds of thousands of televisions region-wide. Charlie had been right. It was the media that could make or break Pompey First and with the local elections just five days away, the campaign was going exactly to plan.

Barnaby felt the lightest of touches on his arm. Hendricks, the programme's editor, was holding the bottle of Sauvignon over his empty glass.

'May I?'

'Thanks.'

Barnaby's eyes were back on the studio floor. The design for the seating plan had come from Hendricks and it served Pompey First wonderfully well. Kate Frankham sat on the left of the presenter, faced with her local opponents from the three major parties. She was wearing a beautifully cut skirt and jacket whose colour – sea-green – perfectly complemented the huge black and white blow-up of HMS *Victory* that dominated the backdrop. By contrast, the others looked dowdy, two men in suits and a shrill woman from the Labour Party, who was talking now about Labour's policies on devolution. Of course people wanted power back from London. And Blair's plans for regional assemblies would guarantee them just that. She leaned back, confident that she'd stolen Pompey First's thunder, her smile issuing a direct challenge to Kate, to whom the presenter threw an enquiring glance. Kate pointed out at once that Labour's regional assemblies were simply a talking shop, a sop to public opinion. They had no powers to raise taxes or pass legislation. They wouldn't even be able to replace the budgets and functions of the regional quangos that Labour claimed were so repugnant. On the contrary, they'd be as much the prisoner of Whitehall as the towns and cities they were supposed to represent. The Labour woman began visibly to bristle. Was Kate suggesting that Labour had no faith in local government? Was this another of the lies that Pompey First was peddling?

Kate smiled. Hayden had warned her to expect exactly this line of attack. She'd turned her back on Labour. She'd deserted them. She could no longer be trusted. The presenter was still waiting for her answer. 'Well?' he prompted. 'Is that fair comment?'

Kate shook her head. 'Absolutely not. New Labour are as frightened of local government as the Tories. They don't say so, not in so many words, but behind the scenes everyone knows it's true. High-spending authorities will wreck their image. There's even talk of sending in the commissioners if things get really sticky. That's the language of war, not peace. No,' her face expressed mild regret, 'I don't expect Portsmouth will find many friends in a Labour government.'

Barnaby heard Hendricks chuckle. 'She's good,' he said. 'She's very good indeed. You're lucky to have found her.'

Barnaby raised his glass in a silent toast. Charlie's insistence on a media training course had paid enormous dividends. The afternoons in a stuffy little studio above Wardour Street, face to face with a succession of off-duty ITN interviewers, had turned Kate into a television veteran. Quicker than most, she'd come to understand what an intimate medium it was. How there was no place for formal speeches. How the tiniest detail of body language could signal nervousness or insincerity. How humour and warmth would win infinitely more votes than yards and yards of dogma.

The presenter was quizzing her again on the perils of going it alone. Without being anchored to a national party, didn't Pompey First risk turning the city's back on the UK? Barnaby tensed. Four months of brainstorming this issue, of bouncing the suggestion off colleague after colleague, had taught him an important lesson. The people of Portsmouth weren't ready for independence. Not real independence. Not yet.

The other guests on the rostrum were looking hard at Kate. They, too, knew that this was the chink in Pompey First's armour, their one real chance to halt the enormous momentum that Charlie Epple's juggernaut had built up. The electorate in Portsmouth were deeply wary of change. They had a deference to authority bred from generations of reliance on the naval dockyard. Didn't Pompey First put this precious loyalty under threat?

'Definitely not.' Kate looked almost amused. 'Very definitely not. What we have is a strong belief in city governance. We believe in focus, in concentrating all our time and effort on the people we represent. What we don't believe in is diluting those efforts by playing to two audiences. Not being part of a national party, part of some remote machine, is a strength, not a weakness.'

'So where's the big idea?'

'We're the big idea. Our very smallness, our *lack* of scale is the big idea. We're small-print politicians, neighbourhood politicians, family across-the-street politicians. We're not into gesture politics. We've no time for Smith Square or Walworth Road. But we do our homework. And we'll get things done.'

Hendricks was miming applause. He was looking at the screen now, a head-and-shoulders close-up of Kate as she listened to the Tory councillor tallying the blessings that had lately come Portsmouth's way. Millions of pounds from the Millennium Fund. The huge D-Day celebrations, televised across the world. A whole stage of the Tour de France, beginning and ending on Southsea Common. Wasn't this evidence that the city was on the up? Wasn't the truth that the people of Portsmouth were grateful for all this coverage?

'Of course we're grateful,' Kate answered briskly. 'And of course we welcome the publicity. But we get all this attention because we have lots to offer. That's our point. That's what lies behind Pompey First. We're tired of going cap in hand to other people. We're tired of Whitehall telling us what we can and can't do. All we want, all we're asking for, is the chance to make our own decisions, to take control of our own lives.'

The presenter leaned forward. 'By going it alone?'

'By voicing an alternative.'

'All by yourselves?'

'Of course.' She smiled. 'If you're not prepared to walk alone in politics, you'll never get off your knees.'

Barnaby shook his head in admiration. The line was perfect, securing an emphatic nod of agreement from the presenter, who turned at once to the Liberal-Democrat, a heavily bearded lecturer at Portsmouth University. Didn't Pompey First have a point? Might next week's election not be the beginning of a watershed in British politics?

Barnaby stepped away from the window. Trays of canapés and sandwiches were laid out on a table beside the television. He picked up a plate. The sheer pressure of campaigning over the last few weeks had made regular meals a distant memory. He bit into a chicken leg, watching the Liberal-Democrat bewailing the ethics of Pompey First. Like the Labour Party, the Lib-Dems had watched some of their best candidates turn their backs on years of mainstream politics and throw in their hands with Charlie Epple's boisterous infant. The notion of serving only the city, so beautifully simple, had touched a nerve in almost every corner of Portsmouth, and Barnaby had been astonished at the calibre of the membership they'd attracted.

If anything, they'd been spoiled for choice when it came to the selection of candidates, and only yesterday he and Charlie had been congratulated by Harry Wilcox, no less, on the small army of men and women they were fielding in the city's wards. In Harry's words, the Pompey First team had depth, legs and real quality. A dozen or so came from business backgrounds, middle-level executives from some of Portsmouth's blue riband companies.

By and large, they were disaffected Tories or Lib-Dems, and to them the prospect of a can-do Pompey First council made perfect sense. Other faces on the sea-green Pompey First posters belonged to union activists, and blue-collar workers, and the unwaged, most of them refugees from the left, glad at last to have slipped the harness of the Labour machine. Others still, a substantial handful, had been previously apolitical, members of no party, individuals whose indifference to politics had melted into frustration and then rage. They were tired of the name-calling and the inter-party squabbles. They wanted, quite simply, to get things done. In this sense, Pompey First's slate of candidates was a collective vote against the state of contemporary politics, a voice that spoke loudest to people like Hendricks.

He was still standing by the window. Barnaby offered him a choice of sandwiches. Below, on the rostrum, Kate had found herself pincered between political opponents. The Tory and the Labour candidates, for once, were in agreement. Pompey First was a sham, a mirage, a confection.

'Well?' Barnaby murmured. 'Do you agree?'

'Christ, no.' Hendricks was beaming. 'Far from it. If this isn't for real, you tell me what is.'

'You think we may be in with a shout?'

'I think you'll win.'

'You're serious?'

'Yes. And delighted, too.' He grinned, still watching the set below, and Barnaby wondered how much of his enthusiasm was mischievous. Media people were like kids. They got bored easily. They enjoyed putting grit in the machine. Charlie Epple was exactly the same.

Hendricks was asking about Kate again. If she won a seat in her own ward and if he was right about Pompey First ending up with a majority on the city council, would she be elected leader?

'Definitely.'

'You're sure?'

'I guarantee it.'

Hendricks looked briefly amused and then asked whether Barnaby was in the market for a follow-up.

'A what?'

'A follow-up. We'd come down to Pompey and put a camera on Kate for a week or two. See how you lot cope with the curse of real power. Can do?'

Barnaby was watching the television monitor. Kate was in close-up again, the studio lighting modelling the planes of her face. He'd rarely seen her so engaged, so luminous, so alive. She was laughing at some *bon mot* or other, and looking at her, Barnaby understood exactly the kinship between sex and power. She was in command. She held the ring, a beautiful woman in a roomful of men. Nothing was beyond her reach.

Hendricks was still at Barnaby's elbow. 'She wouldn't mind, would she?'

'Mind what?'

'Us doing a little profile. Afterwards.'

Barnaby laughed softly, still watching the television. 'God no,' he said. 'She'd love it.'

Liz Barnaby was washing a lettuce when she heard the knock on the door. To her surprise it was Jessie, alone for once, no dog, no Lolly.

She had a huge bunch of flowers. She thrust it at her mother, giving her an awkward kiss. She was wearing jeans and a halter-top. She'd been out in the sunshine. She looked wonderful.

'I've been meaning to for ages,' she said. 'I'm just so lazy.'

'Meaning to what?'

'Give you these.' She followed her mother across the living room and into the kitchen, watching while Liz filled the sink with water.

'I'm touched,' she said, 'but what's brought this on?'

Jessie had helped herself to a banana. One of the differences Liz had noticed since she'd returned from Merrist House was how ravenous her appetite had become. She was always hungry, always eating, always on the cadge for food.

'I just want you to know we care,' she said, through a mouthful of banana. 'Me and Lolly.'

'About what?'

'About you. And Dad.'

Liz glanced back at her. She and Hayden had now been separated for nearly a month. She'd accused him of having another affair with Kate and the fact that he'd barely bothered to deny it had made the parting inevitable. When he'd asked how she'd known, she'd told him it was common knowledge. That wasn't strictly true but at Mike Tully's insistence she'd kept quiet about the intercepted phone conversations she'd overheard, Charlie ribbing Hayden on the fleshier implications of party solidarity.

'Your father's done it before,' she said quietly. 'You ought to know that.'

'He has?'

'Yes, with the same woman as it happens. He was never one to give up easily.'

'Well, I think he's mad.'

'So do I.'

'He'll be back soon. I know he will.'

'You think so?'

'Yes.' Jessie nodded vigorously, reaching for an apple. 'Just pretend he's away somewhere on business.'

Liz turned back to the sink and plunged the flowers in the water. Sometimes Jessie's maturity astonished her. Other times, like now, she could be a child again. Was it really that simple? Kiss and make up? Pretend Kate Frankham had never happened?

'Actually, I don't want him back,' she said slowly. 'Not now, not ever. He's made up his mind, whether he knows it or not. I can't live with someone like that. Mine one minute, someone else's the next. We're grown-up people, Jess. And grown-up people deserve a little better than this.'

She rubbed her nose with the back of her hand, and Jessie was beside her in seconds, misinterpreting the gesture.

'Mum, I'm sorry, I really am.'

'Don't be. I'm angry, not sad.'

'But it'll be all right, I know it will. All men are the same. They just go off their heads from time to time. It'll pass. It always does.'

Liz turned round from the sink, the flowers dripping in her arms. The sight of her daughter's face, so open now, made her smile. 'You know that, do you?'

Jessie looked back at her. 'Yeah,' she grinned, 'I do.'

Hendricks and Kate waited outside the Meridian reception area, watching Barnaby manoeuvring the Mercedes around one of the big outside broadcast vehicles. Over sandwiches and more wine, they'd sat through a replay of the programme, and Kate had been mesmerized by her own performance. She'd looked like a stranger, cool, relaxed and totally in command. The cameras hadn't picked up a trace of the way she'd really felt.

'You were very kind to me,' she said. 'I think I got off lightly.'

Hendricks chuckled. He'd already given her the telephone number of the *pied-à-terre* he used in Southampton during the week, making it plain that Pompey First's on-screen prospects might benefit from a closer relationship. 'You were terrific,' he said. 'I can't believe you haven't done this before.'

'I haven't. I'd tell you if I had.'

'Then you're a natural. And the more you do, the better you'll get.' He bent to kiss her cheek as the Mercedes pulled up beside them. Then he reached for the rear door and opened it with a flourish. Barnaby was already out of the car, watching the pantomime. Hendricks caught his eye. 'Pretend you're the chauffeur,' he said. 'It's the least you owe her.'

Barnaby and Kate exchanged glances, then Kate giggled and slipped into the back seat. She'd had barely anything to eat and a second glass of Sauvignon had gone to her head. Barnaby rounded the bonnet and shook Hendricks's hand. 'Thanks for everything. You've been an enormous help.'

Hendricks was still looking at Kate.

'It's a pleasure,' he said. 'I'll be in touch.'

Back on the motorway, returning to Portsmouth, Kate was still in the back seat. As he drove through the suburbs of Southampton,

Barnaby had talked about her performance, and she'd responded to his compliments with a smile and a nod, saying little, refusing to play the excited *ingénue*. What mattered, she'd murmured, was the next appearance and the appearance after that. If Pompey First was to be more than a gleam in Charlie Epple's eye, then they had to think long-term. This time round, they'd been lucky. Hendricks and the production team had made it easy. Perhaps Hendricks might come up with another invitation.

Barnaby eyed her in the rear-view mirror. 'He wants to do a profile,' he said. 'I'm surprised he didn't mention it.'

'A what?'

'A profile. That's if we win, of course. He wants to shadow you with a crew. See how you cope with real power.'

'He does?'

'Yes.'

'And would he be there? In person?'

'I imagine so.'

Kate said nothing, gazing out of the window at the blur of warehouses on the outskirts of Fareham. The expression on her face, reflective, content, enigmatic, reminded Barnaby of Sunday mornings after they'd made love. There were parts of Kate it was impossible to touch, and he knew with absolute certainty that, no matter what he did, they'd always be beyond his reach. He could spend his whole life trying but he'd never truly know her. That, at least, was now clear.

Kate breathed on the window then drew a little cartoon face with her fingertip, its mouth bowed upwards in a grin.

'You should have done that interview,' she said. 'You're the one with the real brains.'

'Nonsense. You were great.'

'I'm serious. Why should I get all the fun? All the glory? It's not your style, darling, all this back-seat stuff.'

Barnaby laughed. She was in the back seat. He was at the wheel.

'That's not what I meant.' She wiped away the face. 'You've spoken at meetings. I've heard you. You do it brilliantly. It's what you're best at. People believe you, they listen to you.'

She leaned forward, her arms folded over the back of the passenger seat. Barnaby could smell the wine on her breath as she bent towards him, dancing her fingertips along the line of his collar.

'No?'

'No what?'

'Don't you miss it? Resent it? Just a little bit? People like me hogging it all? Some of the other guys, too. When you've done all the work.'

Kate mentioned a handful of the other candidates, men and women who'd spent the last month or so devoting their spare time to bedding down the Pompey First campaign. Thanks to Harry Wilcox, the *Sentinel* had carried little stories on each, accompanied by the photos Charlie Epple had so carefully commissioned. The sight of their own faces in the local paper, alongside a column or two of helpful prose, had sent party morale through the roof. This was evidence that Pompey First was truly under way, proof that, individually, their touch on the wheel mattered.

'You think I should have been a candidate?'

'Definitely. And I still don't understand why you're not. You had the pick of the ward seats. You could practically guarantee a result.'

Barnaby accepted the point. Back in the spring, he'd toyed with the idea, but the harder he'd thought about the realities of the job the less keen he'd become. Being a local councillor meant grubbing around in people's lives, sorting out their problems, mediating in their quarrels, defending them from the chaos that increasingly threatened to overwhelm them. As a solicitor, he'd shouldered this kind of burden for years, applying Legal Aid to society's walking wounded, and he knew exactly how frustrating and exhausting the burden could be. Far better, he'd decided, to remain behind the scenes, directing strategy, allocating resources, acting as a counterweight to Charlie's wayward brilliance. This, he was certain, was where the real power lay. Not in the weekly trudge to draughty ward surgeries and endless committee rooms, but back at party headquarters, updating the political map, plotting the line of the next assault. He was a general, he'd decided, not one of the sharp-end troops. Though generals, too, might command a little of the limelight.

Kate was sitting back again, watching his eyes in the mirror. When the mobile rang, she reached between the front seats, lifting the handset. The message was brief. At the end of it she glanced at her watch. 'Give us ten minutes,' she said. 'We'll see you there.'

Charlie Epple was waiting on the main London road, deep in Portsmouth's northern suburbs. Above his head, on a huge billboard, a man on a ladder was flattening the last wrinkles on the latest of Charlie's posters. Since March, he'd been buying space on prime sites across the city, firing broadside after broadside in Pompey First's assault on the local political establishment. This one, in its cheeky irreverence, was typical. Against the now-familiar sea-green background, in bold white lettering, it read HONK TWICE FOR POMPEY FIRST.

Barnaby touched the Mercedes' horn as the car slid to a halt beside the kerb. Charlie bent to the window. The last week or so, he'd taken to wearing a Pompey football-club tracksuit, complete with grass stains on both knees. He was a walking reminder, he said, that the big game was getting closer. Now he was indicating a group of men across the road. They were standing on the pavement outside an open door, staring at the poster.

'Don't you love it?' he said. 'Just look at them.'

Barnaby followed his pointing finger, recognizing the newly painted premises of the Labour Party headquarters. Few of Charlie's ideas lacked impact but this one was less subtle than most. In the back of the car, Kate's head was in her hands and she was sobbing with laughter. Another car swept past, hooting derisively.

'They'll have to move,' Charlie said. 'They'll never put up with that.'

'They can't move. There's only five days to go.'

'Exactly.' Charlie banged the car roof, then asked Kate about the TV recording.

'She was brilliant,' Barnaby said. 'Absolutely brilliant. Wiped the floor with them.'

'You did?' Charlie reached into the car, cupped Kate's face in his hands, kissed her on the lips and then changed the subject yet again.

There'd been another breakthrough on the media front. A leading Sunday tabloid had been on, looking for a new angle for the local elections. One of the city's Tory MPs, Philip Biscoe, had lodged an official complaint about another of Charlie's posters. This one had featured a photo of the House of Commons in full cry. Charlie's graphics team had added balloons and silly hats to the bedlam in the Chamber and top and bottom Charlie had penned yet more copy that summed up the public's contempt for mainstream politicians. PARTY TIME, the line had read, DON'T THEY JUST LOVE IT? Beneath the photo, in a smaller typeface, Charlie had added the inevitable conclusion, VOTE POMPEY FIRST. THE PARTY FOR GROWN-UPS. And on a new line, ACTION, NOT WORDS. Hard on the heels of similar digs, this poster had evidently stretched Tory patience to the limit and, rather later than Charlie had expected, the big guys had cracked.

'So what's Biscoe done?'

'Gone to the ASA.'

'On what grounds?'

'Infringement of Commons copyright. He says it's not our photo to deface.'

'Is he right?'

'Yeah.' Charlie chortled. 'Of course he's right. But that's not the point. The point is, he can't take the pressure. The point is, we've dug a hole and he's fallen bloody in. I talked to the *Sunday Mirror* this morning. They're promising a centre spread. Biscoe's gone barmy.' He grinned. 'Two million people read the *Mirror*. Are you telling me that's bad news?'

Barnaby shook his head, trying to assess the damage. The Advertising Standards Authority seldom went further than a slap on the wrist but getting up Parliament's nose was a different matter. In theory, they had the power to summon Charlie to answer before the House of Commons, an order that Barnaby knew Charlie would be only too happy to obey. Publicity, in his view, was the fuel that powered Pompey First. The more you put in the tank, the quicker you'd change the world.

Kate wanted to know more about the centre spread in the *Sunday Mirror*. Were they serious about a double page? Or was that more journalistic licence?

'It's kosher,' Charlie said. 'They're trying to line up the heavy guys to have a pop at us.'

'Heavy guys?'

'London politicos. If they've got any sense, they won't touch us with a barge pole but it's a funny old time. The *Mirror* still goes to a lot of Labour families, and that size of readership might be hard to resist—' He broke off to yell abuse at a passing motorist who'd neglected to sound his horn.

'But if they *did* do a double spread?' Kate insisted.

'Yeah, it'd be brilliant, that kind of space . . . ' Charlie was back with Barnaby. 'But we still haven't quite got it, have we? We're still not quite there. We need a headline, an issue, something really solid, something for the broadsheets. It's out there somewhere. It has to be. But I'm buggered if I know where.'

Barnaby was checking his watch. When he looked up again, he was smiling. 'I think I may have found it,' he said, 'I'll phone you later.'

Barnaby dropped Kate outside her house. He didn't tell her where he was going next and she didn't ask, understanding that this was the real answer to the question she'd posed earlier about Barnaby's political ambitions. There were some moves he preferred to make in private, without consultation or interference. When she'd tackled him before about this, demanding to be part of whatever it was he had in mind, he'd shaken his head and talked about the importance of taking risks and about not wanting to load the responsibility for failure onto others.

At the time she'd assumed this independence of his was strictly professional but since then she'd gathered that this was pretty much the way he led the rest of his life, playing the tables alone, piling the chips onto a particular colour or a lucky square, and hoping to God that the numbers came up. Kate adored this addiction to chance, the preparedness to look disaster in the face. Indeed, it was one of the reasons she'd felt so attracted to Barnaby in the first place. But lately she'd spotted something else in his make-up: that playing the tables was one thing but winning was quite another. Given a lucky roll of the dice, Barnaby was incapable of dealing with what followed. It had been the same with his marriage, the same in their own relationship. Once the hunt was over and the quarry run to earth, the man became somehow caged, the prisoner of his own success.

Kate watched the Mercedes round the corner and disappear, wondering whether it was anything as simple as boredom. Success, after all, could be claustrophobic: lots of money, lots of security, the sudden prospect of a risk-free life. The latter was especially relevant just now. Kate was still no closer to knowing how Liz had found out about their renewed affair but by kicking her husband out she'd certainly changed everything. For three difficult weeks, Barnaby had camped in her house, sharing her bed, her bathroom and the intimate routines she called her day. If she'd believed a tenth of the promises he'd made, the letters he'd penned, the poems he'd Blu-tacked to the windscreen of her car, this sudden plunge into domesticity should have knotted them closer than ever.

Yet the reverse had happened. He'd become secretive, and slightly irritable. He'd talked incessantly about Jessie. And last weekend, when he'd finally decamped, having taken a six-month lease on a luxury seafront apartment, it had been with barely an hour's notice. He had some things to work out, some issues to resolve in his head. It wasn't anything to do with her. It was simply a period of introspection, of retrieving a little perspective, a little focus. Kate had listened to it all, watching him ferrying his bags to the car and, to his visible relief, she'd expressed neither anger nor surprise. In truth, she'd felt both, though the house – and her own life – had been infinitely less oppressive since.

She felt in her bag for the front-door key, wondering where he was off to now. She admired the intelligence and sheer energy that he and Charlie Epple had brought to Pompey First. That kind of talent, in her experience, was rare in local politics. But local politics, with all its trivia, involved real consequences for real people, and she'd come to realize that the problem with the Hayden Barnabys of this world was their self-absorption. They were clever and hard-working and never ran out of zippy ideas but, in the end, she suspected, they didn't really care at all. Not because they didn't want to, but because they simply didn't know how.

Harry Wilcox was sitting in the bar at the Imperial Hotel when Barnaby walked in. Wilcox nodded at one of the waitresses and the glass of Tiger beer was already on the table by the time Barnaby had peeled off his coat and sat down. Wilcox listened to his account of the afternoon at the TV studios, lifting his glass to Kate at the end. For public consumption, Wilcox was obliged to keep his personal political leanings a closely guarded secret but he'd never left Barnaby in any doubt that his heart was with Pompey First. It was, he'd confided from the outset, a defining idea. 'And Zhu?' he enquired. 'Our Raymond?'

Barnaby glanced at his watch. 'He'll join us for the meal. We'll go through in a minute.'

'Any idea what he's up to? He gestured towards the restaurant. 'Why the invite?'

'Haven't a clue.'

Barnaby reached for his glass and swallowed a mouthful of the sharp, ice-cold Tiger beer that Zhu imported by the containerload from Singapore. In reality, he knew very well why Zhu had asked for a chat with the *Sentinel*'s editor but it would be both rude and imprudent to steal his host's thunder. Zhu had been in London for most of the last week, dealing with various arms of the Ministry of Defence secretariat, and the hour he'd spent with the newly appointed minister had drained even his reserves of patience. These people, Barnaby suspected, had to be taught a lesson. And Wilcox had been chosen to do just that.

Wilcox was musing aloud about Charlie's posters. His favourite had appeared on hoardings in the city's shopping precinct. No parliamentary photos this time, and no anguished bleatings from the city's self-styled 'real' politicians. Instead, a simple question, *WHY PUT POMPEY FIRST?* with the answer, *BECAUSE NO ONE ELSE WILL* stripped in below.

To Wilcox, these two lines had caught the essence of the new politics. From his perch on top of the city's daily newspaper, he'd been ideally placed to monitor the astonishing upsurge of grass-roots political activity. The *Sentinel's* files were stuffed full of copy from community schools, urban villages, self-help groups, neighbourhood patrols, housing co-operatives, credit unions and local campaigning organizations of all kinds. These were people who'd grown tired of waiting for help from Westminster or Whitehall. Instead, they were making things happen for themselves. Together, this swelling tide of community involvement was now cutting across traditional party lines and, if it lacked anything, then it was a coherent political voice. By putting the interests of the city before all others, Pompey First supplied exactly that voice. Hence, in Wilcox's judgement, the extraordinary calibre of the candidates who'd stepped forward to put their names and faces on Charlie Epple's ward-by-ward posters.

'Power's leaking upwards and downwards,' he'd told Barnaby, 'upwards to Brussels and downwards to the street. One day the London politicians will wake up to all this and it'll frighten them shitless. You mark my words. Shitless.'

That had been on the phone. Next day, over a drink, he'd gone even further.

'Pompey First,' he'd confirmed, 'could change the political map. Potentially you're playing with dynamite.'

Now, his glass nearly empty, he was asking about funding. 'Your billboards must cost a fortune,' he said. 'So who's paying?'

Barnaby did his best to sidestep the question. Membership had been far healthier than anyone had anticipated. Charlie had done a wonderful deal with the billboard people. Contacts of his in the printing trade had cut production costs to the bone.

Wilcox butted in. 'You're not telling me that subs pay for all that advertising?'

'Not all of it, no.'

'Half? A quarter? Ten per cent?'

'A proportion,' Barnaby conceded.

'And the rest?'

'We have our backers.'

'I'm sure,' Wilcox grunted. 'Like who?'

Barnaby named a couple of ageing rock stars who'd left the city for greater things. Charlie knew them both and had extracted smallish sums on the promise of a monster victory party and an endless supply of art college students the night the polls were declared.

'A grand's fuck all.' Wilcox was playing the hard-bitten reporter. 'What about the rest of it?'

Barnaby said nothing. Wilcox emptied his glass. Then Zhu appeared from the restaurant, shuffling slowly towards them. Last month he'd flown to mainland China on a lengthy business trip and had returned with a broken ankle. Three weeks later, he was still walking with a stick.

Barnaby got up, buttoning his jacket and extending a hand. Wilcox did the same. Zhu touched each hand briefly, in an almost regal gesture, and offered a small, formal bow in return.

'You're welcome,' he said to Wilcox, slipping his arm through Barnaby's for support as he turned to limp back to the restaurant.

Like most Englishmen Barnaby knew, Harry Wilcox was awed by the presence of serious money. For the first half of the meal, while the surrounding tables filled up with Saturday-evening couples, he treated Zhu to an expansive review of Pompey life, calculated to flatter both men's sense of self-importance. How the city had been crying out for a bit of class and a bit of style. How impressed friends of his had been with the Imperial's unflagging excellence. How relieved he was to be able to guarantee visiting VIPs an overnight berth in a truly first-class hotel. Much of this nonsense was lost on Zhu, who picked at his boiled rice with tepid enthusiasm, favouring Wilcox with an occasional smile.

At length, as Wilcox spooned up the last of the sauce from his garlic and chilli prawns, Zhu leaned forward over the table and left a twist of paper beside his plate. Wilcox wiped his mouth with his napkin and picked it up. Unwrapping it, he found a metal bolt inside, the size of his little finger.

He held it up, looking puzzled. The bolt, flaky and ochre with rust, had seen better days.

'For you.' Zhu nodded. 'To keep.'

Glancing at Barnaby, Zhu explained that the bolt had come from the naval dockyard, a gift from an old man in one of the plating shops. 'A gift to whom?' Wilcox was lost now.

'Your Mr Samuels. Your new minister.'

'The old man gave it to Samuels?'

'Yes.'

'And Samuels . . .'

'Gave it to me.' Zhu nodded again. 'Yes.'

Wilcox picked up the bolt, revolving it in his fingers as Zhu recounted its history. According to the old man, the bolt had come from HMS *Hood*, extracted for replacement during the battle-cruiser's last pre-war refit. The old man's uncle had been part of the refit crew and the bolt, in due course, had become a family heirloom.

Barnaby watched Wilcox wiping the rust stains from his hands. Clive Samuels was the new Secretary of State for defence, a young right-wing ideologue who'd come from nowhere to a seat in the cabinet.

Barnaby caught Zhu's eye. The bolt was back on the table-cloth.

'So when did Samuels lay hands on it?' he asked.

'Wednesday. When he came down to the dockyard.'

'And he gave it away again? Just like that?'

For once, Zhu looked flustered. Embarrassment simply wasn't part of his make-up but Barnaby was sure he detected a slight pinking of the pale yellow skin stretched tight across his cheekbones.

Wilcox interrupted, keen to make his mark. 'The *Hood* went down in nineteen forty-one,' he growled. 'She was sunk by the *Bismarck*. Fourteen hundred blokes went down with her.' He poked a finger at the bolt. 'Which must make this little fella pretty lucky.'

Zhu was still nodding. 'I think your Mr Samuels is super-stitious,' he said. 'He told me about the *Hood*. He said he wanted the bolt to come back to Portsmouth. Please,' he smiled, 'keep it.'

Wilcox wrapped it up again, beaming with pleasure. Slipping it into his pocket, he asked about Samuels. Wednesday's *Sentinel* had carried a report on the ministerial visit to the dockyard. Asked about rumours of a sale, or possible closure, Samuels had categor-ically denied both.

Wilcox looked at Zhu. 'True or false?' he asked.

Zhu went through the motions of looking pained at Wilcox's bluntness, though Barnaby suspected that this was precisely the question he'd convened the meal to answer. For a moment or two, he tidied the remains of his rice. Then he looked up. 'Your government are strange people. Sometimes nothing happens. Sometimes they hurry, hurry. Why?' He shrugged, letting the ques-tion answer itself. Negotiating with Whitehall was plainly a nightmare. One week, one priority. The next week, another.

'And the dockyard? This week?' Wilcox pressed.

'This week it's for sale, very definitely for sale.'

'He said that? Samuels? He told you?'

'Of course. That's why we talk. That's why I spend so much time with his people. Talk, talk, talk. Sell, sell, sell.'

'But he denied it,' Wilcox pointed out. 'On Wednesday, he denied it.'

'So I understand.'

'He was lying, then?'

'Perhaps not. Perhaps on Wednesday he believed it. Who knows?' Zhu leaned back, his hands an inch apart, a prayerful gesture that seemed to ask for some kind of forgiveness. Presum-ably on Samuels's behalf.

Wilcox was confused. It had been common knowledge for months that Zhu was bidding for the dockyard but the Ministry of Defence had always denied that negotiations had advanced beyond the bare preliminaries. The naval dockyard was a national asset. The sale had to go out to tender. Other bidders would be involved. There were formal procedures here and it would take more than Dr Zhu to hurry Whitehall into a hasty decision.

Wilcox had abandoned the last of his noodles, determined to tie down the details.

'Just run me through this thing one more time,' he said. 'We know you're bidding to buy the dockyard.'

'That's right. It's been complicated, of course, but in essence that's correct.'

'Is there now a sum involved? Have you got that far?'

'Oh, yes.'

'May I ask how much?'

Zhu hesitated for long enough to keep Wilcox on the hook. Then he produced a small notepad. Scribbling a figure, he passed it across.

Wilcox stared at it. 'A hundred million? Isn't that on the cheap side?'

Zhu smiled. 'They're paying me.' He corrected himself, '*You*'re paying me.'

'*We*'re paying you?'

'Yes, this is taxpayer's money. There's a saving, of course. The money it costs each year to run the yard. And that, as it happens, is slightly more than a hundred million.'

'But what's the money for?'

'Mr Samuels calls it a green dowry. Your dockyard has all kinds of problems, poisons mainly. A hundred million is a down payment for the liability, for the sins of your fathers.' He beamed with pleasure at the phrase. 'Maybe you should see the environmental report. Mr Samuels is lucky to find a buyer at all.'

'But you're going ahead?'

'Of course. Subject to contract.'

'And he's driven it through? Samuels?'

'Absolutely. I understand there's an election ahead. I think he needs the money he'll save.'

'But he's spending money, not saving it.'

'He's only spending money once, Mr Wilcox. Every year that passes he saves a good deal more. That money might be useful . . . especially if taxes are to fall.'

Wilcox had located the phone, tucked discreetly into an alcove at the back of the restaurant. Barnaby wondered whether he'd have the bottle to use it. The *Sentinel* didn't publish until Monday. Could Wilcox's little scoop wait that long?

Zhu was describing his plans for the dockyard. He planned to maintain some of the major ship-repair services, perhaps even expand them. Part of the deal with Samuels hinged on a guaranteed facility for naval warships.

At this, Wilcox pulled his chair a little closer to the table. 'You're telling me the Navy stays? As your guests?'

'As my customers,' Zhu answered him. 'Of course.'

'What about a war? Some kind of emergency? Say the Argies have another go at the Falklands?'

'Then we'd do our best to help,' Zhu smiled, 'everything else permitting.'

'Everything else *permitting*? What permitting?'

Zhu looked briefly grave and Barnaby wondered whether he'd rehearsed for this. He was playing his role for all it was worth, the diligent businessman musing about a tricky investment.

'Tell me,' Wilcox insisted. 'Please.'

'About a war situation?'

'Yes.'

'I can't. We'd do our best, of course. Contractually, we'd have no choice.'

Wilcox stared at him, then sat back in the chair, mopping his face with his napkin.

'Is this on the record?' he said at last.

'Record?'

'Can I write it down? Quote you? Put it in the paper?'

'Of course.'

'It won't damage your . . . ah . . . negotiations?'

'Not at all.'

Barnaby glanced at Zhu. Even he hadn't expected quite such candour. Wilcox had produced a pad. His shorthand was slow. Eventually, he asked Zhu about the rest of his plans for the dockyard, and the Chinese obliged with a list of would-be developments. They included hotels, offices and a major expansion for the city's commercial ferryport.

Wilcox's biro paused. 'Have you talked to anyone about the ferryport?'

'No.' Zhu smiled. 'But it's very sensible. The figures speak for themselves.'

'And these offices? These hotels? Are we talking a major investment here?'

'Absolutely. A brand new financial district.'

'But what about jobs?' Wilcox asked. 'All those mateys in the dockyard.'

Zhu was grave again. 'We'll be adding jobs. Not taking them away.'

'But different jobs, surely. Different *kinds* of jobs.'

'Of course. We must be flexible.'

'So some of the present jobs will go?'

'Some of them, perhaps, yes.'

'And Samuels knows this?'

'I'm sure he must be aware that things will change, yes.'

'With respect that's not an answer.'

Zhu held out his hand. Wilcox gazed at it. 'The bolt, please.'

Wilcox produced the twist of paper. Zhu disentangled the bolt, depositing it in the china ashtray between them. 'Your Mr Samuels believes that history is moving on,' he said quietly. 'And I have to say that I agree with him.'

Later the same evening, responding to a summons by telephone, the sitting MP for Portsmouth West, Philip Biscoe, slipped out of a Knightsbridge dinner party and took a taxi to Conservative Party Central Office in Smith Square. There, a young researcher met him in the lobby. She worked on one of the local government desks in the campaign department, and the exhaustion on her face confirmed everything that Biscoe had feared. After the carnage of last year's local elections, with the Tories reduced to third place nationwide, the rout was evidently due for completion. Confidential polling samples were indicating an electoral wipe-out of historic proportions, with Tory local councillors becoming an endangered species. This, of course, wasn't a direct threat to Biscoe's constituency seat but a disaster next week could all too easily set the scene for something similar at a general election. In which case he'd be looking for a job, rather than fantasizing about red briefcases and a seat in the back of the ministerial limo.

The chairman's office was on the first floor. They took the lift, Briscoe running through the bullet points in his mind. The researcher had been more than candid on the phone. The chairman wasn't prepared to give him more than five minutes, and even that – on this particular weekend – was a profoundly generous concession.

The chairman was on the phone when the researcher slipped Biscoe in through the door. She went at once to the desk, picked up the crystal tumbler and topped it up with whisky from a decanter on the cabinet behind the long crescent of sofa. The chairman watched her, nodding when she'd poured two fingers. The phone call over, he stood up and ran a tired hand over his face before joining Biscoe on the sofa.

'How's tricks?'

'Could be worse.'

'But not much, eh?' The chairman accepted the whisky from the researcher. 'So what's the problem?'

Biscoe set out his case, tallying the points one by one. Portsmouth had spawned a brand new party. Four months ago they hadn't existed. Three months ago they'd been a joke in his secretary's constituency minutes. Now they were probably placed to win a minimum of twenty seats.

'Who says?'

'We do. We ran a telephone poll last week.'

The chairman shook his head, the whisky still untouched.

'Phone polls are crap,' he said. 'People lie all the time.'

'Maybe. But it's not just the polls. The local paper's behind them and there's been a lot of defections, the opposition mainly, but us as well. We're talking serious people here, real talent, folk we can't afford to lose.' He paused. 'This new lot seem to have caught the mood in the city. And they're bloody well organized too. Here, take a look for yourself.'

Biscoe produced a sheaf of photos. Each one showed a different billboard, and as the chairman leafed through, his interest quickened. He held up the poster that featured the Commons at bay.

'They've got a bloody nerve,' he said, 'I'll give them that.'

'I've lodged a complaint.'

'Was that wise? Extra publicity?'

'I'm not sure we had a choice. We had to do something.'

The chairman was back with the photos. He looked far from convinced. 'So who did these?' he asked at last.

'Guy called Charlie Epple'

'Who's he with?'

'Pompey First.'

'No.' The chairman sounded impatient. 'I meant which agency.'

'Pompey First. He doesn't work for an agency. He's full-time. One of the founding fathers.'

'Really?'

The chairman looked away, distracted by a signal from the researcher, who was tapping her watch. He nodded and turned back to Biscoe.

'So what are you telling me? That we're in trouble? My friend, we're in trouble everywhere. I could show you projections downstairs that would lose us more than half the seats we're defending. That means we'd kiss goodbye to five hundred councillors. And you're telling me that this . . . Pompey First outfit are a problem?'

'I'm telling you, with respect, that they're more than a problem. I'm telling you they may be the shape of things to come.'

'Meaning?'

Biscoe pursed his lips, taking his time, knowing that this was probably his one and only chance to concentrate minds at the top of the party before it was too late. 'Whether they know it or not, I think there's an agenda behind our new friends. Think the thing through, and it can't possibly stop at the town hall. Say they win. Say they demand more local power. Say, God forbid, they get it. Then what happens along the coast? What happens in Southampton? Brighton? Poole? There's an organization called Metropole. It's a grouping of south-coast cities. Are the guys in Bournemouth going to be happy if Portsmouth steals a lead? Won't

320

they want something similar for themselves? And won't they be right to want it?' He paused, aware that the chairman was fidgeting. He was a gifted fixer but he had difficulty coping with anything longer term than a couple of days.

Biscoe reached for the photos, undaunted. 'And then there's the dockyard.'

The chairman seized the initiative again. Here was something, at last, that he understood. 'The dockyard's on hold,' he said at once. 'I saw Clive Samuels myself yesterday. Nothing on the record until after next week. That's for very definite.'

'And what happens then? Do you mind if I ask?'

'Not at all. We sell the bugger. We have to. There's no other way. Not if we want to free up money for the tax cuts. But don't worry, my friend,' he picked up his glass and sipped the whisky, 'we'll give it the right spin. Jobs, opportunities, lots of foreign money. Fair few votes in that, eh?' He got up, bringing the interview to an end. Biscoe began to thank him for his time but the chairman was already back behind the desk, the phone in his hand. As Biscoe opened the door, he looked up, waiting for his call to answer. 'I'll be watching your results.' He winked. 'Be interesting to see if you're right.'

Biscoe muttered goodnight and left. The chairman put down the phone and checked his watch. Then he shuffled through his drawer for a directory. It wasn't there, so he told the researcher to look in the safe beside the cabinet. She did so and produced a small, loose-leaf binder. The chairman named a senior backbench MP, and the researcher obliged with a number. A woman's voice answered. Sir Giles was upstairs. She'd give him a call. The chairman waited for perhaps thirty seconds, drumming his fingers on the desk, staring at the name he'd scribbled on the pad. Charlie Epple rang a bell, but he couldn't remember why. One of the privatization campaigns? British Gas? The electricity flotation? He heard Sir Giles picking up the telephone. Briefly, he explained about Biscoe's visit and his problems with Pompey First.

'These clowns are evidently pushing the democracy line,' he said. 'You know, returning power to the people. That's subversion, isn't it?' There was a roar of laughter at the other end and the chairman smiled as he reached for his glass. 'Quite,' he said, after a while. 'And I thought you might try your MI5 chum as well, the one you brought up here last week.' He swallowed a mouthful of whisky, his eyes narrowing. 'Chap called Jephson, wasn't it?'

Past midnight, on a small industrial estate deep in a northern suburb of Portsmouth, an ancient Transit van coasted to a halt in a cul-de-sac beside a row of factory units. The one at the end belonged to a firm of printers. Most of their start-up capital had gone on the purchase of two reconditioned colour presses, and the contract for printing Charlie Epple's Pompey First posters had at last begun to make a dent in the daunting bank loan on which the business had been floated.

The van gently nuzzled the roll-down doors that sealed the delivery bay. The driver kept the engine in first gear, easing out the clutch. There were heavy bull bars on the front of the van but it was several seconds before the doors began to buckle inward, triggering an alarm. The driver got out and pulled on a black balaclava and a pair of rubber gloves. From the seat beside him, he hauled out what looked like a gallon can of oil.

Inside the unit, he made his way to the production floor, unscrewing the can as he ran. The machines were smaller than he'd expected. His torch lingered for a second on the control panel, a matrix of multi-coloured buttons, then he bent for the can, holding it at arm's length, his head turned away. Up-ending it, he began to pour the contents over the working surfaces, taking care to avoid splashes. The liquid spilled over the control panel, draining deep into the machine, and the woollen balaclava muffled a laugh as he scented the acrid tang of burning plastic. The rest of the liquid he saved for the other machine, repeating the procedure, cursing in the darkness as the liquid dripped onto his new trainers.

Back in the van, the can abandoned, he kept the gloves on while he tore off the trainers. The torch revealed the damage, the nylon eaten away, the stitching gone. He tossed the ruined Nikes into the darkness before gunning the engine and accelerating backwards into a savage U-turn.

Minutes later, deep in the maze of streets that surrounded the industrial estate, he pulled the van to a halt, winding down the window and listening to the police patrol cars as they converged on the pealing alarm.

Chapter Thirteen

Sunday lunchtime found Mike Tully *en route*, as usual, to the pub. It was the one day of the week when he permitted himself a pint or two of beer, burying himself in the papers in a quiet corner of the saloon. Occasionally he'd join the other drinkers round the bar but what he liked, above all, about the Pembroke was the general consensus that a man's Sunday belonged to no one but himself. If you'd come for a pint and the chance to exchange gossip, there was nowhere better. If you wanted to retire behind the *Observer* or the *Independent on Sunday*, so be it.

The nearest newsagent occupied a corner site opposite the cathedral. Outside on the pavement, the *Sentinel*'s usual weekday placard announced a special Sunday edition. DOCKYARD BOMBSHELL ROCKS CITY, read the scrawl. Tully added the paper to his usual order, trying to shield the thin eight-page supplement from the rain as he crossed the road towards the pub. Billed as an exclusive, the dockyard story spilled across the front page, columns of breathless prose heaped around two photos. One showed the saturnine features of Clive Samuels, the new Minister of Defence. The other, unmistakably, was Raymond Zhu.

Tully collected his pint from the barman and settled behind a table in the corner. The circle of drinkers at the bar had already been through the *Sentinel*'s special edition and were busy trading opinions. These men were local to Old Portsmouth, mostly middle-aged or retired. They led solid, decent lives cushioned by success and a degree of modest wealth. One or two, like Tully himself, had served in the Navy or the Royal Marines and these were the men who salted the conversation with the riper expletives. Samuels was a jumped-up little creep who'd come from nowhere. Zhu was a Chinkie caterer from the other side of God knows where. What did either of these Johnny-come-latelies know about running the bloody dockyard?

Tully finished the front page and opened the paper for the promised inside story. The *Sentinel*'s exclusive evidently revolved around a conversation with Zhu himself, and the details held few surprises for Tully. Ever since his meeting with Ellis at the turn of the year he'd been expecting something similar. Zhu, as he knew only too well, was an entrepreneur of genius and if he was sinking his roots as deeply as he claimed in the city, then bidding for the dockyard was an obvious commercial move.

The inside pages spelled out the details of the *Sentinel*'s scoop. The naval dockyard had been effectively gifted to Zhu with a hefty down-payment against future environmental liabilities. This multi-million-pound deal had been secretly agreed by both parties, giving the lie to Samuels's recent denials of either closure or sale. In Zhu's hands, the dockyard was to become the centre of a huge new commercial development. There were plans for a financial district, office blocks, hotels, a retail park. Spare land would be set aside for an extension to the commercial ferryport and there was the promise of major investment in the naval heritage area.

Tully turned the page to find an artist's impression of the physical shape Zhu's dreams might have taken by the end of the century. The linework was detailed, the product of weeks of work, and had plainly come from Zhu's files. Beyond the soaring masts of HMS *Victory* stretched acres and acres of gleaming new office blocks, elegant towers in steel and glass, cleverly showcasing the best of the dockyard's architectural gems. Buffering the old from the new were treelined walkways and water-filled dry docks. Half closing his eyes, Tully was reminded of similar schemes he'd seen in the Far East. This was exactly what you'd do in Hong Kong or Singapore, he thought, wrapping the heritage of empire in a tissue of hi-tech glitz.

Beside the sketch, the *Sentinel* had run a terse editorial. The paper had become the voice of the city, demanding answers to questions it considered too important to defer even for twenty-four hours. Why had negotiations been such a closely guarded secret? Why hadn't local interests been consulted? What were the implications for jobs? What would happen to other naval establishments in the area? And, most important of all, why had the minister told such a bare-faced lie?

Overnight, reporters on the *Sentinel* had even had time to phone around for reaction, and the back pages of the supplement was given over to a range of local voices. Predictably, the unions were hostile. This was yet another sell-out from a government that gave no thought to the working man. Contracts would be renegotiated, rights lost, security threatened. Elsewhere on the back pages there were howls of rage from anguished patriots: how could any government simply abandon the country's oldest naval port? Were we really so broke that we had to surrender the nation's heritage to a foreigner?

Tully reached for his beer and took a tiny sip, knowing that these were the questions that had so troubled him earlier in the year. He was as realistic as the next man, and he knew how fast the world was changing, but his years in the service had left him with a profound respect for the uniform and the flag. People were right to value discipline and self-respect. The guys at the bar had a point when they banged on about loyalty and national pride. These were things that mattered, the glue that kept society together. Chuck away these values, turn everything into figures on a balance sheet, and you'd be left with nothing but trading estates, video shops and fifty million people dedicated to grabbing what they could. Was that all it meant to be British? Was that what Mr Samuels and his friends really wanted?

Tully picked up the paper again. The word 'betrayal' was everywhere. Promises betrayed. People betrayed. Tradition betrayed. The city betrayed. He returned to the front page and the two photos. Throughout the supplement, the *Sentinel* had been careful not to criticize Zhu. His role in capturing the dockyard had, if anything, been almost passive. He was simply doing what any entrepreneur would do. He'd been pushing at an open door, and if the editorial finger pointed anywhere, then it pointed to the men inside. Once again, the city had been steam-rollered. Once again, Westminster and Whitehall knew best.

Behind the bar, the landlord was trying to intervene in an increasingly heated confrontation. One of the regulars, a recently retired surgeon, was standing as a ward candidate for Pompey First and had been quick to seize on the dockyard's importance in the battle for city votes. This was dynamite, he kept insisting, proof-positive that the old politics had failed. Where were the local MPs in all this? Who was going to man the city's defences? A Tory on the next stool told him he was talking through his arse. What mattered now were global markets, tidal waves of money washing back and forth across the face of the planet. No party, no politician, no bloody country, even, could stand in the way of all that. It didn't matter a toss if this guy was Chinese or Martian or whatever the hell he was. Just as long as he had the money.

Listening to the chorus of protesting voices, Tully winced. Money wasn't everything. There was room, even now, for a bit of sentiment. The retired surgeon took up the running again, waving a flag for the man in the street, and Tully sat back in his chair, watching the koi carp hanging motionless in the fish tank beside the telephone, wondering whether the ex-surgeon really knew what he might be letting the city in for.

On a shelf above his desk at home was a collection of audio cassettes. They'd all come from Liz, recordings of conversations transmitted from Charlie Epple's place, and he'd spent hours sieving through them for incoming calls from Haagen Schreck. In this respect the intercept had been something of a failure. Calls had been recorded, more than a dozen, but not one had given Tully any clue to Haagen's movements. On the contrary, they seemed to be couched in some kind of code. Without exception, Haagen talked about the weather. Some days he complained that it was raining. Some days there seemed to be a chance of some sunshine. Once or twice it couldn't have been nicer. Quite what the vagaries of the Dutch weather had to do with Jessie Tully had yet to fathom, but there was certainly no sign that Haagen planned to risk the move back to the UK. Other conversations, though, involving Charlie, had been of profound interest, not just to Tully but to Liz as well.

There was a roar of laughter from the bar, the political wrangle dissolving into another round of drinks, and Tully retreated behind the paper, remembering Liz's face the first time he'd called round to collect a completed audio-cassette. A device in the recorder enabled her to monitor conversations, and she'd evidently been going through the wardrobe in the spare room when she'd heard her husband's voice. He'd been on the phone to Charlie and Kate Frankham's name had come up. She'd known, of course, that Kate was part of Pompey First. Barnaby had never made a secret of it. But she hadn't realized, fool that she was, that political solidarity extended as far as a full-blown affair. At the time, Tully had been sceptical. He'd listened to the tape and while the references to Kate suggested a certain intimacy it was far from proof. Would Barnaby really be that foolish? Wasn't he playing Charlie along? The way men do? At this, Liz had offered him a tired smile. Barnaby and Kate Frankham had been at it before. In fact their first affair had come close to ending her marriage. Hadn't he heard the rumours? Picked up the tittle-tattle?

Tully took a long pull at his beer, still shamed by his own ignorance, his own gullibility. Like Liz, he'd trusted Barnaby, and he'd admired him too. The man wasn't short of self-confidence and he seemed to find it hard to pass a mirror, but he worked like a demon and he had a razor-sharp intelligence that Tully knew was all too rare. On countless occasions, he'd passed work his way, recommended him to clients, and not once had Tully been let down. The news that he'd betrayed Liz and Jessie not once but twice he found curiously disturbing, a feeling that had grown with every new conversation his equipment had recorded. Within days, it had been obvious that Liz was right and when she'd finally asked Barnaby to leave, Tully had felt profoundly sorry for her. She was a good person, a strong person. He liked her as much as he'd liked any woman in his life, and he'd begun to stay for the odd cup of tea, sometimes even a bite to eat, the evenings when he called round to collect the latest cassette.

Liz, he knew, was becoming increasingly uncomfortable with

the bug on Charlie's line and, for his part, Tully also had qualms about persevering with the intercept. But as the real agenda behind Pompey First became clearer and clearer, he'd come to regard it almost as a duty. As the months went by, it had become plain that Hayden Barnaby and Charlie Epple's political ambitions wouldn't stop with leadership of the city council. What they were really after – what really turned them on – was the possibility of UDI, a city wholly independent of the UK. This was alarming enough, especially in the light of the way Barnaby had chosen to conduct his private life. But what drove Tully to transcribe and cross-index the more damning conversations was what lay behind a bid for independence. Where would they find the money to fund this huge gamble? Who'd organize the billions of pounds you'd need to push off from the motherland and float away the infant statelet? Tully studied the *Sentinel*'s front page again, holding it at arm's length, concentrating on the photo of Zhu. The smile, as usual, gave nothing away.

Back home, in his maisonette, Tully slid a dish of shepherd's pie into the microwave and put a match to the gas beneath the saucepan of frozen peas. The telephone lay on his desk next door. The numbers Ellis had left him were sellotaped to the calendar on the wall. He hesitated, eyeing the line of carefully labelled audio-tapes on the shelf above the desk. The transmitter was still func-tioning, and with luck the batteries should last another couple of months.

His hand went to the telephone and he dialled the first of the numbers. In his head, he could still hear the voices of the men arguing in the pub, the faith they placed in other people's promises, the eagerness with which they traded the glib, catch-all phrases. Grass-roots democracy. Partnership. Powersharing. Was it really as simple as this? Could mere words sort anything out? The number began to ring, then there was a click as an answerphone engaged. At once, Tully recognized Ellis's flat London vowels. He was abroad on business. He'd attend to messages as soon as he got back. Tully scowled and put down the phone. The second number had an outer London prefix. When he dialled, it answered almost at once. A woman's voice, rich, warm.

329

Tully introduced himself and explained that he was trying to get in touch with Ellis. It seemed that he was out of the country.

'I'm afraid so. He's in Singapore just now. Back tomorrow, oddly enough.'

Tully reached for a pen. He had no idea who this woman might be but when he asked for her name she obliged at once. 'Louise Carlton,' she said. 'May I help at all?'

'I'm afraid not. It's Mr Ellis I'm after.'

'Of course.' Louise gave a little chuckle. 'I'll say you called. I'm sure he'll be glad to see you again.'

Tully had nearly finished the shepherd's pie when the doorbell rang. A glance through the window revealed Liz Barnaby. He let her in. When she saw the remains of the meal she apologized and suggested she came back later, but Tully wouldn't hear of it. He'd had more than enough. They could share a pot of coffee.

Liz accompanied him into the kitchen. She'd just had another visit from Lolly. The poor girl was at her wit's end. She was sure that Jessie was seeing Haagen.

Tully was trying to find the coffee filters. He looked round, surprised. 'She's been over to Holland?'

'No, Lolly thinks he's here.'

'*Here?*'

'Yes.'

'How come?'

Liz settled on a stool. 'It's little things. Things she says. Mood swings. Unexplained absences. Apparently Jessie goes out a lot, always with the dog, always alone. And when she comes back, she's . . . different.'

'What do you mean, different?'

'Happy, bubbly, relaxed.' She frowned. 'I've noticed it, too,' she added thoughtfully.

'Drugs again?'

'No, thank God. That's what went through my mind but Lolly said no, definitely not. She says she'd have spotted anything like that. She says she'd know.'

Tully found the box of filters. The kettle had begun to boil. 'It could be anyone,' he said, 'couldn't it?'

'That's exactly what I thought.' Liz reached for the kettle, turning it off. 'But then she found the chocolate. Jess had left it in the fridge. It was Dutch. You can't get it here. And there's the phone calls.'

'What phone calls?'

'Every time Jess goes out on these little trips of hers, there's always been a phone call. They don't last long. Half a minute at the most. But Jessie's out of the door like a shot, so Lolly says. It happened again this morning.' Liz produced an audio-cassette from the pocket of her cardigan. 'I thought this might be useful.'

Tully kept his audio equipment next door. Liz stood watching while he loaded the cassette, respooling it through several messages. When he pushed the play button, he heard Barnaby's voice. He was leaving a message for Charlie. The message was timed at seven twenty-one. The girls must still have been asleep.

'There's a problem at Wallington's,' Barnaby was saying. 'They had a break-in last night. Someone poured acid all over their bloody machines. Gary's saying it's down to us, provoking the opposition, but it's a pain because we'll have to find somewhere else. Just wondered if you had any thoughts.' Tully's finger found the fast-forward button.

Liz was staring at the machine. 'Who's Gary?'

'Gary Wallington. Runs a printing firm. Epple must get his posters done there—' Tully broke off. He had the next conversation cued up. Liz stiffened at the new voice, male again, but younger.

'Haagen,' she said at once.

Tully picked up a pen. Haagen was in a good mood. The weather, he said, was perfect, absolutely perfect. Sunny, warm, not a cloud in the sky. There was a pause, then the sound of Jessie giggling before the connection went dead.

Tully looked up. 'That was this morning,' he said. 'Had to be.'

'Of course it was.'

'But it was raining.'

'Exactly.'

'And Jessie?'

'Out of the door in seconds. According to Lolly.'

Tully was looking up at the row of cassettes above his desk. For once the expression on his face betrayed his frustration.

'Shit,' he said quietly, apologizing at once.

'What's the matter?'

'Nothing. Nothing I can't put right.' He glanced round at Liz, suddenly businesslike. 'What's Lolly's line on all this? Will she confront Jess? Have it out?'

'No.' Liz sighed. 'She says she's through with heavy scenes. She says she's tried all that before and it doesn't seem to work. She just wants Haagen out of it and I gather she thinks I'm her best hope.' She smiled. 'I think she really loves Jess. It's quite touching.'

Tully extracted the cassette and left it on the desk. Then he disappeared into the kitchen. When he returned with the coffee, Liz was reading the *Sentinel*'s special edition.

'What do you think?' she asked. 'Can you sort something out?'

'No problem. Give me a couple of days.'

Jessie was still in bed when Lolly came racing up the stairs.

'Your dad!' she shouted. 'He's on telly.'

Jessie made her way downstairs. The dog was sprawled on the carpet, tearing at the rag doll Lolly had found at the cathedral bring-and-buy.

'Oz,' Lolly hauled him towards the door, 'bugger off.'

Jessie settled on the sofa. She had brought the duvet from the bedroom and pulled it around her, holding it tight under her chin. Lolly was back with the remains of the doll. 'See?' She pointed at the television. Hayden Barnaby was being interviewed outside the dockyard gates. Visible in the background was a small demonstration. One of the hastily scrawled placards read HANDS OFF OUR JOBS.

Jessie slipped off the sofa and turned up the volume. In his buttonhole her father was wearing the paper rosette she'd made for him only last week. It was a lovely pale green, close to the shade that Charlie had chosen for Pompey First but, in Jessie's opinion, infinitely more tasteful. She pointed it out to Lolly, glad that he cared enough to wear it.

'Listen,' Lolly hissed, 'he's doing really well.'

Barnaby was answering a question about what lay behind the dockyard sale. 'It's a political decision,' he said, 'made by a politician. But that's exactly the problem. Politicians are here for five years. The Navy's been around for five hundred.'

Lolly clapped, shrieking with delight. Jessie could hear the dog pawing at the door. Barnaby had changed tack now, listing some of the other ways that Whitehall had sought to bring the city to its knees, and Jessie marvelled at how a man she knew so well, so intimately, could appear on television like this, so authoritative, so cool.

Since he'd moved into his new flat, she'd been seeing a great deal more of him. He'd given her a key and encouraged her to pop in whenever she liked. She'd put herself in charge of his domestic arrangements, adding her own brand of chaos to her father's half-hearted attempts to keep the place in some kind of order. Some evenings she went over and cooked for him, simple stuff like pasta or risotto, and afterwards they'd linger at the table by the big front window and talk for hours about the way things had been. The break-up had hurt her mum a good deal, and Jessie was glad she'd got round to giving her the flowers, but when she tried to talk to her dad about it, he always changed the subject.

What seemed to interest him far more was the progress of Pompey First. Jessie had no interest in politics but these last few weeks she'd begun to understand how much this new party meant to him. It was like having a new baby, she'd decided. It preoccupied him day and night, the tiniest details, and it had transformed his life.

'Look!' Lolly was pointing at the screen again. Barnaby was walking down the bridge that led to the harbour station pontoon. The camera tightened on his face as he paused by the rail, gazing out across the harbour. On the soundtrack, the reporter was speculating about the impact of the dockyard controversy on Pompey First's chances in Thurday's elections. Citywide, he was saying, there was a mood of deep anger. If ever there was a time for a fresh start in local politics, that time was surely now. Perhaps this man would soon be the new voice of Portsmouth. Exactly on cue, as if he'd anticipated the thought, Barnaby permitted himself a small smile, then turned and thrust his hands in his pockets. Jessie felt the warmth flood through her as she watched him walk away.

The dog had started to bark now, and Lolly reached for her plimsolls. 'I'll take him out,' she said. 'It's my turn.'

Billy Goodman was reading the *Sunday Mirror* when Kate buzzed the entryphone with the takeaway curry. Leaving the paper spread on the carpet in front of his armchair, he let her in and she carried the food through to the kitchen, scolding him for not warming the plates. She filled the washing-up bowl with hot water and plunged them in. Billy was back in the armchair.

'You read this stuff?' he called. 'Listen.'

Kate returned to the lounge. She'd bought four copies of the *Mirror* already and had read the piece umpteen times, but it still made her laugh.

> Cheeky Charlie Epple and his hit squad of home-grown Portsmouth politicians have got right up the nose of some of Britain's leading establishment figures. Dismissed as 'cowboys' and 'amateurs' by Tory MPs, Charlie's mob (they call themselves Pompey First!) have been taking the mickey something rotten – as our selection of Charlie's posters shows. But Pompey First may yet have the last laugh. The *Mirror*'s own poll shows that Charlie's DIY cowboys stand every chance of winning next week's head-to-head . . . by giving the has-beens a thrashing.

Billy looked up. 'It's cartoon-speak,' he said. 'How could you?'

'How could we what?'

'Let them get away with that drivel? I thought you lot were serious. In it for real.'

'We are.' She waved at the paper. 'That won't do us any harm.'

Billy wagged his head, folded the paper and let it drop onto the pile beside his chair. Kate knew him well enough to see through the gruff disapproval and, deep down, suspected he was quietly impressed. However inane the treatment, Charlie Epple had put Pompey First on millions of breakfast tables nationwide.

She spooned the curry onto the plates and carried them through. The last of the rain had gone now and the room was flooded with sunshine.

Billy was standing by the sideboard, slopping vodka into tall glasses. 'It's lemonade or lemonade,' he said briefly, 'else you can take it neat.'

They ate the curry in near silence. Afterwards, over the third glass of vodka, she told him about the studio recording. She'd brought round a video. It had arrived in the post yesterday morning. She thought maybe he'd like to watch it. Billy grunted, as noncommittal as ever, and she gave him the video to load in the player while she rinsed the plates in the kitchen. Through the open door, she could hear herself performing and three shots of Billy's vodka made the experience feel somehow remote. Already, since yesterday, a million things had happened, and this morning, after the *Sentinel*'s supplement, the phone had rung non-stop. She'd coped as best she could, sticking to what she imagined might be the party line, but she was getting increasingly irritated at being left so exposed. Whenever she'd tried to phone Barnaby, his mobile had been engaged, and her attempts to contact Charlie had got absolutely nowhere. Jessie, answering his home telephone, thought he might be in London. Beyond that, no one seemed to know.

Kate softened a little, thinking of Charlie. She'd loved his spirit from the start. He affected a kind of manic craziness, a total commitment to excess, but the more she got to know him, the saner he seemed to be. His attitude to politics – that it was giddy, corrupt and wildly enjoyable – was a stark contrast to Barnaby's trudge to the summit. Given a choice her instincts told her that Charlie was probably right. Changing the world was never going to be easy. But who said you couldn't have a laugh or two on the way?

The washing-up finished, Kate rejoined Billy in the lounge. He was fast-forwarding the interview, pausing from time to time to listen to the bits when Kate was talking. At the end, he reached for the remote control and switched off the television. Kate looked at him from across the room. These times she spent with him were precious, little islands of sanity beyond the reach of the bullshitters. However brutal it might be, Billy would never spare her the truth.

'Go on,' she said. 'What do you think?'

'I think you were bloody good.'

'Yeah? And what do you really think?'

'I just told you.'

Kate felt the grin spread over her face. Billy had never said anything as positive as this. Ever. 'Is that it?' she said. 'Gold star?'

'Yeah.' He nodded. 'Definitely. It's just a shame, that's all.'

'Shame? I don't get it.'

'No.' He grasped the vodka bottle. 'And you won't either. Not now. Not once you're in with this lot.' She listened to him, stony-faced, as he listed the ways she'd betrayed what he called her political birthright. He'd heard her talking about her dad, his years in the union, organizing the print boys, taking on the management, squeezing the best possible deal for the blokes he represented. She'd been part of that. He knew she had because she'd told him so. As a youngster, she'd helped keep the books, counting out the weekly subs, arranging the Christmas raffle, understanding what it was to be part of a working-class community. Her socialism, he said, had been of the best kind, unquestioning, instinctive, natural. That was one of the reasons he'd admired her, one of the reasons she'd won his respect. She'd got stuck in. She'd taken people on, face to face. And she'd meant it.

Kate cut in. She was angry now, tired of Billy's unending sentimentality. Sentimentality was easy. Sentimentality was where you hid when you'd turned your back on real life.

'Real life?' Billy's eyes returned to the screen. 'That?'

'Yes.'

'No.' Billy dismissed the proposition. 'That was circus, make-believe. I'm talking about politics, real people, flesh and blood. Not television.'

'They are flesh and blood. We were flesh and blood. I was there. That was me, believe it or not.'

336

'No.' Billy shook his head wearily, the way a teacher might with a particularly backward pupil. 'There's a difference, and it's television that makes the difference. You're becoming someone else, love. You're a confection, a sweetie for the masses. They'll dress you nicely, light you nicely, make you look tasty, make you say the right things, and all of that's fucking wonderful for a week or so. But do yourself a favour, eh? Never confuse it with real life.'

Kate felt too upset to argue. Then she bent to the video and extracted the cassette. Standing up again, she pulled on her coat. By the door, she paused. 'Just say I believe you. Just say I think you're right. I'm a puppet. A dummy. So who's pulling the strings? Tell me that.'

Billy had moved the armchair round. Now he was staring out of the window, the bottle tipped to his lips. He took a pull at the vodka, then wiped his mouth. 'The note's in the video box,' he said softly. 'Don't fucking tell me you haven't read it.'

'Video box?'

Kate looked at it. Tucked down the side was a piece of paper. She unfolded it. The handwriting was unfamiliar but as soon as she read it she could hear Hendricks's voice. *You were better than ever second time round,* he'd written. *Where could all this lead?* She examined the note a moment longer. He'd no right to put kisses on the end, she thought, no right at all.

She began to unbutton her coat. Billy was lying back in the armchair.

'It's a fantasy,' she said savagely. 'It's pathetic.'

Billy smiled at last, his eyes closed. 'Then we agree,' he muttered, offering her the bottle.

It was nearly three before Jephson picked up Louise from her house in Cheam. The director of F branch had phoned before lunch, alarmed by the second call in an hour from Sir Giles Jeffrey. Not only was the Portsmouth situation troublesome but, thanks to an extraordinary breach of commercial confidence, it now had all the makings of a major crisis.

Jephson threaded the BMW through the tangle of slip-roads

that led to the M25. Giles Jeffrey lived in some style on a forty-acre estate out near Henley. He'd only been in residence for a couple of months and he'd warned Jephson that things might be a little chaotic. They were expected for afternoon tea.

'It's evidently our friend Zhu,' Jephson was saying. 'He's been talking to the local paper. As far as I can make out, they printed pretty well everything. Hardly helpful, under the circumstances.'

Louise was watching the speedometer. To her surprise, 110 m.p.h. felt perfectly safe.

'Is it true?' she enquired. 'About the sale?'

'Absolutely.'

'And the terms? Zhu's got it right?'

'Sadly, yes.' Jephson flicked his headlights at a dawdling Porsche in the fast lane. 'Samuels won't bother to deny it either. Backing down isn't his style.'

He and Louise exchanged looks.

'But why us? Why call for Five?'

Jephson laughed. He shared his contempt for politicians with few, but Louise was someone he'd come to trust. 'The Tories are in big trouble,' he said, 'and they know it. Their little boat's sinking and they haven't a clue what to do. If you think it's pathetic, I'm afraid you'd be right.' He paused. 'They've sent up a distress flare. They're desperate for help.'

'But why us?' Louise asked again. 'What are we supposed to do?'

'God knows.' Jephson glanced sideways at her. 'That's why I've asked you along. I thought you might have a few ideas.'

When they arrived, Sir Giles Jeffrey was waiting for them in the drawing room. To Louise's eye, the house was beautiful, a rambling confection of half a dozen period styles, doubtless the work of successive generations. The windows in one wing were still boarded up and there were builder's skips amongst the new owner's fleet of family cars on the broad sweep of gravelled drive.

Louise and Jephson settled into comfortable armchairs while Jeffrey's new wife knelt in front of the fire, toasting crumpets.

'To be frank, Central Office thought nothing of it,' Sir Giles was saying.

'Until when?'

'Last night. Philip Biscoe had the sense to mark the chairman's card. He's sharp, young Biscoe. When chaps like him get rattled, I fancy it's time to listen.'

'And the chairman?'

'Gave me a ring. And again this morning, of course. Once the wretched dockyard thing had broken.'

Louise was watching Sir Giles's wife buttering the first round of crumpets. The national news organizations had picked up the Samuels exposé from the *Sentinel*'s morning exclusive, and after Jephson had rung she'd listened to the midday news. Pressed for reaction, Tory Central Office had thrown up the shutters, retreating behind a curt statement that 'the situation was under urgent review'. In Whitehall parlance, that was as close as politicians ever came to an admission of guilt, and it was a measure of the situation's gravity that Sir Giles had felt it necessary to surrender an hour or so of his precious Sunday afternoon.

He passed round the crumpets while his wife loaded the toasting fork again. Louise bit deep, savouring her first mouthful. 'We have assets down there,' she said absently. 'We may be able to help.'

'Assets where?' Sir Giles was trying to refill the milk jug from a carton beside his chair.

'Portsmouth.'

'Oh? Anything helpful?'

Louise glanced at Jephson. In the car, they'd agreed that she should lead. She was running Ellis. She was the one who'd heard from the man Tully. She knew best.

'Possibly,' she said. 'But it rather depends on your timetable. I imagine it's a bit tight.'

'Bloody right it's a bit tight.' He glared at the puddle of milk that had appeared on the carpet beneath the carton. 'We have to get something into Number Ten by Tuesday lunchtime. Twelve o'clock absolute latest.'

'May I ask why?'

'PM's Questions,' he said briefly, looking helplessly at his wife. 'Tuesdays and Thursdays in the bearpit. Blair's bound to lead on the dockyard story. National heritage. Jobs. Misleading statements from government ministers. It's a real dog's breakfast, whichever way you look at it.' He watched his wife as she hurried from the room. Seconds later she returned with a cloth, pushing her husband gently aside and mopping up the milk. 'We're so bloody disorganized,' he was saying, 'that's the real problem. The fuss about the dockyard's a killer but at least there's a clear line of ministerial responsibility. It's down to Samuels and he's got to bloody sort it out. But that's only half the story. It's the other bit that bothers me.'

'Other bit?'

'Pompey First. In my book, Biscoe's right. Give these chaps a crack at real power, and there won't be a city in the country safe from something similar. These people mean what they say. They're fed up with us. I'm not joking. It's bloody sinister. And bloody worrying, too.' He went on, 'Problem is, there's no one obvious to sort it all out. It's not a departmental matter. It doesn't fit anyone's brief, and to be absolutely honest everyone's a bit woolly about Portsmouth.' He looked across at Jephson. 'So what do you think, David? Can do? By Tuesday? Sparrow fart?'

Jephson was looking engaged. His favourite hobby was moving Five's tanks onto other people's lawns and this, quite literally, was an open invitation. The government was facing humiliation at Thursday's polls. In time those wounds would heal but Sir Giles was right. Pompey First could turn a temporary setback into something far more permanent. The loss of a major city to a party no one had ever heard of was unprecedented.

Sir Giles's wife was on her feet again. Jephson watched her disappear towards the kitchen.

'We're debriefing someone tomorrow morning,' he said slowly. 'He's flying home from Singapore overnight.'

'Singapore?' Sir Giles was baffled. 'Is that relevant?'

'Yes.' Jephson looked at Louise. 'I understand it might be.'

Lolly was dragging Oz along the beach when the bull terrier saw the little girl at the water's edge. She must have been three or four, certainly no more, and she was standing beside an older child, possibly her brother. The older child had thrown an empty can into the water and the pair of them were trying to hit it with handfuls of tiny pebbles.

Attracted by the splash of the pebbles in the water, Oz made for the little girl, tugging Lolly behind him. The child was wearing a pair of yellow wellington boots, and when she turned to face the dog, Lolly saw the red Comic Relief ball on the end of her nose. It dwarfed the rest of her face, and her hand went up to it instinctively, holding it on. She looked, thought Lolly, just like her own Candelle.

The child stared at Oz, stepping back when he tried to sniff her. She reached for him, tentative, uncertain, trying to pat his head, then she bent to the beach picked up another handful of pebbles. As she did so, Oz snapped at the red plastic nose. Lolly heard a gristly noise and then a piercing scream as the little girl's hand went to her face again.

She fell on her back, inches from the water, looking up at her hand, rigid with shock. Lolly kicked the dog, and tried to haul him off, but Oz was too strong for her. Straddling the child's body, it lunged again at the torn red plastic, sinking its teeth into the fleshy softness of her cheeks. The child was shaking her head from side to side, trying to get away, trying to stop the pain, but the movement drove the bull terrier to fresh efforts and he snapped again at the scarlet pulp that had once been her nose.

The older child was struggling up the beach, shouting for his dad. On the promenade, passers-by had stopped to watch. Then a man in a silver shell suit appeared from nowhere. He had two ice creams, one in either hand, and they left a trail of drips on the pebbles as he ran towards the water's edge. Beside his daughter, he abandoned the ice creams, falling on the dog, trying to prise open the massive jaws. The little girl had stopped crying now, and she was lying on the wet pebbles, motionless, her face a mask of blood.

*

It was Harry Wilcox's phone call that brought Charlie Epple to the *Sentinel*'s offices. With the dockyard special safely on the streets, the editor was holding an impromptu party, and the dozen or so journalists and production staff who'd worked through the night were now demolishing an assortment of takeaway pizzas delivered from a restaurant round the corner.

Spotting Charlie making his way across the newsroom, Wilcox emerged from his office. His jacket was off and his tie was loosened at the collar. In one hand he had a bottle of pils while the other encircled the girl from the subs desk who'd sorted out most of the interviews that had featured so prominently in the supplement's back pages.

'Fucking wonderful,' Harry was saying. 'Fucking shafted the bastard.'

'What bastard?'

'Samuels.'

Charlie was delighted. The phone call to his mobile had found him on the train down from London. He'd picked up a copy of the *Sentinel* at the station and read it in the back of the cab. Wilcox was right. The *Sentinel* had cleared the B-52s for take-off. Pompey First could at last go nuclear.

'Go what?' Wilcox was drunk.

'Nuclear.' Charlie was grinning at the young sub. 'Air war's over. Ground war begins. Dagga-dagga-dagga . . .' He drew a bead on a passing journalist. 'Time for the big push.'

Wilcox wove back towards his office, returning with a bottle of Scotch. The sub was laughing, amused by Charlie's playful offer to protect her in the event of hostilities. Wilcox uncapped the bottle and passed it to Charlie.

'Here,' he said, 'have one on us.'

Charlie raised the bottle in a toast and enquired about photos. He fancied something in the dockyard, something that included Samuels. Wilcox nodded at once. 'How about Wednesday? Ministerial visit? Lord High-fucking-Executioner?'

'Nice line.' Charlie swallowed a mouthful of whisky, feeling it torch his empty stomach. 'Might even use it.'

'For what?'

'The ground war.' Charlie winked at the sub. 'Where do you keep the pictures?'

Wilcox hesitated. As drunk as he was, he still knew the dangers of blurring the line between benign neutrality and open support. Quiet encouragement to the likes of Hayden Barnaby was one thing. Offering help and succour to this lunatic was quite another.

The sub had spotted a winking light on a keyboard on a nearby desk. She bent to answer it, pulling a pad towards her as she did so. Lines of shorthand appeared. Wilcox wanted to know more about the pictures.

'Just curious to see what you've got,' Charlie said.

'Then what?'

'Fuck knows.'

The sub was looking up. She had a hand over the phone's mouthpiece. 'Little girl on the beach,' she said. 'Savaged by a dog.'

Hearing the call of the trumpets again, Wilcox seized the phone. The sub felt the gentle tug of Charlie's hand on her arm.

'Boss says it's cool,' he murmured. 'Show me where you keep the photos.'

The picture library was housed in a long narrow office at the back of the newsroom. The sub, whose name was Gina, knew exactly where to look for Wednesday's coverage of the dockyard visit. Charlie pulled up a chair and cleared a space beside the light box. He'd picked up a thick wedge of pizza on his way through the newsroom and he began to eat it, brushing crumbs off a pile of discarded prints.

'Here.'

Gina was going through a file of contact sheets. She passed one to Charlie. The contacts featured tiny black-and-white prints from strips of negatives. There were twenty-four in all and Charlie worked quickly through them, his finger returning to a shot of Samuels looking more than usually pleased with himself. In the background, a gaggle of workmen were trudging away towards a distant gate, most carrying the heavy canvas bags in which they stored their tools. Like all the best photos, it captured the entire story in a single image.

Charlie looked up. A glass partition separated the picture

library from the newsroom and Gina was staring at the circle of journalists around Wilcox. He was off the phone now and Charlie could tell from the expression on his face that the party mood was evaporating fast. Someone appeared from his office with a jacket. Wilcox grabbed it.

Charlie tapped Gina's arm. Time was running out. He showed her the contact sheet.

'Number twelve,' he said. 'Any chance of a ten by eight?'

Gina returned to the file. Blown up, the picture was even better. Charlie laid it on the desk, beside the remains of his pizza.

'Brilliant,' he muttered. 'One in the bollocks for Mr Smug.' He had another thought. He'd been talking to Barnaby on the mobile. There'd been some trouble last night – vandalism at a local printer's, the place they used for the posters – and he was keen to keep the cap on the story. 'Anything tasty last night?' he asked idly. 'Anything for tomorrow's paper?'

'Not to my knowledge. I've been here all day. I'd have heard if there was.'

At the other end of the office the door opened and Charlie looked up to find Wilcox bearing down on him. He was trying hard to sober up. He'd phoned one of the staff photographers. The guy would meet them at the hospital. He'd asked for a couple of rolls of HP4, in case the colour shots were too horrible.

Wilcox was staring at the photo of Samuels. Charlie remembered the child attacked by the dog. Wilcox's face was quite blank.

'The kid's only three,' he said to Gina. 'You'd better come too.'

In Singapore, it was 10.15 p.m. Ellis sat in the lobby of the Furama Hotel, waiting for Lim, the young investigator from the Commercial Affairs Department who'd volunteered to take him to the airport. The last London-bound flight left in two hours. With luck, for once, they might resist talking business.

Lim's Proton saloon stood outside. A gusty wind off the sea stirred the single palm tree in the tiny crescent of garden. Outside the hotel, the bustle and swirl of Chinatown crowded the narrow pavements, and gazing out, Ellis regretted that he hadn't been more adventurous. Maybe, after all, he should have risked a night on the town. Maybe, for just an hour or two, he should have forgotten about Louise Carlton and his ever-fattening file on Raymond Zhu. The receptionist at the hotel had given him her latest telex only minutes ago. Something had blown up in the UK, something pretty major, and his return was now urgent. On no account was he to miss the midnight flight. A Thames House driver would be meeting him at Terminal Three. He was to look for a placard bearing his name.

Ellis spotted the first of the overhead signs for the East Coast Parkway, a splash of green against the night sky. He wound down the window and closed his eyes, hoping Lim wouldn't mind half an hour without air-conditioning. He loved the feel of the sweaty heat on his face. Even now, a week after he'd arrived, it still felt immensely exotic.

Lim was asking about Zhu. He was a relative junior in the CAD team and he'd always been puzzled by the sheer depth of Ellis's interest in the man. The trading regulations in Singapore were as stringent as anywhere in the world, and if Zhu had been anything but 100 per cent clean, the zealots at the CAD would have been the first to know. In the financial columns of the *Straits Times*, quite properly, Raymond Zhu was a hero, a giant. So how come the British were so keen to nail down every last biographical fact? Why the interest? Why the suspicion?

Ellis wearily described Zhu's designs on Portsmouth's naval dockyard. The dockyard was still important, if not strategically then certainly in terms of sentiment. Given the likelihood of new ownership, it might pay to make a few checks.

'Sentiment?' Lim looked amused. 'Or votes?'

'Both. We live in a democracy. You might try it some time.' Ellis looked across at Lim, softening the comment with a smile. 'Zhu is simply someone we need to know about. It's not sinister. And we're not suspicious.'

'You're not? And you come all this way? Trade all this information? And you're telling me it doesn't matter?'

Lim shook his head, more in sorrow than in anger, and Ellis

fell silent, listening to Lim rephrasing the question. The Commercial Affairs Department had only been prepared to open the files on Zhu in return for payment in kind, and the material he'd brought out on Barings' London operations was far too high-grade to swap for anything trivial. For some reason the Brits were after Zhu. But why?

'I've been telling you all week,' Ellis said patiently. 'He's brought us a lot of business. We may be trusting him with a national asset. Wouldn't you feel happier with the full story?'

'Of course.'

They were on the Parkway, speeding towards the airport. Lim lit a cigarette.

'So are you content now? Do you have enough?'

'I think so.'

'Any surprises? Things you didn't know?'

Ellis looked away, staring into the hot darkness, wondering where to start. Conversations in Singapore, however well intentioned, had a habit of turning inquisitorial, a process of challenge and disclosure that Ellis found immensely tiring.

'It's good to know he comes from Shanghai,' he began. 'We rather thought he was a southerner, from Amoy.'

'Is Shanghai important? Lots of Singaporean Chinese are from Shanghai. Lots of Hong Kong Chinese, too.'

'Like Zhu, you mean?'

'Exactly. They follow the money. After the Communists came, the money went to Hong Kong. Just now, the money's coming here. One day . . . who knows? Maybe the money moves on somewhere else.' He glanced sideways at Ellis, then tipped back his head, expelling a thin plume of cigarette smoke. 'We Chinese aren't sentimental. Superstitious, yes, but not sentimental. Money has no smell. Zhu knows that.'

Ellis smiled. He liked the thought of money having no smell. It was dry, desiccated, neutral, a little like Zhu himself. Lim was talking about Shanghai again. Ellis's last session with the CAD team had concentrated on Zhu's interests in Pudong, an area across the Yangtse from the high-rise sprawl of Shanghai's financial district. Pudong was generating explosive rates of growth, outstripping any other development in South-east Asia, and Zhu had secured a substantial slice of the action. Most of his investment was in construction, the raw material of the New China, but he'd also staked out a dominant position in transportation, specifically shipping. The number-crunchers at the Commercial Affairs Department had been reluctant to put a figure on the size of Zhu's investment but it was clear that they were talking billions of dollars.

Ellis nodded. The last few days had confirmed what he'd always suspected: that mainland China was the ultimate destination for the order Zhu had placed for riot gear back in 1995. Packed into containers, and despatched by sea, the stuff had trans-shipped through Singapore and ended up with the quartermasters of the Chinese People's Militia. According to the CAD, final landfall had been Shanghai. In one sense, this was the best possible news. Given their reservations about democracy, the Chinese People's Militia would have a limitless appetite for comms gear, riot shields and hi-tech insurgency sprays. In another sense, though, Zhu's reticence on the subject was troubling. Why, confidentially, hadn't he been straight? Why all the camouflage?

Ellis voiced the thought, watching a big 747 wallowing down the glide path into Changi International. Lim eased the car into the slow lane.

'Don't you think it was a modest order?' he asked at last. 'For mainland China.'

'Of course,' Ellis replied. 'But we're rather assuming he'll be back for more.'

'I doubt it.'

Something in Lim's voice drew Ellis's attention away from the 747. New information, he thought. Something they haven't told me. Something they want to plant now, away from the secretaries around the conference table, away from prying ears.

'The order was for fifty thousand sets,' Ellis recollected, 'and that included a reserve for spares.'

'Exactly.' Lim was smiling now. 'And you know the size of the force Beijing's putting into Hong Kong next year? Once the British have gone?'

He was silent, letting the implications sink in. Finally Ellis wound up the window. The noise of the slipstream was too loud for comfort. He wanted to be absolutely sure. 'You're saying that Zhu bought that equipment in case of riots in Hong Kong?'

'Of course. And he chose British suppliers . . .' he looked across, smiling, ' . . . because he has a sense of humour.'

The last guests had left the big front lounge at the Imperial Hotel when the petrol bomb came crashing through the window. It was a crude design, a milk bottle stuffed with burning rags, but the petrol inside spilled across the carpet, igniting at once. The noise brought the night porter running through from his cubby-hole beside the reception desk and he tackled the blaze quickly, smothering the sheet of flame with foam from a nearby extinguisher, kicking aside an armchair that was already beginning to smoulder.

Within moments the fire was out, and the porter bent to the carpet, picking up shards of broken glass from the window, wondering whether to leave the remains of the bottle for police examination. He was back on his feet, gazing out at the darkness beyond the forecourt, when he became aware of movement behind him.

Zhu was standing in the lounge, looking down at the blackened crater in the carpet. Most of the foam had settled and there was a strong smell of petrol. The porter told him briefly what had happened and Zhu nodded. The dressing gown was too big for him, hanging limply on his thin frame. He poked at the carpet with his slippered foot, his face devoid of expression. The porter began to move towards the door. He'd yet to phone for the police. He should get them here as soon as possible.

Zhu put out a restraining hand. 'It was an accident,' he said quietly. 'Just clear it up.'

Chapter Fourteen

Hayden Barnaby was at Charlie Epple's front door before half past seven next morning. Charlie answered his knock. The two men conferred in the hall.

'What's Wilcox saying?'

Barnaby took a deep breath. He'd been on and off the phone since six, trying to prise Wilcox away from the obvious headlines. Negotiations hadn't gone well, not least because Wilcox was fighting a savage hangover.

'He's saying he has no choice. The kid'll survive but her face is a mess. The consultant says it's early days but the outlook's pretty grim. Privately, he's saying there isn't a plastic surgeon in the country who can make much difference. Apart from filling in the holes.'

'Yuk.' Charlie disappeared into the kitchen, returning with a drying-up cloth. He mopped commas of shaving foam from his chin. 'So how's he going to play it?'

'Big spread. Front page.' Barnaby paused. 'The father wants the dog put down and Wilcox is running an editorial, saying the same thing.'

'Good fucking riddance. I've been trying for months,' Charlie said. 'What else?'

Barbaby looked up the stairs. The door to Lolly's bedroom was closed. 'It's a question of ownership,' he said slowly. 'Lolly's name's still in the frame. They think it's hers. As long as she sticks with her story, we're probably in the clear.' He frowned. 'Fall-back, I'll tell Harry it was Haagen's. In fact, I might do that anyway.'

'And Jess?'

'Jess won't know anything about it.'

'Hang on.' Charlie reached out, steadying Barnaby as he began to turn for the door. 'I meant about the dog. Having it put down. Shouldn't you talk to her? Break the news? Fuck knows why, but she'll be bloody upset.'

Barnaby was buttoning his Burberry. 'You tell her,' he said briefly. 'I'm late already.'

When Charlie went up to her room Jessie was still asleep. She'd spent most of the evening with Lolly, trying to calm her down after the incident on the beach. The dog had gone off in a police van to a cage in the RSPCA compound.

'Tea,' Charlie murmured, shaking her gently.

Jessie rubbed her eyes, propping herself up on one elbow. 'I've got to phone them,' she said at once. 'I'll do it this morning.'

'Phone who?'

'That poor little girl's parents. What can they think? Oz can be such a handful.'

Charlie looked at her. Plainly she had no idea of the real extent of the child's injuries. Lolly, hysterical, hadn't got much further than telling her how traumatic the whole thing had been. He picked up the tea, nudging the mug into her hand.

'Drink this,' he said. 'We ought to talk.'

Jessie blinked up at him. The pillow had left a crease line down her cheek, and it gave her face a childlike, slightly lopsided look.

'What's the matter?' she asked. 'What have I done?'

Charlie explained about the news from the hospital. He spared her most of the details but left her in no doubt that the child would probably be scarred for life.

'Christ.' Jessie's eyes were wide. 'That's terrible.'

'It is. You're right.'

'I'll phone them now. Here—' She gave Charlie the mug, trying to swing her legs out of bed.

Charlie restrained her. 'Don't,' he said. 'Not yet.'

'Why not?'

'It's early. It's not eight yet.'

'But they'll be out of their heads with worry. Wouldn't you?'

'Sure, of course.'

'Then I'll phone. Have you got a number?'

'No, and I haven't got a name, either.'

'Shit.' Jessie collapsed back against the pillow, staring at the ceiling. Then she was up again. 'I'll phone the police. They'll know. They're bound to know. I was going to phone them anyway. It's my dog. Sort of. Not Lolly's.'

Charlie held her down. On occasions like these he'd learned that there was nothing kinder than the truth. 'They want to put Oz down,' he told her, 'and you can understand why.'

'Put him down? You mean destroy him?'

'Yeah. I know it's primitive. I know it's unfair. But their little girl . . . you know . . .' He watched Jessie struggle with the implications of what he'd just said. Oz gone. Another bit of her life wrenched away. Another hole for grief or drugs or God knows what to fill. 'We'll get something else,' Charlie muttered. 'A cat, a hamster, a tame crocodile, anything. Just as long as it doesn't bite anyone.'

Jessie was staring up at him, her eyes glistening. She hadn't heard a word. At length, she sniffed, dabbing at her nose with a corner of the sheet. 'It's Haagen,' she said softly. 'What do I tell him? How can I explain?'

Mike Tully had the dates neatly listed on a notepad when he approached the woman at the information desk. He used the Central Library a great deal. The international reference section alone occupied nearly half a floor.

He gave the woman the list. He was interested in Dutch national newspapers for the dates shown. The woman apologized at once. The library didn't subscribe to any. The best she could do was *Die Welt* from neighbouring Germany.

Tully found himself a place at a nearby table. The newspapers arrived in a thick bundle, secured with string. He undid the knot and sorted out the editions he wanted. Beside each date he'd made a separate note of the weather Haagen Schreck had described. By matching these descriptions against the next day's weather reports, Tully could put the obvious explanation to the test. In his heart he knew the answer already but decades of investigative casework had taught him the value of double-checking. There was no room in his world for guesswork.

The first cluster of dates was in early spring, two days in the same week. On both occasions, Haagen had moaned about winds and constant rain. Tully checked the dates of the calls against the forecast, and then against the subsequent weather reports. The results brought a smile to his face. During the second week in March, Western Europe had enjoyed an early taste of summer under a huge anti-cyclone. Temperatures in Cologne had nudged 20 degrees Celsius. In Amsterdam, it had been even higher.

Tully glanced down at his list, knowing there was no point in going any further. Haagen wasn't in Holland at all. The calls to Jessie had indeed been in code, a simple series of agreed messages to signal when it was safe for her to visit. Tully sat back and reached for the string, wondering where the boy had gone to ground.

Louise Carlton drove herself down from Cheam. South of Petersfield, as the dual carriageway cut through the chalky flank of Butser Hill, she realized that she'd never been to Portsmouth. In every conversation she'd had, the place itself had been of little importance. It was simply a source of departmental opportunity, or a target for overseas investment, or – as now – a political predicament. Not once, oddly, had she devoted any thought to what it might look like.

She glanced down at the directions she'd scribbled across the top of *The Times*. Jephson had phoned first thing, giving her the name of a contact at the Defence Research Agency. It was evidently an establishment of some size, situated on the hill that looked down over the city. Once an arm of the MoD, it had now been given agency status, and a modest foothold in the private sector. The links with Whitehall, naturally, were still strong, and Jephson had talked vaguely of the support they'd be able to give her. There'd be an office she could use. Communications in and out were secure and there were people on hand who'd know their way around the city. It would, he'd said, be an ideal perch from which she'd be able to get a feel for what he called 'the reality of the situation'.

At the coast, Louise joined the east–west motorway. To the left, beyond the salt marsh and a gleaming stretch of water, she could see the blue-grey shadows of a major city. To the right, a fold of downland was slashed to the bone by earlier quarrying for chalk. On top of the hill, visible to the naked eye, was a sprawl of buildings.

She consulted the directions again, taking a slip-road off the motorway and grinding up the hill. A route along the top gave her a fine view to the south and she drove slowly, taking in the distant sprawl of Portsmouth. Rarely had she seen a city so well defined. Even in the north, looking down on Yorkshire mill towns from the flanks of the Pennines, there wasn't this sense of containment, of semi-isolation. She thought of Jephson again, and of the Portsmouth MP who'd sounded the alarm bells at Central Office, and she was forced to acknowledge that he might have a point. If you really wanted to turn your back on the UK, there was probably no better place to do it.

The DRA lay on the western crest of the hill. A mile of chain-link fencing, topped with barbed wire, protected acres of pre-fabs and low, red-brick offices. She began to slow, then turned in through the agency's main gate. Yellow-jacketed security men waved her to a halt, and while they inspected her pass she gazed up at the Union Jack, snapping in the wind.

The main block was Building 91. The car park lay beside it. One of the agency's administrative officers shook her hand and led the way inside. The place looked worn and slightly shabby. There were fire doors everywhere and the scuffed walls and endless flights of stairs reminded Louise of the old MI5 building in Gower Street. The man stopped at a door and produced a key. Inside, Louise found herself inspecting a small office. Sunshine flooded in through the steel-framed window. There was a desk, two telephones, two filing cabinets and an electric kettle. The man indicated a small safe behind the door. His name was Milne. 'We only got the message this morning,' he said. 'I hope this one's big enough.'

Louise peered at the safe. Jephson, she thought. Lately, he'd become obsessed with locking things away.

Milne was checking the telephones, lifting each in turn to his ear. 'These are both direct lines. Everything routed out is XPX standard seven. If you want extra screening I'm afraid you'll have to give us a couple of days.'

Louise was standing behind him, gazing out at the view. A submarine lay moored in the harbour below, the black silhouette unmistakable. Beyond it, she could see a big white ship easing into a ferry berth. Milne was still worrying about secure communications. Louise put her handbag on the desk. 'My mobile's digital,' she said. 'I'll probably use that.'

Milne beamed at her, visibly relieved. 'Do you need a PC at all? Secretarial back-up?'

'I've got a laptop.'

'Are you sure?' He hesitated, looking at the kettle. 'There's tea and coffee downstairs. I'll get some sent up. Any preferences?'

Louise opened her handbag. She'd brought sachets of camomile tea from her supplies at home and she piled them beside one of the telephones.

'Biscuits would be nice,' she said. 'Plain chocolate wholemeal if you have them.'

'Of course.'

Milne couldn't take his eyes off the Harrods bag in which Louise was carrying a collection of files. At length, she began to unpack them, storing them in an unlocked drawer. 'Do you have a key for this? As a matter of interest?'

'I'll find one.' He hesitated, looking at her. 'I understand it's coded CROMWELL,' he said shyly, 'whatever it is you're up to.'

Louise wondered where this information had come from. Normally Jephson wouldn't dream of sharing more than was necessary. Operational codewords were strictly for family use.

'That's right,' Louise said slowly. 'CROMWELL pretty well covers it.'

Milne was beaming again. He moved away from the desk,

giving her room to sit down. He was a local-history buff. He was in and out of the city archives every week. The use of CROMWELL as a code-word rang a bell.

'Churchill's plan to repel boarders, wasn't it? Battle of Britain and all that?' He was standing by the door. 'What a nice idea.'

Hayden Barnaby chaired the Pompey First morning press conference. Zhu had closed off one of the Imperial's private banqueting suites for the duration of the campaign, permitting Charlie to convert it into a fully staffed press centre. Barnaby loved this conscious echo of the way the national parties tried to shape the media agenda, and he found himself spending more and more time at the hotel. The operation was staffed by volunteers – a couple of young journalists on unpaid leave from the *Sentinel* and a freelance PR consultant who shared her life with one of the Pompey First ward candidates. The team had dubbed themselves Charlie's Angels, and between them made sure that the phones were manned fourteen hours a day.

The press conference started at ten. They'd been running for nearly a week now and the attendance had confounded the cynics who'd accused Pompey First, yet again, of losing touch with the real world. Local politics, they said, was meaningless. The percentage of people bothering to vote was the lowest in Europe. No one understood the issues, and even if they did they'd lost all faith in politicians' ability to deliver. Local veterans, with half a dozen campaigns under their belts, scoffed at Charlie's plans for daily briefings, hot-response desks and a brand of grass-roots involvement he'd dubbed 'retail politics', yet the rows of curious faces in the banqueting suite had grown and grown, attracted by word of mouth and by the ever-fattening file of news stories, many torn from the pages of the national press. Far from collapsing under the weight of its own self-importance, Pompey First was fast becoming the story no one could afford to ignore. Things were happening down on the south coast. No matter how absurd, how parochial, Pompey First was definitely worth a look.

Barnaby began by announcing the day's campaigning theme.

Shopping areas in the city centre were becoming derelict. Streets that featured proudly in the sepia prints of Edwardian Southsea – handsome, fashionable, busy – had been ravaged by urban blight. Charlie had commissioned students from the university's Department of Architecture to prepare a series of slides, and on a signal from Barnaby, the lights dimmed and a projector at the back of the room threw image after image onto the screen behind the top table. The images were scored to a jazz track, a long saxophone solo, and the journalists in the audience sat back, swamped by boarded-up shops, abandoned supermarket trolleys and whorls of vicious graffiti on the rain-streaked concrete. Regulars at the morning press conferences had got used to Charlie's passion for slick, hard-hitting presentational novelties like this, and if he occasionally went over the top, compressing a dozen urban miseries into a couple of nightmare minutes, they were more than willing to forgive him. Most of the political messages were simple enough to play well in print or on-screen, and the coffee and Danish served afterwards were invariably excellent. In the seven brief days since the press conferences had started, Pompey First had stolen a huge march on the opposition. Almost overnight, local politics had been transformed.

The lights went up and Barnaby introduced the candidate for the ward featured in the slide show. He was on his feet, tearing into the eighties addiction to out-of-town shopping, when a hand went up in the second row. Barnaby knew the journalist: he was a local stringer who occasionally supplied copy to the weightier broadsheets. He'd already done a nice piece for the *Guardian* on Charlie's brand of local electioneering. Entitled 'Son et Lumière', it had compared Pompey First's strategy to similarly impassioned campaigns in France. 'Who knows?' he'd concluded. 'If journalists start to think seriously about the issues, maybe real people will, too.'

Now he was holding up a copy of yesterday's *Sunday Mirror*. As promised, the spread on Poster Wars occupied the centre pages. Coupled with the *Sentinel*'s exposé of the dockyard sale, the weekend had put Portsmouth squarely on the national map. The journalist had a question: how much of all this was conscious provocation?

The candidate at the top table, still on his feet, looked down at Barnaby for guidance. Barnaby was signalling to Charlie, who'd slipped into the room during the slide show. Charlie loped down the aisle between the rows of seats. Turnout today was well into double figures.

Charlie joined Barnaby on the rostrum. He had a roll of posters under his arm and he slid one out, displaying it. Underneath the *Sentinel*'s photo of Clive Samuels in the dockyard, Charlie had added a line of copy: *NAPOLEON TRIED IT. HITLER TRIED IT. WELL DONE, MR SAMUELS.* The message took a second or two to sink in. Barnaby could hear the cameraman from the German TV crew asking for a translation. Then people began to laugh. The laughter was followed by applause. Charlie offered a mock bow. Barnaby had felt this moment coming for several days. These media people, normally so hard-bitten, so cynical, saw things the way they did. They were tired of the sleaze and the posturing, bored with the lies and the excuses. The daily briefings had paid off. Pompey First had touched a nerve.

The stringer was on his feet now. He had another question. 'How many are you printing?' he asked, nodding at the poster. Charlie glanced at Barnaby. Barnaby made a delicate gesture with his hand.

'As many as we need,' Charlie said.

'How many's that?'

'Full size? Maybe fifty. Smaller ones? Couple of hundred, no more.'

'Where are they going?'

'All over. Wherever they can find a home.'

The stringer nodded, making a note. Then he glanced up.

'So who's paying for all this? Who picks up the tab?'

Barnaby took over again. The question had come up before, but never this direct. There were, after all, limits to spending in local elections.

'We're picking up contributions from a number of sources,' he said smoothly. 'You'd be surprised how much backing we've got and where it comes from.'

'I would?' The stringer's smile wasn't altogether reassuring. 'Surprise me, then.'

'It's not that easy, I'm afraid. If people contribute privately, if they want a measure of confidentiality, of course we have to respect their wishes.'

Barnaby turned quickly to another questioner. The reporter with the German news crew wanted to know about right-wing elements in the city. She'd made a note of some of the graffiti featured in the slide show. One spray-painted shop front had read 'Kill all Nazi scum *now*'. She gestured round. She'd heard from others that there'd been some kind of riot earlier in the year. Here, outside the hotel. Was this a sign of things to come? And, if so, what did Pompey First intend to do about it?

Barnaby began to regret not having pressed on with the morning's briefing. Planning consent for retail parks was a great deal less contentious than the likes of Haagen Schreck. He talked for a minute or two about last year's little upset, blaming it, as ever, on elements from London. One of the driving forces behind Pompey First, he said, was the overwhelming urge to govern the city in its own interests. If that meant an element of protection from political extremism, then so be it.

'Govern?' The German reporter was questioning the verb.

'Administer,' Barnaby corrected himself. 'Lead. Guide. Represent.'

'But you said govern.' The German girl was emphatic. 'And to do the things you want to do,' she gestured at the screen, 'then surely you are right. What you need is government. Independence. For your shopping. For your hospitals. For everything. To govern is to choose, *nein*?'

'Of course,' Barnaby replied. 'Of course we'd like to do those things. But politics is the art of the possible. We work within national constraints. There's no frontier here, no border. We're not a law unto ourselves. We simply want a fair shout, that's all. And if important things happen and they're out of our control, then naturally . . .' he tapped Charlie's latest poster '. . . we'd like to bring it to people's attention. That's our democratic right. It's still a free country. I think.'

A hollow laugh rang round the room and Barnaby seized his chance to resume the briefing. The ward candidate stood up again, reinforcing his plea for shops to return to the inner city. Taking the car to hypermarkets off the island for the weekly trolleyful of groceries might be wonderfully convenient but it didn't do much for the families left behind. What if you couldn't afford a car? What if the Tory version of progress had left you with the handful of corner shops that had managed, so far, to buck the trend? Their prices were outrageous, choice was limited, and soon, no doubt, they too would be driven to the wall. What would happen then? In the densest populated city in the UK?

The language, as ever, was apocalyptic, a working habit that Pompey First candidates were rapidly turning into an art form. Barnaby sat behind the table, wondering how soon they'd be back on the issue of the dockyard. Zhu's indiscretions over the weekend had shaken London's tree, and the windfalls were everywhere. Before lunch, he was due to meet a BBC crew for a *Newsnight* interview. This afternoon, from a radio studio in the Guildhall, he'd be participating in a three-way debate with fellow politicians from Devonport and Rosyth. This evening, if Charlie could swing it, there was the chance of a live inject into *News at Ten*.

He smiled to himself, then stiffened as the *Guardian* stringer caught his eye. The man was tapping his watch, miming a phone call. He had to leave early. There were important calls to make. He beckoned for Barnaby to join him outside and Barnaby got to his feet, handing over control of the conference to Charlie.

Outside, in the corridor, the stringer was already on his mobile. Barnaby caught the phrase 'features editor' before the stringer saw him coming and brought the conversation to an end.

'Anything I can do for you?' Barnaby was steering him towards the all-day breakfast bar. A week in this game was long enough to understand the power of free food and drink.

The stringer stepped through the double doors. 'I'm still interested in the money,' he said. 'Care to give me a steer?'

Barnaby began to talk about membership lists and fund-raising events. It all added up. With goodwill and a fair head of steam it was amazing what you could afford.

The stringer interrupted. 'This is a poor city,' he reminded Barnaby. 'Lots of repossessions, not too many jobs. Are you really telling me it's all down to raffles and bring-and-buys?'

'No, of course not.' Barnaby looked him in the eye. 'But I meant what I said. If some people prefer to stay anonymous, what chance do I have?'

The stringer gazed at him. He had a cherubic face, apple-cheeked, bright-eyed, though Barnaby suspected he was a good deal older than he looked. He buttoned his coat and extended a hand.

'Good luck,' he said. 'You lot deserve everything you'll get.'

'Thanks.'

'Don't mention it.' He smiled, tapping the pocket where he kept his notebook. 'You're beginning to sound like the Tories already.'

Tully had been waiting in the car for less than a hour when Jessie emerged from Charlie Epple's house. He'd reclaimed the recorder from Liz and it sat beside him on the passenger seat. Haagen had rung within the last five minutes. The weather, he'd said, was wonderful.

Jessie was wearing a heavy sweater against the bitter wind and she hurried across the road, running up the steps that led to the promenade. Passing the car, she looked pale and preoccupied, and Tully wondered what kind of scene awaited her at journey's end. Liz had told him this morning about Haagen's dog. As far as she knew, it had already been put down.

Jessie's route took her east, along the seafront. Tully followed at a discreet distance. An hour later, at the end of the promenade, she cut inland, following the main road and then crossing a park. Tully knew the area well. Beyond a tangle of residential streets lay a feature known locally as the Glory Hole, a stretch of Langstone harbour protected from the tidal stream by a long, curling finger of shingle. There was a sailing club here, and a line of scruffy houseboats beached on the mud-flats beneath the road. It was one of the few quiet corners the city had to offer, a retreat from the endless noise of traffic, and Tully himself had once owned a boat here, a modest 25-foot ketch he'd occasionally sailed at weekends.

A single road led down to the water and Tully slowed, knowing that Jessie must be close now. The Glory Hole was already in sight. The road came to an end at a stubby pier used by local fishing boats and the ferry to neighbouring Hayling Island. Jessie was walking on the seaward side, passing the first of the houseboats. Most were semi-derelict, paintwork peeling, wood beginning to rot. At the far end of the curve of muddy shingle, Jessie stopped beside the last houseboat but one. It was slightly bigger than the rest, an old naval launch with a botched extension lashed on the forrard deck. A single plank bridged the gap to the road and Tully watched as Jessie made her way aboard. Not until she was safely on deck did the door beside the curtained window open. A face briefly appeared, too distant for Tully to secure a positive identification, then Jessie had gone.

It was nearly an hour before the door opened again. Tully had found himself a hide in the boatyard across the road. Concealed behind a dinghy, he was as close as he judged prudent to the houseboat. He raised the camera. In the telephoto lens, Haagen's face was clearly visible. Tully had last seen him in the photos Liz had shown him. Since then, he'd put on a little weight. Jessie was giving him a kiss. She lingered long enough for Tully to take two more shots, then the door was shut again, Jessie edging carefully back to dry land. When she passed the boatyard, she was barely twenty feet from Tully. He was studying her face. She looked radiant.

One of the uniformed men who supervised the security checks on the main gate rang through to tell Louise that her visitor had arrived. He was waiting for his pass. Someone would bring him up directly.

'Thank you.'

Louise rang off, finishing another biscuit. So far, the morning had gone well. Jephson had been on twice, once to check that everything was OK, and again to confirm that they were booked in at Downing Street for noon the next day. Government whips were certain that the Prime Minister would be facing hostile questions about the dockyard, and the political office at Number Ten was requesting a full brief before the Commons session in the afternoon. It was imperative, Jephson stressed, that the brief be as comprehensive as possible. The Tory machine was confronting two threats on the south coast, in the shape of the dockyard and Pompey First, and it was absolutely in Five's interests to be seen to be dealing with both.

Louise stood up, brushing the crumbs from her skirt. Another call from Thames House had confirmed that Ellis's flight was due to land at ten forty. Customs and traffic permitting, he should be down for the debrief by one o'clock.

There was a knock at the door. Louise opened it. Without a word, the security guard handed over the visitor. 'Mr Owens?' Louise smiled and invited him in.

Owens was tall and thin, with a chalk-white face and a high, domed forehead. His hair, thinning, was combed sideways across his scalp and there were flecks of dandruff on the shoulders of his coat.

He sat down beside the desk. The sunlight through the window emphasized his pallor. He produced a file from his briefcase and gave it to Louise. A stamp on the cover read 'Special Branch, Hampshire Constabulary'.

'I thought you'd seen these before,' he said. 'I know I sent a set to the Yard.'

Louise shook her head, opened the file and pulled out a sheaf of photos. 'I've seen your report,' she said, 'but not these.'

She began to leaf through the back-and-white photos. They all featured a slight, thin, crop-haired youth. In the occasional close-up, a scar was visible on his face, a line of clumsy sutures that ran diagonally from the corner of his mouth.

She held one up. It showed him emerging from a basement flat, carrying a holdall. 'Did you ever talk to him? This Haagen Schreck?'

'No, Never had a chance. After the riot he did a runner. Apparently, he's still abroad.'

Louise held up another photo. It showed a shopping precinct, and Owens reached across, indicating a middle-aged woman in a belted white raincoat.

'Mrs Barnaby,' he said helpfully. 'And I never talked to her, either. Guvnor's orders.'

'Good.' Louise nodded in approval.

She laid the photograph on the desk, removed her glasses and gave them a polish before studying it in detail. One of her files contained a page and a half on Mrs Barnaby and she was still intrigued to know exactly where she fitted into this sad little tale. According to the surveillance reports, her daughter had been living with the German lad and had got involved in heroin. But why, in that case, should her mother be funding a drugs expedition to Amsterdam? She gazed at the photo a moment longer, knowing that the answer didn't matter. All she needed was the link, and the evidence to back it up.

Owens had produced an envelope. Close to, he smelt powerfully of dog. Louise opened the envelope. Inside was a photocopy of a cheque. Mrs Barnaby's handwriting was stylish and firm. She'd had trouble with the name Schreck.

Owens was writing on the envelope.

'What's that?' Louise was peering at the row of figures.

'Her home telephone number. Her husband's moved out. They've had a domestic.'

His hand was back in his briefcase. He pulled out a sheet of paper and Louise found herself looking at a poster for Pompey First. The candidate's photo was bordered in a tasteful shade of green. She had a strong, open face framed by a tumble of loose curls. It was rare, Louise thought, to find such an attractive woman in politics.

Owens was back on his feet, pulling on a pair of gloves. 'You wanted a poster. She happens to be my ward candidate. You can keep it. She left the missus two.'

He stepped towards the door and Louise got to her feet. She

was grateful to him for sparing the time to drive up. She'd pop the poster on the wall.

Owens knotted his scarf. 'I've put ours in the window,' he said. 'Bloody good idea, if you ask me.'

'What is?'

'Pompey First.'

When he'd gone, Louise sat down again. The photograph of Mrs Barnaby was still on the desk. She pored over it for a full minute, moving it into the pool of sunshine where the last of the chocolate biscuits was slowly melting. Then she picked up Owen's envelope, checking the phone number, and reached for her mobile. The *Sentinel*'s switchboard answered at once.

'Editorial, please,' Louise was looking at the photo again, 'whoever deals with drugs stories.'

The *Newsnight* crew were late for the twelve o'clock interview. They were spending the entire day in Portsmouth, exploring every nuance of Charlie Epple's 'new politics', and Barnaby had agreed to meet them in the car park near Southsea Castle. At twenty past twelve he was still sitting in his car, the seat reclined, his head back, his eyes closed. If this is really politics, he was thinking, then I'm only sorry I started so late.

A tap at the window brought him upright. A young man in a red scarf was standing in the car park. When he wound down the window, Barnaby recognized the voice on the phone.

'We thought we'd do it out there on the grass,' the reporter said briskly. 'Castle in the background.'

Barnaby joined him for the walk across. The camera crew had already set up their equipment and were running sound checks. The interview would be open-ended but the edited piece would probably last no more than a couple of minutes.

Barnaby stood in front of the camera, letting the young reporter angle his body until the cameraman was happy with the balance of light and shade on his face. After yesterday, outside the dockyard, and another TV interview earlier in the week, Barnaby was getting used to this. Kate had been right when she said he was a natural. All you had to do was tell it the way it was, spell it out the way you felt it, and the curious chemistry of television would do the rest.

The interview lasted nearly fifteen minutes. Although *Newsnight* were chiefly interested in the difference Pompey First was making locally, Barnaby was quickly conscious that they were really talking about national issues. Ministerial responsibility. The quango state. The sheer thickness of the curtain that had descended between the people in charge and the men and women who had to live with the consequences of their decisions. Each time the agenda widened, the young reporter tried to nudge Barnaby back to local politics but the longer the interview went on the more it became obvious that these weren't anxieties you could limit to a single city. Up and down the country, local councillors, local officials, and local voters were tussling with the same problem. Power had leaked away. There was a massive haemorrhage of the nation's civic lifeblood. Not out to the provinces, where it belonged, but inwards, to what Barnaby termed 'the dead centre' of British political life. Even in London, he said, even in the nation's capital city, no one was trusted with power. There was no voice for London, no elected body in whom the people could place their faith. Alone amongst the great capital cities of the world, London had no voice of its own.

The reporter nodded, agreeing. He'd liked the line about the nation's civic lifeblood. Was Barnaby serious? In terms of democracy, was he saying that the situation was terminal?

'I simply don't know,' Barnaby answered. 'I don't know where it will end. All I know is that down here, in our own small way, we're trying to make a difference. A month ago people thought Pompey First was a joke. It isn't. It's a reality. It's something you can feel and measure. In votes. And, come Thursday, that's exactly what we'll do.'

The young reporter stepped back, delighted. Barnaby shook his outstretched hand. The camera crew were already packing up their gear, returning the sound equipment to its silver box and collapsing the big tripod. Barnaby gave them a final wave as they drove away, and then climbed the path that led to the castle battlements. From here, the southernmost point of Portsea Island, he could see east to the pier and the long sweep of shingle beach that stretched away towards Hayling Island. Behind him, furrowed by a passing warship, were the approaches to the harbour mouth.

He began to walk, feeling the warmth of the sun on his face, happier than he could ever remember. Whole areas of his life – his marriage, for instance – were in chaos but with Pompey First he'd caught a wave that had somehow lifted him above the daily grind and was pushing him forward, faster and faster. Adjoining the seafront were the wide green spaces of Southsea Common and he paused, shading his eyes, remembering the way it had looked a couple of years back, June 1994, the weekend Bill Clinton and his entourage had descended on the city for the D-Day Commemoration. The memories of that weekend, the feeling of sour frustration, of creeping middle age, of having missed some indefinable opportunity, now seemed to belong to another life. He'd heard the trumpets, he thought, he'd answered the call and, God willing, life would never expose him to that kind of humiliation again. He mattered. He truly mattered. There were people, clever people, who'd just driven seventy miles to listen to what he had to say. His name was in print, in local papers, national papers, even the international press, doubtless cross-indexed in countless cuttings files. Soon, perhaps, there'd be similar clips on video, archived for ever.

Barnaby glanced down at the patch of worn grass where he'd just conducted the *Newsnight* interview, reflecting on the slightly unreal sequence of events that had brought him in front of the camera. Then he retraced his steps towards the Mercedes, thinking once again of Bill Clinton. Two years ago, he'd seemed a remote figure, defined solely by the world's headlines. Now, to Barnaby's intense satisfaction, he was simply flesh and blood.

The meeting with Zhu was brief. Tully took the lift to his top-floor suite at the Imperial, accompanied by Mr Hua, Zhu's chauf-

feur. Zhu was sitting at a desk in the window. It was the first time
Tully had seen him wearing glasses.

Zhu offered him a small cup of Chinese tea but Tully shook
his head. He'd developed the prints himself. He laid them on
Zhu's desk. To Tully's quiet satisfaction, they were excellent.

Zhu examined them for, perhaps, a minute. Finally, he looked
up. 'This is the man you described?'

'Yes, sir.'

'The one who. . . .' Zhu looked pained '. . . wrecked our
opening day?'

'Yes, sir.'

'And he's here?'

'Very definitely.'

'You have an address? Directions? Where to find him?'

'Of course.'

'Good.' Zhu indicated the stocky figure by the door. 'Leave
the details with Mr Hua.' He smiled. 'I'm deeply grateful.'

Louise took Ellis for a late lunch at a pub along the hill from
the Defence Research Agency. He'd arrived only minutes before,
stepping out of a car at the main gate, pale with exhaustion. Now
he sat beside her, looking out at the countryside to the north of
the hill, amazed at how this fold of chalk could separate such
wholly different landscapes.

'Big, isn't it?' Louise was looking at the city. 'Much bigger
than I'd thought.'

'You're right.' Ellis closed his eyes. 'And not too pretty, either.'

The pub had a modest restaurant. Louise studied the menu
while Ellis did his best to brief her. The investigators at the Commercial Affairs Department had been pleased with the file he'd
delivered on Barings. It filled in various holes in their own enquiry
and resolved one or two key issues on which they'd found no
collateral evidence. In return, with some bewilderment, they'd told
him a good deal about Raymond Zhu.

'Bewilderment?'

'They think he's straight. In fact, they think he's the jewel in their crown. Mr Private Enterprise. Very canny. Very shrewd.'

'Very rich?'

'Immensely. Even richer than we thought. They capitalized him at between three and four billion. That's dollars, of course.' He waited while Louise examined the menu. Today's special was monkfish in batter.

'Nothing for us, then?' she asked at last.

'Nothing startling.' Ellis consulted the summary he'd prepared overnight on the plane. 'Except the command and control equipment.'

'Oh?'

Ellis described what Lim had told him in the car on the way to the airport. Zhu had evidently bought the riot gear, plus ancillary communications, on behalf of officials in Beijing. He was using Singapore as a conduit country, camouflaging the real end-user.

'Was this a surprise at the DTI?'

'Frankly, yes. The order wasn't that big. It could have gone to any one of half a dozen regional players. Or it could have stayed in Singapore. China barely figured.'

'So why Beijing?'

The waiter had arrived for the order but Louise was ignoring him, a sure sign to Ellis that her interest was aroused.

'The Chinese have tasked a military force to take over in Hong Kong,' he said slowly. 'We're talking police duties, maintenance of civil order. There's nothing covert about it. It's been in the papers. Photos, even. I've seen them myself.'

'And?'

'They need equipment. State-of-the-art stuff.' His hand went to the file. 'Zhu bought British.'

'On their behalf?'

'So it seems.'

'How interesting.' Louise at last placed her order. Ellis settled for a salad. The waiter disappeared.

Ellis opened the file, offering it to Louise, but she shook her head.

'Talk to me,' she said. 'Tell me more about Hong Kong.'

Ellis bent forward across the table. 'Hong Kong's crucial,' he said. 'Hong Kong's where it begins and ends. It turns out Zhu was born in Shanghai. He fled during the revolution, in 'forty-nine. His parents were killed by the Communists. He and his brother got out of Shanghai on a barge of some sort.'

'They went to Hong Kong?'

'Yes, along with thousands of others. He stayed until the mid-sixties. That's when he and his brother set up Celestial Holdings. Until then they'd been general traders. Celestial took them into the big time. Construction to begin with. Then associated development. The guys at Commercial Affairs have the brothers down as typical Shanghai Chinese. Very nimble, very sharp, always looking for the next opportunity.' He paused. 'In 'sixty-eight we announced we were pulling out of Singapore. Several months later, Zhu applied for citizenship.'

'Of?'

'Singapore. The place was newly independent. Economically, it was buzzing. Cheap labour. Lots of foreign investment. Annual growth rates of twenty-three per cent. For someone like Zhu, all that would have been irresistible.' He paused. 'His brother stayed in Hong Kong but Zhu registered Celestial Holdings in Singapore as soon as he got his citizenship. That's why we got confused about his passport, incidentally.'

'I'm sorry?'

'We thought he was born in southern China, not Shanghai, but it seems he put Amoy to get himself sponsored. At the time, Singapore was awash with Chinese from the south. Not that it matters now.'

'And the brother?'

'He's still running the Hong Kong end of Celestial and he's doing very well. That's partly why Zhu's worth so much. Hong Kong generates a lot of the profits but the brothers obviously feel that Singapore's a safer home for the cash than Hong Kong. And given next year, he's probably right.'

'So Celestial clean up in Hong Kong while they can?'

'Exactly.'

'And the Commercial Affairs people don't mind?'

'Not at all. Money's money. The more of it ends up in Singapore the better.'

Louise nodded, testing a bread roll with her fingers. 'This riot equipment,' she mused, 'the stuff that's going to Hong Kong. Doesn't Zhu have a conscience about that? Arming the Chinese militia against his own kith and kin? Or am I being naïve?'

'You're being naïve. Big business and the Communists have a great deal in common. Neither are very keen on democracy. Especially if it hurts the profit stream. The last thing Zhu wants is a breakdown in law and order.'

Louise was pleased. Very pleased indeed.

Ellis consulted his summary. She wanted more detail on the sources of Zhu's fortune in Hong Kong, how exactly he and his brother were making their money, and Ellis listed the areas he'd targeted for his major investments. Shipping and transportation was one.

Louise stopped him, laying her hand on his. 'What kind of scale?'

'Big. Everything Zhu does is big.'

'Hong Kong to where?'

'Anywhere. US. Europe. Australia. The Zhus are merchants. They trade wherever they can turn a profit.'

'So Zhu's been shipping goods here? Into the UK?'

'Yes.'

'And he's still doing it?'

'Absolutely.'

Louise leaned back in her chair, looking pleased again. Her prawn cocktail had arrived, a tent of shredded lettuce, oozing pink sauce. She tapped her watch. 'Your Mr Tully,' she said briskly.

'Who?'

'Tully. The one you told me about. Your ex-Marine.' She plunged her spoon into the prawn cocktail. 'He's expecting you at three. I must remember to give you the address.' She added, 'I sense he's got a lot to get off his chest.'

*

When the phone rang Liz Barnaby was on the point of going out. She closed the door again and retraced her steps across the lounge. The caller introduced herself. She said she was a reporter. She worked on the *Sentinel*. She wondered if Liz could spare a couple of minutes on the phone.

'Of course.' Liz pulled a stool towards her. The reporter wanted to check that she was married to Hayden Barnaby. 'Yes,' Liz frowned, 'I am.'

'The same Hayden Barnaby who's involved with Pompey First?' 'Yes.'

There was a pause. Then the reporter was back again. She understood that Liz had a connection with a young German, Haagen Schreck. True or false?

Liz blinked. Had Mike Tully run Haagen to earth? Was he under arrest? 'Why?' she asked. 'Why on earth do you want to know?'

The reporter sidestepped the question. She wanted to confirm that Haagen Schreck was the same young man who'd been involved in the riot outside the Imperial Hotel. Back last year.

'Yes,' Liz said. 'He is. But why? Why all these questions?'

'I'm sorry, Mrs Barnaby, I'm just confirming a report.'

Liz was alarmed now. The last few months hadn't been easy and she'd developed an instinct for impending disaster. I shouldn't have answered the phone, she thought. I should have shut the door and left home.

The reporter was asking her to go back to last year. In March, she'd written a cheque for £3,000. The cheque had been made out to Haagen Schreck and had been lodged with a local travel agency.

Liz shut her eyes. Her attempts to get Haagen out of the country had haunted her for months. Not because they had failed, but because she'd felt such a fool to trust him. Her instincts had been right but her faith in human nature, as ever, had been sadly misplaced. Haagen had taken the ticket and the currency. God knows, he may even have gone to Germany. But he'd certainly reappeared, making the headlines outside the Imperial Hotel.

The reporter was talking about drugs.

371

'*Drugs?* What kind of drugs?'

'Heroin, Mrs Barnaby. We have evidence that Haagen Schreck bought heroin. In Amsterdam. With your money. It's a serious allegation, Mrs Barnaby. And, as I say, we have the evidence to prove it.'

'What is this evidence?'

'Photographs, Mrs Barnaby, and a copy of the cheque. Do you have a white raincoat, by any chance? And are you still banking with NatWest?'

Ellis took a cab to the address Louise had given him for Tully. Number 66 Selbourne Place was a three-storey building at the end of an attractive terrace. The brass plate beside the door read 'Quex Ltd. Corporate Security'.

Tully answered Ellis's ring. He was already wearing a raincoat and he looked left and right up the street before leading Ellis to a 200-series Rover parked across the road. He unlocked the passenger door, standing back to let Ellis clamber in. Only when he was behind the wheel, reaching for the seat belt, did he bother with conversation.

'What's her name?'

'Who?'

'That boss of yours.'

'Louise Carlton.'

'OK.' He reached for the ignition key.

Tully had a maisonette in a new development five minutes' drive away. There were clumps of dead daffodils in the neatly edged flower beds and two bottles of milk on the doorstep. Tully unlocked the front door and stooped to pick up the milk.

The tiny sitting room was upstairs, adjoining the kitchen. A desk occupied one corner of the room and there was a cheap MFI sofa beneath the window. Tully waved Ellis onto the sofa and retreated to the kitchen. Ellis looked round. On the mantelpiece, over the gas fire, was a framed photograph. It showed a younger, leaner Tully. He was wearing some form of tropical battledress. He had a carbine in one hand and a radio in the other. In the background, rolling away into the distance, was a series of thickly wooded hills.

Ellis got up to study the photo more closely. He didn't hear Tully returning from the kitchen.

'Brunei,' he said briefly, ''seventy-two.'

Ellis took the proffered mug of tea. It was far too sweet for his taste but he was grateful nonetheless. Tully sat down at the desk. He unlocked a drawer and took out a loose-leaf binder. Inside it were pages of lined paper. A thick vertical line formed a margin on the left-hand side of the top page, and the rest had been divided into blocks of information. Ellis looked at the lines of impeccably neat handwriting. Tully's, he thought. Had to be.

Tully reached for one of the audio-cassettes stored on the shelf above the desk. He weighed it in his hand very carefully, as if something inside might spill. 'There are twelve of these,' he said. 'Did that boss of yours tell you?'

Ellis shook his head. 'I've just come back from Singapore,' he said defensively. 'Flew in this morning.'

'She didn't mention anything?'

'No.'

Tully shook his head in disbelief, then gave Ellis a little of the background. Haagen Schreck was the junkie boyfriend of the daughter of a woman called Liz Barnaby. Liz was a friend of Tully's. Schreck was big trouble and Liz was keen to keep him away from her daughter. Hence the tapes.

'I don't follow,' Ellis muttered.

Tully explained about Charlie Epple's house and the intercept he'd plumbed in. The electronic trawl had netted a number of items including a great deal about an outfit called Pompey First. Pompey First was a brand new political party. And Charlie Epple was one of the founding fathers.

Ellis at last began to understand. Over lunch, Louise had told him about the dockyard fiasco and about the extraordinary rise of Pompey First. Together, these two events signalled a major crisis for Tory Central Office and the shadow extended as far as Downing Street. Tomorrow she and Jephson were due to brief the Prime

Minister ahead of parliamentary questions. Whatever Tully had to say might contribute to that brief.

Ellis was looking at the row of cassettes. If each one lasted ninety minutes, he and Tully could be here for days.

Tully tapped the binder. 'Most of the conversations are between Epple and a bloke called Hayden Barnaby.' Ellis nodded. Louise had mentioned Barnaby. He was a local solicitor. He'd been in at the birth of Pompey First. Lately, he'd taken to styling himself 'President-Elect'.

Tully showed the binder to Ellis. In the left-hand column, he'd listed various headings. They began with 'Constitution'. Underneath came 'Suffrage', 'Currency', 'Defence', 'Education', 'Health', 'Pensions', 'Investment', 'Utilities' and 'External Relations'. Beside each heading, Tully had meticulously noted details of tapes, dates and specific conversations. Each conversation had a separate index number which, Ellis assumed, referred to a transcript or perhaps a summary. The analysis was extraordinarily detailed. It must have taken Tully weeks to sort it out.

'Why go to so much trouble?' Ellis queried. 'What's the point?'

'Point?' Tully looked shocked. He picked up the file. 'Choose a heading. Anything. Go on.'

He pushed the file at Ellis. Ellis's finger stopped on 'Utilities'. Tully began to leaf through the file. More writing, pages and pages of it. At last he found what he was looking for, quotes from dozens of conversations, carefully correlated, all addressing the provision of electricity, water or gas.

'Take electricity,' he said. 'Epple's been talking to Southern Electric. He calls it exploratory conversations. What he's really doing is research. He's trying to sort something out for afterwards.'

'After what?'

'Independence. UDI.'

Ellis stared at him. Then his eyes returned to the binder.

'Here?' he said. 'In Portsmouth? They want to go it alone? Set up outside the UK?'

'That's right. When they tell you it's Pompey First, they mean it. At least they're honest. That's quite unusual, isn't it? In politicians?'

'But they're admitting this? You're telling me it's in their. . .'
he shrugged ' . . . manifesto?'

'Christ, no. That's the point. That's why I tried to phone you
yesterday. I've been worrying about it for months. At first I thought
it was a piss-take.' He poked at the pad. 'It's not. And after
yesterday's *Sentinel*, I don't really have much choice. Zhu won't
stop with the dockyard. He wants to buy the lot.'

'Zhu?'

'Yes.'

'He's behind all this?'

'He's supplying the cash.'

'And he wants everything?'

'Yeah.' Tully nodded, glum now. 'The whole bloody city.'

He told Ellis to read the intercepts on electricity. Ellis did so.
The fragments of conversations, so carefully excerpted, told their
own story. Over a period of months, Charlie Epple had established
that the private electricity companies were flogging power in a
totally unregulated market. They could contract with as many
customers as they could satisfy. Nothing in law, no Act of Parliament, prevented them from concluding a deal with Charlie Epple's
infant city-state. On the contrary, given the buying power of
180,000 people, Charlie could probably negotiate a fat discount.

Ellis reread the conversations, putting on his DTI hat, trying
to spot the problems. Tully was watching him, a thin smile on his
face.

'What about the plant? The power lines? The delivery systems?
All the stuff the electricity people own? Here in Portsmouth.'

Tully nodded at the binder. 'Next page.'

Ellis turned over. Charlie Epple, answering exactly the same
question from Hayden Barnaby, had come up with a series of
options. They began with sequestration. On a formal declaration
of independence, the sovereign state of Portsmouth could simply
seize everything within the city limits.

'That's theft,' Ellis looked up, 'in my book.'

'They'd call it nationalization, but you're right.' Tully was still
looking at the binder. 'Read on.'

Ellis finished Tully's analysis. Power-supply options included negotiations with other regional companies or even the purchase of French electricity through the seabed interconnector, but the perfect solution had only occurred to Charlie ten days ago. Ellis read this conversational exchange twice, making sure he had it right. Then he looked up again. Tully was in the kitchen, rummaging for biscuits. Ellis joined him, still holding the binder.

'Zhu would *buy* Southern Electric?'

Tully was ripping the cellophane from a packet of custard creams. 'Sure.'

'How much would it cost him?'

'There's a bid from National Power already on the table. Two point eight billion. He'd have to top that.'

Ellis did the sums in his head: £2.8 billion was a fortune, even to someone as wealthy as Zhu, but after privatization the regional electricity companies had become a licence to print money, one of the reasons why American companies were queuing up with bids of their own. In terms of simple investment Zhu couldn't go wrong, and if National Power beat him to the draw then there was no obvious reason why he shouldn't buy them instead. That way, he'd end up selling electricity to most of the UK. At a profit, of course.

Ellis returned to the file, putting Zhu to one side, trying to absorb the scale of the task these novice politicians had set themselves. He had yet to hear Charlie Epple's voice but the way he used the language, the stop-start pattern of his sentences, spoke of someone prepared to shimmy their way around any problem.

The conversations bubbled with ideas and through all of them ran a thread of pure mischief. Here was someone who simply didn't believe that prospects for the city and its people couldn't be bettered. Under the Tories, he said, life had become a simple two-way bet. A few won. Most lost. In his view, that meant the guys in London had been running the casino for far too long. It was time, at last, for the punters to have a shout. At least, that way, something might be done about the odds.

Ellis found himself nodding. Might this not work? Didn't Charlie Epple have a point?

Tully abandoned the biscuits and retrieved the file from Ellis, flicking quickly through. An obvious problem was the welfare state. How would Pompey First go about funding hospitals, schools, pensions, income support? Wouldn't that cost a fortune? Charlie Epple, once again, had anticipated the challenge. Conversations in February recounted his progress with a number of leading insurance companies. He'd asked each to prepare private schemes to enable a young married couple to see themselves and their kids through bad health, education, unemployment and retirement. In each of these areas, the companies had prepared insurance plans. Together, these proposals would replace the welfare state. Ellis blinked, tallying the various quotes. The lowest came to £874.56. A month.

Ellis put his finger on the figure, pointing it out to Tully.

'It wouldn't work,' he said. 'No one's got that sort of money.'

'You're right,' Tully grunted. 'But that's where Zhu comes in.'

They returned to the lounge with the custard creams. According to one of Charlie's conversations with Hayden Barnaby, only last week Zhu had outlined a scheme whereby the city could pay its own way. Given real independence, and a benign tax regime, international investment would flood in. There were companies in Hong Kong desperate to find a new home for their capital. This was serious money, billions and billions of dollars. With that kind of funding, and the jobs that came with it, Pompey could afford something infinitely superior to the threadbare welfare state the Tories were in the process of dismantling.

This prospect had triggered a longer conversation than usual, and Charlie had spent the best part of an hour rhapsodizing about new schools, decent money for teachers, first-class equipment, the chance for every child in the city to excel. The same vision awaited the city's hospitals, the city's old. Pensions would be doubled. Unemployment benefit, for the handful without jobs, would be turned into a decent living wage. The list went on and on, promissory notes scribbled on Zhu's account, and at the end of it Ellis found himself battling to put these glittering prizes in some sort of perspective. He was looking at a blueprint for a new society. But where would it lead?

'It's a new Singapore,' he said slowly, 'without the sunshine.'

Tully was munching a custard cream. 'Exactly,' he said. 'Think that through, add Hong Kong to the equation, and you'll realize why I made the call.'

When the phone rang, Barnaby was settling down to watch *Newsnight*. Earlier, he'd asked Jessie to come over but for some reason she'd said no. Kate, too, had been tied up with a prior engagement, and of Charlie there'd been no trace.

The mobile was still in the kitchen. Barnaby picked it up. There was something familiar about the voice at the other end. Seconds later, he placed it. The young reporter from *Newsnight*. Barnaby glanced at his watch. The programme started in ten minutes. What had gone wrong?

The reporter was apologetic. He'd been meaning to phone earlier but he'd been tied up in post-production. They'd commissioned a poll in Portsmouth, asking people about their voting intentions. He'd meant to mention it this morning but it had slipped his mind.

Barnaby bent to the phone. He'd resigned himself to bad news. Maybe he'd been premature. 'Well?' he said.

The reporter chuckled. There were two figures, he said. One was a big surprise. The other was truly amazing. So amazing, that the programme editor had ordered a recut on the programme's opening titles sequence.

'Well?' Barnaby said again.

'Sixty-eight per cent.'

'Sixty-eight per cent what?'

'Sixty-eight per cent turnout. That's sixty-eight per cent intending to vote.'

Barnaby felt the warmth flooding through him: 68 per cent was unheard-of, more than double the usual vote.

'And?' he said.

There was a pause. Barnaby could hear a second conversation in the background. Then the reporter returned to the phone.

'Seventy-three per cent committed to Pompey First,' he said. 'Just thought I'd pass it on. 'Bye now. And well done.'

The phone went dead. Barnaby gazed through the open door that led to the living room. Beyond the big picture window, and the blackness of the Common, was the frieze of coloured lights along the seafront. During the evening the wind had got up and the bulbs were swaying on the cables strung between the lamp-posts. Barnaby looked at them for a long time then he yelled and punched the air, returning to the kitchen for the mobile, wondering who to phone.

To his surprise, Kate was still at home. He could hear the noise of a bath being filled. He told her the news. At first she didn't believe it, then he heard her telling someone else. 'Seventy-three per cent,' she whispered, 'down to us.'

There was a cackle of laughter in the background, abruptly muffled by a hand on the receiver.

Charlie Epple, Barnaby thought uneasily, glancing at his watch.

Jessie took a taxi out to the Glory Hole. She'd spent the entire evening quarrelling with Lolly. A tiny spat about a TV programme had flared into a major row, and Lolly had capped it all by calling her a slag. She knew about Haagen. She knew what Jessie was getting up to. She knew she came back with big eyes and wet knickers. She was a whore, a shag-bag. She'd fuck anyone. Even a dosser like Haagen.

Jessie sat in the back of the taxi, surprised by the coldness inside her. She felt nothing for Lolly, absolutely nothing. She'd tried to please her, tried to look after her, tried to meet her every need, and all the thanks she'd ever got was major hassle and major grief. Lolly's life revolved around Lolly. Nothing she could say or do would ever alter that fact.

She asked the cabbie to drop her at the end of the road that skirted the Glory Hole. Haagen, she knew, would be tucked up with his music and a big fat doobie. The last thing he'd appreciate would be a taxi at his door. She began to walk, letting her eyes accustom themselves to the darkness. Gradually, she made out the shapes of houseboats to her left. Most, she knew, were unoccupied, rotting hulks that Haagen occasionally raided for wood for his stove. She thought of him today, how well he'd taken the news about Oz. She'd been expecting something awful, one of his tantrums, but the news seemed to have come as no surprise. Oz, he'd said, always pushed life to the limits. She smiled, remembering her own relief. Maybe he had been less fond of the dog than he'd always pretended. Maybe that was why he'd agreed so readily that Jess should carry on looking after him.

She was close to the houseboat now. She could see the distinctive hump of the extension at the front where Haagen had built his bunk. She stepped off the road, feeling the wet grass through her plimsolls. Walking the plank in the dark was tricky. She took it slowly, inching sideways. The deck felt slippery underfoot. To her surprise, the door to the cabin hung open. She hesitated, then peered in. Had something happened? Had Lolly finally flipped? Called the police? Grassed Haagen up?

'Haagen?' she whispered.

Nothing happened. She looked round. The tide was low. She could hear ducks chattering softly in the darkness.

'Haagen,' louder this time, 'Haagen.'

Still nothing. She ventured into the cabin. The light switch was taped to the bulkhead. She closed the door and found the switch. The cabin was empty. Haagen's sleeping bag lay unzipped on the bunk. Beside the pillow, turned inside out, was a black balaclava helmet she'd never seen before. She picked it up, curious. It smelled sour, a smell she couldn't place. She stepped outside onto the deck again, her body throwing a long shadow on the glistening mud. She stood perfectly still, listening to the sigh of the wind. Then, for the first time, she heard a moaning noise. It sounded sub-human. It signalled pain or exhaustion. It came from nearby.

Frightened now, Jessie returned to the cabin. Haagen normally kept his torch beside the little transistor radio she'd given him. She found it, switched it on and retraced her steps along the gangplank. The grassy bank fell away to the mud-flats below. She walked slowly along the top of the bank, the beam of the torch pooling below. The moaning was louder. She swung the torch to the right, up onto the neighbouring houseboat. At first she could make no sense of what she saw. Two arms outstretched. A body stripped to the waist, the narrow back crisscrossed with scarlet weals. The head moved in the torchlight, then flopped forward again, and she heard the dull thud of bone against the houseboat's wooden hull. Her hand began to shake. Then she was plunging down the bank, her feet sinking ankle deep in the mud at the bottom. She struggled towards the body. It was Haagen. She knew it was. Someone had come for him. Someone had taken a lash to him, flaying him half to death.

Beside the houseboat, she bent double, gasping for breath. The torch up again, she found Haagen's head. A length of dirty cloth gagged his mouth. She fought with the knot. His back was wet with blood, glistening in the light from the torch. Finally, the gag came free. She used it to wipe his face. He was barely conscious, his eyes closed, his breath coming in tiny gasps.

She kissed him, telling him not worry, telling him she loved him, wondering whether or not to release his wrists. They were lashed to a primitive wooden frame, a simple cross, propped against the houseboat's hull. Her fingers found the first knot and she began to loosen it, then she stopped. Unsupported, she'd never cope with his weight. He wasn't big but the bank was steep and slippery and he was in no state to help her. God knew what lay beneath the raw, exposed flesh on his back. He might have broken bones, or internal injuries. It might be even worse than that.

She put her mouth to his ear. 'I'm going for help,' she whispered. 'I'll be back.'

Haagen stirred. One eye opened. In the light from the torch, he looked terrified.

'No,' he mumbled. 'Don't.'

Jessie stared at him a moment longer then fought her way up the bank. There was a telephone box at the end of the road. She ran all the way, oblivious to everything but the need to summon help. When she got to it she dialled 999.

'Ambulance,' she gasped, when the operator answered. 'I think he's dying.'

Chapter Fifteen

Next morning, Jephson had the use of the Director's Rover to cover the mile and a half from Thames House to Downing Street. Louise sat beside him in the back of the big saloon, and it was three minutes to midday by Big Ben when they rounded Parliament Square and swept up Whitehall.

In the front hall at Number Ten Biscoe was waiting for them. The Portsmouth West MP was carrying a battered orange file and a folded copy of a tabloid newspaper. In the big front-page photo, under the *Sentinel*'s masthead, Louise recognized Clive Samuels's distinctive smile, part mirth, part menace.

Jephson did the introductions. Louise shook Biscoe's outstretched hand. All three followed the messenger up a long, straight, rather narrow corridor until it widened into a lobby at the end. Here, they waited while the messenger knocked on a door and disappeared inside. Seconds later, he was out again, shepherding them into a nearby waiting room. The Prime Minister was busy on a phone call. His political secretary would be out to collect them as soon as he'd finished.

In the waiting room, Jephson stood aside, allowing Louise the choice of seats. She settled herself in a high-backed leather-covered armchair that was, in truth, a little too small for comfort. On the table in the middle of the room was a pile of magazines, old copies of *The Economist* and *Country Life*.

Jephson and Biscoe remained standing. Biscoe was ruefully describing the morning's media invasion of Portsmouth. The *Newsnight* poll of Pompey First's electoral chances had triggered a stampede of journalists and video crews and he'd awoken to the sight of a BBC radio car parked outside his front door. Normally, of course, he'd have been delighted to debate the issues with Radio Four's *Today* programme but throughout this morning's live interview he'd never quite got off the back foot. The evidence that Pompey First would do well was by now overwhelming, and all he could do to stem the flood of further defections was to issue the usual warning against a menu without prices. A vote for Pompey First, he'd kept saying, was like putting your signature to a blank cheque. Not once, as far as he was aware, had any of these new-wave politicians indicated where the money might be coming from. This, he insisted to Jephson, was true, and he was still shaking his head at the fraudulence of it all when a young man in a burgundy jacket put his head round the door and invited them into the Cabinet Room.

The moment they appeared the Prime Minister got to his feet. He'd been sitting at the middle of the long, coffin-shaped table. The room was infinitely lighter and more pleasant than the lobby outside, and through the french windows at the end, Louise could see a terrace and an expanse of walled garden. The Prime Minister shook hands, introduced his PPS and asked whether they'd had coffee. The table in front of him was littered with paperwork and when the political secretary enquired about their preference in sandwiches, he rubbed his hands together in gleeful anticipation. He'd got up far too early. Breakfast had been rushed. The sandwiches weren't entirely reliable but today they might just strike lucky.

Louise took the seat across the table, flanked by Jephson and Biscoe. The Prime Minister had evidently met Jephson before and they were sharing a joke about some scandal amongst the cricket Test selectors. There was laughter from Jephson, then the PPS pulled a briefing note towards him, quickly running through events on the south coast.

Louise sat back, listening. Earlier this morning, once she and Jephson had agreed the line they were taking, she'd managed to confirm exactly why the Downing Street deadlines were so tight. The probability of an electoral drubbing at the hands of Pompey First, coupled with the publicity Clive Samuels had attracted over the sale of the naval dockyard, had put Portsmouth firmly on the parliamentary agenda and Jephson knew for certain that Tory Central Office had been ordered to pull together a comprehensive strategy for damage limitation. Hence Biscoe's summons to attend his masters, and hence their own invitation to Downing Street. It was, Jephson had concluded with a smile, a wonderful opportunity to put Downing Street in MI5's debt, and with luck the next half-hour would achieve just that. Not by battling against opposition gibes, but by turning damage limitation into a pre-emptive strike.

The PPS had finished his précis. The polls, he said, told their own story. Pompey First were way, way ahead. They were well organized and highly innovative. They were riding an enormous wave of local support and they'd spent a great deal of money turning an unfocused resentment into solid votes. Biscoe, to his credit, had been right. These people were a real threat. Not just to Pompey Tories, but to local politicians everywhere.

The Prime Minister nodded. Behind the smile and the easy small-talk, Louise sensed a deep exhaustion. He tapped the briefing summary the PPS had passed to him. He was looking at Biscoe. 'The dockyard business is unfortunate. We'll come to that in a minute. What are the issues here? What's really hurting us?'

Louise felt Biscoe stiffen beside her. Instinctively, she liked this man. He had the air of someone whose patience had finally run out. If the PM wanted the truth, he could have it.

'It's difficult to know where to start, Prime Minister.' He opened his file, then closed it again. 'Number one, we're simply not popular. The trust has gone, the willingness to put up with the tough times because there's something better round the corner.'

'But there *is* something better round the corner.' The Prime Minister was looking concerned, a kindly GP offering reassurance, and Biscoe nodded at once.

'I agree,' he said, 'I'm sure you're right. But for whom? Take employment. Getting a job's really tricky, and even if you find something the money's often pathetic. I see these people week in, week out. They've got kids, bills, a couple of thousand owing on the mortgage. It's bloody hard just making ends meet and, whatever we say, it's not getting any better. Except for other people. Often in London.'

'I take your point.' The Prime Minister was frowning. 'But what about specifics? Education, say, or the health service?'

'Disaster areas. The schools are falling apart and the people up at the university seem close to packing it in. These people are angry, Prime Minister, and they've found a home to go to. That's what's so alarming about Pompey First. It's not just our lot. It's the opposition, too. These people are fed up with all of us. They've lost faith. If someone offers them an alternative, no matter how radical, they're going to take it. Not simply in Portsmouth, but very possibly elsewhere.'

The Prime Minister looked glum. Then grave. He'd managed to snatch the last general election by playing the union card, by wrapping himself in the flag, and the anthem, and all those precious memories of what it really meant to be British. Yet here he was, suddenly facing a situation that could, conceivably, unpick it all.

Jephson's cue could hardly have been more perfect. Biscoe was looking in his file for some figures. Jephson leaned across, restraining him. 'Prime Minister,' he began, 'if I may . . .'

The Prime Minister looked up, visibly relieved. 'Please,' he said, 'go ahead.'

Jephson began to describe what lay behind Pompey First's attacks on Westminster and Whitehall, the real agenda they intended to pursue once they were in power. Evidence had come to hand, he said, that they were pushing not simply for a greater say in the city's affairs but for wholesale independence. They'd developed strategies in great depth and detail. They had forward plans for a local health service, for supplementary school funding, for city-wide pension provision. On the back of the government's privatization programme, they'd had a number of conversations with the utility companies, assuring supplies of electricity, gas and water. They were even in the process of finalizing plans for a new flag.

'It's blue and white with a hint of red,' he said helpfully. 'Just like the Pompey football strip.'

The Prime Minister was looking at his PPS. The PPS plainly

thought that Jephson had lost touch with reality. 'You're joking,' he said. 'You have to be.'

'Not at all.' Jephson produced an audio-cassette and laid it carefully on the table in front of him. Louise had given it to him in the car – it had come from Mike Tully's collection. 'I'll spare you the chore of listening,' he said, 'but I assure you we're talking hard intelligence.'

The PPS began to ask where the cassette had come from. The Prime Minister waved the question aside. 'You're sure about all this?' he queried.

'Prime Minister, I'm certain.'

'And you think they could really do it?'

'I think they could really try.'

The Prime Minister thought about the proposition. 'But that has to be illegal, doesn't it? An act of sedition? An act of rebellion against the lawfully elected government?'

Jephson leaned forward. 'And a threat to national security, too, the way we're reading it.'

'Hence your interest?' The Prime Minister gestured vaguely at Jephson and Louise.

'Of course.'

The Prime Minister blinked, aghast yet fascinated. 'And you think they have the backing? Financially?'

'I suspect so.'

'How?'

Jephson didn't answer. Earlier, he and Louise had agreed that the advantage for MI5 lay in a slow drip-feed of relief, parcelling out the story chunk by chunk. Keep the politicians caged as long as possible, Jephson had told her. Otherwise they'll so easily forget who's found the key.

'How?' the Prime Minister repeated. 'How would they ever raise the money to make it all work?'

'There are ways and means, Prime Minister. We haven't quite got the whole picture yet but we're moving as fast as we can. Rest assured.' He smiled.

The PPS took up the running. 'What about this afternoon?' he said. 'PMQs?' He waved a hand at the mountain of paperwork, the bullets for the Prime Minister's parliamentary gun when he faced the leader of the opposition in the Commons.

Jephson frowned, the diligent civil servant keen to help wherever he could. 'My sense is that the key issue will be the dockyard. Everything else, at this point, is speculation.'

'I think you're right,' the PPS agreed. 'But we were rather hoping . . .' He peered at a line on the typescript. 'Mr Zhu, wasn't it?'

'Yes.'

'Anything on him?'

'Nothing firm. Nothing a hundred per cent.'

'Soon?'

'I very much hope so.' Jephson picked up the audio-cassette. 'It's only a suggestion, of course, but, as far as the dockyard's concerned, might it be possible to announce a suspension of negotiations? Pending the outcome of certain enquiries.'

'You think that might help?'

'Absolutely. And it also happens to be true.'

The Prime Minister and his PPS exchanged glances. Jephson was right. It was a little premature for the PM to comment on the dockyard sale and, in any case, these matters were of a commercial nature and therefore subject to the usual strictures on confidentiality. Likewise the issue of Pompey First. At this stage, their success was pure speculation.

He glanced across at Jephson. 'It's good to see you so well briefed,' he said. 'I'm grateful.'

Jephson smiled, then gestured towards Louise. 'I'm lucky to have such professional support, Prime Minister,' he said. 'Miss Carlton's played a blinder.'

Mike Tully was typing an affidavit when he heard the approaching loudspeaker in the street below. He pencilled a mark on his notes, then pushed his chair back from the desk. It was a woman's voice. She was talking about the way the city's budget had been slashed. This year, the government had snatched away half a million pounds. Pompey's money. Your money.

Tully looked down from the window. One of the old open-top buses had come into view around the corner. It was plastered with Pompey First posters and amongst the gaggle of candidates on the top deck, Tully could see the woman with the microphone. He stepped back from the window. Kate Frankham, he thought. Hayden Barnaby's bit of stuff.

Further down the street, a gang of contractors was digging up the road. There was a tail-back from the temporary traffic lights and the Pompey First bandwagon came to rest outside Tully's office. Kate had handed over the microphone to someone else, and while the new candidate droned on about Opportunity '96, another Pompey First initiative, Tully watched Kate pour a cup of coffee from a Thermos. She was deep in conversation with a tall man in jeans and a linen jacket. He had a wide grin and a mop of blond curls and as she beckoned him closer he began to laugh. Her gloved hand touched him lightly on the arm, and Tully saw the coffee spill as the bus inched towards the traffic lights.

He returned to his desk, trying to shut his mind to the howl of the Tannoy below. The candidate was talking about the dockyard, stirring up the controversy over Samuels's breach of faith, and Tully felt a fuse burning deep within him. He'd barely stopped thinking about the dockyard since he'd read Sunday's *Sentinel*, and the longer he brooded, the more he became convinced that Barnaby must have been privy to the secret negotiations. He was Zhu's chief of staff, for God's sake. There was surely nothing that the Chinese got up to in Portsmouth that Barnaby wouldn't, at the very least, suspect. Yet here he was, leading a party committed to a clean break and a fresh start, pretending that the *Sentinel*'s little scoop about the dockyard had come as a terrible shock. Did Barnaby seriously think he could have it both ways? Would he do to the city what he'd done to Liz?

Tully got up from the desk again. Yesterday, before Ellis had disappeared back to London, he'd done his best to find out what would happen to the information he'd passed on. He wanted a guarantee of action, an assurance that something would be done, but although Ellis had obviously understood what he meant, he'd been unable to offer anything firmer than a nod, and a mumbled aside about 'appropriate channels'. Quite where these channels might lead was anyone's guess, and it was beginning to dawn on Tully that Ellis's pals in the intelligence community might well be playing a game of their own. From occasionally bitter experience, Tully knew far too much about the secret world for his own peace of mind. That's the way these things work, he told himself. Debts settled here. Obligations established there. But absolutely nothing set in motion that might attract unwanted attention.

Tully glanced at his watch. Time was running out. It was already Tuesday. People would be going to the polls on Thursday. If they chose to vote for Pompey First then surely the city deserved to know exactly what the leadership had in mind. Tully entered a number into the electronic lock that secured his filing cabinet. He kept a duplicate set of audio-tapes in the middle drawer. Consulting his master list, he selected a recent set of conversations from late April and closed the drawer again. He picked up the phone. The number was some time answering. In the street below, Pompey First were still trawling for votes. Finally, on the phone, a woman's voice.

'The editor, please,' Tully said, 'and tell him it's urgent.'

Harry Wilcox was watching Prime Minister's Questions on the parliamentary cable TV feed when the call came in. He reached back, plucking the phone from the desk. The Prime Minister was on his feet again. Wilcox's pen hovered over the pad on his knee.

'Yes?'

Wilcox listened for perhaps thirty seconds, scribbling as he did so. On television the Prime Minister was explaining that the Minister of Defence would be dealing with questions arising from the potential sale of Portsmouth dockyard as and when he deemed appropriate. Details of the negotiations were presently confidential. Members of the House would not expect Her Majesty's Government to breach that confidentiality. The Prime Minister sat down while a Tory backbencher took up the running. His question addressed the latest inflation figures. Were they not another confirmation that the country was on course to become the most successful economy in Western Europe?'

Wilcox's finger found the off button on the remote control. The screen went blank. 'Very interesting,' he said to the caller on the line. 'By all means come on over.'

Twenty minutes later, Tully was sitting in Wilcox's office. The two men had met before, at the Imperial Hotel on the day of the riot, and the conversation quickly turned to Hayden Barnaby. 'I thought he was mad,' Tully said candidly, 'or drunk. Situation like that, you weigh the odds. They were appalling. He was bloody lucky not to get himself killed.' He paused. 'But then he's like that, isn't he? Death or glory? All or nothing?'

'You're right. He's exactly like that. You know him well?'

'Not really.' Tully produced an audio-cassette, leaving it in his lap where Wilcox could see it. 'He puts a bit of business my way from time to time and we've had the odd drink but I wouldn't say I know him, not well at any rate.'

Wilcox caught the tiny lift in Tully's voice, a signal, he thought, of disapproval. He nodded at the cassette. 'What's that?'

Tully ignored the question. He was looking at the framed front page hanging on the wall behind Wilcox's desk. Already, Sunday's exclusive belonged behind glass.

'What's your line on Pompey First?' he asked.

Wilcox reached for a paperclip. Everywhere he went people were asking the same question and he'd not once wavered in his answer.

'From where I sit they're a blessing,' he said. 'If nothing else, they've made us think about ourselves. That's rare in local politics, believe me.'

'I meant personally. What do you think of them personally?'

Wilcox was looking at the cassette again, no longer sure where the conversation was headed. Had this man Tully heard the story he'd just picked up from the newsroom? About Liz and Haagen? And Amsterdam? He decided to stall. 'Are you asking me about my vote?'

'Not at all. I'm asking you about Pompey First. You know

Hayden Barnaby. You probably know this Charlie Epple. What's the verdict?'

'Hayden's a friend of mine,' Wilcox said carefully. 'That makes it difficult.'

'Why?'

'Because it makes me prejudiced.' He shifted his bulk in the chair. 'He's a bright man. And he's committed, too.'

'Committed to what?'

It was Wilcox's turn to let the question drift past. He looked at Tully for a long time. Then he leaned forward, shadowing the desk. 'Mr Tully, what exactly do you want? I'm a busy man. You told me you had something I'd be interested in seeing.'

'Hearing.'

'What?'

'Hearing.' Tully tapped the cassette. 'Have you got a player for this?'

Wilcox was briefly disconcerted. Then his curiosity got the better of him and he left the office. Tully watched him bend over an empty desk in the newsroom and pull at the drawers. When he returned with a player, Tully gave him the tape. 'It's cued up,' he said. 'Side A.'

Wilcox was going to say something but thought better of it. He inserted the tape and pressed the play button. At once, there was a distinctive bark of laughter.

'Charlie Epple,' Tully explained. 'The other voice you'll know.'

Wilcox sat back in his chair, revolving it slowly, first one way, then the other. Charlie was humming. At length, he broke into song. It sounded like a chorus, at once intimate and exhortatory.

> '*Nothing in shadow, nothing to hide,*
> *Heaven's Light Our Guide . . . yeah!*'

There was more laughter, then Barnaby's voice. He was telling Charlie to hang onto the day job. If he wanted a failed rock star to lead the Department of Culture and Arts, he'd bear him in mind. In the meantime, maybe they could get on with the business in hand. Had Charlie pursued the currency thing? Had he talked to the economics guy at the university? The conversation rambled on. Charlie said he knew fuck all about ecus but the bloke with the doctorate insisted it was the obvious route. Even if the Treasury didn't cut up rough about hanging on to sterling, the ecu was still favourite.

'Why?'

'Something to do with stability. It's not a floater. It doesn't bounce around, like the pound. You understand any of this stuff?'

'Not really, but Zhu does and he says the same thing. Either the ecu or the Swiss franc. Hates dealing in anything else. You happy to go with the ecu?'

There was a pause on the tape, then more laughter from Charlie.

'Fine by me, Mr President. You name it, I'll sell it.'

Wilcox indicated that he'd heard enough. Tully stopped the tape.

'Where did you get that?'

'I can't tell you.'

'It's recent?'

'Last month.' Tully showed him the spine of the cassette. 'April the twelfth.'

Wilcox nodded. His hands were knotted behind his head and he was staring out across the newsroom. 'So what's the point you've come to make?' he asked.

Tully wondered whether he'd chosen the right excerpt. Maybe he should have gone for something less technical. Like Charlie's plans to enter the city's swimming team for the next Olympic games.

'They were discussing a national anthem,' he said, 'and a new local currency. These guys want to pull us out of the UK, lock, stock and barrel. It's all there, hours and hours of it. A blueprint for UDI.'

Wilcox shook his head emphatically. 'It's a piss-take,' he said. 'They're fucking about.'

'You think so?'

'I know it, I know these guys, they're at it all the time, especially Charlie Epple. He's a headbanger. Always was.'

'And Barnaby?'

'Barnaby's different. He's a regular bloke. He's reliable. He delivers. With Barnaby you get what you see. He cares about the city. He wants things to change. But there's no secret agenda.'

'Is that what his wife thinks?'

'That's cheap.'

'Not to her, Mr Wilcox.' Tully glowered at him, then stood up and reclaimed his cassette from the machine. He was half-way to the door before Wilcox called him back. He was still sprawled behind the desk but Tully could see the uncertainty on his face. People were right about him and Pompey First. He was wedded to the cause. But he was a newsman, too. And he couldn't resist the scent of a really big story.

He was fiddling with the cassette machine. 'You say there are more tapes?'

'Plenty.'

'Can I listen to them?'

'No,' Tully lied. 'I've passed them up the line.'

'What line?'

This, at last, was the question Tully had anticipated. He'd scrawled the number in his diary before he'd left the office. He read it out to Wilcox, suggesting he get in touch at once. Wilcox pretended he hadn't heard and reached for the phone. He hated being told what to do.

When the number answered, he introduced himself then mentioned Tully's name. He'd been listening to a tape-recording. It had to do with an outfit called Pompey First. He pulled a pad towards him. When he'd put the phone down, he looked up.

'So who the fuck's Louise Carlton?' he said. 'And why's she so keen on tea at the Imperial?'

Barnaby's council of war in the Pompey First press room had already turned into a victory celebration.

Charlie Epple had spent most of the day in the editing suite, assembling all the campaign's TV reports onto a single tape, and the fact that he could end the montage with a one-minute clip from Prime Minister's Questions was the icing on the cake. Six months ago, Pompey First hadn't existed. Yet here he was, viewing nearly an hour of campaign highlights, courtesy of various television networks.

The early material, admittedly, was locally sourced, and he'd used clips from Kate's performance on *The South Decides* as a kind of running gag, but the interest he'd attracted over the last seven days had come from the big national operations and it was this kind of heavy-duty coverage that had surely swung the votes to Pompey First. As well as *Newsnight*, Charlie had supplied interviewees to *News at Ten*, *Sky Tonight*, and a Channel Four political slot, *Grass-roots*.

Word had even spread as far as BBC network radio. *Call Nick Ross*, that very morning, had devoted an entire hour to the subject of what they'd christened 'stand-alone political parties', and Charlie had been heartened by the stampede of disgruntled callers that news of Pompey First's success had released. All over the country, it seemed, people had tumbled the myth of parliamentary sovereignty. The government had been ignoring the people for well over a decade, and after its contemptuous dismissal of the Scott Report ordinary voters had finally had enough.

Charlie raised the remains of his bottle of champagne as the Prime Minister sat down. At a nearby desk, Barnaby was trying to collate his notes. All the candidates were due at the hotel by half past three. Most had to be away within the hour. This would be his last chance to confirm arrangements and set the mood for the campaign's final push.

Charlie had retrieved the video-cassette from the player. He showed it to Barnaby. 'I'll get another two duped as back-ups,' he said, 'plus fifty more for press giveaways.'

'Fifty enough?'

'A hundred, then. We'll be running the master on small monitors at the Guildhall tomorrow night.'

Barnaby nodded, scribbling a note to himself about the Guildhall. From the start of the campaign, he and Charlie had always planned to end with a modest eve-of-poll rally at which all the Pompey First candidates would be present. Anyone who fancied it could attend, and candidates were pledged to answer any question that came their way. On the basis of early indications, Charlie had hired a church hall in Fratton but the events of the past week had tempted them into the Guildhall, Pompey's pride and joy, a big 2,000-seater auditorium with a stage and a proscenium arch, a full lighting rig and a professional sound system. The decision hadn't been cheap, and hundreds of empty seats could still make them look silly, but Charlie had taken the precaution of halving the prices in the Guildhall bars and word had gone round that Pompey First was on a roll. With luck, given the torrent of press coverage, Charlie was predicting a turnout of around nine hundred. With the upstairs seating closed off, it would look like a full house.

Candidates were arriving at the hotel now, and Barnaby glimpsed Zhu outside in the corridor, shaking each one gravely by the hand. Normally impenetrable, the excitements of the past few days had made a visible impression on him. Barnaby wasn't entirely sure, but he sensed that Zhu viewed Pompey First as the child he'd never had: boisterous, noisy, occasionally wayward, but full of promise. The stream of camera vehicles arriving every morning for the regular press conferences had at first amused him. Like so many others, he seemed surprised that these people should come so far for so little. Yet only this morning, overhearing Charlie and Barnaby discussing the fee for the hire of the Guildhall, he'd stolen quietly away, returning minutes later with yet another four-figure contribution to campaign funds. He'd always believed, he said, in enterprise and commitment. Pompey First, in his view, embodied both.

Kate Frankham was the last to arrive. Breathless and excited, she'd just done a stand-up interview with a visiting American TV crew on the pavement outside the hotel. They'd been tracking the Republican campaign in the US election and they'd told her what a pleasure it was to have found some real people at last. She'd responded to their flattery with a scorching denunciation of big-money politics, and at the end of the piece, the interviewer had kissed her hand.

Charlie's eyes revolved. 'Americans'll do anything for a shag,' he said. 'You should have asked for money.'

Finally, later than he'd intended, Barnaby called the gathering

to order. Candidates settled on chairs or sat around the edges of
the room, their backs against the wall, while Barnaby asked Charlie
Epple to outline the programme for the last forty-eight hours of
the campaign. Tomorrow, Wednesday, candidates and a swelling
army of supporters would be blitzing their respective wards. Charlie
had done a deal on 74,000 felt-tips, one for each of the city's
households. The pens carried the Pompey First logo and each
would be posted through a letter-box with a single sheet of sea-
green paper listing the ten deadly ways the big national parties had
sinned against the local community. At noon, weather permitting,
an airship would appear over the city, flying slow figures-of-eight
for most of the afternoon. Suspended beneath it, a giant flag
carrying the star and the crescent moon, the city's emblem, plus
the invitation to *REACH FOR THE SKY – VOTE POMPEY FIRST!*.

Charlie's battle order unfolded still further. Throughout the
day, local commercial radio stations would be offering information
about Thursday's polling arrangements, and Charlie's careful
courtship of a handful of the key DJs would ensure sympathetic
mention of Pompey First. Normally, media coverage of elections
was restricted by rules about political endorsement, but Pompey
First had become a news item in its own right and Charlie seemed
confident that the party could only benefit. The *Newsnight* poll
certainly suggested it, and their predicted Pompey First vote – 73
per cent – would form a giant backdrop to the eve-of-poll rally at
the Guildhall. Once again, the media would be there in force. To
date, the press centre had processed sixteen requests for facilities.

Barnaby moved the meeting on to arrangements for polling
day, and Charlie handed round an armful of sea-green folders with
a ward-by-ward analysis of exactly how he planned to maximize
the Pompey First vote. Yet another deal had given him access to a
fleet of minibuses, and these would be offering free trips to local
supermarkets via designated polling stations. Computer printouts
listed the names and addresses of confirmed Pompey First supporters, and these trusties would be offered separate lifts in private
cars. A final round-up of electoral waifs and strays was planned for
8 p.m., an hour before the polls closed, and with luck Charlie
anticipated a turnout of pledged votes that might be as high as 90

per cent. The operation had, he said ruefully, given him renewed respect for the guys who'd masterminded D-Day.

There was laughter around the room, and a round of applause for his efforts. Then Barnaby got to his feet again, applauding his troops in return. Collectively, these people had become friends, allies in an extraordinary war that he and Charlie had declared against the sprawl of vested interests in London. They shared his impatience, his disgust, and they shared as well his conviction that men and women of goodwill could make an infinitely better job of governance than the faceless mandarins and tired politicians in the metropolis.

He paused for breath, looking round the crowded room, then ended his impromptu speech with a reminder that even victory wouldn't bring the battle to an end. Back in the sixties, a Labour politician, T. Dan Smith, had attempted something similar. He'd mustered support in the north-east and led local voters towards a vision of semi-independence. He'd talked of 'vertical structures', local decision-making, the beginnings of a kind of autonomy. The threat to the centre was obvious and London had destroyed him with a ruthless mix of rumour, innuendo, and finally prosecution and arrest. His political career had ended in the law courts, answering charges of corruption, and for a generation the dream of a thriving local democracy had gone away. Now, thanks to the efforts of Pompey First, the return of power to the people was back on the agenda, but they'd taken the battle deep into enemy territory and the last thing they could afford now was complacency.

Barnaby was suddenly sombre. The enemy, he said, was everywhere. But with luck, and a great deal of effort, they'd battle through. It was what the people wanted. And the people, on Thursday, would have their shout.

Kate Frankham was standing beside the top table. Barnaby reached out to her, inviting her up, holding her hand high. Charlie did the same with her other hand and there was more clapping, and then whooping and war cries, and finally a great roar of applause. Barnaby looked down at Kate, squeezing her hand, but she was gazing up at Charlie, her head back, a huge grin on her face.

*

Wilcox was standing in the hotel lobby when he heard the commotion down the corridor. He raised an eyebrow at the smiling faces behind the reception desk but when the duty manager explained about Hayden Barnaby's council of war he resisted the temptation to stroll down and take a look for himself. This afternoon's meeting with Tully, and now the prospect of more revelations, had sounded an alarm bell deep in his head and he wondered again whether he shouldn't suggest afternoon tea at some other venue.

When she arrived minutes later, Louise Carlton wouldn't hear of it. She peered round, unbuttoning her coat and carefully folding the Paisley silk scarf into a pocket. Tea was always served in the Nelson lounge, an ample, beautifully restored room on the south side of the hotel, and she tucked her hand through Wilcox's arm, insisting he walk her through. To Wilcox's surprise, Zhu was occupying an armchair at the far end. Beside him, deep in conversation, was a squat, harassed-looking businessman, whom Wilcox recognized at once. As leader of the city's Tory councillors, he was fighting for his political life.

Louise ordered tea, scones and a plateful of cakes, waving away Wilcox's protests that he'd eaten already. From her bag, she produced a long brown envelope, leaving it on the table between them. Wilcox examined his name on the label, looking for clues to this strange woman with her granny bun and huge glasses. Who was she? And what gave her the right to take command like this?

Louise was asking him whether he'd like to make notes. The envelope contained material he'd doubtless find interesting but there was nothing to beat an *aide-mémoire*.

Wilcox glanced across at Zhu. Unusually, he was laughing.

'I don't want to sound rude,' he said, looking at Louise again, 'but who are you?'

Louise tut-tutted to herself and plunged a hand into the bag by her side. From a leather wallet, she produced a slim ID.

Wilcox took it. 'Security Service?' he said blankly. 'Thames House?'

'I'm with MI5. I'm sorry. I should have explained.'

Wilcox was looking at the envelope again, thinking about Tully.

Was he MI5 as well? Was this an official operation? Intelligence-driven?

Louise's hand was back in the bag. She offered a ring binder pad to Wilcox, plain white cover, brand new.

'Just in case you'd forgotten your own.' She beamed at him, a plump, middle-aged woman, enjoying her afternoon by the sea. 'Shall we begin?'

Wilcox uncapped his pen while Louise outlined the operation she'd been running these last six months. From the day he'd flown into Heathrow, Raymond Zhu had been awarded VCIP status. As a Very Commercially Important Person, he'd been given priority access to the higher reaches of the DTI. They'd smoothed his path to certain manufacturers and he'd duly placed a modest order for equipment of what Louise termed a 'paramilitary nature'. At the same time, he'd begun to invest heavily in Portsmouth, a decision that no one at the DTI could satisfactorily explain.

The comment stung Wilcox. This was exactly the kind of Whitehall dismissiveness that had led to the birth of Pompey First. Barnaby and Charlie Epple were right. The bastards really did think we still lived in caves.

Wilcox's gaze had returned to Zhu. 'What's so crazy about investing in Portsmouth?' he enquired. 'It's a free world, isn't it?'

Louise patted his knee.

'Of course it is,' she said. 'But it was the *amount* he was investing that concerned us. In our trade, Mr Wilcox, we look for anomalies, bumps in the usual graph line. Mr Zhu represented a very big bump indeed. We simply wanted to know why.'

'And?'

'We started making enquiries. As you might expect.'

Her hands returned to her lap. Wilcox noted the absence of rings on her fingers and found himself speculating on her seniority within MI5. She didn't somehow fit his image of a sharp-end agent. She was too old, too comfortable, too self-confident. But did that mean she occupied a perch in the upper echelons? And, if so, what might that say about the importance of this mission of hers?

Louise was talking about the dockyard now. The *Sentinel*'s

intervention in the negotiations had, to be frank, been extremely premature. The details fuelling Sunday's exclusive had plainly come from Zhu, and that in itself rather confirmed one of the preliminary conclusions she'd reached about the man.

'Such as?'

'Well,' she lowered her voice, 'he plainly sees no divide between business and politics. He briefed you on the dockyard in the sure knowledge that you'd use it. That, in turn, rather made Mr Barnaby's point.' She smiled. 'Didn't it?'

'You know Barnaby?'

'I know of him.'

'And you're saying he and Zhu are close?'

'Obviously.'

'And you're saying that's deliberate? On Zhu's part?'

'Yes.'

'And that's a problem?'

'Yes.' She nodded. 'I think it might be.'

'Why?'

'Because politics and business don't mix. Or shouldn't.'

Wilcox permitted himself a short, mirthless snort of laughter. 'Are you kidding? Where have you been these last sixteen years?'

Louise pursed her lips. 'Domestic politics are different. Domestically, we assume a common interest.'

'Do we?'

'Yes. Mr Zhu, I'm afraid, doesn't offer the same guarantee.'

'Is that why we're selling him the dockyard?'

'That's a matter of interpretation. Mr Zhu's, to be precise.'

'You're saying he hasn't bought it?'

'I'm saying negotiations are still in progress. But that's not the point. The issue is rather longer-term. We need to understand where Mr Zhu is heading. And, to do that, we need to take rather a good look at where he's been.' Louise reached forward, touching the envelope. 'I think you'll find the evidence pretty conclusive.'

'What evidence?'

Wilcox picked up the envelope, weighing it in his hand. For the first time, it occurred to him that Zhu might have some connection with the drugs exposé the young reporter on the crime desk was investigating. So far, she hadn't got much further than showing him the photos that had arrived anonymously on the *Sentinel*'s front desk. The prints had tracked the German boy to Amsterdam. One had featured Liz Barnaby leaving a Southsea travel agency. According to the carefully typed notes that came with the photos, the link between Liz and Haagen was pretty firm. Her cheque had funded the ticket to Amsterdam with plenty in reserve for the twenty grams of heroin and somewhat larger consignment of cannabis that Haagen had allegedly bought. Might Zhu be involved in narcotics? Turning Portsmouth into some kind of bridgehead for hard drugs? Was there a Triad dimension here?

Wilcox wondered how much of this to share with Louise. He badly wanted to regain the initiative. He opened the envelope.

'We've had a tip-off about a drugs story,' he said.

'Oh, really?'

Wilcox told her briefly what had happened. There was no suggestion that Barnaby had been involved but they were still talking to his estranged wife.

'And what does she say?'

'She claims she was trying to buy the boy off. He was a junkie. He shared a flat with Barnaby's daughter, who was crazy about him.'

'How much money was involved?'

'Three thousand pounds.'

'She gave him that to clear off?'

'That's what she's saying.'

'Without telling her husband?'

'Yes.'

'And this lad spent it on drugs?'

'So it seems,' Wilcox confirmed. 'He was certainly back in the city because I saw him that weekend. The day this place opened.'

Louise steepled her fingers. At length, she sighed. 'And you believe her husband never knew? A sum as big as that?'

'I've no idea. It's certainly possible. Then again . . .'

'Let's say he did. Let's say he sanctioned the arrangement. Doesn't say much for his judgement, does it?'

Wilcox accepted the hint and emptied the contents of the

envelope onto the table. There were sheets of paper, dense lines of typescript. The top page headlined the various ways Zhu had supported Pompey First. In cash terms, he'd so far written cheques for nearly £98,000.

Wilcox stared at the figure. A waiter had arrived with a tray of tea. Scones and cakes would follow. He cleared a space on the table, handing the papers to Wilcox.

'Where did you get this figure?' he asked.

Louise was eyeing the mountain of clotted cream beside the dish of strawberry jam. 'Take a look at the rest,' she said. 'It's important you understand the context.'

Wilcox read on. The second page traced Zhu's various holdings in Hong Kong. Through his brother, he'd built up interests in a number of conglomerates and, as far as Wilcox could judge, he still held major stakes. Page three was more technical, an analysis of cash-flow into three bank accounts in Singapore. All were registered in the name of Celestial Holdings and the figures were enormous. The smallest account topped $898 million.

The scones had arrived. Louise loaded one with cream and jam and passed it across to Wilcox, who didn't move. 'The man's made a lot of money,' he said. 'So what?'

'Page four,' Louise said, smiling across the room at Zhu, 'is especially interesting.'

Wilcox returned to the stapled sheets of paper. Page four listed bids Zhu was making for major British utilities. Southern Electric was one, Southern Water another. He was even building up a sizeable position in Nynex, the cable operator with a network in Portsmouth. All the bids had been made in the name of nominees but accompanying notes followed the paper trail back to Celestial Holdings.

'Why?' Wilcox looked up again. 'Why does he want all this?'

'It's partly good business,' Louise admitted. 'Water and electrical distribution are still monopolies. They're out-performing the market. The Americans are snapping them up.'

'But?'

'No buts.' Louise was brisk now. 'Just logic. Why would you

need to secure power and water? Why would you want to control the cable network?'

Wilcox's eyes returned to the tables of figures. Buried in there, he was beginning to realize, was a far bigger story than even the dockyard exposé. But why had Zhu chosen Portsmouth? And why all the backing for Pompey First?

He picked up the scone. Louise's mouth was full. She took a sip of tea.

'Hong Kong's the key,' she said at last. 'As you've no doubt guessed.'

'But I thought Zhu came from Singapore?'

'He does. Before that, he lived in Hong Kong. His brother's still there. The other half of the empire.'

Wilcox nodded, the light beginning to dawn. His eyes were back on the figures, tallying the tidal wave of money flooding into Celestial Holdings.

'Zhu's building a lifeboat,' he said softly. 'He's shipping out all this cash. Money from Hong Kong. His and other people's.'

'Of course.' Louise paused. 'So what else would he need?'

'Somewhere to keep it. Somewhere to invest it.'

'And?'

'A brand new home for him and his chums. Somewhere small. Somewhere on the edge of Europe. Somewhere. . . .' he looked up ' . . . they could call their own.'

Across the room, Zhu was still deep in conversation with the leader of the Tory Group. He wants to build a new Hong Kong, Wilcox thought, and Pompey First will hand him the city on a plate.

'So what does that make Barnaby?' he mused aloud, still looking at Zhu. 'An accomplice?'

'Of course.' Louise was reaching for another scone. 'Either that or a dupe.' She smiled. 'Good story?'

For the second time in two years, Jessie found herself in the Queen Alexandra Hospital. Haagen occupied a bed in a private room on the third floor. A young uniformed policeman sat outside, and when Jessie gave him her name he checked it against a list of permitted visitors. She had spent most of the day at the city's central police station. To most of their questions, she couldn't begin to supply an answer.

The policeman spoke into his radio. A door opened down the corridor and a policewoman appeared. She searched Jessie from head to foot, and examined the contents of her bag. The policeman unlocked the door to Haagen's room. 'Five minutes,' he said.

Haagen appeared to be asleep. He was lying on his belly, naked to the waist. The lash marks had scabbed on his back and the bruising had already acquired a yellowish tinge. Standing by the bed, Jessie wondered whether she should wake him. His head was turned to the window and his eyes were closed. Then, barely audible, he spoke. 'Is the door shut?'

'Yes.'

Jessie found herself a chair. She wanted to kiss him, but when she tried he shook his head. The beating had extended to his face. There was a heavy swelling over one eye.

'How are you?'

'Shit.'

'What have they done?'

Haagen didn't answer. His eyes, open now, were cold. 'Have you got a pen?'

'Why?'

'I want you to write down an address.'

'They're watching. Through the window.'

'Yeah?' He smiled. 'Just memorize it, then.'

For a long moment, he said nothing. Then he gave her an address. 89 Tokar Street. 'Got that?'

'Yes. Tokar Street. Number eighty-nine.'

'Know where it is?'

'I'll find it.'

Jessie could hear a woman's voice in the corridor outside. She was saying that Haagen should be OK in a couple of days. OK enough to be transferred into police custody.

'There's a guy called Monty,' Haagen muttered. 'Just tell him to make sure it's on.'

'What's on?'

'Doesn't matter. Just tell him that. Just make sure he gets the message. Tokar Street. Number eighty-nine. OK?'

Haagen's eyes closed again. He appeared to have lost interest in the conversation and when the policeman knocked on the glass and Jessie bent to kiss him goodbye, he shook his head again, burying his face in the pillow.

Chapter Sixteen

A grey day, dawn curtained by flurries of rain.

Before seven Barnaby was awake in his flat, rummaging in the tiny bathroom for a bottle of paracetamol. He swallowed two and took a second glass of water back to bed. Kate was still asleep, her body curled in a tight ball. Unusually, after last night's impromptu session at the Imperial, she'd consented to spend the night with him. Drunk, they'd made love. He couldn't remember much about the details except the face beneath him on the pillow. For the first time ever, she hadn't said a word.

There was a radio clock beside the bed. At seven o'clock, it turned itself on and Barnaby listened to the headlines on the *Today* programme. This had always been routine for him but lately he'd developed a near-addiction to breaking news. Only once had Pompey First ever featured on this flagship show but that had been enough to open the door to the world Barnaby wanted so desperately to join. If the last four weeks had taught him anything, it had been that nothing was beyond his reach. If you wanted something badly enough, you could make it happen.

He sat on the edge of the bed, debating what to wear. At first he didn't hear the phone ringing in the lounge across the hall. When he finally found the mobile, tucked behind a cushion on the sofa, it was Wilcox.

'There's a car park on Portsdown Hill,' he grunted, 'up by the roundabout. I'll be there at eight.'

Automatically Barnaby checked his watch. It was still barely seven. He still had time to shave and shower.

'Why the hurry?' he said.

'Don't ask. Just be there.'

Wilcox put the phone down. He'd sounded gruff and angry, as if someone had awakened him prematurely from a deep sleep, and Barnaby stood at the window for a full minute, wondering why he hadn't come down to the hotel and joined the party in the bar last night.

At length, he heard movement behind him. Kate was standing in the open doorway. She was wearing nothing except an old T-shirt of Jessie's. Across the chest, in faded black letters, it read 'All Property is Theft'.

'I feel terrible,' she said. 'I think I'm going to throw up.'

Wilcox was already in the car park when Barnaby swung the Mercedes in from the roundabout. The wind had got up but the rain had stopped and Barnaby could feel the warmth of the sun through the thin veil of cloud. He stood beside the car, staring down at the city below. Patches of sunshine mottled the grey silhouettes in the dockyard. Over the Isle of Wight, the horizon was purpled with a passing squall. Barnaby had rarely seen such dramatic contrasts in the weather. It was, he thought, astonishingly beautiful.

There was a photographer with Wilcox. He got out of the car and began to unpack equipment from the boot. Wilcox walked across. His coat was streaked with rain.

'Fucking awful morning,' he said briefly. 'Mind if the snapper takes some shots?'

Barnaby shook his head. Something had happened to Wilcox, something profound, and he couldn't work out what it was. The hostility he'd sensed earlier on the phone was visible on his face, in his body movements, in the way he barked at the photographer when he began to moan about the light. Wilcox wanted shots of Barnaby against the city below. He didn't care a fuck about the readings on the meter. If the photographer had to use flash to fill in the shadows on Barnaby's face, so be it.

The photographer shrugged, taking Barnaby by the arm and positioning him at the edge of the car park where the sodden downland fell away to the housing estate below. Barnaby adjusted his tie and ran a comb through his hair, still watching Wilcox. The photographer was asking how many shots he wanted.

'Lots.'

Wilcox returned to his car. Barnaby mustered a smile while the photographer motioned him left and right. After one set of photos, he changed cameras and took another. Eventually, he told Barnaby he'd finished.

Barnaby walked across to Wilcox's car. The *Sentinel*'s first edition appeared on the city's streets at noon. He wanted to be sure that there'd be a mention of the evening rally at the Guildhall.

'Get in.' Wilcox jerked his thumb towards the passenger seat.

Barnaby did as he was told, his bafflement giving way to irritation. It was still bloody early. He'd been more than obliging. Why the aggression?

Wilcox had produced a small cassette recorder. He wedged it on the dashboard and pressed the record button. Then he turned to Barnaby. 'OK,' he said. 'Let's have your version.'

'My version of what?'

'Your version of what this whole charade's been about. Zhu's moving millions into the city. At the moment we're talking money. Soon it'll be Hong Kong Chinese. Thousands of them. Hundreds of thousands.' He nodded at the recorder. 'We're on the record, remember. So don't fuck about.'

Barnaby was at Charlie Epple's house before nine. Jessie opened the door, her bare toes curling on the plastic matting. Her face was a mask, pale and drawn. When she saw her father, she forced a smile. 'I tried to ring you last night,' she said.

Barnaby gazed at her. The last thing he needed was another episode with Jessie. 'What happened?'

'Haagen.'

'What about him?'

'It's complicated. I need to talk to you.'

'Later,' he said briskly. 'Is Charlie in?'

'He's up in the bathroom.'

Barnaby pushed through, hearing the door close behind him

as he mounted the stairs. Charlie was sitting on the lavatory, naked. Barnaby wedged himself in the space between the wash-basin and the window. Charlie tapped ash into a soap dish.

'We've got a problem,' Barnaby told him. 'Has Wilcox been on?'

Charlie reached for the lavatory paper. 'No,' he said. 'Why?'

Barnaby explained about the encounter on the hill. Wilcox had been talking to some source or other. He believed Zhu was fronting for Hong Kong interests. At best, Pompey First had been set up. At worst, the new politics was a cover for a wholesale invasion.

'Of what?'

'Hong Kong Chinese. Wilcox thinks we're angling for independence. And he thinks Zhu's put us up to it.'

'What did you say?'

'I said it was bollocks.'

'It is. It's a lovely thought but it's still bollocks.' Charlie finished with the lavatory paper and stood up. 'What's this source, then?'

'He wouldn't say.'

'So what's the evidence?'

'He says he's heard tapes.'

'Tapes of what?'

'You and me. Talking about UDI.'

'Face to face?'

'On the phone.'

'Fuck.'

Charlie reached for a towel and wrapped it round his waist. Downstairs, on his hands and knees beside the telephone socket in the hall, his fingers found a thin whisker of wire. He fetched a butter knife from the kitchen and used it to unscrew the cover of the socket. Then he peered inside. 'We've been bugged,' he announced.

Barnaby became aware of Jessie watching them from the kitchen. It took him several seconds to realize she was crying.

'Bugged by who?'

'Fuck knows.' Charlie was on his feet again. 'What are we supposed to have said?'

409

'Wilcox wouldn't tell me, not in detail, but he says it all stands up. We've betrayed the people. We've sold them a pup. That's the line he's taking.'

'Where?'

'In the paper.'

'*Today?*'

'Yes.'

Charlie groaned and took a step backwards, sinking onto the stairs. From the kitchen, Barnaby could hear Jessie making tea. Charlie was trying to recall the conversations they'd had. Of course they'd talked about the future, about the possibility of independence, about going it alone. That was logical, that was where the fun was. Fuck, no one went into politics to keep the world spinning the same old way. Otherwise why bother?

'Fuck.' He shook his head, trying to dislodge Barnaby's news. 'Fuck, fuck.'

Jessie arrived with tea. Without a word Barnaby took a mug. He didn't take his eyes off Charlie.

'This stuff about Zhu,' Charlie was saying. 'It's crap, isn't it?'

Barnaby hesitated. 'I'm not sure. To be honest.'

Charlie stared up at him. 'You're not sure? What the fuck does that mean?'

'It means what it says. I'm not married to the man. I'm not privy to everything he gets up to.'

'So you think it might be true?'

'I don't know.'

'But what did you tell Wilcox?'

'I told him exactly that. That I didn't know.'

Charlie closed his eyes in disbelief, his hands cupping the mug.

'He's a newsman, for Chrissakes. Saying you don't know is next best to admitting it. Jesus, where have you been all these weeks?'

'Trying to win an election,' Barnaby said heavily. 'Since you ask.'

The two men gazed at each other, then Charlie looked at his feet, lost for words.

'I thought he was a supporter,' Barnaby muttered. 'I thought he was a mate. I thought he cared.'

'He's a journalist,' Charlie said. 'Journalists don't have mates. They have sources, contacts, careers. There's a difference. Trust a fucking journalist, and you're dead meat. As we're about to find out.'

'Maybe he won't print. He's got to talk to Zhu yet. He's bound to deny it. Bound to.'

'Deny what?'

'Whatever Wilcox has been fed. He says Zhu's been bidding for the utilities. Water, electricity, Nynex, companies that keep this place going. Listen to Wilcox and it all makes perfect sense. The master plan for UDI. He even quoted from that daft song you wrote, "Heaven's Light". He says it's going on the front page. Pompey First's national anthem. Exhibit A.'

Charlie groaned again, putting his head down and hugging his knees. At length he looked up. 'But that was shit,' he said ruefully. 'I could have done much better if I'd known.'

Louise Carlton bent to the phone, glad to have found Ellis at home. In the absence of other instructions, he'd elected to have the day off. Louise pulled a copy of *Yellow Pages* towards her, leafing through until she found the entry for restaurants. Pompey First's final rally would probably end around ten. She wanted a little guidance on what they should eat first.

'First?'

'Before we go back to the hotel.'

There was a long silence. Through the window, beyond the sprawl of the city, Louise could see clear down the Solent to the northern tip of the Isle of Wight. After the early-morning gloom, it was a beautiful day.

Louise tucked the phone into her shoulder. She'd found a Spanish restaurant called Bodega Hermosa. She scribbled down the number. 'You've done extremely well,' she murmured to Ellis. 'It'll be my treat.'

*

By mid-morning, the Pompey First election machine was in top gear. Charlie had arranged for all candidates to carry mobiles and, as promised, they were making regular progress reports to one of the three rapid-response desks he had set up in the press centre. A couple of TV crews were prowling around, picking up shots for the early-evening bulletins, and Barnaby was aware of roving microphones eavesdropping on his telephone conversations. The more sensitive calls he made from a bedroom upstairs, reserved for his use, but the sheer pressure of events demanded his presence at the operation's nerve centre.

Charlie had just arrived from the *Sentinel*'s offices. He'd been engaged, in his own words, in a little damage limitation. His face betrayed the way the conversation had gone.

'No go?'

'Hopeless.' Charlie kept his voice low, eyeing the TV crews. 'Even worse than I expected.'

'He's printing?'

'As we speak.'

'Shit.'

'Exactly.'

The two men retired to the bedroom upstairs, leaving the girls on the response desks to field incoming calls. Barnaby had drafted a press statement and Charlie scorched through it with a felt tip, changing a phrase here, stiffening an adjective there. The best form of defence, he told Barnaby, was attack. The slur on their efforts was monstrous – yet more evidence of the battle they had to fight. Given that Pompey First might win the support of the people, London had reacted the only way they knew. By lying.

'You'll go with that?' Charlie looked up.

Barnaby was standing by the window. In the last hour or so he'd begun to lose touch with events. The world he'd created, the activity around him, was no longer real. He gazed across the Common, towards the sea.

'Say what you like.' He sighed. 'I'm leaving it to you.'

'Thanks.' Charlie was already heading for the door. 'Managed to find Zhu yet?'

'Who?'

'Zhu.' He made a dismissive gesture with Barnaby's press statement. 'Our guiding light.'

Mike Tully had been alerted to the *Sentinel*'s midday edition by a phone call from the paper's newsroom. A reporter had presented the editor's compliments and advised him to nip down to the newsagent. Now, past noon, Tully heard his secretary hurrying up the stairs outside his office. When she opened the door, she gave him the paper, pausing to tell him about the convoy of outside-broadcast vehicles she'd seen nosing into the Guildhall Square. Something big, she'd said. Something for the telly.

The story dominated the *Sentinel*'s first four pages. Under the giant headline SELL OUT! a team of reporters detailed Zhu's involvement in the Pompey First campaign. His donations approached six figures. By funding the poster sites, the felt-tip giveaways, the air-ship and a dozen other electoral come-ons, he'd tried to buy the votes that would prise the city away from the motherland and expose it to a flood of immigrant Hong Kong Chinese. His strategy had been subtle and immensely cunning. The jury was still out on the involvement of Pompey First's leaders, but they were either fools or knaves. If the latter, then the city had very nearly been the victim of a ruthless international conspiracy. If the former, then readers must surely draw their own conclusions. Did they really deserve to be led by dupes?

Tully turned the page to find Hayden Barnaby gazing uncertainly at the camera. Behind him, in the distance, the distinctive Portsmouth skyline. A caption beneath asked, MR POMPEY? WHO ARE YOU KIDDING? Tully tried to suppress a smile. He should have made allowances for this kind of tabloid excess. No one deserved so crude a public execution. He turned the page again, glad to see that Wilcox had kept his promise. The editor had mentioned the alleged involvement of Liz in some drugs scam, and Tully had only agreed to hand over the audio-tapes on condition that she be spared the attentions of the *Sentinel*'s news machine. When Wilcox had pressed him for more details, he'd refused to say another word and it had amused Tully to watch him battle to suppress his curiosity. Journalists were like kids, he'd decided. Give them a sniff at the cookie jar and they couldn't keep their fingers to themselves.

Charlie had called the press conference for 3 p.m. The phones at the press centre had started ringing at a couple of minutes past twelve, and he had been driven to drafting in extra pairs of hands, stationing them beside telephones in bedroom suites upstairs to cope with the torrent of calls. To no one's surprise, Wilcox had sold his exclusive to the wire services, and now there wasn't a news organization in the country that didn't want to put its own spin on what the subs at the *Sun* were already calling THE ZHU COUP. If a local party had found so many takers in Portsmouth, how many other cities might share this hunger for independence?

It was this element that braced Charlie when he stood to face the roomful of journalists and TV crews, and the longer the press conference went on, the more exultant he felt. He began by reading a statement. It was brief and punchy. Pompey First had given Whitehall a black eye. Whitehall was a bad loser. There were a million ways of abusing the newly born, but what they'd done to Pompey First was close to infanticide.

A reporter for BBC News, drafted in from Southampton, asked if Charlie was denying the allegations.

'One hundred per cent,' Charlie yelled defiantly. 'They're doing what they know best. They're lying.'

'Who's they?'

'You tell me. That's the whole fucking problem.' Charlie's language caused a ripple of laughter, not all of it amused. Answers like this, sadly, would never make it to the screen.

'So where's Zhu?' shouted a voice from the back.

'Pass.'

'Have you talked to him?'

'No.'

'Why not?'

'Because he's not around.'

'Doesn't that tell you something?'

'Yes, it tells me he's got taste. Who'd be here? Putting up with you lot?'

More laughter. Charlie ignored it, treating the next accusation with contempt. The reporter came from the *Sentinel*. Throughout the campaign, he'd enthused about local democracy, about returning power to the people. Yet now, along with the rest of the pack, he was riding hard for the kill. His question was simple. Hadn't Pompey First betrayed the city?

Charlie gave him a hard stare. It was a good question, he said, coming from a paper that had thrown its weight behind the campaign. For once in his life he'd begun to believe in journalists who'd put the real issues before the usual media garbage. Now, though, he knew he'd been naïve. The editor of the *Sentinel* was as wedded to fantasy as the source to whom he'd surrendered most of this morning's paper.

Charlie reached inside his jacket, produced a folded copy of the *Sentinel* and held up the front page.

'This is crap,' he said. 'This is what you get when no one bothers to think too hard, when no one bothers to ask the obvious questions.'

'What questions?'

'My friend, the fact that you even have to ask says it all. Who planted this stuff? Who manufactured it? And what made them so sure you'd print it?'

'You're denying it?'

'Categorically.'

'Zhu hasn't funded your campaign?'

'Mr Zhu has made some generous donations. We treat them as loans.'

'Repayable?'

'Of course.'

'When?'

Charlie grinned at him, refusing to answer, one derisive finger in the air. The storm of flash-bulbs drove him to fresh excess.

'Wilcox is a tart,' he announced. 'I just hope he gets well fucked.'

Another question came in, a change of tack. Would Pompey First's rally still be on? At the Guildhall? Or was the contest over?

'Over? Far from it.' Charlie laughed. 'Ladies and gentlemen, the gig goes on.'

Wilcox was on the phone to the Meridian newsroom when the reporter returned from the Pompey First press conference. The phone conversation over, he gave the editor a brief summary of the line Charlie Epple was taking. There was no conspiracy, no disguised bid for independence. With Pompey First, you got what you saw: governance the city could truly call its own.

Wilcox had his jacket off, his sleeves rolled up. He glowered at the reporter. 'You asked him about betrayal?'

'Of course.'

Wilcox indicated the shorthand pad. 'What did he say? Verbatim?'

The reporter began to look uneasy.

Wilcox had a notoriously short fuse. He stared at the reporter until the man shrugged and began to flip through the pad. He read out Charlie's thoughts on the *Sentinel* and its editor. Word for word. Wilcox watched him, unblinking. 'He said that?'

'Yes.'

Wilcox pulled out a drawer. He consulted a small address book, scribbled a number on a sheet of paper and passed it over the desk. 'That's Barnaby's mobile,' he said. 'Ask him why his wife spent three grand buying heroin in Amsterdam. Tell him we have photographs. And ask him for a comment. OK?' He slammed the drawer, then yelled for his secretary. Meridian were doing a special. They were sending a crew over. He wanted everyone in ties by the time they arrived.

Barnaby was still trying to find Zhu when the call came from the *Sentinel*. He'd phoned everywhere, trying to pin down the Singaporean, but for some reason both his mobiles were turned off and all attempts to raise his driver's pager had come to nothing. The latest call had gone to Zhu's home in Surrey. There, his personal assistant had been polite but evasive. Mr Zhu was currently in transit. Between where and where she wasn't prepared to say. Only when Barnaby asked if he was still in the country did she offer any guidance. Mr Zhu had no immediate plans to leave the UK, she said.

The reporter on the *Sentinel* was brisk. Barnaby listened to what he had to say. At the end, without waiting for the inevitable question, he put the phone down.

Below, in the hotel lobby, Charlie intercepted him *en route* to the revolving door.

'Zhu's due at six,' he said. 'The manager tipped me the wink.'

'Where's he been?'

'Heathrow. Apparently he picked someone up. Now we need to keep him away from those animals.' Charlie nodded down the corridor towards a group of journalists nursing glasses of Scotch while they compared notes. Charlie had just broken out Pompey First's reserves of single malt. He saw no reason why a disaster shouldn't be turned into a wake.

Barnaby glanced at his watch. It was already twenty past four. 'He's turned off his mobiles. So how do we get through to him before he arrives?'

'No idea. But I'll think of a way.' Charlie paused. 'The troops are getting restless. Word's gone round already.'

Barnaby knew. Worried calls from Pompey First candidates were beginning to arrive in the press centre. The *Sentinel*'s reach was longer than he'd thought and they were taking a lot of heavy flak on the doorsteps. One or two were already starting to question the wisdom of pressing ahead with the Guildhall rally and, whatever reassurances he offered, Barnaby sensed a reluctance to appear on the same platform as the man whose face peered out from the *Sentinel*'s midday edition.

Charlie was still musing about Zhu. He'd post sentries. He'd lay an ambush. Somehow he'd shield him from the wolves down the corridor. He saw Barnaby reach for the revolving door. 'Where you off to?'

Barnaby laid a hand on his shoulder. 'Out,' he said.

*

When Barnaby rang the front doorbell Liz was in the back garden. She appeared in jeans and an old sweater, her hair tied back with a scrap of scarlet ribbon. At the sight of him, she stiffened, saying nothing. 'You've seen the *Sentinel*?'

Liz nodded. 'Sort of. A friend phoned me up. Read me out the best bits.'

'And what did you think?'

'It made me laugh.' She smiled at last. 'Sup with the devil . . .'

'Zhu's straight. I swear he is.'

'I didn't mean Zhu.'

'Oh?'

Barnaby blinked. Liz had been in the sun and it showed on her forearms and he found himself wondering quite how far the tan extended. She was still looking at him, still waiting for an explanation for this sudden visit.

'We have to talk,' he said. 'I'm afraid it's urgent.'

'Talk about what?'

'Drugs. And three thousand pounds of my money.'

Liz pursed her lips. Then she pulled off her gardening gloves, shaking the loose soil onto the flower beds beside the front door. Inside, the house smelled different, as if it belonged to a stranger, and for the first time it occurred to Barnaby that Liz might be living with someone else.

'Still by yourself?' he asked, watching her fill the kettle.

'I'm afraid so.'

'No toy boys?'

She turned her back on him, unamused, the way you might ignore a child's curse.

Uninvited, Barnaby sank onto the sofa. We used to sit here in the evenings, he thought. We used to be happy.

'Have you eaten?'

'Yes, thanks.'

Liz pulled up a chair and sat down. She took an orange from the fruit bowl and began to peel it. Barnaby watched her fingers, the way they dug into the skin, easing back the pith, leaving each segment undamaged. He'd come for a row, a confrontation. Yet all he wanted to do was watch.

'You mentioned something about money,' Liz said.

Barnaby told her about the reporter from the *Sentinel*. The accusation was brutally simple: Liz had given Haagen three thousand pounds. And Haagen had spent it on heroin.

'True or false?'

'Depends.'

'On what?'

'On whether you're a lawyer or a human being.' Liz tidied the peel and dropped it into the bin. 'You choose.'

'Neither. I'm under attack, that's all.'

'Who by? Who from?'

'More or less everyone. You want a list?'

'No, thanks.'

'OK.' Barnaby shrugged. 'But I'd still like an answer, if you don't mind. To be honest, it makes me feel a bit of a prat, not knowing.'

'I bet.' Liz began to divide the orange into segments. 'Pretty unpleasant, isn't it?'

'What?'

'Not knowing what your partner's up to. Getting calls out of the blue. Trying to come up with some explanation.'

Barnaby acknowledged the reproof with a slight tilt of his head. This was a new Liz, he thought. A year ago she'd have been halfway through the bottle by now, hopelessly off the pace.

'I'm sorry,' he said softly, 'if that helps.'

He looked up in time to catch the smile that ghosted across her face. She began to tell him about Haagen and about the money. The man on the phone had been right. She'd spent £3,000 trying to get him out of the country. She'd told herself he'd be as good as his word. She'd told herself it was an investment. She'd been wrong.

'An investment in what?'

'Jessie,' she said. 'And us.'

'You didn't know about the heroin?'

'No.'

'You thought he'd pack up and go? Just like that?'

'Yes.'

419

'Why?'

'Because I wanted him to, needed him to. I'm a simple woman, a mother. You do strange things when—' She broke off, refusing to bother with excuses.

Barnaby reached for one of the orange segments. He put it in his mouth and sucked it, surprised at its sweetness. Bits of him were less dead than he'd thought.

Liz was talking about Jessie again. She'd been round for most of the morning. She was very upset.

'Why?'

Liz shook her head in a gesture of profound sympathy. For a long time she was quiet. At last, she looked up. 'You don't know, do you? You really don't understand. Your daughter's been to damnation and back and yet there's no way you'll open your eyes, and take a second or two off, and see her for who she really is.'

Barnaby began to defend himself. Jessie was coming round to the flat. They were talking. Comparing notes. Getting closer.

'To you, yes. To her? I doubt it.'

'Who says?'

'I say. Not her, me. She's loyal to you, fiercely loyal. God knows why, but she is. She thinks the world of you, and all you do is tell her how much you want to make it better.'

'Make what better?'

'The world. Not hers. Not ours. But someone else's. And I'm talking politics, not Kate Frankham.' She stared at him, her eyes blazing, then looked away. Moments later, the anger had gone, leaving in its place something infinitely more sombre. 'Haagen's back,' she said.

'Back where?'

'Here. Back in Portsmouth, living on some houseboat or other. Jessie's been seeing him regularly, keeping it a secret, not wanting to upset anyone.'

'*Upset* anyone? Like who?'

'Lolly. Me. Even you.'

Barnaby stared at her, a pattern of events beginning to resolve itself in his mind. Someone had wrecked their printing machines.

There were rumours of a fire bomb at the Imperial. And Haagen was back in town.

He leaned forward on the sofa, helplessly inquisitorial.

'Why?' he asked. 'Why did she want to see him so badly?'

'I suppose she loves him. In her own way.'

'But what do they talk about?'

'God knows.'

Barnaby sat back, numbed. Jessie knew everything about Pompey First, every last detail of the schedule, every last change of plan. He'd bored her stiff with his new baby for weeks, months. How much of this had she passed on to Haagen? How much had he coaxed out of her?

He looked up, aware that Liz was still gazing at him.

'It's a great pity,' she said. 'A real shame.'

'What is?'

'You. You're a bright man. Often you're a kind man. You can make us laugh. You can make us feel wonderful. We love you. We both love you. But it's not enough, is it?' She gazed at him. 'At first I thought it was just greed. You wanted more. More money. More sex. More conquests. More clients. More of everything. But now? Now, I'm not so sure. I think about it a lot. You, I mean. And sometimes I think you might be just a little bit autistic.'

'*Autistic?*'

'Yes. There are bits of you that seem completely dead, completely unformed. The light just doesn't get through. And that means, poor thing, that you're going to miss a lot. Us, for a start.'

The phone on the table between them began to trill. For once, Barnaby didn't stir. His mind was quite blank.

Liz picked the phone up. She listened, then nodded. 'It's Charlie,' she said drily. 'He's saying he's kidnapped Zhu.'

Jephson insisted Louise accept the Director's offer of his driver and his car for the return trip to the south coast. For the second time in twenty-four hours, she stretched her legs in the back of the big Rover, watching the suburbs of Mitcham glide past.

Her three hours at Thames House had reminded her powerfully of Christmas. There'd been drinks up on the top floor and a graceful speech from Jephson, the new director-designate. He'd said some witty things about democracy and subversion, and had raised his glass in a toast to Pompey First. Never before, he remarked, had the service owed so much to so few. It proved, if proof were needed, that the most successful operations were often conducted at negligible financial cost. Not only that but the noises emerging from Downing Street indicated that Five's credit was massively in surplus. The prospect for future battles, of which there would doubtless be many, had never looked rosier.

Louise had acknowledged the congratulations with a show of unaffected pleasure. It warmed her that the operation had gone so well, that the material Ellis had brought back from Singapore had meshed so nicely with the script she'd prepared for the *Sentinel*. Just sometimes, she confessed to her colleagues, the media had its uses.

Now, in the outskirts of Carshalton, she leaned forward, switched on the overhead light and read out directions to Ellis's house. The MI5 driver had relatives in the area and he picked his way through leafy avenues of semis until the big car slowed to a halt and Louise recognized the sagging front gate that guarded the path to Ellis's door.

He took an age to answer the bell. When he opened the door, he was wearing a dressing gown over a pair of striped pyjamas. He smiled awkwardly at Louise, apologizing at once. He'd been trying to ring her. He had a touch of flu. It had been in the offing for days.

Louise beamed at him. She had a driver. They'd be snug in the back of the car. Portsmouth was barely an hour and a half away. Ellis began to protest but she reached forward, a comforting hand on his arm. While he got dressed, she'd see to a couple of hot-water bottles. Did he have a Thermos? Should she make cocoa?

Ellis was staring at her. She'd never heard him stammer before.

'What are you telling me?' he said. 'What are you saying?'

Louise stepped into the house, encouraging him towards the stairs. He wasn't to worry about the rumoured redundancies at the DTI. She'd been with Jephson only that afternoon and scope for recruitment at MI5 was a good deal more ample than she'd been led to believe.

The Seaspray Hotel lay in the middle of a scruffy Victorian terrace, overlooking South Parade pier. A neon sign in the ground-floor window advertised single rooms for £16 per night, and something large had made a jagged hole in the plastic canopy shadowing the open front door.

Barnaby met Charlie in the front hall. He was trying to charm a fat, belligerent woman in a pink apron. The bar, she said, was for residents only. Was he intending to book in?

Charlie produced a twenty-pound note from his wallet, ignoring her invitation to sign the register. Zhu and his guest were in the lounge. In theory, the bar should now be open.

Barnaby was frowning. 'Guest?'

Charlie rolled his eyes towards the ceiling. He'd managed to intercept Zhu half a mile short of the Imperial. Sitting beside him in the back of the Daimler was an oriental vision. He hadn't caught her name but she was clearly unimpressed by the Seaspray. Circumstances hadn't given Charlie much choice. This was one place the media would never dream of looking for Zhu.

Charlie took Barnaby by the elbow and steered him into the lounge. Zhu was sitting on a sofa covered in threadbare Dralon. There was a semi-circle of cigarette burns in the carpet at his feet, and from somewhere close came the smell of old cooking oil. Zhu was reading a copy of the *Sentinel*'s midday edition. When Barnaby and Charlie came in, he stood up at once, extending a small, formal bow. As ever, his expression gave nothing away.

Barnaby was staring at the woman at the other end of the sofa. The dramatic fall of jet-black hair was even longer than he remembered but the challenging smile and the tall, slender figure were unmistakable. Flora Li. The woman from the Singapore Ministry of Home Affairs. His guide around Changi prison.

She got to her feet, smoothing the creases on her trouser suit. Charlie watched Barnaby kiss her on both cheeks.

'Something else you never told me?' he enquired.

They all sat down, Charlie folding himself into a plastic-covered armchair beneath the window. Zhu carefully folded the copy of the *Sentinel* and put it on the carpet beside his feet. Flora, it was quickly obvious, had already been through it.

'What's been happening?' she asked Barnaby. 'Why so much trouble?'

Barnaby looked at Zhu, trying to work out what lay behind the question. Was this really such a great surprise? Was Zhu really this ignorant? He explained the basis for the *Sentinel*'s attack on Pompey First: that the party had been funded by Zhu, that he'd built up shareholdings in major British utilities, that Pompey First was merely a stepping-stone to some kind of full-blown independence, a raft for tens of thousands of exiled Hong Kong Chinese. He got to the end of his exposition and apologized for his frankness, aware of Flora's steady gaze.

Zhu began to go through the *Sentinel*'s list of accusations. He had the air of a man with limitless patience and limitless time. Of course they were right to say that he'd helped Pompey First. He'd been pleased to do so. He agreed with people taking charge of their own lives. It was his democratic right to offer financial support.

'And the other business? Electricity? Water?' This was territory Barnaby had never entered before. 'You've bought into these shares? Heavily?'

'Of course,' Zhu replied. 'Your government makes it so attractive. I'm a businessman. Why not?'

'But you did it for gain? For profit? Not because . . . you had some other motive?'

Zhu leaned forward, his elbows on his knees, giving the proposition some thought. At length, he looked up.

'Your friend with the newspaper, Mr Wilcox. The man we met on Saturday?'

'Yes?'

'He's crazy.' Zhu lifted the copy of the *Sentinel*, then let it fall to the carpet again. 'Of course I invest. Wherever I go, I invest. Without seed, there's no corn. Without investment, there's no growth, no future. But investment isn't the same as ownership. I don't need to own your city. I just need to make money here. And profits can be good. For everyone.'

'I know. That's what we've been saying for months. Investing in people. Investing in jobs.'

'Of course.' Zhu spread his hands wide. 'And I'm happy to help. Is that such a bad thing to do?'

'Not at all.' Barnaby glanced at Charlie. 'Not in our book.'

'So why all this?' Zhu pushed the paper with the toe of his shoe. 'You remember what happened when we opened the hotel? The trouble outside? This is no better. This is exactly the same. Your people don't want us here. We're not stupid. We're not blind. We understand what you're saying. And believe me, my friend, there are plenty of other places in the world we can go.' He sat back, nodding. 'I was born in Shanghai, Mr Barnaby. When the Communists came, I had to flee. My brother and I, we had nothing, just a single bracelet, my mother's bracelet. We ran like everyone else. And you know where we went? Hong Kong. An experience like that teaches you a great deal. Nowhere in the world is home. Nowhere. The only thing that matters is *kiasu*. You remember *kiasu*?'

Barnaby had heard the word in Singapore, during the conversation over dinner that first night. He stole a glance at Flora. She was studying her fingernails.

'Winning,' she said quietly. 'It means winning.'

'*Kiasu*,' Zhu confirmed. 'So maybe that's a lesson for you English. Maybe you should run a little harder. Maybe you should know what it's like to be chased, to be homeless. My brother and I, we made our money in Hong Kong. That's where we ran. And now we run from there, too. Not that it matters, not that it means we won't survive.'

Barnaby extended a calming hand. He'd never seen Zhu like this, so angry, so upset.

'It's not our people,' he said. 'Our people are happy to have you. You bring work. You bring money. You get things done. It's not us, not our people.'

'Who, then? Who is it?'

Barnaby leaned back, helpless. It was a question to which he didn't have an answer. Not if Zhu was as honourable as he claimed. Not if his civic interests extended no further than Pompey First. He glanced across at Charlie. The *Sentinel*'s brand of flag-waving was dangerously close to racism. The least they owed Zhu was an apology.

'If we win tomorrow,' Charlie said quietly, 'you'll stay?'

'Of course.' Zhu nodded. 'But you won't win, Mr Epple. Not after this.'

There was a long silence. The landlady appeared behind the bar and switched on the row of fairy lights above the optics. On the wall behind the bar was a framed photograph of a warship at anchor in a foreign port. The white ensign hung limply at the battleship's stern. Matelots in white shorts stood at the rail. Rick-saws lined the quayside.

Zhu was also looking at the photograph. He cleared his throat. There was a smile back on his face. He leaned forward, touching Barnaby lightly on the knee.

'Flora flew over for tomorrow,' he said. 'We had news to break.'

'What news?'

'We wanted to start a factory. A big factory. Many jobs. Here in Portsmouth.'

'Making what?'

'Police equipment. Riot shields. Helmets. Radios. Batons.' He glanced fondly at Flora. 'She's been looking forward to it. A new start.'

Barnaby looked at Flora, confused now. 'But I thought you worked for the Singapore government?'

'I do.' She corrected herself, 'I did. But my father prefers now that I work for him. Perhaps here. Perhaps . . .' she shrugged, looking round, 'wherever.'

Barnaby was staring at her. 'Your *father*?'

'Yes.' She reached across, squeezing Zhu's hand. 'Didn't he ever tell you?'

Mike Tully sat in a corner of the lobby at the Imperial Hotel, still uncertain, reading the *Sentinel*'s late edition for the third time.

426

Since noon, the front page had been radically altered. Over a huge photo of Charlie Epple, the new headline read, *THE PARTY'S OVER!* Tully peered at the photo. Epple was standing behind a table. His shirt was tieless and his jacket hung loosely from his shoulders. His head was back, and he was grinning at the camera, his middle finger raised in a derisive salute. If a single image could stop Pompey First in its tracks, Tully thought, then this was surely it.

He opened the paper again, returning to the other photograph, the big blow-up that had brought him to the hotel. Liz Barnaby was pictured leaving a travel agency in Southsea's shopping precinct. She was wearing a long white trenchcoat and she looked harassed. The accompanying story outlined her alleged involvement in a drugs conspiracy. The police might forward evidence to the Crown Prosecution Service, and that – in turn – might result in charges against her. Three times, over the two-column report, Liz was flagged as the wife of Pompey First's founding father and the piece ended with dark hints of a possible Triad involvement, a slur that clearly extended as far as Zhu. Hong Kong was awash with hard drugs. Zhu was big in transportation. His container ships called weekly at nearby Southampton. Need the *Sentinel* say more?

Tully shook his head. As far as he knew, this was pure invention on Wilcox's part and simply added to Tully's growing unease at what he seemed to have triggered. He was no closer to trusting either Barnaby or Charlie Epple. On purpose or otherwise, they'd put some major question marks against a lot of what Tully himself held dear. But the treatment they were now getting at the hands of the *Sentinel* was rough to the point of brutality, and he had no taste for the kind of baseless innuendo that seemed to pass for tabloid journalism. Finding Liz on the inside pages, clearly identified, was the last straw. Wilcox had made a promise. And now he'd broken it.

Tully became aware of two figures pushing in through the revolving door. One of them was a woman. She was well past middle age. She had a soft, round face, and her eyes were bright behind a pair of enormous glasses. Her hair was greying, gathered into a bun, and she walked with a slight roll. Behind her, carrying a small suitcase, came the man Tully had talked to only a couple of days back. Ellis, he thought. Whitehall's bagman.

The two of them were standing by the reception desk. The woman was checking a prior booking. Tully heard her mention the Raffles suite, and he watched while the receptionist handed over a key and what looked like a set of faxes. The woman lingered a moment, reading the faxes, her other hand reaching for Ellis. Ellis had spotted a pile of *Sentinels* on the reception desk and was deep in the front page. If he'd been tasked to shaft Pompey First, Tully thought, it doesn't seem to have brought him much pleasure.

The woman looked at her watch, then linked arms with Ellis and tugged him towards the stairs. Half-way across the lobby, she stopped and turned round. She wanted to know about the Guildhall. Was it far? Was it walkable? The receptionist recommended a taxi and the woman agreed. She'd need one at seven, she said. They had to be there by quarter past. She checked her watch a second time, permitting herself a girlish laugh. Ellis had freed himself and was consulting the dinner menu outside the restaurant. When the woman joined him, they had a brief, whispered conversation. Then, with the greatest reluctance, Ellis picked up the suitcase and headed once again for the stairs.

Tully remained in the lobby for nearly half an hour. Twice he asked for Hayden Barnaby, and both times the receptionist said he was expected in time. When he finally arrived, hurrying across the forecourt to escape a brief flurry of rain, Tully met him at the door.

The two men eyed each other. In the one conversation they'd had since Barnaby left Liz, Tully had made no secret of his feelings. She was a good woman. It was a great shame.

Tully folded his copy of the *Sentinel* and pushed it deep into the pocket of his raincoat. 'Your do at the Guildhall still on?'

'Of course. Why not?'

'What time does it start?'

'Half seven.'

'OK,' Tully said. 'Then maybe we ought to talk.'

Epilogue

'Southsea . . . a residential suburb of terraces with a half-hearted
resort strewn along its shingle beach, where a mass of B&Bs
face stoic naval monuments and tawdry seaside amusements.'
England, the Rough Guide, 1996

It was nearly six by the time Jessie made it to Tokar Street. Number
89 was at the eastern end, a narrow-fronted terrace house beneath
the shadow of the Royal Marine barracks. She paused outside. The
curtains in the windows were pulled tight but she could hear wild
laughter and the thump of heavy rock music inside. At length, she
tapped on the door.

Within seconds it opened. An enormous man stared down at
her. He had a can of Tennant's in one hand and a mobile phone
in the other. Braces over his collarless shirt supported a pair of
skintight jeans and his head had been shaved to make way for an
elaborate Union Jack tattoo. A grubby plaster cast encased one
forearm, and amongst the scribbled messages Jessie recognized
Haagen's signature.

The phone began to trill. He put it to his ear, still looking
down at Jessie. 'Yeah. OK.'

He thumbed a button, ending the conversation. Jessie introduced herself. She'd come with a message. For Monty.

'That's me.'

'Haagen says to make sure it's on.'

Monty permitted himself the beginnings of a smile. Most of
his teeth were missing. He offered Jessie the can of Tennant's.

When she shook her head, he shrugged. 'Tell Haagen it ain't a problem. It's done, sorted. Tell him we're ready for the off.' He jerked a thumb behind him. 'OK?'

Jessie nodded. Beyond Monty, in the narrow hall, other bodies had appeared. More tattoos. More flags. Sullen faces. Dead eyes. Jessie wanted to go. She'd had enough. She wanted to be back home. With Lolly. With her mum. With anyone but these nightmare people.

Monty caught her arm. She froze.

'What's he think he's up to, then? That old man of yours? All this Pompey First crap?'

Jessie looked up at him. 'I don't know,' she said. 'And that's the truth.'

Faced with open rebellion amongst the Pompey First candidates, Barnaby had no choice. He'd locked himself away with them in a dressing room behind the Guildhall stage but forty minutes' heated argument hadn't altered anything. The huge majority of candidates felt compromised and betrayed. The last thing they intended to share was a public platform with Charlie Epple and Hayden Barnaby. The *Sentinel* had been right. The party was, indeed, over.

Barnaby glanced at his watch. The last he'd seen of Charlie was back at the hotel. He'd caught the gist of Mike Tully's story, something about an MI5 involvement, but frankly he'd had neither the time nor the energy to give it the attention it deserved. A phone call from the *Panorama* office had dragged him away and he'd ended a fierce debate about the case the *Sentinel* was trying to make by putting the phone down. There was no hidden agenda. There were no plans to swamp Pompey with Hong Kong Chinese. The allegations were offensive and absurd.

Now, looking dazedly at the men and women around him, he heard a knock at the door. Charlie was standing outside in the corridor. He was wearing leather trousers and a black shirt studded with fake diamonds. His left ear sported a big gold ring, and his hand-tooled boots were blocked with one-inch heels. He looked, Barnaby thought, like a refugee from a sixties rock band.

Kate was standing beside him and stepped back as the room began to empty. Charlie watched the candidates flooding away towards the fire exits. 'Off home, then?' he shouted. 'Early night?'

He turned back, not waiting for an answer. The Guildhall was filling nicely, he said. The *Sentinel* had nearly doubled the media attendance and there was a good turnout from the far right. A lot of them, it seemed, had turned up in England football shirts, eager to rehearse for the coming European championships. With luck, amongst these lunatics, the occasion might also have attracted one or two locals who fancied working things out for themselves. In this respect, Charlie promised, he'd be only too happy to oblige.

The remark drew a warm smile from Kate. She hadn't attended the meeting in the dressing room but now she seemed as bullish as Charlie about the course of the next couple of hours.

Charlie had a seating plan in his hand. He gave it to Barnaby. A block of seats up in the wings had been ringed in red.

Barnaby stared at the plan, uncomprehending. 'What's this?'

Charlie jerked a thumb up the corridor. In the shadows at the end, beside the door that led to the stage, Barnaby recognized the sturdy figure of Mike Tully.

'You're on guard duty,' Charlie was saying, 'you and my new friend there.'

'Guard duty for whom?'

'Tell you later. Mike's got the script.'

'What script?'

Barnaby stepped towards Charlie, beginning to lose his temper.

Kate edged her body between them. 'Charlie's out front for the rally,' she said firmly. 'It's all agreed.'

'What?'

'Me, mate.' Charlie threw his head back, swallowing a small yellow tablet. 'I'm out there, I'm doing it. Don't think it's a coup because it isn't. There's fuck all left to squabble about. Thanks to our Whitehall friends.'

He offered Barnaby his hand. Barnaby ignored it, watching Kate. She gave him a strange half-smile, then slipped her arm through Charlie's. They set off down the corridor, perfectly in step, without a backward glance. Nothing left to squabble about, Barnaby thought. Absolutely right.

Tully was advancing down the corridor towards him. They were to take the lift to the second floor. A door would give them access to the seats ringed in red. Their targets had been up there since ten past seven. He'd checked again only minutes ago.

'Targets?' Barnaby followed Tully through a warren of corridors. In the lift, he was aware of Tully watching him. The expression on his face spoke of righteousness and an ounce or two of pity. There were debts to be settled here, and they weren't altogether political.

A pair of swing doors gave access to the top tier of seats in the wings. Between here and the balcony, the seats were empty except for a couple huddled at the front. The man had his arm around the woman. They were laughing together, their heads touching.

Tully motioned Barnaby closer. 'You're on her side,' he whispered. 'I'll take Ellis.'

'Who's Ellis?'

'Doesn't matter. Just sit beside the woman. And make sure she doesn't leave.'

Barnaby looked at him, then shrugged. In certain moods, Tully could be truly intimidating. The Marine background, he thought. And eyes that brooked no argument.

They made their way down towards the balcony, then shuffled sideways along the front row, Tully from one end, Barnaby from the other. Ellis saw them first and alerted the woman. When Barnaby sat down beside her, she looked at him. The eyes behind the huge glasses were the palest blue. 'May I help you?'

Barnaby shook his head, saying nothing. When she repeated the question, he ignored her, leaning forward, his elbows on the balcony, gazing down on the sea of bodies below. Charlie had been right. For a local election, it was an astonishing turnout, the seats in the stalls almost entirely occupied. Here and there, beneath little thickets of Union Jacks, sat gangs of crop-haired youths in light grey football shirts, their forearms heavily tattooed. There were video crews at the front, a tangle of cables and tripods, and every time they swung their cameras round, hunting for shots to establish the atmosphere, the flags begin to wave. It was like a wind blowing through the auditorium, and with it came a low chant that swelled and swelled and then died again as the cameras panned away.

'*Eng-ger-land . . . Eng-ger-land . . .*'

Abruptly, the lights dimmed and the heavy blue curtains parted. A single spotlight followed Charlie Epple as he made his entrance. The youths began to chant again, louder this time – and watching Charlie's extravagant bows, his outstretched arms, the way he saluted the crowd, Barnaby realized that he'd finally achieved his dream. This was the moment when politics toppled into show business, the moment when Charlie Epple became the rock star of his dreams.

There was a microphone on a stand in the middle of the stage. Charlie adjusted it, taking his time, then began to talk. Despite everything, he said, it's come true. Despite all the pressures, all the doubts, all the guys who said it couldn't be done, it's here for real. Tomorrow night's poll may be a different story but already someone's bothered to ask a question or two and, in their own small way, the people have spoken. He stepped back with a flourish and a line of lights at the back of the stage softly illuminated Charlie's precious statistic, a giant 73 per cent, dwarfing the figure on the stage.

Charlie's hands were high in the air again, applauding the audience the way footballers applaud the crowd after a game, and his gesture stirred another round of chants. Feet were stamping this time, and Barnaby could feel the auditorium tremble under the heavy boots. Charlie tried to still the uproar and, for a moment, Barnaby thought they were back outside the Imperial, all control lost, but then the shouts and insults began to fade. A new figure stood on the stage, smaller and slighter than Charlie. Kate.

Barnaby stared down as Charlie introduced her. Despite the day's events, she still had enough credit to carry the audience and, for ten minutes or so, she recalled exactly why she'd been attracted to Pompey First. In the circumstances, the speech was beautifully judged. She made no apologies, offered no excuses. She'd done what she'd done for the good of the city. She believed absolutely that money was power and that both had been fenced off by a government that wasn't prepared to trust the people. The Labour Party, her old spiritual home, wouldn't redress that balance. On the contrary, they might be driven to adjust it even further in Whitehall's favour. No, she concluded, the truly new politics lay with the people. It was they who deserved a voice, they who deserved a party of their own. And, in Pompey First, she'd done her best to create just that.

She stepped back from the microphone. There was a moment's silence, then ripples of applause that grew and grew. Peering down, Barnaby could even see the odd flag waving back and forth, and he found himself clapping as well. Kate had administered the last rites. Singlehanded, with quiet simplicity, she'd put Pompey First to rest.

Charlie was back at the microphone. He ran briskly through the *Sentinel*'s charges. OK, Zhu had given Pompey First financial support. But this money wasn't tainted, unlike the huge donations the Tories had wrung from their own overseas supporters. Men like Octav Botner, who'd fled the country after allegations of a £97 million tax fraud. Or Asil Nadir, who was hiding away in Cyprus. Or Azil Virani, who'd been slung into jail after the BCCI rip-off. They were the real menace to democracy. They were the men who'd handed over money in the hope of political favours.

Zhu's share purchases came next. Of course he'd bought into British utilities. Anyone would, once they knew the terms on which the government had chosen to get rid of them. Gas, and water, and electricity were giveaways, choice hunks of British industry tossed to the private sector. That's why the Americans were snapping them up. So what was so different about Zhu to turn a shrewd investment into something sinister? Was it his colour? His race? Or was it the fact that he cared enough about Portsmouth to offer it the promise of a half-decent future?

The audience stirred again. Charlie wrenched the microphone from the stand, advancing to the front of the stage, warming to his theme. Britain was bloody lucky that men like Zhu, entrepreneurs with a bit of heart and a bit of social conscience, even bothered to get off the plane. These were the guys that were bringing in the real money, the real investment. So why all the paranoia? Why the headlines about Selling Out? And Zhu Coups? And why, tackiest of all, did elements of the press sink to winks and nudges about drugs and Triads?

Charlie's finger stabbed the air, buttonholing the audience, piling the questions up, one after the other. Pompey First had been destroyed. Last night, foolishly, they'd celebrated certain victory. Twenty-four hours later, thanks to the local press, they barely existed at all. Why? Who'd supplied the information? The spin? The tissue of lies that had engulfed the people's party? Why was democracy, real democracy, *local* democracy, such a threat?

Barnaby watched as Charlie began to turn towards their perch up in the wings. Then, abruptly, he was blinded by a powerful spotlight, mounted across the auditorium. Instinctively, his hands went to his face, shielding his eyes. Beside him, he could feel the woman doing the same. Then she got to her feet and tried to push past him, and he remembered Tully's instructions and reached up, pulling her down again. On stage, he could hear Charlie talking about visitors from London, envoys from Whitehall, spooks from God knows what branch of the intelligence services. The two in the middle, he said, had doubtless been told to spoil the party. And with tremendous efficiency, they'd done just that. So here they were. In at the death.

The woman beside Barnaby flinched. Then she was on her feet again. This time she didn't try to get away but simply stood there, her hands held high acknowledging her role in Charlie's script. Charlie stared up at her a moment, then stepped back with a whoop, and through his parted fingers Barnaby saw thousands of balloons cascading down from a net in the roof. The balloons were sea-green and the youths in the football shirts began to puncture them, a fusillade of bangs that sounded like rifle fire. In the aisle, a huge man with a plaster cast was bending over an enormous ghetto-blaster, and suddenly there came the thunder of Elgar at full volume, 'Land of Hope and Glory'. The groups with the Union Jacks were on their feet now, stamping and singing, their faces raised to the woman in the wings, and minutes later, as the spotlight dimmed and the curtains closed on Charlie Epple, they were still there, roaring.

Barnaby got home past midnight. He'd walked miles and miles, brooding. Towards the end, crossing Southsea Common, he paused in the bitter wind, trying one last time to visualize the way it must have been for Bill Clinton and Hillary and all the other heads of state. Shivering in his thin coat, he told himself that the bottle of whisky he'd just shared with Liz and Jessie should have made it easier, should have parted the curtains on the memories of that extraordinary weekend but, try as he might, the images wouldn't come. The Common stayed the Common, empty and pale in the moonlight, shadowed by the racing clouds.